The Horus Heresy series

Book 1 – HORUS RISING
Dan Abnett

Book 2 – FALSE GODS
Graham McNeill

Book 3 – GALAXY IN FLAMES
Ben Counter

Book 4 – THE FLIGHT OF THE EISENSTEIN
James Swallow

Book 5 – FULGRIM
Graham McNeill

Book 6 – DESCENT OF ANGELS
Mitchel Scanlon

Book 7 – LEGION
Dan Abnett

Book 8 – BATTLE FOR THE ABYSS
Ben Counter

Book 9 – MECHANICUM
Graham McNeill

Book 10 – TALES OF HERESY
edited by Nick Kyme and Lindsey Priestley

THE HORUS HERESY

Mike Lee

FALLEN ANGELS

A BLACK LIBRARY PUBLICATION

First published in Great Britain in 2009 by
BL Publishing,
Games Workshop Ltd.,
Willow Road, Nottingham,
NG7 2WS, UK.

10 9 8 7 6 5 4 3 2 1

Cover and page 1 illustration by Neil Roberts.

A CIP record for this book is available from the British Library.

UK ISBN 13: 978 1 84416 728 9
US ISBN 13: 978 1 84416 729 6

See the Black Library on the Internet at

www.blacklibrary.com

Find out more about Games Workshop
and the world of Warhammer 40,000 at

www.games-workshop.com

Printed in the UK by CPI Bookmarque, Croydon, CR0 4TD

The Horus Heresy

It is a time of legend.

Mighty heroes battle for the right to rule the galaxy. The vast armies of the Emperor of Earth have conquered the galaxy in a Great Crusade – the myriad alien races have been smashed by the Emperor's elite warriors and wiped from the face of history.

The dawn of a new age of supremacy for humanity beckons.

Gleaming citadels of marble and gold celebrate the many victories of the Emperor. Triumphs are raised on a million worlds to record the epic deeds of his most powerful and deadly warriors.

First and foremost amongst these are the primarchs, superheroic beings who have led the Emperor's armies of Space Marines in victory after victory. They are unstoppable and magnificent, the pinnacle of the Emperor's genetic experimentation. The Space Marines are the mightiest human warriors the galaxy has ever known, each capable of besting a hundred normal men or more in combat.

Organised into vast armies of tens of thousands called Legions, the Space Marines and their primarch leaders conquer the galaxy in the name of the Emperor.

Chief amongst the primarchs is Horus, called the Glorious, the Brightest Star, favourite of the Emperor, and like a son unto him. He is the Warmaster, the commander-in-chief of the Emperor's military might, subjugator of a thousand thousand worlds and conqueror of the galaxy. He is a warrior without peer, a diplomat supreme.

As the flames of war spread through the Imperium, mankind's champions will all be put to the ultimate test.

~ DRAMATIS PERSONAE ~

With the Emperor's 4th Expeditionary Fleet:

LION EL'JONSON	Son of the Emperor, Primarch of the First Legion
BROTHER-REDEMPTOR NEMIEL	Chaplain
CAPTAIN STENIUS	Master of the battle barge *Invincible Reason*
SERGEANT KOHL	Terran, veteran of many campaigns
TECHMARINE ASKELON	Member of Sergeant Kohl's veteran squad
MARTHES	Member of Sergeant Kohl's veteran squad
VARDUS	Member of Sergeant Kohl's veteran squad
EPHRIAL	Member of Sergeant Kohl's veteran squad
YUNG	Member of Sergeant Kohl's veteran squad
CORTUS	Member of Sergeant Kohl's veteran squad
TITUS	Dreadnought

On Caliban

LUTHER	Once a great knight; now, in Jonson's absence, Master of Caliban
LORD CYPHER	The Keeper of Secrets

Brother-Librarian Israfael	Chief Epistolary at Caliban
Brother-Librarian Zahariel	Librarian in training
Chapter Master Astellan	Terran, one of Luther's training masters
Master Remiel	An elderly and esteemed training master for the Legion
Brother Attias	Veteran of Sarosh and member of the training cadre
General Morten	Terran, Commander of the Calibanite Jaegers
Magos Administratum Talia Bosk	Terran, chief Imperial bureaucrat on Caliban
Sar Daviel	Former knight of the Order
Lord Thuriel	Scion of a once-powerful noble house
Lady Alera	Noble lady and mistress of her house
Lord Malchial	Son of a famous knight, now fallen on hard times

On Diamat

Governor Taddeus Kulik	Imperial Governor of Diamat
Magos Archoi	Master of the Forge at Diamat

PROLOGUE

Loyalty and Honour

Caliban
In the 147th year of the Emperor's Great Crusade

THERE WERE NO trumpets to announce their arrival, no cheering crowds to welcome them home. They returned to Caliban in the dead of night, dropping down through the sullen clouds of a late autumn storm.

One by one the drop ships broke through the heavy overcast, their white undercarriage lights knifing through the gloom as they swept down to the landing field below. For a few moments the black hulls of the Stormbirds were highlighted by the harsh yellow glow of the space port lights, picking out the winged sword insignia of the Emperor's First Legion on the transports' broad wings.

The assault ships flared their thrusters and settled onto the landing pad amid billowing clouds of hissing steam. Moments later came the iron clang of assault ramps striking permacrete, followed by the heavy tread of armoured feet; huge, broad-shouldered giants emerged from the roiling mists. Rain lashed at the curved plates of the Dark Angels' black power armour and soaked the white surplices of the warrior-initiates. Here and there, orbs of blurry crimson light leaked from the oculars of battle helms, but for the most part the Astartes had bared their faces to the storm. Water beaded on heavy brows and blunt cheekbones, on gleaming data plugs and shaven pates. To a man, their expressions were as stern and impassive as stone.

The Astartes marched to the far end of the permacrete and formed into silent ranks facing the Stormbirds, their boltguns held at port arms. There were no proud banners to raise above the serried lines, nor bold champions to anchor the files with their ceremonial harness and master-crafted blades. All those honours had been left behind with their parent chapters, still fighting with the primarch and the Fourth Expeditionary Fleet at Sarosh. Their armour was polished and unadorned; only a few bore the traces of battle scars mended during the long journey. Since leaving Caliban to join the Emperor's Crusade they had participated in just a single campaign; few of them had seen any combat at all before receiving the order to return home.

Thrusters roared as empty Stormbirds lifted ponderously into the air, making room for still more drop ships descending through the iron-grey cloud cover. The ranks of the returning warriors swelled, rapidly filling the northern edge of the landing field. It took more than four hours to transport the entire contingent to the planet's surface, with the assault ships working in steady rotation; the assembled warriors waited and watched in complete silence, stolid and immovable as statues while the wind howled and the storm raged about them.

Two hours before dawn, the last of the transport flights touched down. The ranks of Astartes stirred slightly as warriors roused themselves from meditative rotes and came to full attention as the last four Stormbirds lowered their ramps and their passengers disembarked.

First came the wounded; Astartes who had suffered grievous injuries during the combat landings at Sarosh, their comatose forms borne on grav-sleds and watched over by attentive Legion Apothecaries. Next was the guard of honour, comprised of the most senior warrior-initiates in the cadre. In the lead marched Brother-Librarian Israfael, his dour face hidden within the depths of a wide samite hood. Each of the Astartes in the guard of honour wore surplices hemmed with ruby, sapphire, emerald, adamantine or gold, signifying their devotion to one of the Higher Mysteries. All, that is, except one.

Zahariel marched ten steps behind Brother Israfael, his head hooded like that of his mentor and his armoured hands tucked into the broad sleeves of his plain surplice. He felt self-conscious and out of place among the champions and senior initiates, but Israfael had been adamant.

'You saved everyone on Sarosh,' the Librarian had declared, back aboard the *Wrath of Caliban*, 'including the primarch himself. And you spend more time at Luther's side these days than all the rest of us combined. If you don't deserve to stand in the honour guard, none of us do.'

The guard of honour followed at a measured pace behind their wounded brothers, who passed slowly by the waiting ranks of Dark Angels and then took their leave, headed for Aldurukh's extensive medicae wards. Israfael halted the guard of honour before the assembled Astartes and with a murmured command ordered a sharp about-face. Twelve boots crashed down in unison on the rain-slick permacrete and every warrior stiffened to attention. Rain drummed against Zahariel's hood, plastering it slowly to the top of his shaved head.

Across the landing field the assault ramp on the Stormbird lowered with a faint hiss of hydraulics. Ruddy light spilled down the ramp, casting a long, martial shadow onto the scorched pavement as a single, armoured figure emerged into the stormy night.

At just that moment, the driving rain slackened and the howling wind receded like an indrawn breath as Luther set foot on Caliban once more. The former knight was clad in gleaming armour of black and gold, forged in the close-fitting Calibanite fashion rather than the larger, bulkier Crusader-pattern suits favoured by the Astartes. A curved adamantine combat shield bearing the insignia of a Calibanite wyrm was strapped to the knight's upper left arm, while his right pauldron bore the winged sword insignia of the Emperor's First Legion on a dark green field. On Luther's left hip rode Nightfall, the fearsome hand-and-a-half power sword gifted to him in happier days by Lion El'Jonson himself; in a holster on his right sat an old and well-worn pistol that had seen much use in the monster-haunted forests of

Caliban. A winged great helm concealed the knight's features and a heavy black cloak swirled about his feet as he strode swiftly to the assembled warriors.

Every eye was upon Luther as he came to a halt precisely twenty paces from the Astartes and surveyed their ranks with glowing, implacable eyes. Though he had been given many of the same physical augmentations as Zahariel and the rest, Luther had been too old to receive the gene-seed as they had. They towered head and shoulders over him, and yet his sheer physical presence seemed to fill the space around him, making him seem far larger than he actually was. Even Israfael, a Terran by birth, seemed slightly awed by Jonson's second-in-command. He was the sort of man that came along once in a thousand years, a man who might have united all of Caliban but for the appearance of another, even greater figure: Lion El'Jonson himself.

Luther surveyed the Astartes for a moment longer, then reached up and drew off his helm. He had a handsome, square-jawed face, with strong cheekbones and an aquiline nose. His eyes were dark and piercing, like chips of polished obsidian. His hair was black as jet and cropped close to his skull.

Thunder rumbled off to the south and the wind began to pick up again, blowing a curtain of cold rain across the landing field. Luther turned his face to the heavens and closed his eyes, and Zahariel thought he saw the ghost of a smile play across his face as the drops struck his cheeks. The precipitation grew into a steady, pelting shower once more.

Zahariel watched as Luther took a deep breath and glanced back at the assembled troops. This time his grin was broad and comradely, but Zahariel saw that the smile didn't reach all the way to Luther's eyes.

'Welcome home, brothers,' Luther said, his powerful speaking voice carrying easily over the rain and the wind, and eliciting rueful chuckles from the Astartes in the front ranks. 'I regret that I can't promise you a grand feast, such as welcomed the questing knights of old. If we're lucky and we're bold, perhaps we can stage a quick raid on Master Luwin's kitchen and make off with some fresh victuals before the day's work begins.'

Many of the Dark Angels laughed at the thought, remembering Luwin, the roaring tyrant of the kitchens at old Aldurukh. Zahariel chuckled in spite of himself, thinking back to his days as an aspirant and remembering fondly the halls and courtyards of the fortress. For the first time since leaving Sarosh, he found himself looking forward to seeing Aldurukh again.

Before the laughter could entirely subside, Luther tucked his helmet under his right arm and nodded to his honour guard. 'All right,' he said. 'Let's go see how much the old rock has changed in our absence.'

Without another word, Luther turned on his heel and set off for the landing field's access road, his shoulders straight and his head held high. Immediately his honour guard fell into step behind him, and then moments later the pavement resounded with the thunder of hundreds of armoured feet as the rest of the cadre began the march to the distant fortress.

Luther marched at the head of the column like a conquering hero, returning to Caliban in glory rather than exile. It was an impressive performance,

Zahariel thought, but he wondered if any of his brothers were fooled by it.

OFFICIALLY, THEY HAD been ordered back to Caliban because the Great Crusade was about to enter a new operational phase, and the First Legion was in dire need of new recruits to meet the tasks the Emperor had planned for them. The Lion declared that experienced warriors were needed at home to speed up the training process, and a list of names was drawn up and circulated throughout the fleet. Little more than a week after being deployed on their first campaign, Zahariel and more than five hundred of his brothers – over half a chapter – discovered they had been dismissed.

The news had stunned them all. Zahariel had seen it in the eyes of his battle brothers as they'd mustered on the embarkation deck to begin the long trip back to Caliban. If the Legion needed warriors so badly, why were they being pulled from the front lines? Training recruits was a job for elders, men who were full of wisdom but past their physical prime. That was the way it had been on their homeworld for generations – and it had escaped no one that virtually all of the Astartes being sent home were from Caliban rather than Terra.

Ironically, it was the announcement that Luther himself would take charge of the recruitment effort that convinced them something was wrong. Luther, the man who had been Jonson's right hand for decades, and who had risen to become the Legion's second-in-command despite not being an Astartes himself, had no business leaving the Crusade to train young recruits at Aldurukh. He was being sent as far from the Lion as possible, and the rest of the cadre were being exiled along with him.

They followed their orders to the letter, without question or hesitation, as they had been trained to do. But Zahariel could see the doubts that had taken root inside each of his battle brothers. What did we do? How have we failed him? But Luther gave the Astartes little opportunity to speculate; once the *Wrath of Caliban* entered the warp he established a rigorous regimen of equipment maintenance, combat training and readiness drills that kept idle time to an absolute minimum. To all intents and purposes, it appeared that the Legion's second-in-command took the primarch at his word and intended to fulfil his assigned task to the best of his ability. When he wasn't taking an active role inspecting wargear or supervising combat exercises, Luther spent the rest of his time secluded in his quarters, drafting plans for overhauling the training practices at Aldurukh.

Zahariel was kept as busy as the rest, although he quickly found himself exempted from the more mundane aspects of the shipboard inspections and readiness drills in favour of training his psychic powers under the tutelage of Brother-Librarian Israfael – and acting as Luther's unofficial aide-de-camp.

The order had come down shortly after the voyage began. Luther required an assistant to help draft the orders for the new training scheme and organise the ongoing activities aboard ship. He had chosen Zahariel personally for the job. Most assumed that he'd chosen the young Astartes because of their shared exploits during the Saroshi assassination attempt aboard the primarch's flagship, the *Invincible Reason*. They were correct in their assumption, but not for the reasons they imagined.

The Saroshi had been a highly cultured people who hid a terrible canker at the heart of their civilization. Sometime during the nightmare known as the Age of Strife they had sealed a pact with a horrific entity in exchange for their survival. When the Dark Angels had assumed the task of formalising Saroshi compliance, the Saroshi leaders had attempted to assassinate their primarch by smuggling an atomic warhead onto the flagship. Had the bomb not been discovered and dealt with by Luther and Zahariel, the Legion would have been dealt a catastrophic blow – or so the story went.

Luther never brought up the incident during the length of the voyage back to Caliban, but the question hung in the air between them. Had Jonson suspected the truth? Was that why Luther had been sent away, and was Zahariel being punished by virtue of his association to the event?

There was no way to know.

THE SPACE PORT was one of five within a two-hundred-square-kilometre perimeter around the Legion fortress of Aldurukh. Zahariel could remember a time when the land had been covered in dense forest that teemed with deadly plant and animal life. Caliban was considered by Imperial planetologists to be a 'death world' – a planet that wasn't merely dangerous but actively inimical to human life. Every day had been a struggle for survival, and life was both brutal and often very short. It was only through the courage and sacrifice of the planet's knightly orders that humanity survived at all.

Lion El'Jonson had united all the knightly orders under his leadership and had led a successful campaign to eradicate the deadliest of Caliban's monsters, but the final blow had come in the form of the Imperium. The Emperor's servants had descended on the planet with enormous machines that cleared dozens of kilometres of forest a day and left flat, lifeless earth in their wake. Mines, refineries and manufactorums had followed, ready to transform the planet's abundant resources into vital war materiel for the Emperor's Crusade. Cities were built to supply the sprawling industrial sites, growing upwards and outwards with each passing year as villages and towns were emptied and their citizens relocated to better serve the Imperium.

In the past, more than two dozen villages and settlements had supported the fortress of Aldurukh, providing everything from food to clothing, metal ore and medicines so that the knights were free to hone their skills and defend the land from the beasts. All of them were gone now; the land surrounding the fortress had been levelled and transformed into a vast military and logistical complex. Zahariel would have been hard-put to recall where any of the villages had once stood. Now, in addition to the space ports, there were training centres, barracks, arsenals, storehouses and maintenance yards stretching as far as the eye could see, all dedicated to supplying the

Legion with the men and equipment it needed to fulfil its role in the Great Crusade.

Even at such a late hour, the cadre went almost unnoticed in the bustling activity surrounding the fortress. Cargo lifters and shuttles came and went between the space ports and the harbours in high orbit, ferrying supplies and personnel destined for the front lines. The Dark Angels passed long convoys of ordnance haulers and supply trucks on their way to and from the landing fields. Platoons of armoured vehicles roared past, heading for the marshalling yards south of the fortress or to the training grounds for the Legion's auxiliary Imperial Army units. Once, a regiment of new Army recruits stopped in its tracks and shuffled quickly off the road to let the Astartes pass. The young men and women in their crisp new battle-dress stared open-mouthed at the marching giants and the golden-armoured figure who led them.

They marched through the rain and the wind for ten kilometres, passing through curtain walls made from permacrete and studded with defensive shield projectors and automated weapon emplacements. The closer they drew to Aldurukh, the denser and higher the structures grew, until finally the Astartes found themselves marching down man-made canyons lit solely by globes of artificial light.

Yet Aldurukh rose above all else, a bastion of strength and tradition surrounded by a sea of constant change. Its granite flanks had been scraped bare by Imperial construction machines; even now, titanic excavators scaled its sheer sides, carving out ledges and boring tunnels deep into the rock as the fortress continued to expand into the heart of the mountain itself. Zahariel had heard of plans to one day create a series of gates at the foot of the mountain that would provide access to the fortress's subterranean levels as well as lifts that would carry passengers up into the centre of the fortress within seconds. For all its efficiency, the notion seemed vaguely offensive to him; the path up the Errant's Road to the castle gates had been trod by the knights of the Order for centuries, and had taken on great spiritual significance in their legends and lore. His brothers could ride the lifts if they preferred; he intended to walk the path built by his elders for as long as he was able.

To his relief, the fortress hadn't yet changed so much in the years he'd been away. At the base of the mountain, rising incongruously to either side of a narrow, paved lane that passed between two towering barracks facilities, stood the ancient, weathered menhirs that marked the foot of the old road. The old stones depicted the beginning and ending stages of a knight's journey: the left menhir was carved in the likeness of a proud knight striding forth into the world, pistol and chainsword in hand; the one on the right showed a battered and weary warrior, his armour splintered and his weapons broken, kneeling wearily but with head held high as he contemplated his return home. Zahariel smiled to see Luther brush his fingertips lightly against the right-hand menhir as he passed by, a tradition that reached back to the earliest days of their brotherhood. He repeated the gesture, feeling the smooth stone beneath his fingertips and thinking of the generations of his forbears who had done the same, stretching back for millennia.

The storm broke as they trod the narrow, winding road, though the wind still tangled their surplices and tugged at their hoods as the clouds paled with the first light of dawn. The climb, though long, passed quicker than Zahariel expected. After what seemed like only a couple of hours he found himself upon a broad, paved square that in times past had been a forested clearing, where aspirants to the Order once spent a long and harrowing night before the castle gates.

Now those gates were thrown wide open as the Dark Angels approached, and Zahariel saw with surprise that the courtyard beyond was filled with ranks of young recruits, arrayed to create a processional that led to the feet of the castle's outer citadel. The recruits had been assembled in haste; many of them stared at the new arrivals with an equal mix of curiosity and surprise.

Luther led his warriors down the length of the processional as though he'd expected the impromptu assembly all along. At the far end of the long line of recruits waited two figures: one wasted and bent with age, the other clad in dark armour and a surplice hemmed with gold. He stopped at a respectful distance from the two, and behind him the cadre of Astartes came to a thundering halt.

As if on cue, the assembled recruits sank to one knee and bowed their heads to the golden knight. A trumpet pealed from the castle gatehouse, the traditional signal for a knight home from a long and dangerous quest. Master Remiel, of late the Castellan of Aldurukh, knelt before Luther as well. Behind Remiel, Lord Cypher inclined his head respectfully to the Legion's second-in-command, though Zahariel could not help but notice a faint glitter of amusement in the warrior's eyes.

Cypher was not a name, but a title; one that went back to the earliest days of the Order. His role was to maintain the traditions, customs and history of the brotherhood, as well as maintaining the integrity of the Higher Mysteries – the advanced tactics and teachings shared with the senior initiates. Because he was the literal personification of the Order and its beliefs, once a man took the role of Cypher he gave up his proper name from that moment forward. He was the brotherhood's touchstone, a knight of great experience and wisdom who held little real power but wielded enormous influence within the organisation.

The current Lord Cypher was even more of an enigma than most, not least because of his youth and lack of seniority within the brotherhood. When Lion El'Jonson became Grand Master of the Order it had been expected that he would name Master Remiel to the position; instead, he raised up a little-known knight younger than Luther or many other high-ranking peers. It was said that the new Cypher had been trained at one of the Order's lesser fortresses, near the beast-haunted Northwilds, but even that was little more than rumour. No one could fathom Jonson's decision, but no one had found cause to complain about it, either. By all accounts, the current Cypher was more of a reclusive, scholarly figure than previous bearers of the title, spending long hours poring through the libraries and record vaults hidden within the castle – though the paired pistols at his belt hinted that he was as capable a fighter as anyone else in the brotherhood.

Luther seemed genuinely surprised by Master Remiel's gesture of fealty. He stepped forward quickly, extending his hand. 'Do your knees trouble you, Master?' he said. 'Please, let me help you up.' He looked left and right, taking in the ranks of kneeling recruits. 'Rise, all of you, in the Lion's name,' he said, his voice ringing from the walls of the citadel. 'We are all brothers here, with no man set above another. Is that not so, Lord Cypher?'

Cypher inclined his head to Luther once more. 'It is indeed,' he replied in a quiet voice. The faintest of smiles played across Cypher's face. 'Something we would all do well to remember.'

Master Remiel stared at Luther's outstretched hand for a moment. Reluctantly, he accepted the offer and rose stiffly to his feet. He had aged a great deal in the past few years, Zahariel saw, and seemed almost diminutive between the towering figure of Cypher and Luther's enhanced stature. Like most of the senior members of the Order, Remiel had been accepted into the Legion, but was far too old to receive the Dark Angels' gene-seed. Strangely, he had also refused even the basic physical augmentation and rejuvenation that men such as Luther had received. He remained a product of a bygone age, one fading quickly into the mists of time.

'Aldurukh welcomes you, brother,' Remiel said to Luther. His voice was hoarse with age, which made his tone all the more stern and forbidding. 'The captain aboard the *Wrath of Caliban* informed us of your impeding arrival, but there wasn't enough time to arrange a proper welcome.' He stared up at Luther, his pointed chin thrust out in a proud, almost defiant pose. 'The recruits stand ready for inspection. I look forward to hearing your appraisal.'

For the first time Zahariel noted the faint air of tension in the courtyard; from the slight straightening of Luther's shoulders, it was clear he sensed it as well. The young Astartes surveyed the assembly carefully, and realised that Remiel's impromptu welcome might be designed to send a message to the cadre as well.

Master Remiel thinks the Lion has lost faith in him as well, Zahariel thought. Why else send Luther and half a chapter of Astartes all the way back to Caliban to take over the training of recruits?

Never before had Zahariel questioned the orders of his primarch. The very idea that Jonson could make a mistake seemed inconceivable. But now, a cold sense of foreboding sent a shiver along his spine.

Luther, however, seemed unaffected by Remiel's tone. He chuckled, gripping the master's arm warmly. 'You have forgotten more about the training of fighting men than I will ever know, Master,' he said, loud enough for everyone to hear. 'We're here to help train more recruits, not train them better.' Luther turned to the assembled men and smiled proudly. 'The Emperor himself has spoken, brothers! He expects great things from our Legion, and we will show him that the men of Caliban are worthy of his esteem! Glory awaits you, brothers; have you the loyalty and honour to earn it?'

'Aye!' the recruits answered in a ragged shout.

Luther nodded proudly. 'I expected no less from Master Remiel's students,' he said. 'But time is short, and there's much work still to be done. The Great Crusade waits on no man, and before long I and my brothers here will be called back to the thick of the fighting. We intend to bring as many of you with us as we can. The Lion needs you. We need you. And starting today you will be tested as you never have before.'

A stir went through the assembly – not just the recruits, but the Dark Angels surrounding Zahariel as well. Everywhere he looked, he saw expressions of determination and pride. Luther's challenge had transformed the atmosphere of the courtyard in a single instant; even Master Remiel seemed moved by the conviction in Luther's voice. The cadre felt it, too. For the first time, they saw a noble purpose in what they'd been sent to do. They hadn't been forgotten. Rather they would soon return to their brothers out among the stars at the head of an army that they'd helped create, one that would propel the First Legion into the annals of legend.

Luther spoke again, this time with an iron tone of command in his voice. 'Brothers, you are dismissed,' he ordered. 'Return to your morning meditations and prepare yourselves for the today's training cycle. You can expect to encounter a host of new challenges as the day progresses, so be prepared for anything.'

Under Master Remiel's watchful eye, the recruits dispersed quickly and quietly from the courtyard. The Astartes of the training cadre remained in ranks, awaiting word from Luther. Zahariel watched him speak a few quiet words to Remiel after the last of the recruits had left. Lord Cypher had vanished at some point during Luther's short speech; Zahariel couldn't say how or when he'd left.

After a few moments, Remiel bowed to Luther and took his leave. Luther turned to the waiting Astartes, his expression businesslike. 'All right, brothers, now you can see the challenge that lies before us,' he said with a faint grin. 'The sooner we're done here, the sooner we can return to the fight, so I don't plan on wasting a single minute. Report to the training grounds at once. We're going to put these young ones through their paces.'

Luther's honour guard bowed their heads and broke ranks, and the rest of the cadre followed in quick succession. Zahariel was turning to go when Luther caught his eye. 'A word, brother,' the knight said, beckoning to him.

Zahariel joined Luther as the cadre filed from the courtyard. Speaking quickly, Luther summarised the parts of his training plan that he intended to implement over the course of the day. 'Coordinate with Master Remiel to ensure that all of the instructors are informed of the changes,' he said. 'I'm going to have to leave matters of implementation entirely in your hands, brother. For the time being I'm going to have my hands full reviewing everything that's happened here at the fortress in our absence.'

'I'll see to it,' Zahariel said, both surprised and honoured that Luther would place so much trust in him. Despite the responsibility that had been placed on his shoulders, he was surprised to find that his spirits were lighter than they had been since the battle at Sarosh.

For the moment, the two were alone in the vast courtyard. Luther was gazing across the empty space, his mind turning to other matters. On impulse, Zahariel said, 'That was well done, brother.'

Luther glanced quizzically at the young Astartes. 'What do you mean?'

'What you said a moment ago,' Zahariel replied. 'It was inspiring. To tell the truth, many of us have been in low spirits since we left the fleet. We... well, it's good to know that we won't be here for long. All of us are eager to get back to the Crusade.'

As Zahariel spoke, the light seemed to go out of Luther's eyes. 'Ah, that,' he said, his voice strangely subdued. To Zahariel's surprise, Luther turned away, glancing up at the cloudy sky. 'That was all a lie, brother,' he said with a sigh. 'We've fallen from grace, and nothing we do here will change that. For us, the Great Crusade is over.'

ONE

Alarums and Excursions

Gordia IV
In the 200th year of the Emperor's Great Crusade

The primarch's summons found Brother-Redemptor Nemiel at the Seventh Chapter's forward base in the Huldaran foothills, just twenty kilometres south of the planetary capital. Dawn was only two hours away, and the chapter's battle brothers were completing their final checks on their weapons and equipment. The last survivors of the Gordians' battered heavy divisions had finally halted their long, bitter retreat and decided to make a stand amid the steep, iron-grey hills. The Dark Angels sensed that this would be the last battle in the months-long campaign to bring the stubborn world into compliance.

It had been a hectic night on the windswept plains. The Seventh Chapter had travelled two hundred kilometres on the previous day, harrying the Gordian rearguard, and there was little time to prepare for a dawn assault against fortified enemy positions. Nemiel had spent much of the time shuttling back and forth between the chapter's four assembly areas, speaking with each of the squads, evaluating their readiness and, when asked, receiving their battle-oaths in the name of the Lion and the Emperor. He had only just reported to Chapter Master Torannen and certified the chapter fit for combat when the message was sent down from the fleet: Brother-Redemptor Nemiel and squad to report aboard the flagship immediately. Transport en route.

The Stormbird touched down less than fifteen minutes later, just as the Imperials' preliminary bombardment began to fall on the enemy's forward positions. Surprised and somewhat bemused, Nemiel could only clasp hands with Torannen and accept the chapter master's battle-oath, then watch the Seventh Chapter's armoured vehicles rumble northward without him and his men.

Within minutes, the dropship was climbing skyward again. After a single orbit of the war-torn planet, climbing high over its storm-tossed oceans and soaring, white-capped mountain ranges, the Stormbird's pilot had adjusted his course and was closing on the Imperial squadrons anchored above Gordia IV – only to be shunted into a temporary holding pattern while the battle barge completed a resupply evolution and cleared its embarkation deck. After all the haste and urgency, Nemiel was left to sit and wait, contemplating the grey-green world below and wondering how the battle was faring for Torannen and his chapter.

A half-hour passed. Nemiel listened idly to the vox chatter over the fleet command net and turned his attention to the constellation of warships and transports that surrounded the primarch's battle barge. He could remember a time, fifty years past, when the 4th Expeditionary Fleet numbered no more than seven vessels; at Gordia IV the flagship was accompanied by twenty-five ships of various types, and that was barely a third of the fleet's total complement. The remainder were organised into discrete battle groups that were in action across the length and breadth of the Shield Worlds, fighting the Gordian League and their degenerate xenos allies.

The warships anchored around the flagship constituted the fleet's reserve squadrons, plus vessels damaged in recent actions against the League's small but powerful space navy. Tenders were pulled alongside the grand cruisers *Iron Duke* and *Duchess Arbellatris* while repairs were underway on their battle-scarred flanks. Plasma torches twinkled coldly in the dark as hundreds of servitors repaired damaged hull plating and wrecked weapons emplacements. After several minutes of idle study, Nemiel noticed frantic activity around a dozen other warships as well. Cargo lifters and supply shuttles were flying back and forth from the fleet's huge replenishment vessels, delivering everything from reactor fuel to ration tins at breakneck speed. For the first time he felt a twinge of uneasiness, wondering if the League had managed to launch a surprise counter-offensive that had caught the Legion off-guard.

When the Stormbird was finally granted priority clearance to land, the tension Nemiel felt in the air of the cavernous embarkation deck only served to deepen his unease. Harried-looking officers and ratings were hard at work organising hundreds of tonnes of supplies and getting them stowed as rapidly as possible. Shouted orders and angry tirades from impatient petty officers were drowned out by the loud crackle of the deck's magnetic barrier as two more Stormbirds came aboard in rapid succession and touched down directly behind Nemiel's ship.

The drop ship's assault ramp quivered beneath the weight of armoured feet, and Brother-Sergeant Kohl led his squad out onto the deck. The Terran had removed his helmet and clipped it to his belt, and he surveyed the frenetic activity with a bemused scowl. Nemiel glanced over at Kohl as the squad leader joined him at the base of the ramp. 'What do you make of all this?' he asked.

Kohl shook his head. The sergeant was one of the oldest surviving Astartes in the Legion, having fought in the very first battles of the Great Crusade, two hundred years before. His broad face was all flat planes and jutting angles, creased with old scars and weathered by centuries of hard fighting in the service of the Emperor. His black hair hung in tight braids close to his bull-like neck, and four polished service studs gleamed above his right brow. When he spoke, this voice was a gravelly basso.

'Never seen anything like it,' Kohl said warily. 'Something's happened, that's for certain. The fleet looks like they're getting ready for a fight.'

The embarkation deck's containment field crackled again, admitting two more Stormbirds onto the increasingly-crowded deck. Assault ramps deployed, and more Astartes squads – veterans one and all, judging by the battle honours decorating their breastplates and pauldrons – disembarked with the same mix of bemusement and professional alacrity.

An alert tone echoed from vox speakers set in the overhead. 'All squad leaders and command staff report to the strategium immediately.'

Nemiel frowned up at the overhead. Even the bridge announcer's voice sounded unusually anxious. 'Everyone seems to know something we don't,' he muttered.

Kohl shook his head. 'Welcome to the Great Crusade, brother,' he replied.

Nemiel chuckled, shaking his head in mock exasperation. He'd fought beside Kohl and his squad many times over the past few decades, and had learned to appreciate his sarcastic wit, but this time Nemiel couldn't help but notice the faint undercurrent of tension in the veteran sergeant's voice. 'Come on,' he said, setting off towards the lifts at the far side of the embarkation deck. 'Let's go find out what all this is about.'

Human crewmen stood to attention as Nemiel passed, and fellow Astartes bowed their heads respectfully. Fifty years of hard campaigning had left their mark on the young Calibanite. His armour, fresh from the forges of Mars a half-century ago, was now scarred and blemished from countless battlefields. His left pauldron, replaced by the Legion armourers after the combat drop on Cyboris, had been engraved with battle scenes commemorating his chapter's charge against the Cyborian hunter-killers. Parchment ribbons fluttered from the edges of his right pauldron, affixed with stamps of melted gold and silver to commemorate deeds of valour against humanity's many foes. The cloak of a senior initiate hung about his shoulders, edged with double bands of red and gold to mark his rank in the Higher Mysteries – a tradition from the old Order on Caliban that had been implemented by their primarch. He'd grown his hair long, like his Terran brothers, and wore it in tight braids bound by silver wire. But of all the awards and accolades that Nemiel had earned over the last half-century, it was the gleaming staff clutched in his right hand that he was proudest of.

The crozius aquilum marked him as one of the Legion's select order of Chaplains, charged with maintaining the fighting spirit of their battle brothers and preserving the ancient traditions of their brotherhood. It had been ten years since he'd been nominated for the position following the grim siege of Barrakan, when his chapter had been cut off by the greenskins and trapped at Firebase Endriago for eighteen months. By the end they were fighting off the alien assaults with fists and pieces of sharpened steel scavenged from bombed-out strongpoints, but through it all Nemiel had never wavered. He'd taunted the greenskins relentlessly and exhorted his brothers to acts of ever-greater defiance in the face of insurmountable odds. When a greenskin's crude axe had shattered his knee he'd grabbed the beast by one of its tusks and kicked it to death just for spite. When the last line of defence was broken, he'd stood his ground in the face of a massive xenos champion and fought an epic duel that had given the chapter time to launch a counter-attack that finally exhausted the last of the enemy's strength. The next day, when relief forces finally managed to fight their way through to the firebase, Nemiel had stood on the ramparts and cheered with the rest of his brothers. It took several minutes before he registered the slaps on his shoulders and back and realised that the chapter wasn't cheering for victory – they were cheering for him. Not long after, the chapter voted unanimously for him to take the place of Brother-Redemptor Barthiel, who had fallen during the darkest hours of the siege.

The whole thing still seemed a bit unreal to him, a full decade later. Him, a paragon of the Legion's ideals? As far as he was concerned, he'd just been too angry and stubborn to let a bunch of dirty greenskins get the better of him. In private moments, he'd hold up the crozius and shake his head in bemusement, as though it belonged to someone else.

This should have been Zahariel's, he'd often think to himself. *He was the idealist, the true believer. I just wanted to be a knight.*

Not a month went by that he didn't wonder what his cousin was doing back on Caliban, and he regretted not saying farewell back on Sarosh. The departure of Luther and the rest had been sudden, almost businesslike, and at the time Nemiel had assumed, like everyone else, that they would be back with the fleet before long. But Jonson had never spoken of them again – he no longer even read the regular dispatches from Caliban, relegating that task to members of his staff. Luther and the rest seemed to have been entirely banished from the primarch's mind, and as the years lengthened into decades, rumour and speculation had begun to circulate through the ranks. Some suggested a falling-out between Jonson and

Luther over the near-disaster at Sarosh, of old jealousies and petty enmities rising to the fore. Others speculated that Luther and the rest bore the blame for allowing the Saroshi bomb aboard the *Invincible Reason*, which led to sometimes-heated debates between the Terran and Calibanite factions within the Legion. Primarch Jonson made no attempt to address any of the rumours, and over time they were forgotten. No one spoke of the exiles much any more, except as a cautionary tale to new initiates: once you fell from grace with Lion El'Jonson, you were never likely to rise again.

I should send Zahariel a letter, he thought absently. He'd started several over the years, only to set them aside as the chapter prepared to deploy to yet another conflict. Then he'd begun his tutelage as a Chaplain, which occupied every spare moment that wasn't spent fighting or training to fight, and before he knew it, the time had just slipped by. He resolved to try again, just as soon as they'd gotten the current crisis under control.

Whatever the situation was, Nemiel thought grimly, he was certain that Jonson and the 4th Fleet were up to the task.

THE BATTLE BARGE's strategium, which overlooked the warship's bridge and served as the combat control centre for both the *Invincible Reason* and the 4th Fleet as a whole, was already filled to capacity by the time that Nemiel arrived. The human officers on deck bowed their heads and stepped aside as he and Kohl went to join their brethren by the strategium's primary hololith tank. The mood on deck was tense;

unease showed on the faces of the Astartes and the human officers, no matter how much they tried to conceal it. Some tried to mask their concerns with rough banter; others withdrew, focussing their attentions on their data-slates or receiving reports from their subordinates via vox-bead, but the signs were there for a trained Redemptor to read.

Moments after Nemiel's arrival, a stir went through the assembly. The assembly stiffened to attention as Lion El'Jonson, primarch of the First Legion, appeared at the entrance to the strategium.

Like all of the Emperor's sons, Jonson was the product of the most advanced genetic science known to mankind. He hadn't been born; he had been sculpted, at the cellular level, by the hands of a genius. His hair was shining gold, falling in heavy curls to his broad shoulders, and his skin was pale and smooth as alabaster. Green eyes caught the light and seemed to glow from within, like polished emeralds. His gaze was sharp and penetrating, laser-like in its intensity.

Normally, Jonson preferred to wear a simple white surplice bound with a belt of gold chains, which only served to accentuate his towering physical presence and genetically perfect physique. This time, however, he was clad for war, cased in the intricately-crafted power armour that had been gifted to him by the Emperor himself. Ornate gold scrollwork had been worked into the curved, ceramite plates, detailing forest scenes from distant Caliban. Across the breastplate was a vivid depiction of a younger Jonson wrestling with a fearsome Calibanite Lion; the monster's back was bowed and its paws raked furiously at the sky, its neck strained to breaking point by the primarch's powerful arms. At his hip, Jonson carried the Lion Sword, a glorious blade forged on Terra by the Emperor's own master armourers. A heavy cloak of emerald green swirled at the primarch's back, and he walked with the portentous tread of an avenging angel.

Voices fell silent at Jonson's approach. Nemiel watched the expressions of man and Astartes alike change at the sight of the primarch. Even to this day, after fighting alongside Jonson for so many decades, Nemiel still felt a bit awed every time he stood in the Lion's presence. He'd often said to Kohl and the rest that it was a good thing the Emperor had dedicated himself to ridding the human race of religious superstition – otherwise it would be all too easy to look upon the primarchs and worship them like gods.

For his part, Jonson seemed completely unaware of his effect on his subordinates – or else was so accustomed to it that he simply accepted it as a fundamental fact, like light or gravity. He acknowledged senior officers and long-time veterans like Kohl with sombre nods before taking his place at the strategium's circular hololith projector. Jonson fitted a data crystal into the projector's inload socket, paused scarcely a moment to marshal his thoughts, and began to speak.

'Well met, brothers,' Jonson began. His normally melodious voice was subdued, like someone who has just been dealt a terrible blow. 'I regret to have called you away from your duties, but this morning we received grim tidings from the Emperor.' He paused, meeting the eyes of the officers and Astartes closest to him. 'The Warmaster Horus and his Legion have renounced their oaths of allegiance, along with Primarch Angron's World Eaters, Mortarion's Death Guard and Fulgrim's Emperor's Children. They have virus-bombed Isstvan III, the most heavily-populated world in the system, and have rendered it lifeless. An estimated twelve billion human lives have been lost.'

Gasps of shock and cries of dismay were uttered by many of the fleet officers. Nemiel scarcely heard them. He felt only the rushing of blood in his temples and the awful coldness that seemed to spread like a wound through his chest. The primarch's words echoed in his mind, but they didn't make any sense. They couldn't make sense. His mind refused to accept them.

He turned to Kohl. The veteran sergeant's expression was stoic, but his eyes were glassy with shock. The rest of the Astartes also bore the news in silence, but Nemiel could see the words sinking into them like a torturer's knife. The Redemptor shook his head slowly, as though he could banish the awful knowledge from his head.

The primarch waited patiently for the assembly to regain a sense of order before continuing. He keyed a series of controls on the side of the hololith projector, and the device flickered into life. A detailed, three-dimensional map of the Eriden sector flickered into existence before the assembly. Imperial systems were displayed in bright blue, while at their heart, the Isstvan system pulsed an angry red. Jonson pressed another set of keys, and many of the star systems surrounding Isstvan changed colour in an irregularly-expanding sphere. Nemiel and many others in the assembly were shocked to see a score of systems switch from blue to red, and scores more flicker from blue to a dull grey.

'The reasons for the Warmaster's rebellion are unclear, but the magnitude of his actions cannot be overstated. News of the rebellion has spread like a cancer through the sector and beyond,' Jonson said, 're-igniting old tensions and territorial ambitions. Some governors have openly declared for Horus, while others see the rebellion as an opportunity to build petty empires of their own. In the short space of just two and a half months, Imperial authority in the Ultima Segmentum has been severely compromised, and dissent is beginning to spread into Segmentum Solar as well.'

Jonson paused, studying the pattern of unrest represented on the map as though it held secrets that only he could see. 'It's likely that agents loyal to the Warmaster are operating all across both Segmenta, helping fuel the growing dissent. Note how the outbreaks of lawlessness spread from system to system along the most stable warp routes leading back to Terra, the direction from which any large-scale retaliation is certain to originate.'

Nemiel took a breath, drawing on the psycholinguistic rotes he'd learned in training to suppress his emotions and focus on the data suspended in the air above the projector. To his eyes, the instances of revolt in the Ultima Segmentum appeared haphazard, but Lion El'Jonson was famous within the Legion – if not elsewhere – for his strategic genius. He had an almost intuitive ability to understand the balance of forces in a conflict and predict its course with stunning accuracy. It made him one of the Emperor's finest generals, second only to Horus himself – and in the opinion of many Dark Angels, perhaps even greater than that.

'As soon as word of the Warmaster's rebellion reached Terra, the Emperor began assembling a punitive force to confront the rebel Legions and take Horus into custody,' Jonson continued gravely. 'According to the despatch we received, a full seven Legions, led by Ferrus Manus and the Iron Hands, are en route to Isstvan, but it will be at least another four to six months before they arrive. In the meantime, Horus has redeployed his forces to Isstvan V, and is in the process of fortifying the planet in anticipation of the coming attack.'

Out of the corner of his eye, Nemiel saw Kohl fold his arms across his chest. He glanced at the Terran sergeant, and saw a bemused frown cross his weathered face.

'The next few months are going to be crucial for Horus and the rebel Legions,' Jonson said. 'The Warmaster knows that the Emperor will respond with all the force he has available. I now believe that our deployment to the Shield Worlds was part of an effort to scatter the Imperium's most loyal servants as far as possible in order to minimize the number of Legions he would have to face at any given time. Even so, a strike force of seven full Legions poses a dire threat to Horus's survival; surviving a planetary siege from such a force, let alone defeating it, will require transforming Isstvan V into a veritable fortress world. That will require an enormous amount of supplies and equipment on very short notice – the sort of materiel that only a fully-operational forge world can provide.'

The primarch adjusted the controls on the projector, and the sector view blurred, focussing in closely on the Eriden subsector and its neighbours. One system very close to Isstvan, stubbornly blue in a sea of grey and red, was suddenly highlighted.

'This is the Tanagra system, located at the edge of the adjoining Ulthoris sub-sector. As you can see, it is only fifty-two-point-seven light years from Isstvan, and lies along the most stable warp route to and from Terra. It also happens to be one of the most heavily industrialised systems in the entire sector, with a Class I-Ultra forge world named Diamat and more than two dozen mining outposts and refineries scattered throughout the system. Historically, Tanagra was rediscovered by Horus's Legion and became compliant relatively early in the Great Crusade. It has been a key logistical centre for the region ever since.' Jonson indicated the highlighted system with a thoughtful nod. 'It is no exaggeration to say that whoever controls the Tanagra system might well determine the fate of the entire Imperium.'

Murmurs spread through the assembly. The primarch's voice carried easily over them all.

'The Warmaster's treachery caught all of us offguard – just as he intended it to do,' Jonson said. His voice took on a cold, angry edge. 'At this stage, our forces are too deeply enmeshed here in the Shield Worlds to respond quickly to Horus's treachery; the best estimates of my staff indicate that it would take us nearly eight months to conclude our offensive operations, even on an emergency basis, and re-position ourselves for a strike against Isstvan. Even if we could move more quickly, Horus's agents would be able to alert the Warmaster in time to organise a counter-move.'

Jonson paused, once more surveying the shocked faces surrounding him, and his lips quirked in a predatory smile. 'A small, hand-picked force, however, might accomplish what an entire Legion cannot.' He pointed to the Tanagra system. 'Diamat is the key. If we can keep its industrial wealth from Horus's hands, he and his Legions will be as good as beaten.'

The murmurs among the assembly grew to an excited buzz. Suddenly, Nemiel understood the frenetic activity occupying much of the fleet, and the primarch's summons from the planet below. He'd been chosen, along with all the other Astartes who'd come aboard. A fierce pride swelled in his breast. Looking about, he could see that many of his brethren were feeling it as well.

Jonson raised a gauntleted hand for silence. 'As many of you already know, I've issued orders for many of our reserve squadrons to resupply and prepare for immediate deployment. I have also summoned two hundred veterans – the most I feel we can spare – from our chapters on the planet below. As you're well aware, the Shield Worlds campaign is at a critical juncture. We've been fighting the Gordians and their degenerate xenos allies for months, and this is our best opportunity to break the alliance once and for all.

My senior staff will be transferring aboard the grand cruiser *Decimator* within the hour, and will remain behind to conclude operations here in the Shield Worlds as quickly as possible. I will personally lead the expedition to Diamat, with a battle group of fifteen warships. We will travel light, leaving the slower tenders and supply vessels behind, and trust that we will be able to replace our stores when we reach Tanagra. Our Navigator believes that if current warp conditions persist, we should reach Diamat within two months.'

Jonson folded his arms and stared at the fleet officers. 'One thing more. As far as the fleet – indeed, the rest of the Legion – is concerned, the *Invincible Reason* and the ships of the battle group are withdrawing for refit and repair at Carnassus. We'll be taking a number of damaged vessels along with us to maintain the ruse. Secrecy is vital. Horus is certain to have agents in the region keeping watch on us, and they must not suspect where we're really headed until it's too late to do anything about it. Is that clear?'

The officers responded at once with nods and muttered assents. Nemiel and the Astartes said nothing. It went without saying that they would comply.

The primarch nodded curtly. 'The battle group will weigh anchor and depart for the system jump point in ten hours and forty-five minutes. All ongoing repairs, resupply efforts and equipment checks must be complete by that time. No exceptions.'

Jonson turned his attention back to the hololith projector. 'I expect by now that the Warmaster has despatched a raiding fleet to Diamat to begin plundering the necessary supplies,' he said. 'When we reach the Tanagra system, eight weeks from now, we need to arrive fully prepared to fight.'

TWO
The Tyranny of Neglect

Caliban
In the 200th year of the Emperor's Great Crusade

The tiny logic engines in the brass holoscriptor whirred softly as they wrote data onto the portable memory core. Zahariel paused while the buffer emptied, taking the time to review the facts and figures stored in his own memory. When the indicator light set atop the 'scriptor flashed from amber to green, he continued his report.

'Brother Luther's planet-wide recruiting efforts continue to show a steady twenty per cent increase each training cycle; for the third time in a row we have had to increase the size of our training chapters to accommodate the new aspirants, and the Magos Apothecarium reports that our new screening model has dramatically reduced incidents of organ rejection among inductees. In fact, not a single fatality has been reported for the last two training cycles, and the magos is confident that this trend can continue indefinitely.'

Zahariel straightened slightly, his hands clutched tightly behind his back and his head held high as he looked into the 'scriptor's lens and imagined himself speaking directly to the primarch and his senior staff. 'I am thus proud to present you with four thousand, two hundred and twelve new Astartes, ready to join their brothers in the Legion's front-line chapters. This represents a certification rate of nearly ninety-eight per cent; an extraordinary achievement by the standards of any of the Emperor's Legions.

'I am also pleased to report that the Magos Logistum has certified two thousand suits of new Mark IV armour, a hundred new suits of Tactical Dreadnought armour and two hundred of the new Thyrsis pattern jump packs for transhipment to the fleet from the forges at Mars. The manufactories here on Caliban are including two thousand new chainswords for the fleet armoury and twelve million rounds of bolt gun shells. We are expecting a shipment of armoured vehicles from the Mechanicum within the next two months, and will expedite the transhipment as soon as they have been certified. If all goes as planned, they will be accompanied from Caliban by two new divisions of Jaegers, who are performing their final training manoeuvres this month.'

Zahariel paused for half a beat, going over the figures in his head to make sure he'd left nothing out. Satisfied, he nodded to the 'scriptor. 'This concludes my report. By the time you receive this, we will have already begun our nineteenth training cycle. Brother Luther and the training masters concur that further reduction of the cycle time would only degrade the fitness of new recruits, so we've reached an optimal training time of twenty-four months, incorporating accelerated surgical implantation into an ongoing regimen of conditioning and instruction. Current projections indicate that we will have another five thousand new Astartes ready for battle by late 315. The Mechanicum has assured us that shipments of wargear will continue on an accelerated basis until you order otherwise.'

His face sobered as he reached the final item of his report. 'As a postscript, I regret to inform you that Master Remiel has taken his leave of the Legion at the age of one hundred and twelve. I am proud to say that he left on horseback, riding the Errant Road with lance in hand. All of us, especially Brother Luther, regrets his loss. We shall not see his like again.

'I trust this report finds you at the forefront of the Emperor's Crusade, driving back the shadows of Old Night and adding to the glories of our venerable Legion. On behalf of Luther the rest of the training cadre, we remain your loyal and dutiful brothers in arms.'

He bowed deeply to the 'scriptor. '*Victoria ut Imperator*. This is Brother-Librarian Zahariel, signing off.'

Zahariel reached forward, shutting off the 'scriptor with a flick of a switch. The logic engines whirred and clattered, transferring the rest of the message to the memory core. As he listened to the machine work, he debated continuing further. Was he tempting the primarch's wrath? There was no way to know. On the other hand, he thought ruefully, what was the worst that could happen if he did?

The 'scriptor finished its work. He paused, composing his thoughts, then adjusted the dials on the face of the machine. As the machine clattered, setting up a new message header, Zahariel stepped back in front of the lens. When the amber light blinked twice, he said. 'Appended message file, classification four-alpha, standard cipher. Recipient: primarch Lion El'Jonson, First Legion.'

When the light turned green again, Zahariel took a deep breath and began his plea.

'I beg your pardon in advance, my lord, and I hope you will not think me speaking out of turn, but I would be remiss in my duties if I didn't make every effort to improve the fortunes of our Legion in these trying times.' He hesitated, considering his words carefully.

'Our training cadre has worked diligently for the last half-century, refining our recruiting and training procedures to meet the challenges that the Emperor has set for us. I believe that my reports – as well as the constant flow of warriors and supplies – testify to our dedication and success. We have achieved a degree of speed and efficiency unmatched by any other Legion, and we are rightly proud of our achievements.

'At this stage, our procedures have been well-established, and we have a highly-capable infrastructure in place to continue the induction process. What the Legion needs most is for veteran warriors to return home and share the experience they've gained over the last fifty years. By the same token, our brothers here on Caliban are acutely aware of the limited nature of their own experience, and are eager to hone their skills against the Emperor's foes on the front line. This especially applies to Brother Luther, whom I believe would serve the Legion far better at your side than conducting recruiting drives here on Caliban.'

Zahariel kept his face calm and composed, even as his mind struggled to find the perfect argument that would sway the primarch. 'I think it fair to say that we have done all we can here, and it would be in the best interests of the Legion if we were rotated back to our parent chapters in the fleet. This goes particularly for Brother Luther, whose skills as a warrior and diplomat are well-known. If you were to summon just one of us back to your side, my lord, let it be him.'

His hands, clasped behind his back, tightened into fists. There was more he wanted to say, but he feared that he had pressed his luck too much already. Zahariel bowed his head before the lens. 'I hope that after you have reviewed my reports you will see the logic of my request. We all have a duty to the Emperor, my lord; all we ask is for the chance to fulfil it as we were meant to – defeating his enemies and redeeming the lost worlds of mankind.'

Zahariel sketched another quick bow, and, lest he be tempted to speak further, he reached forward swiftly and switched off the recorder. Silence fell in the small office, broken only by the whir of the 'scriptor's logic engines and the murmur of voices in the adjoining operations centre. Sighing faintly, the young Librarian turned away from the machine and surveyed the cramped, neatly-kept space, with its polished grey desk-cum-hololith unit and neat stacks of message cores containing status reports on everything from training schedules to munition production quotas. Beyond the desk, a tall, narrow window looked out past the Tower of Angels onto the southern sector of the Legion's vast sprawl of armouries, barracks and training grounds. Tall spires rose out of the late-afternoon smog, navigation hazard lights blinking red and green through the haze. He looked out at the bustling activity, the energetic industry of war, and wondered what had become of old Master Remiel.

There was a clatter of gears and the 'scriptor ejected the memory core. Zahariel plucked the small cylinder carefully from the socket and slipped it onto an ornate brass carrying tube marked with the heraldry of the Legion. Checking his internal chrono, he saw that he had just enough time to reach the detachment before they left for the embarkation field. He keyed his vox-bead and summoned a transport, then drew up the hood of his surplice and headed for the lifts on the opposite side of the operations centre. A sense of foreboding dogged his steps as he entered the lift and descended into the depths of the great mountain.

Zahariel couldn't say why the years had started to weigh on him of late. Most of the last half-century had passed swiftly indeed, lost in a whirlwind of hard work and seemingly endless iterations of recruitment strategies, training schemes and industrial expansion. Luther had seen at once that it wouldn't be enough to simply accelerate the pace of training; fulfilling the primarch's stated objectives demanded the creation of an enormous support structure that stretched across the entire planet. It was a herculean task, and at first Zahariel told himself that it was an honour that Jonson had chosen them for it.

Luther involved himself in every aspect of planetary administration, from tithe structures to industrial and arcology construction, and Zahariel was drawn along in his wake. Luther depended on him more and more, leaving him to make decisions that affected the lives of tens of millions of people each day. At first, the sheer weight of his responsibilities horrified him. But he summoned up his courage and rose to the occasion, determined to redeem himself in the primarch's eyes. Caliban's forests dwindled, replaced by mines, refineries and industrial sprawls. Huge arcologies rose like man-made mountains across the landscape as the planet's population swelled. Civilization spread across the globe, and the ranks of the Legion increased as Luther found ways to reduce the training cycle from eight years to only two. Meanwhile, reports of Jonson's exploits made their way back to Caliban, swelling their hearts with pride as the Dark Angels marched from one victory to the next. Transport ships from hundreds of distant worlds carried battle honours and war trophies back to Aldurukh, testifying to the valour of the primarch and the Legion's fighting chapters. The members of the training cadre admired each and every token sent back by their brothers and made comradely boasts of how they would exceed them all when Jonson summoned them back to the fighting.

Yet the decades passed, and no summons came. Jonson had never returned to Caliban; two planned visits had been cancelled at the last moment, citing new orders from the Emperor or unexpected developments in the current campaign. With each passing year, Luther's promise to the cadre in the castle courtyard sounded increasingly hollow, but not a warrior among them faulted him for it. If anything, their loyalty to Luther had increased during their exile. He shared their burdens and praised their successes, inspiring them by virtue of hard work, humility and personal charisma. Though they would deny it if asked, Zahariel believed that many of his brothers owed more loyalty to Luther than they did their distant primarch, and that worried him more and more as time went by.

It was only in more private moments, travelling across Caliban on manufactory inspections or working long hours alongside Luther in the Grand Master's sanctum, that Zahariel saw the turmoil in the great man's eyes.

News took a long time to reach Caliban these days, as the expeditionary fleets advanced farther and farther across the galaxy. Transports laden with plunder and trophies had grown less and less frequent of late. Then, recently, they'd received the news that the Emperor had named Horus Lupercal his Warmaster and left the crusading Legions to return to Terra. At first, Luther had hoped to keep the news quiet, but that had been folly. Before long all of their battle brothers had been talking about what had happened, and what it meant for them.

None of them were fools. They could see that the Great Crusade was entering into its final phases, and their last chance for glory was slipping away forever.

After several long minutes the lift deposited Zahariel at the base of the mountain, amidst the Legion's cavernous vehicle assembly areas. Plasma torches hissed and sputtered as Techmarines and servitors laboured to repair severely damaged Rhinos and Predator tanks sent back to Caliban from the front lines. No sooner had he stepped from the lift chamber than a four-wheeled personal transport rolled smoothly out of the vehicle pool and stopped beside the Librarian. He stepped into the open-topped passenger compartment, large enough to accommodate two Astartes in full armour. 'Sector forty-seven, training chapter five, main assembly grounds,' he ordered the servitor in the driver's compartment, and the transport set off at once, gathering speed as it made for one of the cavern's transit tunnels.

Zahariel's thoughts wandered as they sped past ranks of armoured personnel carriers, tanks and assault vehicles. He turned the memory core over and over in his hands, wondering at the unease that lingered in the recesses of his mind. Not even Israfael's meditative techniques had managed to blunt the sense of foreboding he felt. It was like a splinter beneath the skin, reminding him painfully of its presence and defying every attempt to pluck it out.

He could not say why it was so important for Luther to return to Jonson's side. They had all borne their exile with stoicism and dedication to duty, as any Astartes would, and Luther more than most. Of course, Zahariel knew why; the Legion's second-in-command was seeking redemption for what he'd nearly done aboard the *Invincible Reason*. Luther had discovered the bomb that the Saroshi delegation had smuggled onboard the Dark Angels' battle barge – and had done nothing about it. For a brief time he'd let his jealousy of Lion El'Jonson's achievements overcome his better nature, but at the last moment he'd come to his senses and tried to make things right. He and Zahariel had nearly died disposing of the Saroshi bomb, but somehow the primarch suspected Luther's earlier lapse and had exiled him to Caliban. Now Luther worked to extirpate his guilt, but his efforts went unnoticed.

Yet what other choice did Luther have? Even if he wanted to defy Jonson's wishes, what options did he have? A demand for a fair accounting and a return to the front lines? To do that he would have to leave Caliban and seek out the primarch, in direct violation of Jonson's orders, and that meant outright rebellion. Luther would never countenance such a thing. It was inconceivable.

But if Jonson did nothing – if he let these loyal warriors sit here while the Crusade came to a close, it would leave a scar within their brotherhood that would never truly heal. Such wounds tended to fester over time, until the entire body became imperilled. It had happened on Caliban all the time, back in the old days.

Zahariel reached up and rubbed his forehead as the transport exited the tunnel into the afternoon sunlight. He couldn't imagine outright dissent within the Legion, but the thought still nagged at him.

The Librarian clenched the message tube tightly. If he earned the primarch's wrath, so be it. This was far more important.

It took almost an hour to travel from the mountain to the chapter training facilities in sector forty-seven, passing through successive rings of defensive walls and checkpoints before pulling up at the edge of a broad parade ground surrounded on three sides by barracks, firing ranges and combat simulator centres.

Zahariel sat bolt upright as the transport rolled to a stop, his brow creasing in a worried frown. The square was empty.

He checked his chrono again. According to the embarkation schedule, there should be a thousand Astartes in full combat gear waiting to board a transport for high orbit. 'Wait here,' he told the servitor, leaping from the idling vehicle and striding swiftly to the chapter master's quarters. Zahariel keyed the door open and rushed into the ready room to find the chapter master conducting an informal briefing with his newly-trained squad leaders. The young Astartes turned at the Librarian's approach, failing to conceal the bemused looks on their faces.

'Chapter Master Astelan, what's the meaning of this?' Zahariel said, his voice calm but stern. 'Your Astartes should be mustering for embarkation this very minute but the square is empty.'

Astelan's eyes narrowed on the advancing Librarian. He was one of the few Terrans serving with the Legion on Caliban, having been sent to Aldurukh some fifteen years after Luther and the rest of the training cadre. He was a veteran warrior who'd risen quickly to command of a chapter in the years following Jonson's ascension to primarch and his sudden reassignment was every bit as baffling to Zahariel as his own. He presumed that Luther was aware of the circumstances, but if Astelan had been exiled from the expeditionary fleets like the rest of them, the Master of Caliban hadn't made that fact public. Instead, he'd immediately assigned the Terran to lead one of the newly-reorganised training chapters, and treated Astelan with all the respect and esteem that he showed his other battle brothers. Luther's charisma and leadership quickly won him over, and now Zahariel would be hard-pressed to name another member of the Legion more loyal to the Master of Caliban.

'The muster was cancelled two hours ago,' Astelan said in a deep voice. He had a bluff, square-jawed face and deep-set eyes shadowed by a brooding brow. A fine white scar bisected his right eyebrow and stretched across his forehead up to the edge of his scalp. When he'd arrived on Caliban he'd worn his hair in long, tightly-knotted braids, but within the first few days he'd shaved his scalp and kept it that way.

'By whose order?' Zahariel demanded.

'Luther, of course,' Astelan replied. 'Who else?'

The Librarian frowned. 'I don't understand. Your warriors were certified for deployment. I saw the report myself.'

Astelan folded his arms. 'This has nothing to do with my Astartes, brother. Luther has cancelled all deployments offworld.'

Zahariel was suddenly conscious of the message tube clutched in his left hand. 'That can't be right,' he said. 'It's not possible.'

Astelan's scarred eyebrow raised slightly. 'Luther appears to think otherwise,' he said. One of the squad leaders chuckled, but the chapter master silenced him with a sidelong glance. 'He's in command here, is he not?'

Zahariel ignored the challenge in Astelan's tone. 'Why did he cancel the deployments? The fleet is depending on those reinforcements.'

The chapter master shrugged. 'You will have to ask him, brother.'

Biting back a sharp reply, Zahariel spun on his heel. 'I will, Astelan,' he said, heading for the door. 'You can be assured of that.'

HE FOUND LUTHER high in the fortress's topmost tower, at work in the Grand Master's chambers. Jonson and Luther had shared the huge working space in better times, shaping the future of first the Order, then the Legion. As ever, scribes and staff aides bustled through the adjoining rooms, performing the countless daily tasks of Imperial rule.

Luther's desk was a massive bastion of polished Northwild oak, solid enough to stop a boltgun shell even before the heavy hololith projector and cogitators were installed. He used it as a bulwark to keep visiting bureaucrats out of arm's reach, as he often joked.

Just behind the desk stood a narrow archway that led to a small, open balcony. Zahariel saw Luther out in the sunshine, glancing thoughtfully up at the cloudless sky. He rounded the desk and stepped to the edge of the balcony, reluctant to intrude even under the current circumstances. 'May I speak to you for a moment, brother?'

Luther glanced over his shoulder and waved Zahariel forward. 'I take it you've heard about the deployments,' he said.

'What's going on?' Zahariel replied. 'Has there been some word from the primarch?'

'No,' Luther said. 'More's the pity. There have been... developments here on Caliban.'

Zahariel frowned. 'Developments? What does that mean?'

Luther didn't reply at first. He leaned against the balcony's stone railing, staring down at the industrial sprawl thousands of feet below. Zahariel could tell that he was troubled.

'There have been reports of unrest in Stormhold and Windmir,' he said. 'Worker strikes. Protests. Even some cases of sabotage at the weapon manufactories.'

'Sabotage?' Zahariel exclaimed, unable to conceal his surprise. 'How long has this been going on?'

'Several months,' Luther said darkly. 'Perhaps as long as a year. It began with a few isolated incidents, but the problem's worked its way through the outer territories like a reaper vine, digging deep into every chink and crevice. Now it's bleeding us in a hundred places. Work stoppages have cut ammo production by fifteen per cent.'

Zahariel shook his head. He held up the message tube. 'That can't be right. I prepared the reports personally. We're over our quota.'

Luther smiled ruefully. 'That's because I've been making up the shortfall by drawing lots of ammunition from the fortress's emergency stockpiles. Now we're dangerously low.'

The Librarian let out a long breath. The emergency stockpiles were held in reserve to defend Caliban from enemy attack. Jonson would be furious if he knew they'd been cleaned out. 'What about the constabulary? Why haven't they put a stop to this?'

'The constabulary have been less than effective,' Luther said, glancing meaningfully at Zahariel.

'You mean they're helping these… these rebels?'

'Indirectly, yes,' Luther said. 'I have no proof, but I can think of no other way to explain it. There have been few detentions, and little progress on attempts to uncover who is organising the dissenters.'

Zahariel considered the implications. 'The upper echelons of the constabulary are filled with warriors from the defunct knightly orders,' he mused. Once again, the sense of foreboding tingled at the back of his mind. He pressed the fingertips of his right hand to his forehead.

'I was thinking much the same thing,' Luther said. 'There are many former nobles and powerful knights who broke with the Order when we swore our loyalty to the Emperor. Many of them possess considerable wealth and influence in their former domains.'

'But what do these rebels want?'

Luther turned to Zahariel. This time, his dark eyes glinted coldly. 'I don't know yet, brother, but I intend to find out,' he said. 'But I'm going to need warriors I can trust, so I've cancelled all deployments until further notice.'

Zahariel leaned against the balcony. The decision made sense, but he feared that Luther was striding along the edge of a precipice. 'The primarch needs those warriors in the Shield Worlds,' he said. 'If we delay them, it could lead to disastrous consequences.'

'Worse than having Caliban descend into anarchy?' Luther countered. 'Don't worry, brother. I've given this much thought. We'll send in the Jaegers first. If it they appear to have matters well in hand, I'll release the new Astartes for immediate deployment to the fleet.'

Zahariel nodded, still uneasy. 'We need to root out their ringleaders,' he said. 'Drag them out into the open and confront them with their crimes. That will put an end to this lawlessness.'

Luther nodded. 'It's already begun,' he said. 'Lord Cypher is searching for them even as we speak.'

THREE
Hammer and Anvil

Diamat
In the 200th year of the Emperor's Great Crusade

'Vox transmission from Destroyer Squadron Twelve,' Captain Stenius reported, joining the primarch at the strategium's primary hololith display. 'Long-range surveyors are picking up thirty vessels anchored in high orbit above the forge world. Reactor and sensor emissions suggest a mixed group of capital ships and heavy-grade cargo transports.'

Lion El'Jonson rested his hands against the burnished metal rim of the tank. A faint smile played at the corners of his mouth. 'Identification?'

Stenius shook his head. He was another veteran of the Legion's earliest campaigns, and bore the scars of his service proudly. His eyes were silver-rimmed, smoke-grey lenses set deeply into sockets that were seamed with scars. Nerve damage, inflicted by razor-sharp slivers of glass from an exploding hololith display, had transformed his face into a grim, inscrutable mask.

'None of the vessels in orbit are flashing ident codes,' the captain replied. 'But Commander Bracchius, aboard *Rapier*, claims the reactor signatures from two of the larger craft match those of the grand cruisers *Forinax* and *Leonis*.'

The primarch nodded. 'Formidable ships, but well past their prime. I expected as much: Horus has sent a second-line fleet comprised of renegade Imperial warships and Army units to plunder Diamat, while holding back his Astartes to protect Isstvan V.'

Stenius watched gravely as the hololith image above the table updated to reflect the new data. Diamat hung in the centre of the display, rendered in mottled shades of rust, ochre and burnt iron. Tiny red icons dotted the face of the world facing the approaching Dark Angels battle group, marking the approximate size and location of the enemy ships in orbit. Two of the icons had been tentatively classified as the two rebel grand cruisers, while others were given probable classifications based on their size and reactor emissions. Currently, the plot was showing no less than twenty cruiser-sized contacts anchored at Diamat, clustered around another ten heavy transports.

Nemiel, standing to Jonson's left on the other side of the hololith table, saw the concern in the captain's eyes. Second-rate or not, the rebels had twice as many capital ships as they did. For the moment, the Dark Angels enjoyed the advantage of surprise, and the enemy had been caught with little room to manoeuvre, but it was anyone's guess how long that would last.

Tension and uncertainty hung heavy in the dimly-lit chamber; Nemiel had observed it for weeks in the hunched shoulders and hushed exchanges between the fleet officers. During the two-month voyage from the Gordia system the news of Horus's betrayal and the nature of their clandestine mission had left indelible marks on the crew's psyche.

They've lost their faith, Nemiel thought. And why not? The unimaginable had occurred. Warmaster Horus, the Emperor's favoured son, has turned his back on the Emperor, and brother has been set against brother. He studied the faces of the men inside the strategium and saw the same fear lurking in the depths of their eyes. No one knows who to trust any more, he sensed. If someone like Horus could fall, who might be next?

The two hundred Astartes aboard the flagship dealt with their own uncertainties as they always did: honing their skills and preparing themselves mentally and physically for battle. Early in the voyage, Jonson had issued a set of directives organising his hand-picked squads into two small companies and establishing a rigorous training regimen to cement them into a cohesive fighting unit.

As the only Chaplain aboard the battle barge, Nemiel found himself personally tasked by Jonson to monitor the Astartes' training regimen and periodically certify their physical and psychological fitness. Since virtually all of the Legion's senior staff members had been left behind at Gordia IV, Nemiel soon found his responsibilities expanded to include logistics and fleet operations as well. He accepted the extra duties with pride and a certain amount of uneasiness as well, because the more he worked alongside Lion El'Jonson, the less sense the undertaking to Diamat made. Such a relatively small force couldn't possibly hold out for very long against the full strength of four rebel Legions, and Nemiel couldn't imagine that the Emperor would have ordered Jonson to attempt such a thing. The more he thought about it, the more certain he became that the primarch had ordered the expedition to Diamat for reasons that were entirely his own.

Nemiel focused his attention on the tactical plot and tried to put his foreboding aside. 'The rebels have us outnumbered, my lord,' he pointed out.

Jonson gave Nemiel a sidelong look. 'I can perform hyperspatial calculations in my head, brother,' he said wryly. 'I think I can manage to count to thirty unaided.'

Nemiel shifted uncomfortably. 'Yes, of course, my lord,' he said quickly. 'I don't mean to belabour the obvious; I was just curious as to your strategy–'

'Easy, brother,' Jonson chuckled, clapping Nemiel on the shoulder. 'I know what you meant.' He pointed to the cluster of transports above Diamat. 'That's going to be their weak point,' he said. 'The success or failure of their mission depends on the survival of those big, lumbering ships, and they're going to hang like an anchor around the rebel admiral's neck.' He glanced back at Stenius. 'Any picket ships?'

Stenius nodded. 'Bracchius reports three squadrons of escorts in a staggered sentry formation,' he reported. 'They have detected our scouts and are coming about to engage. Time to contact is one hour, fifteen minutes at current course and speed.' He straightened, hands clasped behind his back. 'What are your orders, my lord?' he inquired formally.

The battle group had reached the point of no return. At this point, more than one and a half astronomical units from Diamat, the battle group still had time and manoeuvring room to come about and retreat from the system. If Jonson chose to press ahead, it would commit his small force irrevocably to battle.

Jonson did not hesitate. 'Execute attack plan Alpha,' he said calmly, 'and send the signal to launch all Stormbirds. Bracchius is to maintain speed and engage as soon as the pickets come within range. He'll have the honour of striking the first blow against Horus's rebels.'

Stenius bowed to the primarch and turned about, issuing a stream of orders to the flagship's command staff. Jonson turned his attention back to the tactical plot. 'Brother-Redemptor Nemiel, inform the company commanders to prepare their squads for an orbital assault,' he said. 'I expect we will be in position to launch in just over three hours' time.'

'At once, my lord,' Nemiel replied, and began to relay the command through his vox-bead. The image above the hololith tank updated again, this time depicting the approximate location of the battle group's three small scout squadrons. Ahead of them, three much larger squadrons were displayed in bright red, shifting slowly into a rough crescent formation. The arms of the crescent were oriented towards the oncoming Imperial scouts, like a pair of encircling arms. Blue and red numerical data, depicting the range, course and speed of the two formations changed with steadily-increasing speed.

Lion El'Jonson studied the glowing motes of data and folded his arms, his expression distant and thoughtful. Nemiel watched another ghostly smile play across the primarch's face as both forces arrayed themselves for battle, and fought down another twinge of unease. At that moment he would have given a great deal to know what Jonson saw in the grim picture that he did not.

As SOON AS the Dark Angels' battle group had arrived in the Gehinnon star system it had effectively split into two forces. Six of the group's sixteen ships were sleek, swift destroyers, which the primarch immediately ordered ahead of the main division with a trio of light cruisers to provide support. These scout squadrons quickly pulled ahead of the larger and slower cruisers, their long-range surveyors sweeping the void ahead of them and attempting to fix the size and disposition of the enemy fleet.

Now that the enemy was sighted, vox signals went back and forth between the two destroyer squadrons and the trio of light cruisers hanging back in their wake. As the rebel picket ships – no less than fifteen enemy destroyers, organised into three large squadrons – deployed into a standard crescent formation, Jonson's light cruisers flared their thrusters and moved up to form a battle line with the rest of the scouts.

Thousands of kilometres behind them, the main body of Jonson's battle group was altering formation as well. The *Invincible Reason* and the strike cruisers

Amadis and *Adzikel* drew ahead of the two grand cruisers and two heavy cruisers that comprised the rest of the main force. At the same time, the armoured blast doors covering the three ships' prow hangar bays slid ponderously open and flight after flight of Stormbirds leapt like loosed arrows into the darkness. Within minutes, seven squadrons of the heavily-armed assault craft were speeding ahead of the formation, racing to join up with the distant scouts before the rebel destroyers reached extreme firing range.

With four minutes left to contact, the rebel pickets suddenly increased speed; perhaps the flotilla commander detected the oncoming Stormbirds, or gave in to his eagerness to open the engagement, but it was too little, too late. Jonson's Stormbirds were streaking through the scout squadron's firing line just as the enemy destroyers opened fire.

The rebel ships opened the engagement as Jonson expected they would, opening their bow tubes and launching a salvo of deadly torpedoes at the oncoming scouts. Thirty of the huge missiles – each one powerful enough to blow a destroyer-sized ship apart – sped towards the scouts in a wide arc that left the Imperial ships with no room to escape.

Surveyor arrays aboard the Stormbirds detected the launches at once, and the Astartes pilots spread out their formations as widely as possible to intercept the oncoming torpedoes. They swept through the volley of missiles in the space of a few seconds; lascannons spat bolts of searing light, spearing through the torpedoes' casings and detonating their huge fuel tanks. Massive explosions flickered angrily in the darkness in the Stormbirds' wake, spreading clouds of incandescent gas and debris that faded quickly in the airless void. Almost half of the torpedoes were destroyed; the rest sped onward towards their targets, too fast for the assault ships to alter course and come around for another pass. The Astartes held their course, already picking out targets among the oncoming picket ships.

The scout squadrons opened fire on the incoming missiles as soon as they came within range. Macro cannons and rapid-cycle megalasers filled the vacuum ahead of the small ships with a veritable wall of fire. Energy lances – massive beams of voltaic power – swept in burning arcs ahead of the light cruisers. More globes of flame bloomed along the path of the onrushing scouts, blending together into a seething field of vaporised metal and radioactive gas.

Five torpedoes slipped through the maelstrom. They crossed the remaining space to their targets in less than a second, flying into a second, smaller cloud of exploding shells as the destroyers' flak batteries opened fire. The servitor-crewed guns succeeded in destroying two of the remaining missiles.

Three torpedoes out of thirty struck home. One of the weapons smashed into the prow of the destroyer *Audacious* but failed to detonate; *Hotspur* and *Stiletto*, however, were not so fortunate. The torpedoes' plasma warheads tore the lightly-armoured destroyers apart, transforming them into expanding clouds of gas and debris in a single instant. Horus's rebels had claimed first blood.

The surviving ships passed through the remnant gases of the intercepted torpedoes, wreathing their void shields with streamers of plasma and temporarily fouling their auspex returns. Hungry for vengeance, their surveyor crews strained at their scopes, searching for engine telltales amid the storm of interference. Moments passed; points of heat swelled like stars in the radioactive haze. Ranges and vectors were calculated and relayed down to the torpedomen, who entered the data into their deadly charges. While the enemy pickets were still trying to reload their tubes, the scouts launched a torpedo salvo of their own.

By this time, the two formations were at extreme weapons' range, and the enemy pickets were faced with a dilemma: fire at the oncoming Stormbirds, the torpedo salvo or the scout squadrons behind them. The flotilla commander was forced to make a split-second decision, ordering all gun batteries to target the scouts and leaving the rest to the flak guns.

It was a brave but costly tactic. The Stormbirds reached the pickets first, each squadron orientating on a target and thundering in at full power. Explosive shells and multilaser bolts hammered at the oncoming assault craft, but the heavily-armoured Stormbirds pressed on through the barrage. Here and there an enemy shot struck home; engines exploded or cockpits were shattered by direct hits, but the rest continued their attack. They swept in low across the destroyers' upper decks, pummelling their hull and superstructure with cannon fire and melta rockets. Four of the pickets staggered out of formation, their bridges smashed and their decks ablaze.

Seconds later the Imperial torpedoes struck. Seven of them hit their targets, blowing the rebel destroyers apart. The four surviving ships plunged onwards, doggedly trading blow for blow with the scout squadrons. Their void shields blazed beneath a rain of explosive shells and ravening lance beams as they plunged into the Imperial formation. At such close range the gunners could scarcely miss their targets; one by one the shields of the rebel ships failed and the concentrated Imperial fire ripped them open from stem to stern.

But Horus's ships and their veteran crews died hard. They concentrated their fire on the survivors of Destroyer Squadron Twelve, pouring fire into *Rapier* and *Courageous*. The void shields of the two destroyers collapsed beneath the onslaught; *Courageous* died a moment later as a shell found its way into her main reactor room. *Rapier* fought on a few seconds more, destroying one of the picket ships with her last salvo, before an enemy shell detonated in her torpedo magazine.

Forty seconds had passed since the rebels' first salvo. Captain Ivers, master of the light cruiser *Formidable*, sent a terse vox to the flagship: the way to Diamat was clear.

'INCREASE SPEED,' JONSON ordered, watching the telltales update on the tactical plot. They were less than a quarter of a million kilometres from Diamat now, well within range of the battle group's surveyor arrays, and they were getting positional updates on the enemy fleet in real time.

It had been more than an hour since the initial engagement against the rebel pickets. The Stormbirds had been recovered and were being rearmed for another sortie. Nemiel had expected that the surviving escorts would be withdrawn as well, but Jonson had instead sent the depleted force on a roundabout course that threatened to swing around the far left flank of the enemy squadrons that had weighed anchor and were forming a battle line between Jonson's force and the planet. The rebel transports were still in high orbit above Diamat, surrounded by a protective cordon of eight cruisers.

Nemiel felt the rumble of the battle barge's thrusters reverberate through the deck plates as the *Invincible Reason* went to maximum acceleration. The battle barge and her flanking strike cruisers had adopted a wedge formation, presenting themselves as primary targets to the rebel ships. The Astartes' ships, designed to force their way through a hostile planet's defence network and deploy their landing companies, were even more heavily armoured than typical ships of the line. Jonson calculated that the enemy ships would focus the majority of their fire on the battle barge, buying his other ships precious seconds to close to effective firing range.

'Any response to our hails?' Jonson asked Captain Stenius. They had been trying to raise the Imperial authorities on Diamat as soon as they had come within vox range.

Stenius shook his head. 'Nothing yet,' he replied. 'There's signs of heavy ionization in the atmosphere, though, so we might not get a signal through until we reach orbit.'

'Atomics?' the primarch asked.

The captain nodded. 'It looks like the rebels have launched dozens of orbital strikes, likely targeting troop concentrations and defence installations.'

'Have the rebels succeeded in reaching the forges?' Nemiel asked.

'If not, they must be very close,' Jonson said. 'Otherwise those transports would have broken orbit as soon as we were detected.' He nodded his head at the telltales representing the escorting cruisers. 'They also wouldn't have left behind such a strong reserve force to guard them unless they already contained something valuable, so we have to assume that the enemy has at least managed to breach a number of the planet's secondary forges. If there are any defence forces still in action, they will be concentrated around the primary forge complex and Titan foundry.'

'Titans?' Nemiel asked. 'There is a legion based at Diamat?'

Jonson nodded. 'Legio Gladius,' he replied. 'Unfortunately, their engines are embarked with the 27th Expeditionary Fleet, far to the galactic south. On Horus's orders, I might add.'

'What does that leave the defenders with?'

The primarch paused, consulting his memory. 'Eight regiments of Tanagran Dragoons, plus two armoured regiments and several battalions of heavy artillery.'

Nemiel nodded. It was an impressive array of force. He wondered how much of it still survived. 'What forces can the forges muster?'

Jonson shrugged. 'An unknown number of Mechanicum troops. The scions of Mars are not obliged to share the secrets of their defences.' He paused, studying the plot for several moments before straightening and shaking his head. 'It's looking unlikely that the rebels will detach any units from their main body to try and intercept our escorts. They'll trust the reserve cruisers to keep them at bay, which leaves us facing no less than twelve ships of the line.'

'Ten minutes to contact,' Stenius announced. 'Orders, my lord?'

'Are the Stormbirds ready for another sortie?' Jonson asked.

'We have two squadrons ready for launch, and *Amadis* reports that they have one squadron standing by. *Adzikel* has a fire in her hangar bay from a crash-landed Stormbird. They estimate another fourteen minutes before they can resume flight operations.'

'The battle will be over in ten,' Jonson growled. 'Very well: signal the scout force and order them to ready torpedoes and prepare for a course change on my mark. Transmit the same signal to the main force, and add that no ship is to fire until ordered.'

Stenius bowed curtly and began barking orders across the strategium. On the tactical plot the distance between the two fleets was dwindling rapidly. They would be in extreme weapons range within moments. Nemiel thought back to the savagery of the initial engagement and prepared himself for the coming storm.

The main body of the enemy fleet was centred on four grand cruisers; at this range the officers aboard the flagship had positively identified them as the Avenger-class grand cruisers *Forinax* and *Leonis*, and the Vengeance-class ships *Castigator* and *Vindicare*. To either flank of this powerful group of ships were arrayed a squadron of four cruisers each: a mix of Crusaders, their hulls bristling with weapon batteries, and swift, lance-armed Armigers. Against such a force, the Dark Angels had their battle barge and two strike cruisers, plus the Avenger-class grand cruisers *Iron Duke* and *Duchess Arbellatris* and the Infernus-class heavy cruisers *Flamberge* and *Lord Dante*. Though the rebels had a clear edge in numbers and firepower, they no longer had any ships capable of launching torpedoes - a slim advantage that Jonson intended to capitalise on.

The seconds ticked by. Captain Stenius watched the readouts on the tactical plot. 'We're at extreme torpedo range,' he announced.

'Not yet,' Jonson ordered. He watched the scout force slip past the main body of the rebel fleet, still accelerating towards Diamat and the vulnerable transports.

Stenius nodded. 'Two minutes to extreme firing range.'

'Any signals from the planet's surface?' Jonson asked.

'Negative,' the captain replied.

'Very well.' Jonson turned to Nemiel. 'If we don't hear anything from the governor or his defence forces by the time we reach orbit, I'm going to send the landing force down around the main forge complex. Your orders will be to secure the forge and eliminate any rebel troops in the area. Clear?'

'Clear, my lord,' Nemiel answered at once.

The battle group sped onwards, straight into the guns of the waiting rebel ships. Two minutes later the Aegis Officer called out, 'Incoming fire!'

'All ships brace for impact!' the primarch ordered.

Lance beams leapt from the prows of the rebel cruisers, raking the void with searing beams of force. They slashed across the prow of the *Invincible Reason* and the two strike cruisers, causing their shields to flare with incandescent fury. Violet light blazed beyond the reinforced viewports of the bridge and a powerful blow resounded through the hull of the great ship.

'Hull breach, deck twelve, frame sixty-three!' the Aegis Officer called out. 'No casualties reported.'

Captain Stenius accepted the news with a curt nod. 'Do we return fire?' he asked the primarch.

'Not yet,' Jonson replied. He was studying the read-out on the plot intently. 'Signal the scout force: come about to new heading one-two-zero and commence torpedo runs on rebel grand cruisers.'

The Astartes ships ploughed through glowing clouds of plasma and vaporised deck plating as they continued to close on the rebel ships. As they closed to optimum firing range the enemy force began a slow turn to starboard so they could bring their fearsome broadsides to bear on the Imperial ships. But as they began their turn, Nemiel saw the scouts begin their course change. The nimble escorts swung around in a tight arc directly behind the enemy ships, their presence hidden by the rebels' own reactor emissions.

The trap had been sprung. Jonson smiled coldly. 'Signal *Amadis* and *Adzikel*: target enemy grand cruisers and launch torpedoes. Captain Stenius, you may fire at will.'

More lance shots leapt from the rebel ships, and now the enemy weapon batteries were going into action as well, hurling streams of blazing shells at the oncoming Imperials. At the same time, torpedoes leapt from the tubes of the Astartes ships and the oncoming scout vessels, bracketing the rebel grand cruisers from both fore and aft.

Heavy blows pummelled the battle barge to port and starboard. Alarms wailed. 'Multiple hits, decks five through twenty!' the Aegis Officer called out. 'Fire on deck twelve!'

'Signal the main force,' Jonson said calmly. 'New course three-zero-zero. All units, target enemy cruisers to port. Fire at will.'

Wreathed in a maelstrom of fire, the Imperial ships swung ponderously to port, aiming away from the centre of the enemy formation and instead towards the four rebel cruisers on the enemy's flank. Along the dorsal gun decks of the battle barge, enormous turrets slowly traversed, bringing their massive bombardment cannons to bear on an Armiger-class cruiser. At the same time the battle barge's starboard weapons batteries went into action, hammering at the rebel ship's void shields with a hail of macro cannon shells. The enemy cruiser's shields flickered angrily under the relentless barrage before collapsing entirely. At the same time her lance batteries lashed at the *Invincible Reason*, raking her void shields from stem to stern. Beams of force pierced the defensive field and clawed through the barge's armoured hull.

Seconds later the battle barge replied with a rolling salvo from her bombardment cannons. They boomed through the hull like war drums, each one growing louder as the volley marched closer to the bridge. The shells glowed as they sped through the void and smashed into the flanks of the rebel ship. Nemiel watched in awe as a series of massive explosions rippled through the cruiser's decks, until finally it blew apart in a flare of escaping plasma.

Farther away, the grand cruisers at the centre of the enemy formation were reeling beneath the blows of Imperial torpedoes that struck them both fore and aft. The *Forinax* staggered out of the formation, her bridge aflame, while the *Castigator* saw most of her starboard gun decks smashed by a trio of powerful hits. The scout force reduced speed and continued their run behind the rebels, lashing at the enemy ships with their weapon batteries and energy lances.

The Imperial ships plunged through the rebel formation, exchanging thunderous broadsides with the enemy. The smaller cruisers suffered greatly under the punishing blows of Jonson's larger ships; a Crusader received a broadside from both the *Amadis* and the *Iron Duke* that ripped her open and left her a burning hulk, while the second Armiger blew apart in another massive fireball as her reactor core was breached. Lances and shells hammered the Imperial ships as well; the flagship and the strike cruisers bore the brunt of the enemy fire, their armoured hulls riddled with multiple impacts and the glowing tracks of lance hits. *Duchess Arbellatris* staggered beneath a hail of fire; her hastily-repaired hull plating gave way beneath the onslaught, wracking the proud vessel with devastating internal explosions that left her drifting out of control. *Flamberge* and *Lord Dante* suffered as well, their upper decks and superstructure smashed by a hail of enemy shells, but the battered heavy cruisers held their course and returned fire with every weapon they had left.

The exchange lasted barely fifteen seconds, though to Nemiel it seemed like an eternity. The void was rent with fire and streams of blazing debris. Ships and men died in the blink of an eye before the two forces drew away from one another on opposite courses. The scout force continued to harry the rebels as they sped away and began a slow turn to re-engage the Imperial battle group.

'Damage report!' Jonson ordered. The *Invincible Reason* shuddered like a wounded beast as she sped on towards Diamat. The air in the strategium was growing hazy with smoke as fires spread throughout the ship.

Captain Stenius was bent over the Aegis Officer's station, his augmetic lenses glowing green in the reflected light of the flickering readouts. 'All ships report moderate to severe damage,' he replied. '*Duchess Arbellatris* is not responding to signals. *Flamberge* and *Lord Dante* report heavy casualties. *Iron Duke* and *Amadis* have both sustained damage to their thrusters, and *Amadis* also reports that her flak batteries are out of action. Repairs are underway.'

'What about us?' the primarch said. 'How hard were we hit?'

Stenius grimaced. 'Our armour stopped the worst of it, but we've got hull breaches all over the ship and a fire raging on three decks. The torpedo deck reports that the forward tubes are fouled, but they're working to clear them.' He shrugged. 'It's not good, but it could have been much worse.'

Jonson smiled grimly. 'Don't tempt fate, Captain. We're not finished yet. Signal the main force to alter course to three-three-zero and launch the Storm-birds. We'll head straight for those transports and see if we can force them to weigh anchor. I'm betting the reserve force will opt to disengage rather than risk those ships.'

He turned to Nemiel. 'Brother, it's time you made your way to the drop pods. We'll be over Diamat in another ten minutes.'

FOUR

Uncertain Allegiances

Caliban
In the 200th year of the Emperor's Great Crusade

THERE WAS AN ill wind blowing through the halls of Aldurukh, and Zahariel feared he was the only one who felt it.

The courtyard was much the same as it had been when he was a young aspirant; the white paving stones were kept spotlessly clean, the more to highlight the dark grey stone of the spiral that had been laid there many hundreds of years before. The Order had used it as a training tool, incorporating the curving lines into their sword routines and close-order drills, but Brother-Librarian Israfael claimed that its significance was far more ancient. 'Walk the Labyrinth and meditate daily,' he told his students. 'Fix your eyes upon the path, and it will help to focus your mind.'

Zahariel walked the spiral with slow, deliberate steps, his head covered by a deep woolen cowl and his hands tucked into the sleeves of his surplice. His eyes followed the endlessly curving line of dark stone, no longer truly seeing what was before him. The Librarian's mind was turned inward, buffeted by an unseen storm.

He could feel the energies of the warp whipping about him like a gusting breeze, angry and turbulent. Israfael had warned him on the trip back from Sarosh that the winds of the warp were far stronger on Caliban than any other world he'd ever visited, and the senior Librarian had spent considerable time studying the phenomenon since they'd returned. From Zahariel's own observations, it seemed that the energies surrounding the vast fortress had grown increasingly agitated over the past few months. He knew from his training that the warp was sensitive to strong emotions – particularly the darker passions of fear, sadness and hate. Given the troubling events that were occurring beyond the walls of Aldurukh, the rising wind felt like an ill omen of things to come.

The civil unrest spreading across Caliban baffled and troubled Zahariel, all the more so because it had evidently been building for a long time. He was dismayed to discover that the clues had been there all along. After learning of the situation from Luther, he had spent every free moment sifting through the vast message archives in the fortress's library. The Imperium operated and maintained Caliban's fast-growing vox and data networks, and every bit of message traffic – from personal calls to news broadcasts – were captured and archived as standard procedure. So far he'd managed to work his way back through several years' worth of data, and his Astartes training had taught him exactly what to look for. The patterns were obvious to one educated in the myriad ways of waging war.

There was an insurrection spreading across Caliban. It was well-organised, well-equipped and growing bolder with each passing day. It hadn't been going on for months, or even a year, as Luther claimed, but possibly as long as a decade.

Whoever was behind the unrest had been very careful, starting with small disturbances in scattered settlements and slowly expanding as their skill and experience increased. Reports of industrial accidents at weapon manufactories and other industrial sites had been written off in the past as the unfortunate consequence of a highly aggressive expansion program, but now Zahariel wondered how many of these accidents had actually been staged to cover up the theft of weapons and other military-grade equipment. Investigations by Munitorum officials and the local constabulary had been perfunctory at best, but the Imperial bureaucracy on Caliban was overworked and undermanned and there was good reason to believe that the planet's law enforcement organisation had been compromised. There was certainly enough evidence to indicate that the constabulary had been covering up the extent of the problem for a long time, but yet...

How could Luther not have known?

The ghostly pressure of the warp vanished, like a snuffed candle. Zahariel paused, took a deep breath, and tried to regain his focus once more.

It seemed inconceivable to him that Luther had missed the signs for so long. He was justly famous for his intellect, one of the very few on Caliban who could converse with Jonson on an almost equal footing. Zahariel knew that Luther monitored the reports of the Administratum, the local militia and the constabulary as a matter of course – it was part of his duties as the master of Caliban. If the threat was obvious to him, it should have been glaringly so to a man like Luther. The implications were disturbing, to say the least.

Zahariel wished there was someone he could talk to about his concerns. More than once he'd been tempted to bring the matter up to Brother Israfael, but the Librarian's stern and aloof demeanour had persuaded him against it. The only other member of the Legion he felt he could talk to had been Master Remiel, and now he was gone.

The young Librarian cast his eyes skyward and found himself wishing, once again, that Nemiel had been sent home as well. Zahariel thought his cousin could be overly cynical at times, but right now he needed a pragmatic perspective more than anything else. As much as he wanted to believe that Luther was still a noble and virtuous knight at heart, Zahariel had a sacred duty to his Legion, his primarch, and above all, the Emperor himself. If there was corruption within the ranks he was obligated to do something about it, regardless of who might be involved, but he had to be absolutely certain before he took action. Morale among the brothers was tenuous enough as it was.

Once again, Zahariel breathed deeply and tried to focus once more on his meditations. He closed his eyes, summoning up the mental rotes that Israfael had taught him, if only to drive away the worries that gnawed at his heart. He ruthlessly pushed conscious thought aside and emptied his mind.

The ghostly wind gusted once more, surprising him with its strength. Invisible and insubstantial, it nevertheless pushed roughly against him. The force of it rocked him back on his heels; without thinking, he opened his eyes and found himself staring into the face of the storm.

A pale blue glow suffused the courtyard, similar to moonlight but roiling like oil. Wild currents swirled and eddied around him, outlined in shades of black and grey; if he focused on them, they took on patterns that plucked uncomfortably at his mind. A faint, discordant moaning filled his head. The intensity of the vision startled the young Librarian for an instant. His concentration faltered – yet the sensations grew stronger.

Dark, hooded figures stirred at the edges of his sight, and then a voice, alien and yet chillingly familiar, echoed in his mind.

Remember your oath to us.

Zahariel let out a startled cry and spun on his heel, seeking the source of the voice. Memories of his quest for the Calibanite Lion, more than fifty years past, flooded back to him in an instant. He remembered wandering into a remote part of the forest more haunted and evil than he had ever known before, and the strange, hooded creatures who had confronted him there.

His hearts pounding wildly, Zahariel searched the courtyard's shadows for the Watchers in the Dark. The blue glow and the angry wind vanished from one blink to the next, and when his vision cleared, he found himself staring across the courtyard at the pensive figure of Luther. The master of Caliban was studying Zahariel intently.

'Is something wrong, brother?' Luther said quietly. His voice was full of concern, but the knight's expression was inscrutable.

Zahariel mastered himself quickly, controlling the flow of adrenaline and lowering his heart rate with a few controlled breaths. 'Brother-Librarian Israfael would reprimand me for letting someone catch me unawares while I was meditating,' he said. It shocked him how quickly the lie came to his lips.

Silence fell between the two warriors. Luther studied Zahariel for a long moment, then smiled ruefully. 'We've all got a lot on our minds these days, haven't we?'

'More so than ever before,' Zahariel managed to say.

Luther nodded in agreement. He crossed the courtyard quickly, his manner formal but his expression still guarded. 'I've been looking all over the fortress for you,' he said.

Zahariel frowned. 'Why didn't you contact me on the vox?'

'Because some conversations don't belong on the network,' Luther replied in a low voice. 'I'm about to attend a very important meeting, and I want you there as well.'

The Librarian's frown deepened. 'Of course,' he replied at once. Then, more hesitantly, he said, 'The hour is very late, brother. What's this about? Has something happened?'

Luther's handsome face turned grim. 'An hour ago, insurgents launched attacks on foundries, manufactories and Administratum buildings all over Caliban,' he said. 'Since then, riots have broken out in a number of arcologies, including the new one up in the Northwilds.' His lip curled in an angry snarl. 'The constabulary has been unable to deal with the crisis, so I've despatched ten regiments of Jaegers to restore order.'

The news stunned Zahariel. Suddenly, Luther's decision to withhold the Legion's reinforcements seemed almost prescient. The insurgency on Caliban had entered a dangerous new phase. His mind began to race, recalling reams of data on combat readiness, deployment times and logistics requirements for the Astartes chapters and support units on-planet. 'Will this be an operational meeting, or a strategic one?' he asked. 'I'll need a few minutes to collect the proper data files.'

'Neither,' Luther replied. His expression became guarded. 'The rebel leaders have been in contact with Lord Cypher. They want to meet with me under a flag of parley, and I've agreed. They'll arrive within the hour.'

THE SHUTTLE WAS a standard Imperial design, anonymous and unnoticed among the hundreds of craft coming and going from the landing fields around Aldurukh. At precisely two hours past midnight, the transport touched down and lowered its landing ramp. Its engines subsided to an idle hum as five individuals moved quickly and purposefully down the ramp and crossed the permacrete towards the open doorway of a nearby hangar. They entered the cavernous space warily, scanning the deep shadows for potential threats. Finding none, the rebel leaders and their lone escort crossed to the centre of the building, where Luther and Zahariel stood in the glow of one of the hangar's many floodlights.

Zahariel watched the traitors approach and tried to remain outwardly calm. His mind was in turmoil, torn between outrage and obedience. Luther's decision to meet with the leaders of the insurrection shocked him to the core; it went against everything the Legion had taught him. Defiance of Imperial law demanded swift and ruthless action, without mercy or compromise. Negotiation of any kind was unthinkable, and threatened to undermine the Emperor's authority. Entire worlds had been devastated for less.

But this wasn't some strange, isolated planet like Sarosh. This was Caliban. These were his people, and Zahariel knew in his heart that they weren't corrupt or evil. Perhaps that was what was foremost in Luther's mind as well, he thought. It served no one, least of all the Emperor, if millions of innocent lives were lost thanks to the actions of a misguided few. And if anyone could convince these men to abandon their cause, it was Luther. So Zahariel told himself, and tried to master the doubts that gnawed at his heart.

The five figures each wore an aspirant's hooded surplice, hiding their faces in shadow. None of them were armed, as the ancient traditions of parley demanded. As they stepped into the circle of light, Zahariel felt a rising pain in the back of his head. His vision wavered; the hooded figures seemed to double before his eyes, and the light flickered strangely. The Librarian screwed his eyes shut and used the rotes he'd learned from Israfael to try and clear his mind. When he opened them again, his vision was clear, but the pain refused to go away.

The rebel leaders drew back their hoods, one by one. Lord Cypher was in the lead, his expression flat and unreadable. The others Zahariel recognised with a mix of anger and dismay.

The first of the rebel leaders was Lord Thuriel, scion of a noble family in the southlands that still clung stubbornly to its last vestiges of wealth and power. Behind him came Lord Malchial, the son of a famous knight who had earned much renown during Jonson's crusade against the great beasts. The fact that he and Thuriel had been bitter enemies for decades led Zahariel to wonder what could have possibly united them so.

After Malchial came another surprise: the third rebel leader was a woman. Lady Alera had inherited her title when all four of her brothers had been killed in the Northwilds, and under her leadership her household had prospered until the coming of the Emperor. Now her fortunes were in decline, like all of Caliban's noble families, but she remained a force to be reckoned with.

But the last of the rebels was the most surprising of all. Zahariel recognised the man's ruined face at once: more than a half a century ago, Sar Daviel had been among the knights who had stormed the fortress of the Knights of Lupus, and was one of the warriors who fought the terrible beasts that their foes had loosed upon the Order. A monster's huge paw had crushed the right side of his face, caving in his cheekbone and bursting his eye. The creature's talons had carved Daviel's flesh down to the bone in five ragged arcs that stretched from his right ear all the way to his chin. By some miracle he'd survived the terrible wound, but when the Emperor had come and the Order had been absorbed into the Legion his request to join the ranks of the Astartes had been denied. The young knight had left Aldurukh soon after, and none knew what had become of him. Daviel was an old man now; his hair had grown white and his face seamed with decades of hard living out on Caliban's ever-shrinking frontier, but his body was still lean and strong for a man almost seventy years of age.

Thuriel caught sight of Zahariel, and the noble's sharp, aristocratic features darkened with rage. He rounded on Cypher. 'You assured us that only Luther would attend the parley,' he snapped. Lady Alera and Lord Malchial cast suspicious looks at the Librarian's tall, imposing form.

'That's not for Lord Cypher to decide,' Luther replied in a steely tone. 'Brother-Librarian Zahariel is my lieutenant; anything you say to me can be said to him as well.' He folded his arms and stared forbiddingly at the rebels. 'You requested this parley, so let's hear what you have to say.'

The cool menace in Luther's voice caused Lord Thuriel to pale slightly. Malchial and Alera looked uneasily at one another, but neither seemed willing to speak. Finally Sar Daviel let out an impatient growl and said, 'We speak for the free peoples of

Caliban, my lord, and we declare that the Imperial occupation must end.'

'Occupation?' Luther echoed, his voice faintly incredulous. 'Caliban is an Imperial world now, governed and protected by the Emperor's law and the might of the First Legion.'

'Protected? More like conquered,' Malchial interjected. 'It was Lion El'Jonson who welcomed the Emperor – his father, if rumours be true – to Caliban and delivered the planet into his hands.'

'For all we know, that was their plan all along,' Lady Alera snapped. 'It seems very convenient to me that Jonson arrives on Caliban under very mysterious circumstances, and then, just when he's gained control of the planet's knightly orders, the Emperor just happens to find him.'

'That's the stupidest thing I've ever heard,' Zahariel snapped. 'You people don't know what you're talking about! If you had any idea how vast the Imperium is–'

Luther cut off the Librarian with an upraised hand and a warning glance. 'My lieutenant speaks out of turn,' he said smoothly. 'Nevertheless, your suspicions, Lady Alera, are groundless at best. As to you, Lord Malchial, how do you defend the assertion that my primarch delivered Caliban to the Emperor? Our own legends speak of Caliban's ties to distant Terra. Now, thanks to the Emperor, those ties have been restored, and our planet has entered a new age of prosperity.'

'Prosperity?' Lord Thuriel snarled. The noble's initial pallor had vanished beneath a swelling tide of outrage. 'Is that what you call the wholesale plundering of our world? Perhaps if you'd stuck your head outside the walls of this spreading canker you call a fortress you'd see how Caliban suffers! Our forests are gone, our villages ploughed under, our mountains cracked open like nuts and scraped clean by huge mining machines! Noble families that fought and bled for their lands and their people for generations have been disinherited, their feudal subjects carried off and put to work in Imperial factories and mines. And the knightly orders who might have protected us from all of this have all been disbanded or–' he glanced up at Zahariel's giant form '–altered nearly beyond recognition.'

Zahariel's fists clenched at the implied insult. Only Luther's steady demeanour kept the Librarian's anger in check and the rules of parley intact.

By contrast, the Master of Caliban folded his arms and chuckled softly. 'And now we get to the heart of things,' he said with a mirthless grin. He indicated the rebel leaders with a sweep of his hand. 'Your grievances are personal, not collective; you're not rebelling for the sake of your feudal subjects, as you call them, but because you've lost the wealth and power your families have hoarded over the centuries. Do you imagine that the majority of our people would actually want to become peasant farmers once more? The Emperor has completed the process that Jonson began here with the Order: providing safety, security and above all, equality for everyone, regardless of their class or station.'

Lady Alera looked pointedly from Luther to Zahariel and back again. 'Clearly some people are more equal than others,' she said.

Luther shook his head, refusing to take the bait. 'Appearances can be deceiving,' he replied evenly.

'Indeed they can,' Sar Daviel said, stepping to the front of the group. 'Look at me, brother. I'm no pampered earl's son. I earned these scars by your side in the Northwilds, serving Jonson's vision. And how was I rewarded?'

Luther sighed. 'Brother, it was nothing more than cruel fate that kept you from the ranks of the Legion. Your injuries were too severe to permit the process of transformation, just as I was too advanced in years. It was your decision to leave. You still had a place at Aldurukh.'

'Doing what?' Daviel shot back. 'Polishing the armour of my betters? Scurrying through the halls like a pageboy?' Tears shone at the corners of his remaining eye. 'I'm a knight, Luther. That used to mean something. It meant something to you, once upon a time. You were the greatest among us, and frankly it kills me to see how Jonson has used you all these years.'

Zahariel saw Luther stiffen slightly. Daviel's blow had struck home.

'Have a care, brother,' Luther said, his voice subdued. 'You presume too much. Jonson united this world. He saved us from the threat of the beasts. I could never have done that.'

But Daviel didn't waver. He held Luther's gaze without flinching. 'I think you could have,' he replied. 'Jonson could never have convinced the other knightly orders to support his crusade against the beasts. You did that. The plan might have been his, but you were the one who rallied an entire world behind it. The truth is that Jonson owes you everything. And look how he has repaid you. He's cast you aside, just like me.'

'You don't know what you're talking about!' Luther snarled, his voice sharp with anger.

'Not so,' Daviel said, shaking his head sadly. 'I was there, brother. I watched it happen. When I was a child, my greatest ambition was to become a knight and ride at your side. I know what a great man you are, even if no one on Caliban still remembers. Jonson knows, too. How could he not? You raised him like a son, after all. And now he's left you behind, like the rest of us.'

Lady Alera stepped forward. 'What has the Imperium truly given us? Yes, the forests are gone, and with them the beasts, but now our people have been herded into arcologies and put to work in manufactories or recruited to serve in the Imperial Army. Every hour of every day we see a little more of ourselves carved away and carried off into the stars, to serve a cause that doesn't benefit us in the least.'

'You can scorn the old ways if you wish, Luther,' Lord Thuriel added, 'but before the creation of the Order, the noble houses provided the knights that fought and died for the peasantry. Yes, we took our due, but we gave back as well. We served in our own way. How do Jonson and the Emperor serve us? They take the very best of what we have and give little or nothing in return. Surely you of all people can see that.'

'I see nothing of the kind,' Luther answered, but his expression had grown clouded. 'What about medicines, or better education? What about art and civilization?'

Malchial snorted derisively. 'Medicines and education that make us better labourers, you mean. And what good are art or entertainments when you're too busy slaving in a manufactory to appreciate them?'

'Do you imagine ours is the only world called upon to contribute to the Great Crusade?' Luther replied. 'Zahariel is right. If you only knew the scope of the Emperor's undertaking.'

'What we know is that we're being impoverished for the sake of people we don't know and have never seen,' Thuriel countered.

'We've had our culture and traditions taken from us,' Daviel interjected. 'And now our people are in greater danger than ever before.'

Luther frowned. 'What is that supposed to mean?' he asked, some of the anger returning to his voice.

Daviel started to answer, but Malchial cut him off. 'It means that Caliban's suffering will continue to worsen under Imperial rule. The question is whether or not you will stand by and allow it to happen.'

'You're not our enemy, Sar Luther,' Lady Alera said. 'We know you're a brave and honourable man. Our fight is with the Imperium, not with you or your warriors.'

Zahariel stepped forward. 'We are servants of the Emperor, my lady.'

'But you're also sons of Caliban,' the noble countered. 'And this is your world's darkest hour.'

'Join us, brother,' Sar Daviel said to Luther. 'You've denied your destiny for too long. Embrace it at last. Remember what it was like to be a knight and ride to your people's defence.'

'Defence?' Zahariel said. 'It's you who have taken up arms against your fellow citizens. Even now your rebels are fighting constabulary officers and Jaegers all across the planet, and innocent people are suffering in the riots you've spawned.' He turned angrily to Luther. 'You can see what they're trying to do, can't you? If we move quickly our battle brothers can crush this revolt in a matter of hours. Don't let them play on your jealousies–'

Luther rounded on Zahariel. 'That's enough, brother,' he said, his voice as hard as iron. The sharp tone brought the Librarian up short. The Master of Caliban glared at him a moment longer, then turned back to the rebels.

'This parley is finished,' he declared. 'Lord Cypher will return you from whence you came. After that, you will have twenty-four hours to order your forces to cease all operations and turn themselves in to local authorities.'

The rebel leaders glared angrily at Luther, all except for Daviel, who shook his head sadly. 'How can you do this?' he said.

'How can you think I wouldn't?' Luther shot back. 'If you think I hold my honour so cheaply, then you're no brother of mine,' he said. 'You have twenty-four hours. Use them wisely.'

Thuriel turned to Lady Alera and Lord Malchial. 'You see? I told you this was pointless.' He shot a venomous look at Lord Cypher. 'We're ready to leave,' the noble said, and headed swiftly for the waiting shuttle. One by one, the rebel leaders fell in behind Thuriel and walked out into the pre-dawn darkness. Zahariel felt tension drain from the muscles in his neck as the pain in his head began to ease. He made a mental note to ask Israfael about the episodes. Whatever was causing them, they were clearly getting worse.

Luther walked along behind the departing rebels, his expression lost in thought. After a moment, Zahariel followed. Part of him wanted to insist that Luther arrest the rebel leaders on the spot – the parley was a convention of Caliban's rules of warfare, not those of the Imperium, so the Legion wasn't truly bound by it. But another part of his mind warned that he'd already overstepped his bounds with Luther, and Zahariel was uncertain what might happen if he pressed further.

The engines of the shuttle rose to a pulsing roar as the rebels hurried to the waiting ramp. Zahariel stopped just outside the hangar, but Luther continued on, escorting the leaders across the permacrete.

Daviel was the last to board the shuttle. At the bottom of the ramp he turned to regard Luther. Zahariel could see the old knight say something to the Master of Caliban, but his voice was lost in the shriek of the shuttle's turbines.

When Daviel had disappeared inside the shuttle, Luther turned and made his way back to the hangar. Behind him, the transport lifted off in a cloud of dust and sped off westward, racing ahead of the dawn.

Zahariel watched Luther approach and braced himself for a sharp rebuke. The knight's face was deeply troubled. When he reached the Librarian's side, he turned to watch the dwindling lights of the shuttle's thrusters and sighed. 'We should get back to the strategium,' he said. 'We've got a lot of work to do.'

The Librarian nodded. 'You don't think they'll heed your warning?'

'No, of course not,' Luther replied. 'But the words needed to be said, nonetheless.' After a moment he added, 'Best we kept this meeting to ourselves, brother. I would not want any misunderstandings to impact morale.'

Zahariel knew an order when he heard one. He nodded curtly and watched the shuttle disappear from sight. 'What was it that Sar Daviel said to you, just before he left?' he asked, keeping his voice carefully neutral.

Luther stared out into the darkness. 'He said that Jonson betrayed us all. The forests are gone, but the monsters still remain.'

FIVE

Into the Cauldron

Diamat
In the 200th year of the Emperor's Great Crusade

Nemiel reached the midships ordnance deck at a dead run, his helmet locked in place and counting the seconds he had left until the battle barge entered Diamat's atmosphere. Already he could feel the rhythmic thunder of the ship's gun batteries rumbling through the deck plates beneath his feet, which meant that the battle group was trading fire with the enemy reserve squadron. Jonson was racing forward with his ships as quickly as he could to deploy his Astartes onto the beleaguered forge world, and Nemiel had no intention of keeping the primarch waiting.

Thick, heavy steel hatches were clanging shut in rapid succession along the length of the cavernous drop bay as the assault pods were sealed into their launch tubes like oversized torpedoes. Only one pod still sat in its loading cradle, poised above the last of the portside launch tubes. A single hatch was still open, red light spilling down the steel ramp from the cocoon-like re-entry compartment within.

A single, heavy blow rang sharply through the bulkheads; an enemy shell had penetrated the flagship's armour and detonated on one of the decks above. There was an ordnance crew waiting for Nemiel at the foot of the open pod; they followed him up the ramp, ensured he was locked into the re-entry harness and fitted a series of data cables to interface plugs set into his armour's helmet and power plant. They completed their tasks in just a few seconds and retreated from the pod without a single word. Nemiel barely noticed; he was already tapping into the fleet command net through the pod's vox array.

Readouts flickered coldly across the lenses of his helmet. Icons of red and blue flared to life, silhouetted against the curve of a planet. At first he struggled to make sense of the torrent of information, but within a few seconds a coherent picture of the orbital battle took shape. The reserve squadron had formed a wall of steel between the heavy cargo carriers and Jonson's onrushing ships. The Dark Angels' Stormbirds, however, had already raced past the rebel cordon and were even now launching strafing runs on the largely defenceless transports. With the *Duchess Arbellatris* out of action, Jonson was left with just six ships against eight undamaged enemy cruisers, but the rebel ships were caught at anchor, with little room to manoeuvre against the fast-moving Astartes ships. A salvo of torpedoes was already speeding towards the rebel cruisers' flanks, and the battle barge and her strike cruisers were well within range to open fire with their devastating bombardment cannons. So long as they were committed to protecting the transports, the cruisers were practically stationary targets for the battle group's combined firepower.

No sooner had the ramp sealed shut over Nemiel's re-entry compartment than the whole pod gave a grinding lurch and began to descend into its launch tube. Kohl's gruff, sardonic voice reverberated from Nemiel's vox-bead over the squad net. 'Good to have you join us, brother,' he said sarcastically. 'I was beginning to think you'd gotten lost.'

'We can't all spend our time lounging around in a drop pod, sergeant,' Nemiel said with a chuckle. The pod jolted to a stop with a loud clang, then came the thud of the hatch sealing overhead. 'Some of us have to do proper work so you can live this life of leisure.'

A chorus of deep voices laughed quietly over the vox. Nemiel smiled and glanced over the status readouts of Kohl's Astartes. All nine of the warriors showed green on the display, which was no less than he expected. He had fought alongside them for so long that he'd come to think of them as his own squad, and much preferred their jibes over the deferential respect that most other members of the Legion afforded him.

Kohl began to growl a retort but was cut off by a priority signal over the fleet command channel. 'Battle Force Alpha, this is command,' Captain Stenius called over the vox. 'We are thirty seconds from orbital insertion–' a hollow boom echoed through the battle barge's hull and the signal broke up into squealing static for a second '–are now in contact with Imperial forces on the ground. Inloading new drop coordinates and tactical data to your onboards now. Stand by.'

Seconds later the schematic of the orbital battle disappeared, replaced by a detailed map of a battle-scarred city and the outlying districts of a massive forge complex. The city – identified in the image as Xanthus, Diamat's capital – was built along the shore of a restless, slate-grey ocean, and stretched for dozens of kilometres north and south along the rocky coastline. Twenty kilometres east of the city outskirts, far inland along a desolate plain of black rock and drifts of red oxide, rose the conical slopes of a massive volcano that lay at the heart of the Adeptus Mechanicum's primary forge on Diamat. Many hundreds of years in the past, the scions of Mars had bored into the corpus of the dormant volcano and tapped the geothermal energies within, fuelling the vast smelters, foundries and manufactories that surrounded it. At the far edge of the great plain, the city sprawl and the forge's warehouse complexes met. Squalid subsids and reeking shanty towns fetched up hard against a towering permacrete wall that separated the orderly world of the Mechanicum from the haphazard lives of ordinary humans.

Nemiel took it all in, absorbing every detail with his keenly-trained mind. Icons blinked into life across this grey zone between the city proper and the great forge: blue for the units of the Tanagran Dragoons, and red for Horus's traitors. It took only a moment for the Redemptor to realise that the situation on the ground was desperate indeed.

Xanthus proper had been subjected to prolonged orbital bombardment over the course of several weeks. The city centre was a burnt-out wasteland, and the great, artificial bay of the harbour district was dotted with the hulls of hundreds of broken or capsized ships. To the southeast of the city, connected by tramways to both the city and the great forge complex, lay the planet's primary star port. The port was firmly in rebel hands. Nemiel counted six heavy cargo haulers landed at the site, surrounded by rebel support units and at least a regiment of mechanised troops.

Rebel ground forces had been advancing up the tramway towards the forge complex with four infantry regiments and approximately a regiment of heavy armour, and had apparently managed to break through an Imperial strongpoint covering the forge's southern entrance. There was no data on enemy troop strength or Mechanicum defence forces inside the complex itself. Nemiel suspected that the data had all come from the Imperial forces on-planet, and they had no idea what was going on behind the walls of the Mechanicum preserve.

Blue icons were driving south and east through the grey zone towards the rebels along the tramway; two under-strength regiments supported by a battalion of armour, trying to hit the rebels in the flank and drive them away from the forge. It was a valiant attempt, but the rebels had already stymied the Imperial counter-attack along a rough front some five kilometres north of the tramway.

'Ten seconds to orbital insertion,' Captain Stenius said over the vox. 'Battle Force Alpha, stand by for drop.'

Glowing blue circles appeared on the tactical map, showing the landing zone for the drop. The two companies would come down in a chain of foothills that bordered the very southern edge of the plain, some two kilometres south of the rebel-held tramway. The strategy from there was obvious: the Astartes would advance north and strike the rebels from their other flank, cutting access to the tramway and trapping them against the Imperial forces further north. The elevated terrain south of the tramway provided excellent fields of fire and ample cover for the Dark Angels, allowing them to target the rebel forces at will. Once resistance along the tramway had been eliminated Nemiel reckoned that one company would remain to hold the road against reinforcements approaching from the star port, while the other company would enter the forge complex itself and hunt down any rebel forces operating there.

'Five seconds. Four... three... two... one. Begin drop sequence.'

A massive impact hammered into the *Invincible Reason's* port side, hard enough to slam Nemiel against this re-entry harness, and everything went black.

JONSON HAD BROUGHT his battle group into Diamat at a fairly steep angle, intending to close with the rebels as rapidly as possible and deploy the landing force. Since the cruisers and the transports they guarded were in geo-synchronous orbits over Diamat's main forge complex, this brought the two forces into point-blank range. Weapons batteries and lance turrets blazed away at the Imperial ships, which responded with a spread of torpedoes and the deadly bombardment cannons of the flagship and her strike cruisers.

The battle barge was wreathed in a hail of explosions as she drove ever closer to the enemy battle-line. At the last moment, the *Invincible Reason* and her strike cruisers slewed to starboard, almost paralleling the enemy cruisers as the flagship prepared to release its drop pods.

Less than fifty kilometres to port – appallingly close range for a naval engagement – a rebel Armiger-class cruiser raked the battle barge's flank with its heavy lance batteries. Torpedo impacts had gouged deep craters in the Armiger's hull, igniting fires deep in the bowels of the stricken cruiser.

The flagship's bombardment cannons fired a rolling volley into the Armiger. At such close range, each and every shell found its mark. The giant rounds – five times the mass and explosive power of a standard macro cannon shell – punched through the cruiser's armour and touched off a chain of catastrophic explosions inside the hull that overloaded the ship's plasma reactor. The huge warship disintegrated in a tremendous explosion, hurling molten debris in every direction.

One piece of the destroyed cruiser – a hunk of armoured superstructure as large as a city block – smashed into the flagship's port side just as she began her drop sequence. The *Invincible Reason* lurched to starboard under the tremendous impact, throwing off the precise manoeuvres directed by the ship's Ordnance Officer. But it was too late to abort; the automatic sequence had activated and the pods were firing at a rate of two per second. Within ten seconds all two hundred Astartes had been launched, their pods scattering through the atmosphere over the battle zone.

THE DROP POD's onboard power plant restarted a second after launch. Data displays flickered back to life and attitude thrusters fired, correcting the pod's corkscrewing tumble through the atmosphere. It juddered and shook like a toy in a giant's rough hands. Tortured air howled past the drop pod's rudimentary stabilisers, but their vertiginous spiral finally ceased.

The flagship had been hit hard, Nemiel reckoned, which meant that they had likely been knocked outside their deployment envelope. He scanned the readouts quickly while the pod's logic engines read its trajectory and projected its new landing point.

A yellow circle pulsed on the tactical map. Nemiel frowned. They were going to come down a few kilometres north of the tramway now, right into the middle of the rebel forces who were holding off the Imperial counterattack. That was going to complicate things. Nemiel checked the command frequency, but heard only static. Between the atmospheric ionization and the thick hulls of the drop pods, he wouldn't be able to speak to Force Commander Lamnos until the Astartes had reached the ground.

The Redemptor switched over to the squad net. 'Everyone still here?' he called.

'You were expecting us to go somewhere, brother?' Kohl replied at once.

A new voice came over the vox, mellower than Kohl but just as amused. 'I don't know about the rest of you, but I could stand to stretch my legs,' Askelon, their Techmarine, said with a chuckle. 'All this lying about is bad for the circulation.'

'Says the one who spends all his time with his head and shoulders buried in a maintenance bay,' Kohl retorted.

'Which makes me an authority on the subject, wouldn't you agree?' Askelon replied.

'That'll be the day,' snorted Brother Marthes, the squad's meltagunner. 'The day Sergeant Kohl stops being disagreeable is the day he stops breathing.'

'That's the stupidest thing I ever heard,' Kohl grumbled, and the squad laughed in reply.

The turbulence of re-entry rose to a bone-shaking crescendo and then held steady for a punishing nine-and-a-half minutes until a warning icon flashed on the display and the retro thrusters kicked in. The Ordnance division aboard the flagship had programmed the pods to deploy their thrusters at the last possible moment, just in case there was a significant anti-aircraft threat over the drop zone. The jolt was akin to being kicked in the backside by a Titan, Nemiel mused.

An ear-splitting roar swelled up from beneath their feet as the thrusters flared to full power for three full seconds, right up to the point of impact. Nemiel felt another, much lesser jolt, and dimly heard a rending crash, then a series of small, sharp impacts reverberated through the pod's hull before it finally came to rest.

Nemiel's display blanked, flashing an urgent red. 'Disengage and deploy!' he shouted over the squad net, and hit the quick-release on his re-entry harness.

There was a hiss and a rush of hot, reeking air as the ramp in front of him began to deploy – then stopped at roughly a sixty-degree angle. The hydraulics whined insistently, nearly shifting the pod's bulk with the effort, before the safety interlocks kicked in and aborted the process.

At the back of his mind, Nemiel sensed that the deck beneath him was angled slightly. He growled with irritation, took a step forward and planted a foot against the ramp. He heard a crackle of masonry; the ramp rebounded slightly, then lowered another half a degree.

Acrid smoke and waves of heat were starting to penetrate the inside of the re-entry chamber. Nemiel heard muffled cursing over the vox-net as other members of the squad tried to force their own way out of the pod. He took hold of the entry frame with one hand and the ramp's edge with the other and clambered up and out, then saw at once what had happened.

The pod had come down squarely atop a multi-storey hab unit, punching like a bullet through at least four or five floors before finally coming to rest in the building's decrepit basement. Faint sunlight filtered down through the gaping hole of the floor above, all but occluded by clouds of increasingly thick smoke. The pod's retro thrusters had set the building's upper storeys ablaze.

Several of the pod's ramps had managed to open fully, while others, like Nemiel's, had been blocked by piles of debris. Brother-Sergeant Kohl was braced against the side of the pod and helping free Brother Vardus and his cumbersome heavy bolter.

Brother Askelon came around the side of the pod closest to Nemiel. His powerful servo arm deployed above his shoulder with a faint whine as he placed his feet carefully among the rubble. 'Stand clear!' he called, then opened the gripping claw of his arm and extended it against the side of the pod. Servo-motors hummed with gathering power. Askelon slid backwards a few centimetres; Nemiel stepped forward and tried to help brace him. Then, with a grating of powdered masonry and a groan of metal, the pod shifted slowly upright.

'Well done, brother,' Nemiel said, clapping the Techmarine on the shoulder as the pod's ramps fully deployed. 'Sergeant Kohl, find us a way out of here.'

'Aye, Brother-Redemptor,' Kohl answered, his tone all business now. He snapped orders to his squad, and the Astartes went to work. Already, Nemiel could hear the snap and crackle of lasgun fire outside, followed by the hollow bark of bolters.

Within seconds the squad was scrambling up a fallen slab of permacrete to reach the building's ground floor. Flaming debris fell amongst the Astartes like stray meteors; small pieces clattered harmlessly off their armour. At ground level, Sergeant Kohl pulled an auspex unit from his belt and took a compass reading in the smoky haze. 'Orders?' he asked Nemiel.

The Redemptor made a snap decision. 'We go north,' he said to Kohl.

Kohl checked the glowing readout once more, nodded curtly, and headed off into the blackness. The Astartes didn't bother fumbling about for a doorway – when he encountered an inner wall he barrelled right through the flimsy flakboard with scarcely a pause. In moments, the squad saw a large square of hazy light up ahead. Kohl led the squad through the viewport at a run, emerging onto the street outside in a shower of glittering glass shards and a billow of dirty grey smoke.

They were on a narrow avenue running roughly east-west through the grey zone. Piles of debris and dozens of blackened bodies dotted the road as far as Nemiel could see. Most of the buildings fronting the street were little more than hollowed-out shells, their facades blackened and cratered by small arms fire. A smashed six-wheel military transport lay on its side a few dozen metres to the squad's right, its tyres still burning. The air reverberated with the crackle and thump of weapons fire and the ominous whistle of mortar rounds arcing overhead.

The roar of petrochem engines echoed up a narrow cross-street just twenty metres to the squad's left. Nemiel recognised the sound at once: Imperial military APC's, moving fast. It sounded like four vehicles – a full mechanised platoon.

'Ambush pattern epsilon!' He called out, waving half the squad to the opposite side of the street. Kohl followed after the warriors, his bolt pistol scanning for threats. Brother Marthes knelt behind a pile of blackened rubble to Nemiel's immediate left, bracing his heavy bolter atop the pile. The Redemptor drew his bolt pistol and hit the activation stud on his crozius aquilum. The double-headed eagle atop the staff blazed with crackling blue energies.

The APCs reached the corner in seconds, rumbling fast up the cross-street towards the front line a few more kilometres north. They were lightly-armoured Testudo personnel carriers, armed with a turret auto-cannon and capable of transporting a full squad of troops. Their drivers were going all-out, kicking up thick plumes of black exhaust from their engine decks.

The Dark Angels had gone to ground with admirable speed and skill, concealing their presence behind piles of debris or in the entry niches of several ruined buildings. Just as the APCs appeared, one of the Astartes stepped out of cover and raised the muzzle of his stubby meltagun. Brother Marthes brought the antitank weapon to bear on the flank of the lead Testudo and touched the firing stud, unleashing a blast of high-intensity microwaves that converted the vehicle's metal hull into superheated plasma. The APC's fuel tanks exploded in a ground-shaking *whump,* blowing the Testudo apart in a shower of blazing fragments.

Brother Vardus opened fire a second later, raking the rear Testudo with an extended burst of heavy bolter fire. The mass-reactive rounds exploded against the APC's armoured hide and gouged craters in its solid tyres. Here and there the rounds found a seam in the armour plates and penetrated into the APC, wreaking bloody havoc on the men crammed within. The Testudo lurched to a stop, smoke pouring from the holes punched in its side.

The two middle APC's swerved left to try and avoid the burning wreck of the lead vehicle and escape the kill zone. Their turrets slewed to the right and spat a stream of high-explosive shells down the street, blasting more holes into the burnt-out buildings and digging up sprays of permacrete from the rubble piles. Brother Marthes switched his aim and fired at the next APC in line, but this time his shot went a little high, striking the vehicle's small turret and ripping it open. Autocannon shells cooked off in the blast of heat, wreathing the Testudo's upper deck in angry flashes of red, and the APC abruptly lost speed. The second Testudo, moving too fast to stop, rear-ended the damaged vehicle and spun it ninety degrees to the right, nearly flipping it over.

Vardus levelled the heavy bolter at the two immobilised APCs and hammered them with short, precise bursts. Nemiel watched the rear ramp of the second Testudo come down and raised his bolt pistol. As the panicked squad fled from the stricken vehicle, he and the rest of the squad cut them down with a volley of bolter fire. The last of the rebels had yet to hit the ground when Marthes fired another shot at the damaged APC, this time scoring a direct hit and immolating the men trapped inside.

It was a far cry from the old tales of chivalry he'd been taught on Caliban, Nemiel thought, surveying the carnage with clinical detachment. War was about butchery, plain and simple. Notions of glory came long afterward, he'd come to realise, imagined by those who had never seen the reality with their own eyes.

Nemiel's vox-bead crackled to life. 'All units, location and status check,' Force Commander Lamnos said tersely.

Brother-Sergeant Kohl and two other squad members dashed down the street to check the wrecked vehicles and ensure there were no survivors. Nemiel called up a map of the landing zone on his tactical display and checked his coordinates. They'd come down just a kilometre and a half north of the tramway, close to the forge's southern entrance. 'This is squad Alpha Six. Status is green. Awaiting orders,' he replied, providing their coordinates.

'Affirmative, Alpha Six. Stand by,' Lamnos answered at once. Less than a minute later the Force Commander came back. 'Alpha Six, we're getting a signal that Echo Four's pod is down but failed to deploy. Enemy forces are closing in on Echo's location from the south. Link up with Echo Four and ascertain its status immediately. Stand by for coordinates.'

Nemiel compared the coordinates to his tactical map. Echo Four had come down half a kilometre to the southeast, closer to the forge complex. 'We're on our way. Alpha Six out,' he replied.

Kohl and his warriors returned from the killing ground. 'There's mechanised infantry with Testudo APCs coming up the street from the direction of the tramway,' he reported.

'They'll have to wait,' Nemiel said. 'We're heading east. Echo Four is in some kind of trouble; the pod probably came down inside another building, and the ramps won't deploy. We've got to get there before the rebels do.'

Kohl nodded his helmeted head and addressed the squad. 'Askelon, you wanted a nice walk in the sunshine, so don't let me hear you crying if you can't keep up. Brother Yung and Brother Cortus, you're on point. Let's move!'

Without a word the squad rose from cover and set off east down the street, their boltguns sweeping ahead and to the flanks in search of targets. Nemiel fell into step with Techmarine Askelon and Brother Marthes beside him, while Kohl and three other squad members brought up the rear. Farther east, the grey wall of the forge complex rose above the smoking ruins of the grey zone. Tall, blinking towers made a metal forest beyond that forbidding barrier, girding the flanks of the bound volcano at the heart of the Mechanicum's domain. Plumes of orange and black smoke hung heavily about the complex, giving the place a nightmarish cast.

We came all this way to defend that? Nemiel grinned ruefully within the confines of his helmet. It hardly seemed like the kind of place worth dying for.

SIX
Angels of Death

Caliban
In the 200th year of the Emperor's Great Crusade

'This is Epsilon Three-Niner Heavy, lifting from zone four! I'm taking fire!'

The panicked vox-transmission cut through the hectic buzz of conversation in the fortress strategium, tearing Zahariel's attention from the glowing panes of after-action reports projected above his desk. Gritting his teeth, he blanked his hololith display and stepped swiftly from his office into the bustling chamber beyond.

It was mid-afternoon of the fourteenth day since the insurgents' global campaign began and so far the violence showed no signs of abating. The strategium had been in constant operation ever since, staffed by a mix of Legion officers and aides and senior commanders of the Jaeger regiments in action across Caliban. The men and women of the Jaegers struggled to cope with the constantly shifting nature of the enemy attacks, and the pressure of maintaining civil order while simultaneously trying to come to grips with insurgent cells that avoided direct combat as much as possible. They consumed pots of bitter tea and stim capsules and tried to match the stoic calm of the Astartes that loomed in their midst, but he could feel their frustration as the cargo hauler's distress call broadcast from the vox-unit across the room. Zahariel caught sight of Luther standing near the vox-unit, listening intently. So far as he knew, the Master of Caliban hadn't left the strategium for days on end.

A new voice crackled over the vox as Zahariel worked his way across the chamber. He heard a Legion air defence controller say, 'Epsilon Three-Niner Heavy, be advised, combat air patrol has been alerted and is vectoring on your position. Time to rendezvous is thirty seconds. What are you seeing?'

Epsilon's civilian pilot came back over the vox at once. 'My co-pilot says he's seeing red flashes to the north, out beyond the perimeter. My starboard engine's been hit. Temperature is spiking! I need to divert and make an emergency landing!'

'Negative, Three-Niner Heavy,' the controller shot back. 'Increase speed and altitude. Do not, I repeat, do not attempt to land.'

Zahariel shook his head in irritation. The civilian pilots always tried to set their transports back down at the first sign of trouble, not realising that turning around and slowing down for landing only made them more vulnerable to ground fire. Thunder reverberated through the room as the combat air patrol roared past Aldurukh's spires, heading north at full speed.

'What are the rebels going after this time?' Zahariel asked as he reached Luther's side.

'A Type II cargo hauler loaded with ten thousand tonnes of promethium,' Luther replied grimly, his eyes fixed on the vox-unit's grille. 'They couldn't have picked a better target.'

Zahariel's eyes widened. Epsilon Three-Niner was, for all intents and purposes, a flying bomb. A direct hit on one of the pressurised promethium tanks in its cargo holds would turn the ship into a massive fireball, scattering wreckage and blazing fuel all over the northern landing zones. He thought of all the fuel substations and warehouses in that sector and tried to calculate the devastation such an explosion would cause.

The vox-unit crackled once more. This time, the deep voice of an Astartes sounded from the grille. 'This is Lion Four; I've got a visual on Epsilon Three-Niner at this time. Stand by.' Moments later, the pilot spoke again. 'Contact! I've spotted a group of rebels operating a lascannon from the back of a civilian truck two kilometres outside the perimeter. Engaging now.'

'Hurry up, Lion Four!' shouted Epsilon Three-Niner. 'We just got hit again!'

Lion Four didn't respond. Seconds ticked by, and Zahariel realised the strategium had fallen silent. Then, moments later, the vox crackled once again.

'This is Lion Four. Target destroyed. Repeat, target destroyed. Epsilon Three-Niner is clear.'

A relieved cheer went up from the Jaeger officers and Legion aides; any victory, however small, was worth celebrating under the circumstances. The

Astartes in the chamber received the news impassively and continued with their work. Zahariel took a long breath and glanced at Luther. 'The rebels are getting bolder,' he observed. 'That's the third attempt in the last twelve hours.'

The Master of Caliban frowned thoughtfully. 'We need to push the perimeter out another five kilometres or so, and increase our mobile patrols. Sooner or later they'll realise that vehicle-mounted lascannons are too easy to spot and switch to shoulder-fired missile launchers, which will make our job that much harder.'

Zahariel nodded in agreement. So far they had been fortunate; two shuttles had been shot down over the past two weeks, but none of the larger transports had suffered more than minor damage. Clearly the rebels hoped to interdict all orbital traffic from Aldurukh to the waiting supply ships above Caliban, but Luther was determined to continue operations despite increasingly loud protests from the civilian pilots who were hauling the cargo. Of greater concern to Zahariel was the fact that no new supplies were coming in to replace those being launched into orbit.

'We have four Jaeger regiments in training that are advanced enough to perform basic combat patrols,' the Librarian suggested. 'We could put them on perimeter patrol immediately.'

'What about line regiments?' Luther asked.

Zahariel shook his head. 'All of our combat-capable units have been deployed. Right now the Jaegers are stretched thin.' He paused. 'We have almost an entire Scout chapter ready for action, brother. We could send them out in pairs to patrol the countryside around Aldurukh and hunt down rebel weapon teams instead of calling up the trainees.'

Luther seemed to consider this for a moment. 'If the tempo of rebel attacks increase, I'll consider it,' he said at length. 'In the meantime, set up a patrol rotation for the training regiments.'

'Very well,' Zahariel replied. He tried to keep any trace of exasperation from his voice. Violence had raged across Caliban for two weeks, and the Dark Angels had yet to stir from Aldurukh. He couldn't fathom Luther's reluctance to commit the Legion. Zahariel chose to believe that the Master of Caliban was holding them in reserve for a swift, decisive blow against the insurgents.

The only other possibility was that Luther wasn't certain of his own allegiances, which was simply too terrible to contemplate.

'THE SITUATION IS absolutely intolerable.' Magos Administratum Talia Bosk's metal-capped fingers sliced through the air in a gesture of Imperial pique. She sat perched on the edge of the tall, throne-like chair in the Grand Master's chambers, her slight figure nearly swallowed by the bulk of her layered robes. 'Our production quotas have slipped by sixty-three per cent at this point. Something must be done about these attacks at once, or we won't be able to meet our commitments to the Emperor's Crusade.' From the dread in Bosk's voice she might have been describing the end of life as she knew it – which, from her perspective, was probably close to the truth.

Bosk and most of her staff were from Terra, having been assigned to Caliban by the Administratum to oversee the planet's growing bureaucracy and its breakneck industrialization programme. Gleaming, metal-sheathed cables ran from recessed data ports at the base of her skull and wound about her bird-like neck before disappearing beneath the wide collar of her robes. Her shaven head was adorned with tattoos etched in holographic ink, drawing on her own bio-electric field to project shimmering images of the Imperial Aquila a few millimetres above her skin. The haptic interfaces covering the tips of her fingers were ornamented with tiny jewels and delicate whorls, like fingerprints, etched into their platinum surface. Her augmetic eyes gleamed with a cold, blue light as she regarded Luther across the massive oaken desk.

It was late afternoon, and the slanting light was creeping across the chamber floor from the tall windows on the west side of the room. The chamber, which normally seemed spacious to Zahariel, was crowded with regimental officers, staff aides and Bosk's fretful retinue of bureaucrats. He stood patiently by the window, his broad shoulders outlined by the setting sun, a data-slate gripped loosely in his hand. The meeting, intended to provide Luther with a status report from the planet's senior Imperial officials, wasn't going well.

Luther sat back in the Grand Master's enormous chair. Built for Lion El'Jonson's massive physique, it made the great knight seem almost childlike in comparison. He rested his elbows on the chair's broad arms and regarded Bosk coolly.

'Rest assured, Magos Bosk, there's no one on this planet more conscious of our obligations to the Legion than I,' Luther replied. Only someone who knew him well could detect the undercurrent of tension in his voice. 'General Morten, perhaps you could enlighten us on the current security situation.'

General Morten, outfitted in the dark green uniform of the Caliban Jaegers, cleared his throat and rose slowly from his chair. Like Bosk, he was a Terran, a decorated soldier of many years' service who had been tasked with creating the planet's defence forces. He was a short, stout man, with sagging jowls and a nose that had been broken so many times it was little more than a misshapen bulb in the centre of his weathered face. His voice was a steely rasp, thanks to a year fighting amid the toxic ash plumes of Cambion Prime.

'Caliban's major arcologies remain under martial law, with mandatory curfews in effect,' the general began. 'The riots appear to have run their course, at least for the moment, but we're still seeing isolated rebel attacks on checkpoints, precinct houses and infrastructure targets like water pumps and power substations.' He sighed. 'A heavy troop presence in the arcologies has sharply reduced the number of attacks, but it can't eliminate them completely.'

Luther nodded. 'What about industrial sites?'

'We've had much better luck there,' Morten continued. 'The larger manufactories and mining outposts have been assigned a small garrison for security, with mobile reaction forces standing by to provide reinforcement in case of an attack. As a result, we've managed to defeat a number of major attacks over the course of the last few days.'

'Although it appears that the rebels feel confident enough to start sniping at transports and shuttles coming and going from Aldurukh itself,' Bosk complained. Not half an hour after Epsilon Three-Niner's narrow escape, Bosk's shuttle had been briefly targeted by a rebel autocannon on its approach to the fortress. 'Who are these criminals, and how have they managed to accomplish so much in so little time?'

Luther took a deep breath, clearly choosing his words carefully. 'There are indications that the rebels are made up mostly of disaffected nobles and former knights. We believe they've been laying the groundwork for this campaign for many years, stockpiling weapons and organising their forces.'

'Their discipline is impressive,' Morten said grudgingly. 'And their organisation is highly decentralised. I have no proof, but I strongly suspect that one or more of their senior leaders have received Imperial military training at some point. We haven't been able to gather any useful intelligence on their command and communications network, much less identify any of their leaders.'

Zahariel eyed Luther intently, wondering if he would identify Lord Thuriel and the other rebel leaders, but the knight said nothing.

'What do these criminals want?' Bosk demanded.

Luther regarded the magos inscrutably. 'They want to be relevant once more,' he said.

'Then they can go to work in a munitions plant,' Bosk snapped. 'This planet has obligations – strict obligations – to the Emperor's forces, and it's my responsibility to make sure those obligations are met. What's being done to round up these ringleaders and deal with them?'

Morten sighed. 'That's easier said than done, magos. My troops are already stretched to the limit maintaining order and protecting your industrial sites.'

'Which are sitting idle because there aren't any labourers to man the assembly lines,' Bosk retorted. 'They can't leave their hab units while martial law is in effect.' Layers of fabric rustled as the magos folded her thin arms and glared at Luther. 'Where is the Legion in all this, Master Luther? Why haven't they been unleashed against the rebels?'

Zahariel straightened. Bosk had cut to the heart of the matter. Now perhaps they would hear the truth.

Luther leaned forward, resting his forearms on the massive oak desk, and met the administrator's stare unflinchingly. 'Administrator, my battle brothers are capable of a great many things, but hunting criminals isn't one of them. When the time is right and the proper targets present themselves, the Dark Angels will act – but not before.'

Magos Bosk stiffened at Luther's reply. 'That won't do, Master Luther,' she said curtly. 'This unrest must stop immediately. Caliban's obligations must be fulfilled without delay. If you won't act, then I'll be forced to report the situation to Primarch Jonson and to the Adeptus Terra.'

The air in the chamber was suddenly charged with tension. Luther's gaze turned hard and cold. Zahariel started to step in and try to defuse the situation when the door to the chamber opened and one of Morten's aides hurried inside. With an apologetic bow to Luther, the aide turned to the General and whispered urgently into his ear. Morten frowned, then began asking the aide a number of increasingly urgent questions. Magos Bosk watched the exchange with growing alarm.

'What's happened?' she asked, her metal-clad fingers clicking as she gripped the wooden arms of her chair. 'General Morten? What's going on?'

Morten waved his aide away. He looked questioningly at Luther, who gave his permission with a curt wave of his hand. The general took a deep breath, and addressed the magos.

'There's been... an incident at Sigma Five-One-Seven,' he said.

'An incident?' Bosk said, her voice rising. 'You mean an attack?'

'Possibly,' the general replied. 'At this point we don't know for certain.'

'Well, what exactly do you know?'

Morten couldn't entirely suppress a frown of irritation at the administrator's demanding tone. He related what he knew in a clipped, businesslike manner. 'Approximately forty-eight minutes ago our headquarters received a garbled transmission from the garrison at Sigma Five-One-Seven. The vox operator confirmed that the signaller was using the garrison's proper callsign and encryption code, but couldn't make out what he was trying to say. The transmission lasted thirty-two seconds before being cut off. Nothing has been heard from the garrison since.'

'Jamming?' Luther inquired.

Morten shook his head. 'No sir. The transmission simply stopped. The signaller was cut off in mid-sentence.'

The Master of Caliban turned his attention back to Magos Bosk. 'What exactly is Sigma Five-One-Seven?'

'A materials processing plant in the Northwilds,' she replied. 'It went online last month, and has yet to become fully operational.'

'How many labourers?'

'Four thousand per shift under normal conditions, but as I said, the plant wasn't operational.' Bosk pursed her lips as she accessed her cortical data shunts. 'There were difficulties with the plant's thermal power core. An engineering team was on site, trying to track down the source of the problem, but that was all.'

Luther nodded. 'And the garrison?'

'A platoon of Jaegers and an attached heavy weapons squad,' Morten answered. 'Enough to defend the site against anything but a major rebel attack.'

'Well, obviously that's exactly what happened,' Bosk snapped. 'You said you had mobile troops to reinforce the garrisons in the event of attack. Why haven't you despatched them?'

The general glowered at Bosk. 'We did, magos. They landed at the site five minutes ago.'

'Well, what in the Emperor's name did they find?' Bosk demanded.

Morten's expression turned grim. 'We don't know,' he said reluctantly. 'We lost all contact with them moments after they touched down.'

Luther sat bolt upright in the Grand Master's chair. Zahariel felt a wave of unease wash over him; something very strange was going on. From the dark look in Luther's eyes, it was clear that the Master of Caliban felt much the same.

'How large was the relief force?' Luther asked.

'A reinforced company,' Morten replied. 'Two hundred men, plus heavy weapons and ten Condor airborne assault carriers.'

Zahariel's unease deepened. A force that size would have been more than enough to deal with any rebel attack. 'It's possible that the original transmission was a ruse, and the relief force was lured into an ambush.'

'It's possible,' Luther said, somewhat dubiously. 'But why no vox signals? Surely we would have heard something.' He turned to Morten. 'Are there any other reaction forces in the area?'

'The closest one is more than two hours away,' the general replied. 'I can divert them to the site, but it would leave the Red Hills sector without any reinforcements in the event of another attack.'

Bosk rose angrily to her feet. 'This is outrageous,' she declared. 'Master Luther, I mean you no disrespect, but I have to report this to Primarch Jonson and my superiors on Terra. The situation is worsening by the moment, and it's obvious to me that you're unwilling to commit your Astartes in battle against your own people. Perhaps forces from another Legion can be despatched to put an end to the uprising.'

Luther's handsome face paled with anger. General Morten saw the danger and began to stammer a quick reply, but Zahariel cut him off.

'The defence of Caliban is not a matter for the Adeptus Terra to concern itself with,' he said in a stern voice. 'And our primarch has more important matters to occupy his attentions at present. Master Luther explained to you that he was waiting for the proper time to order our battle brothers into action, and clearly that moment has arrived.'

Luther turned to Zahariel as the Librarian spoke, and the two warriors locked eyes. The Master of Caliban glared at the Astartes for a moment, his dark eyes glittering with anger. Zahariel met the knight's gaze steadily.

After a moment, Luther seemed to master his anger. He nodded slowly, though his expression was still deeply troubled.

'Well said, brother. Assemble a squad of veterans and depart for Sigma Five-One-Seven at once. Eliminate any resistance and secure the site, then report back to me. Understood?'

Inwardly, Zahariel breathed a sigh of relief. He regretted having forced Luther's hand, but he was certain that, in time, the Master of Caliban would forgive him. The Librarian bowed to Luther, then nodded respectfully to General Morten and Magos Bosk before striding purposefully from the room.

His conscience was clear. For the sake of the Emperor and the honour of the Legion, the Dark Angels on Caliban were rousing themselves for war.

SEVEN
Brothers in Arms

Diamat
In the 200th year of the Emperor's Great Crusade

Nemiel's squad raced down the narrow street towards the location of Echo Four's downed pod, expecting to encounter more rebel troops at any moment. Sounds of fighting between Astartes squads and enemy forces echoed across the grey zone with increasing intensity as the rebels began to respond to the danger in their midst. Nemiel heard the bark of autocannons and, here and there, the flat boom of a tank's battle cannon adding to the din.

'Turn south at the next corner,' he called out to his squad. 'Echo Four should be another four hundred metres down the cross-street and somewhere to the left.'

'Acknowledged,' said Brother Yung, one of the two warriors on point. Nemiel watched the Astartes race up to the street corner and put their backs to a burnt-out storefront, their bolters held across their chests. One of the two warriors – Brother Cortus, Nemiel thought – slid to the end of the wall and peered around the corner.

Nemiel heard the battle cannon fire and watched the corner of the building Cortus was standing at disintegrate in the space of a single heartbeat. The two Astartes disappeared in a blizzard of pulverised stone and fragments of structural steel. A billowing cloud of dust and smoke enveloped the intersection and rolled down the street towards the rest of the squad.

The squad took cover on reflex, crouching behind rubble piles or pressing close to a building wall. Nemiel checked his helmet display and saw the status icon for Brother Cortus flash from green to amber. He was wounded, perhaps seriously, but still functional. The walls of the building must have shielded the Astartes from the worst of the blast.

Less than a minute later Brother Yung emerged from the smoke cloud, his black armour caked with brown dust. He was half-carrying, half-dragging Brother Cortus. Nemiel rose from cover and jogged forward as Yung set the wounded warrior down next to the shattered stoop of a hab unit.

Cortus reached up and fumbled with his helmet. One side of the ceramite helm had been partially crushed, shattering the right ocular and splitting it from crown to nape. Yung lent a hand and helped the wounded Astartes pull the helmet free.

'Status?' Nemiel asked.

Brother Cortus sent the smashed helmet bouncing across the street. The skin on the right side of his face had been deeply scored by the impact, peeling away the flesh down to the bone in some places. His right eye was a bloody ruin, but the wound was clotting quickly thanks to Cortus's enhanced healing ability.

'One battle tank and four APCs, three hundred metres south,' he said, his voice rough with pain. 'Approximately a platoon of infantry in hasty defensive positions, maybe more.'

'I was talking about your head, brother.'

Cortus glanced dazedly at the Redemptor, blinking his one good eye. 'Oh, that,' he said dismissively. 'It's nothing. Did anyone see what happened to my bolter?'

'Here,' Yung said laconically, handing over Cortus's dirt-caked weapon.

The wounded warrior's face brightened. 'Thanks for that, brother,' he replied. 'Kohl would have had my skin if I'd lost it.'

'Too right,' Sergeant Kohl growled as he crouched down beside Nemiel. 'It sounds like the rebels have beaten us to Echo Four,' he said to the Redemptor. 'We might already be too late.'

'Or perhaps we're just in time,' Nemiel countered. 'Three hundred metres is too far away to have a good chance at a kill with the meltagun. We'll have to get closer.' He looked back down the way they'd come, searching for an alley they could use to outflank the enemy position, but there was none. 'We'll have to cut through the buildings,' he decided. 'Sergeant, you and Askelon lead the way.'

Kohl nodded and beckoned to the Techmarine. Nemiel helped Cortus to his feet, then followed the sergeant through the hab unit's gaping doorway.

It took ten minutes for the squad to work its way through the partially-collapsed structure. Kohl and

Askelon ploughed through any rubble in their path; in places the Techmarine used his servo arm to reinforce damaged structural supports so that the squad could keep moving without touching off a cave-in. They emerged from the building via a broken out viewport, crossed a narrow, filth-strewn alley, and entered the shell of another structure on the far side.

The second building had almost completely caved in, forcing the Astartes to scramble over enormous piles of rubble to reach the opposite side. Nemiel could hear the idling rumble of petrochem engines now, and the distant sound of shouted orders.

They reached the crest of a rubble pile close to the far corner of the building and hunkered down. Nemiel joined Kohl and Askelon, and peered over the top of the pile. By this point, his armour was so caked in dust that it was nearly invisible against the backdrop of debris.

He could see the enemy positions through the tall, broken viewport frames at the corner of the ruined structure. The battle tank was parked in the centre of another intersection, its flanks wreathed in exhaust fumes. The four APCs were arrayed behind it in a loose formation; their ramps were down and their troops had deployed into cover on either side of the street. At the opposite corner of the intersection stood a ruined hab unit with a huge, ragged hole high on the side of one of its upper storeys. Flames licked hungrily about the hole.

'We've found Echo Four,' Nemiel announced over the vox. 'Vardus, set up your shot. Everyone else, get ready to move.'

Brother Vardus worked his way up the rubble pile and aimed his meltagun through the viewport frame at the tank. The rest of the squad climbed up the slope to either side, their weapons ready.

The meltagunner glanced at Nemiel and gave a nod.

'Fire!' Nemiel said.

The meltagun went off with a hissing shriek of superheated air and struck the tank in the side, right beside the engine. Molten pieces of armour plate and track segments went spinning through the air. Nemiel surged to his feet.

'Loyalty and honour!' the Redemptor cried. 'Charge!'

With a shout, the Dark Angels scrambled down the rubble pile and leapt through the open viewport frames, their boltguns blazing. Rebel troops tumbled to the ground, their light armour no match for the bolters' powerful rounds, but the survivors immediately returned fire. Lasgun rounds buzzed through the air, detonating against the sides of the blackened buildings with a staccato crackle.

Nemiel emerged into the street at a run, charging straight towards the parked APCs. The Testudos were already traversing their gun turrets, but the Astartes were already too close for the vehicles to use their guns effectively. Lasgun bolts seared the air around him; he brought up his bolt pistol and snapped off two quick shots, hitting a trooper crouching in the doorway of a building a little further down the street.

'Get across the intersection!' he ordered over the vox. 'Make for the building on the opposite side; that's where Echo Four went down!' Nemiel said, running past the burning tank. Askelon and Kohl dogged his heels, trading fire with the rebel troops. They ran into the midst of the parked APCs, and the sergeant tossed a fragmentation grenade into the troop compartments of the two vehicles he could reach. Vardus took aim and fired on the move, hitting one of the Testudos a bit farther down the street. The bolt struck the APC square on the front glacis and burned easily through the armour plate, touching off a huge explosion.

Nemiel reached the far side of the intersection in just a few seconds and found himself under fire from three different directions. Another squad had taken cover around the building where Echo Four had gone down, and now they fired point-blank at the onrushing Astartes. A las-bolt struck Nemiel full in the chest; another dug a glowing crater out of his left pauldron, but his ceramite armour withstood the worst of the impacts. Askelon was struck several times as well, but his ornate harness, forged by the master craftsmen on Mars itself, shrugged off the hits with ease.

To Nemiel's right, Brother-Sergeant Kohl shot one rebel soldier point-blank with his bolt pistol, then sliced his power sword through another. Nemiel caught sight of an enemy sergeant off to the left, hastily switching power cells on his laspistol. The Redemptor shot the man twice, then rushed in among the rest of the soldiers, slaying every rebel he could reach with savage blows from his crozius. A las-bolt flashed through the building's open doorway and struck him in the midsection; he felt a searing pain as the bolt found a weak spot in his armour, but the ceramite plating still managed to deflect most of its energy.

Roaring a challenge, Nemiel pressed forward into the building, leaving the survivors of the enemy squad to his brethren. He found himself inside another blasted, fire-scorched shell; the hab unit's roof and three storeys had collapsed some time ago, leaving only the battered outer walls still standing. In the corner of the building, directly opposite the entrance, sat Echo Four. The drop pod had come down at nearly a forty-five degree angle and had dug itself into a mound of crushed flakboard and masonry. There wasn't a single ramp that could properly deploy at that angle, leaving the occupant trapped inside.

Figures scattered about the shadowy interior, firing lasguns and laspistols at Nemiel. One bolt struck his right thigh, while two more punched into his chest. Amber warning telltales flashed on his armour readout, but the suit's integrity was still well within accepted parameters. He charged towards the pod, his powerful legs driving him relentlessly over the shifting piles of rubble. His bolt pistol barked again and again; each shot struck home, killing a rebel soldier as he rose from cover or tried to switch positions to outflank him.

He had just crested the tallest debris pile, only ten short metres from the drop pod, when he saw the flicker of an energy field low and to his left. Without thinking he dodged to the right and brought his crozius down to block the blow, and just barely managed to keep his leg from being cut off at the knee. As it was, the rebel lieutenant's power sword sliced deeply through his left calf and caused him to stumble.

The pain was so intense it took his breath away. Even with the autohypnotic rotes at his command, the wound very nearly sent him into shock. His armour sensed the damage and immediately compensated, stiffening the pseudo-musculature of his left calf and immobilising it, like a ceramite splint. The sudden change in mobility pitched Nemiel forward, sending him sliding face-first down the debris pile into the midst of the platoon's small command squad.

The rebels closed in on Nemiel from all sides, firing their laspistols as they came. He was hit in the head, shoulders and chest; the armour stopped the blasts, but the integrity sensors began to shade from amber to red. He heard the distinctive crackle of the rebel lieutenant's power sword as the man chased down the slope after him.

Nemiel crashed to a stop against a tangle of steel supports at the base of the pile and twisted onto his side just as the enemy officer reached him. The power sword swept down at his chest, and he just managed to twist far enough to parry it with his crozius. Snarling, the lieutenant drew back his blade for a quick thrust, but Nemiel brought around his bolt pistol and shot the man through the heart.

Another rebel soldier rushed past the lieutenant's falling body and tried to drive a bayonet into Nemiel's throat. The Redemptor contemptuously blocked the thrust with his crozius and killed the soldier with a backhanded blow to his head. The remaining soldiers scattered as Brother-Sergeant Kohl reached the crest of the debris pile and opened fire with his bolt pistol. The survivors retreated from sight around another mound of fallen permacrete.

Kohl sheathed his power weapon and dashed nimbly down the slope. 'Are you all right, brother?' he called, extending his hand.

Nemiel waved the offer of assistance away. 'I'm fine,' he said, climbing quickly to his feet. He was about to ask for Brother Askelon when the Techmarine appeared at the top of the pile and quickly moved to join them. Instead of inquiring about Nemiel, however, his eyes were for the drop pod alone.

Askelon indicated an open crate a few metres away. Four disc-shaped melta charges had been carefully unpacked and sat in a neat row on a small slab of flakboard. 'I'd say we were just in time,' he noted, giving Kohl a meaningful look.

'Well, you know what I say, Askelon?' Kohl shot back. But the rest of his retort was swallowed in a thunderous explosion as the tank outside fired its battle cannon into the derelict building. The blast pulverised a ten-metre-wide section of the building's front entrance, showering the Astartes in a hail of jagged stone and metal. When the cloud of dust and smoke cleared, Nemiel could look through the hole the cannon had made and see the enemy tank, still sitting where Marthes had hit it. The melta blast had knocked out the vehicle's engine, but the crew was still very much alive.

'Marthes!' Nemiel called out over the vox.

'I know, brother, I know!' Marthes called back. 'I'm at the southern end of the building with half the squad. Just give me a minute to get into position.'

'We may not have another minute!' Nemiel shot back. But it wasn't himself or his squadmates he was worried about – the downed drop pod made for a much more enticing target. 'Askelon, we've got to get that pod open!' he shouted.

The Techmarine nodded his helmeted head. 'We need to get it level fast, so the ramps can deploy!' he said. His gaze fell to the melta charges. 'Help me with these!' he said, and bent to grab two of the discs.

Nemiel and Kohl each grabbed one of the charges and followed Askelon around to the far side of the pod. The Techmarine surveyed the debris pile, then activated his servo arm and began to dig deep gouges into the rubble at specific points below the canted end of the pod.

'You're not going to be able to dig this pile out fast enough!' Kohl barked.

'I'm not planning to, brother,' Askelon said. He took one of the melta charges, set its timer, and shoved it into one of the gouges, then quickly placed the second one.

Nemiel heard the whine of servos as the tank's turret rotated to bear on its new target. Then came a shriek of superheated air, and a melta blast struck the tank from its right. The detonation reverberated down the street, but when the smoke cleared, Nemiel saw that Marthes had shot from too far away, and the melta blast hadn't fully penetrated the tank's armour. The crew inside had likely been stunned by the hit, but that wouldn't last for more than a few seconds.

Askelon grabbed the charge from Nemiel's fingers. 'I'd find some cover, if I were you,' he said, setting its timer and placing it in the pile.

The three Astartes hurried away from the pod and crouched at the base of the debris pile. No sooner had they settled onto one knee than the four charges detonated in carefully-orchestrated succession.

The blasts went off so close together that the sound merged into a single, thunderous explosion. Molten stone and vaporised earth sheeted out from the pile, channelled away from the pod by the precise placement of the charges. In one stroke, Askelon removed ten cubic metres of rubble from beneath one end of the drop pod. Slowly, then with gathering speed, the elevated end of the pod began to settle, until it landed upright with a hollow metal clang. The flank of the pod slammed into the corner of the building, sending an alarming series of cracks forking across the damaged walls.

Immediately, Nemiel heard the metal thud of harness releases popping, then the buzzing whine of servos as the pod's four large ramps finally deployed, revealing Echo Four's lone passenger.

The huge figure in the centre of the pod was approximately humanoid in shape, with two stubby, powerful legs and a pair of mighty weapon arms attached to a giant, barrel-like torso. A sensor turret, shaped similarly to a helmet-clad head, swivelled left and right from an armoured collar set a little above the torso's middle. The overall effect was of a hulking, hunchbacked giant, with a matte black ceramite hide. Both shoulders bore the winged sword emblem of the First Legion, and a score of noble battle honours fluttered from the Dreadnought's frontal plates. A Mechanicum artisan had applied gilt scrollwork to the glacis, just beneath the Dreadnought's notional head, which bore the name Titus.

Gears and servo-motors whirring, Brother Titus strode from his drop pod just as the tank fired its cannon once more. The shell flew into the pod where Titus had been standing a moment before and blew it apart.

Red-hot shrapnel pinged like raindrops off Brother Titus's shoulders. The Dreadnought cleared the ramp in three long steps and kicked its way through the debris piles towards the rebel tank. Its turret slewed to the right, desperately tracking the oncoming war machine while the crew struggled to load another round into the cannon's breech.

Brother Titus was armed with a standard Dreadnought weapons configuration. His right arm terminated in a large, multi-barrel assault cannon, capable of firing streams of high-velocity shells that were lethal to troops and light vehicles, but far less likely to penetrate the thick armour of a battle tank. Titus's left arm, however, ended in a powerful, four-fingered hand that crackled with pent-up energies like an Astartes power fist. Nemiel and his brothers watched Titus charge through the ragged gap blown in the front of the building and bring that tremendous fist down on the top of the tank's square turret. Armour plates crumpled like tin; there was a bright, violet spark and a tremendous concussion as the turret split apart beneath the blow. Flames leapt from the ruptured seams.

Nemiel shook his head in awe at the Dreadnought's power. 'Brother-Sergeant Kohl, re-form the squad,' he said, and began limping quickly from the building. The pain in his leg had subsided to a dull ache, thanks to injections from his suit's array of pain blockers and his own enhanced healing abilities. He switched to the company command net. 'Force Commander Lamnos, this is Alpha Six,' he said. 'We've reached Echo Four and freed Brother Titus. No enemy forces in our immediate area. What are your orders?'

'Good work Alpha Six,' Lamnos responded. 'Titus was the only one still unaccounted for. The rest of the landing force has engaged rebel units along the tramway, and we've received word that forward elements of the Tanagran Dragoons are working south to link up with us.' There was a short pause while Lamnos consulted with his other squad leaders. 'There are still enemy units present around the entrance to the forge complex, approximately one kilometre to your southeast. Take Titus and engage the rebels.'

'Affirmative,' Nemiel replied. 'Alpha Six, out.'

The Redemptor limped over to Kohl and Askelon, who were standing in the shadow of Brother Titus. Askelon was clearly in awe of the mighty Dreadnought; Kohl was looking up at Titus's sensor turret, his head cocked as though in conversation. They were probably speaking on a private channel, he realised. Dreadnoughts were an uncommon sight in the Legions; since they required a human mind to operate, only severely-injured Astartes were offered the opportunity to continue serving the Emperor by having themselves installed into one of the war machines. Those offered the task were typically warriors who had demonstrated great heroism in battle and were mentally strong enough to endure their entombment in a Dreadnought's sarcophagus. As a result, they were accorded tremendous respect by their brethren.

Titus's head swivelled slightly at Nemiel's approach. 'My thanks to you and your squad, Brother-Redemptor,' he said over the squad channel. Titus's voice was deep and powerful, and entirely synthetic, devoid of human inflection. 'Force Commander Lamnos has directed me to accompany your squad for the time being. What is our objective?'

'The rebels have taken the southern entrance to the forge complex,' Nemiel said, turning and heading off to the southeast. 'We're going to take it back.'

EIGHT
DARK DESIGNS

Caliban
In the 200th year of the Emperor's Great Crusade

A ROILING, GREY overcast hung over the towers of Sigma Five-One-Seven, swallowing the rays of the setting sun and plunging much of the processing plant into shadow as Zahariel and his warriors reached the outskirts of the site.

They made their approach straight down the plant's primary access road with a clatter of steel treads and a billowing wake of oily black smoke from the Land Raider's massive petrochem engine. Sitting in the assault tank's troop compartment, Zahariel adjusted the settings of the tactical display on the bulkhead next to his station and switched from light-enhancement to thermal view. Instantly the blocky outlines of the plant's main buildings and its sifting towers were painted in stark silhouettes against a vivid green background, their flanks studded by bright spots of white that marked the locations of hot chem-lights. Peering carefully at the display, he could make out a faint, white nimbus colouring the air at the centre of the plant; from what he knew of the site's layout, he suspected that was likely the heat rising from the power plants of the relief force's ten Condor transports. According to the blueprints, the site had a large, central landing zone for offloading heavy-lift cargo haulers. The reinforcements could touch down there and unload under cover without worrying about fire from rebel forces around the site perimeter.

Except that there weren't any rebel troops, as near as Zahariel could reckon. The dark foothills, scoured down to bare rock by Imperial crawlers, were silent and still. Stranger still was the lack of any obvious signs of attack: there were no gaps in the plant's tall perimeter fence, nor thermal scars on the buildings from small arms or light artillery fire. More and more, he was coming to believe that the threat to the plant had been internal rather than external. He'd accessed the site's status reports and work logs on the short flight from Aldurukh and discovered that the engineering team working on Sigma Five-One-Seven's thermal plant consisted of twenty-five Terran engineering specialists and a hundred Calibanite labourers. Could the labour pool have been infiltrated by insurgents? Zahariel thought it entirely possible. From there, it would have been easy to smuggle weapons onto the site and hide them in the plant's sub-levels until the time was right. Using the advantage of surprise, such a force could then easily overcome the rest of the engineers and the unsuspecting garrison, and then set an effective ambush for Imperial relief forces.

Zahariel could understand how such a thing could be done. He just couldn't figure out why. An attack of this kind didn't match the insurgents' tactics to date, and it seemed like a disproportionate investment of time and manpower on a target that was far from any of the planet's major population centres. So far, the rebels were doing a very effective job of crippling the planet's industrial base by fomenting riots in the arcologies and staging hit-and-run raids with small, well-armed guerrilla forces. And this particular plant was sitting idle anyway; Zahariel could think of a dozen targets offhand that would have made better candidates for a takeover. There was a great deal about the situation that didn't add up, and he wasn't heading back to Aldurukh until he had some answers in hand.

The voice of the Land Raider's driver crackled over Zahariel's vox-bead. 'Coming up on the site's main gate now,' he said. 'Orders?'

'Increase speed,' Zahariel replied. 'Advance up the main road towards the central landing zone.'

The assault tank's engine roared in reply, and the Astartes in the troop compartment swayed in their seats as the Land Raider surged forward. The vehicle struck the plant's heavy main gate and crumpled it contemptuously. Zahariel heard the faint clang of the impact and the screech of metal as the broken gate was ground beneath the heavy tank's treads, but the barrier scarcely slowed the Land Raider down. As the tank roared along the main road, he switched to the Legion command frequency and reported in to Aldurukh. 'Seraphim, this is Angelus Six,' he called. 'We have reached Objective Alpha and are proceeding to secure the area.'

The reply came back at once. Zahariel was surprised to hear Luther's voice over the vox instead of the strategium's duty officer. 'We read you, Angelus Six. Any sign of the garrison or the relief force?'

'Negative,' Zahariel replied. 'No obvious signs of combat, either. I expect I'll learn more once I reach the central landing zone.'

'Understood,' Luther said. 'Broadsword Flight is on station and standing by if you require support, Angelus Six. Remain in contact at all times.'

The Librarian twisted a dial on the tactical display and brought up a regional map of the Northwilds sector. A green diamond, representing the transport craft that had delivered the Land Raider from Aldurukh was shown exiting the area to the south. There was also a small, red chevron blinking above the mountains northwest of the site, flying in a circular holding pattern between Sigma Five-One-Seven and the recently established Northwilds arcology. The alphanumeric code beneath the chevron told him that Broadsword Flight consisted of three Stormbirds, each loaded with a full suite of air-to-ground ordnance. Luther had put enough firepower at his disposal to destroy an entire armoured regiment. Zahariel was more grateful for the obvious sign of Luther's support than the Stormbirds themselves. 'Understood, Seraphim,' he answered. 'We will keep you advised.'

Zahariel switched the tactical display back to the tank's forward auspex array, then turned away from the screen and bent in his seat to pick his helmet off the Land Raider's deck. 'We're coming up on the edge of the objective area,' he said, pitching his voice to carry over the tank's roaring engine. 'Prepare to deploy. Brother Attias, take the pintle mount.'

Silent and purposeful, the veteran squad fitted on their helmets and checked their weapon loads. Across from Zahariel, Chapter Master Astelan readied his bolt pistol and power sword. When the order had come down to assemble a combat patrol to investigate the site, Astelan had been among the first to volunteer. After nearly a half-century in garrison, every member of Luther's training cadre was eager for action, and Zahariel was glad to have a warrior of Astelan's ability as part of the squad.

At the far end of the troop compartment, Brother Attias rose to his feet and worked his way down the narrow aisle between his squadmates. Attias had been an aspirant of the Order at the same time as Zahariel and Nemiel, and as a youth he'd earned no small amount of grief thanks to his nervous and overly-studious nature. That had changed on Sarosh, when an alien monster had melted his helmet with a torrent of caustic slime. Attias had been lucky to survive, but the Legion Apothecaries had been powerless to heal the damage wrought by the monster's acid. In the end, they had been forced to strip away most of the flesh and muscle and graft polished steel plates directly to Attias's skull, transforming his face into a gleaming death mask. After more than a year recovering from his wounds, he had joined Astelan's training cadre, where he was roundly feared by the chapter's novices. Zahariel had barely spoken to him in the years since returning to Caliban. Outside of training, Attias rarely spoke to anyone at all.

Zahariel watched as Attias stepped past him and took up the remote controls for the Land Raider's pintle-mounted storm bolter. Servo-motors whined on the tank's roof as the weapon elevated and began to cover the rooftops of the plant's outer buildings as they made their way deeper into the site. The heavily-armoured Land Raider was impervious to all but the most powerful anti-tank weapons, but in the confines of the industrial plant a rebel team with melta bombs – or worse, a meltagun – could be a serious threat.

For several minutes there was nothing to do but wait. Zahariel reached over and unclipped his force staff from where it hung against the tank's armoured bulkhead and gripped the cold, adamantine haft with both hands. The staff was both a weapon and a focus for the Librarian's psychic abilities, and Zahariel took a moment to meditate upon it as Israfael had taught him to do. He began with a series of slow, steady breaths as he interfaced first with the crystalline array of the psychic hood built into his power armour. The array, built into a metal shell that rose from the back of his cuirass and partially enclosed his bare head, served as a crucial buffer that shielded his brain from the terrible energies of the warp. Without it, he risked madness – or worse – every time he unleashed his psychic powers in battle.

The interface cables connecting Zahariel to the hood grew warm against the back of his skull as he accessed the array and focused his awareness on the staff. Only then, once he was firmly grounded, did he extend that awareness further and take the measure of the psychic energies surrounding Sigma Five-One-Seven.

The shock was like an icy gale against his skin. Zahariel felt his flesh prickle; his muscles tensed, and a hungry, howling wind thundered in his mind. He felt the crystal array behind his head grow hot as the psychic torrent threatened to overwhelm the hood's dampeners. It was like the raging storm he'd experienced at Aldurukh, only far stronger and wilder. What was worse, the Librarian could feel an otherworldly wrongness about the tempest – a taint that seemed to tug at his very soul.

Zahariel recoiled inwardly from the shock of the psychic storm. Screwing his eyes shut, he drew back his awareness as swiftly as he could, but the vileness in the aether plucked at him like grasping tendrils. For a horrifying second it felt as though there was a sentience behind the psychic force, and he was reminded of the nightmarish spectacle he'd witnessed on Sarosh.

After what seemed like an eternity, he managed to pull himself free from the taint. It withdrew and left him shaken to his core.

'Are you well, brother?'

Zahariel looked up and saw Astelan's concerned expression. He nodded, catching his breath. 'Of course,' he replied, 'merely focusing my thoughts.'

The chapter master raised a dark eyebrow. 'They must be very weighty thoughts. I can see the pulse in your temples from here.'

Zahariel wasn't certain how to respond. Did he share what he'd just experienced? Would it make any difference to Astelan or the rest of the squad? This was a situation he'd never experienced in any training scenario. The matter was taken from his hands, however, when suddenly the driver called out over the intercom. 'We've reached the central landing zone. I see ten Condor aerial transports in tactical landing formation at one hundred and fifty metres.'

The Librarian pushed his doubts and questions aside. If there was one thing he was certain of, it was that hesitation in battle was often fatal. 'Halt and deploy!' he called over the intercom. Leaping to his feet, he drew his bolt pistol from its holster and addressed his squad. 'Tactical pattern delta! Treat all contacts as hostile until otherwise directed.' He raised his staff, noticing for the first time the rime of frost coating the metal shaft. 'Loyalty and honour!'

The Land Raider rumbled to a halt, its front assault ramp deploying with a hiss of powerful hydraulics. Astelan stood, igniting his power sword's energy field. 'For Luther!' he shouted to his men.

As one, the Dark Angels answered Astelan's cry. Zahariel had no time to wonder at the chapter master's strange oath; he was already rushing towards the assault ramp, the golden double eagle at the top of his staff held before him like a talisman.

The landing field was a dark, grey plain of permacrete some five hundred metres square, bounded on three sides by huge, multi-storey mineral refinery and storage plants. Cylindrical sifting towers loomed over the idle refineries, ringed every ten metres by blinking red hazard lights. They cast long shadows across the field, bisecting the orderly rows of Condor transports crouching silently on their squat landing struts.

Zahariel swept the field with his bolt pistol, searching for targets as the squad spread out around him.

The transports' assault ramps were down and all of the craft he could see had one or more of their maintenance hatches open, but there were no signs of activity.

The Librarian felt his scalp prickle as he grew aware of the deathly stillness that hung over the plant. He glanced at one of the warriors in his squad who was busy sweeping the field with a portable auspex unit. 'Any readings?' he asked.

'No movement. No life signs,' the Astartes answered. 'Trace heat on the engines of the transports, but that's all.'

Zahariel's eyes narrowed warily. That wasn't quite all; he could sense the tension in the warrior's voice. There was something else, something invisible that didn't register on any of their equipment. He'd felt it once before, many, many years past, when he'd travelled deep into the forest in search of the last Calibanite Lion.

This was an evil place, Zahariel knew. The air was heavy with a sense of malice and slow, hateful corruption, and it knew he was there.

A dreadful sense of déjà vu swept over him. Zahariel raised his head and looked past the hulking buildings and silent towers, searching the horizon for clues. He studied the broken line of mountains that comprised the nearby Northwilds, and realised that he was very close to that same spot where he'd fought the lion, decades ago. The terrible, twisted trees were gone and the echoing hollows had been scraped bare, but the aura of the place somehow remained.

'Not far from here,' a hollow voice spoke in Zahariel's ear. With a start, he turned to see Attias staring at him, just a couple of metres away. The lenses of Attias's augmetic eyes were flat and depthless in his polished, skull-like face.

'What is that, brother?' Zahariel replied.

'The castle,' Attias replied. The words were flat and emotionless, resonating from the small, silver vox grille embedded in his throat. He raised his chainsword and pointed off to the northeast. 'The fortress of the Knights of Lupus was just a few score kilometres off that way. You remember?'

Zahariel followed the whirring tip of the sword and stared off into the gathering darkness. Sure enough, he could just make out the distant flank of Wolf's Head Mountain, the old peak from which the disgraced knights had taken their name. They had been the last of the knightly orders to defy Jonson's plan of unification against the great beasts that terrorised Caliban's people, and their intransigence had ultimately led to open conflict. He remembered the horrific assault on the fortress as clearly as if it had been yesterday. That had been his first real taste of the brutality of war.

The worst shock, though, had been once the knights of the Order had breached the outer walls and fought their way into the castle proper. The outer courtyard of the fortress had been full of enclosures, most of them filled with twisted monstrosities. Zahariel and his brethren had been horrified to learn that the Knights of Lupus had been collecting as many of the great beasts as they could and preserving them from the wrath of Jonson's forces. Jonson had been so furious he'd ordered the fortress to be completely destroyed. Not one stone had been left atop another, and every trace of the Knights of Lupus had been wiped away.

Except for their library, Zahariel realised. The library of the renegade knights had been vast, larger even than the one at Aldurukh, and filled with a huge assortment of ancient and esoteric tomes. To everyone's surprise, Jonson had ordered the library to be catalogued and transported back to the Rock. No one knew why, and Zahariel never learned what happened to the books after that.

The Northwilds had always been the oldest, wildest and most dangerous wilderness region on Caliban. Now, nearly all of the forest was gone – but had something ancient and inimical somehow remained?

Astelan's voice shook Zahariel from his reverie. 'Is your vox-unit working, brother?' he said. He nodded his head back at the idling Land Raider. 'I've tried to check with the crew, but no one is responding.'

Zahariel turned and stared worriedly at the massive vehicle. He keyed his vox-unit. 'Raider two-one, respond.'

Nothing. No interference, no static. Just dead air.

The Librarian took a step towards the assault tank just as the driver's hatch rose on hydraulic hinges and the warrior's helmeted head appeared. 'We've been trying to call you for a full minute,' the driver said over the rumbling engines. 'Our vox-unit's not working properly.'

Frowning inside his helmet, Zahariel tried to contact Luther. The orbital communications array and the Rock's far more powerful vox-unit should have easily picked up the signal, but once again, all he heard was dead air. The unit was working fine, he knew, and there were no signs of jamming. It was as though their vox signals were simply being swallowed, though he couldn't imagine how such a thing was possible.

'The vox was working fine at the plant's perimeter,' Astelan said, clearly thinking along the same lines. 'We could send the Land Raider back to maintain contact with Aldurukh while we secure the site.'

Zahariel shook his head. The whole point of bringing the Land Raider in the first place was to provide a base of heavy firepower for the squad and to serve as a mobile strongpoint that the Astartes could fall back to in the event of an emergency. Until he knew more, he wanted the tank close by.

'Button up and keep a close eye on the auspex arrays,' he ordered the driver. 'And secure the assault ramp until we signal.'

The driver acknowledged with a curt nod and dropped back inside the tank. Within seconds the circular hatch and the heavy ramp clanged shut, sealing the vehicle tight. Zahariel then turned to Astelan. 'Take two brothers and see what you can find at the plant's control room,' he said. 'There ought to be a log of vox transmissions at the very least.' He indicated the landing field with a sweep of his staff. 'We'll inspect the transports and try to find out what happened to the relief force.'

Astelan acknowledged the order with a nod. 'Jonas and Gideon, you're with me,' he said, and headed off across the landing field at a ground-eating jog with two of the squad's warriors close behind him.

Zahariel waved the rest of the squad forward. 'Spread out,' he ordered. 'But remain in visual contact at all times. If you see anything strange, inform me at once.'

Weapons ready, the Dark Angels advanced across the landing field towards the closest of the Condors. Permacrete crunched underfoot; Zahariel glanced down and saw deep cracks running through the landing field's pavement. Here and there, he saw the tops of slick, brown and black roots pushing their way up through the cracks. Caliban's forests were not surrendering meekly to the Imperium's ground-clearing machines. His home planet was a death world, Zahariel had come to learn, and such places were nearly impossible to tame. Still, it surprised him to see so much damage to a site that couldn't be more than eight months old. Reinforced permacrete was built to resist the elements for centuries.

They came upon the first transport in line, approaching it from the port side. Zahariel saw at once that the Condor's cockpit, set between the craft's building air intakes, was empty. The Librarian circled around aft as the squad surrounded the transport. Bolt pistol ready, he peered up the open assault ramp into the red-lit troop compartment. It was empty, save for an open toolbox sitting in the centre of the bay.

'Access panels are open, starboard side,' Attias said, peering up at the ship's fuselage.

Zahariel walked around the transport and studied the open hatches. 'Auspex and vox arrays,' he said thoughtfully. 'I suspect the crews were running tests on their systems and trying to determine why their vox-units weren't working.'

'And then?' Attias said in his sepulchral voice.

Zahariel shrugged. 'I don't know. There's no sign of a struggle. No weapons damage to the transport. It looks like the crew just walked away.'

'Like Sarosh,' Attias declared.

'No, not like Sarosh,' Zahariel shot back. 'The people of Sarosh went insane. This has to be something different.'

Attias said nothing, his augmetic eyes lifeless and unreadable in a cold steel mask.

The sound of running feet resounded across the permacrete plain. Zahariel turned to see Brother Gabriel approaching at a dead run.

'Astelan says to come at once,' Gabriel called out. 'We've found something.'

NINE

Unto the Breach

Diamat
In the 200th year of the Emperor's Great Crusade

'I SEE THE Dragoons built the rebels some fortifications,' Kohl grumbled.

Nemiel and the sergeant were crouching at the corner of a burnt-out building some two hundred and fifty metres from the entrance to the forge complex, peering across a wasteland of rubble and twisted girders that had once been someone's hab. From their vantage point they could observe approximately five hundred metres of tramway and the tall, wide gateway that led into the outer districts of the great forge. Neither of the Astartes cared for what they saw.

At some point in the recent past the Imperial garrison had heavily fortified the entrance, creating a pair of permacrete bastions to either side of the gateway. Heavy weapons emplacements had been built to create a deadly crossfire covering the approaches to the gate, and revetments had been dug to provide cover for armoured vehicles as well. Buildings had been levelled in a two hundred metre swathe around the fortifications, creating a killing ground devoid of cover or concealment. It was a formidable strongpoint by anyone's estimations, and Nemiel would have been encouraged by its presence, except for the fact that there were rebel troops manning the fortifications now instead of the Tanagran Dragoons.

'It looks like the Tanagrans at least put up a fight,' Nemiel observed. Their enhanced vision allowed them to scrutinise the bastions as well as any man with a set of magnoculars. 'Most of those gun emplacements have been knocked out, and there's a burnt-out tank in each one of those revetments. That's why the rebels have their vehicles parked along the tramway.

Kohl gave a pessimistic grunt. They could see four Testudos lined up along the berm, hull-down, with only their squat autocannon turrets showing. 'Wonder why there aren't any tanks?'

'They were probably called away to reinforce another part of the line,' Nemiel suggested.

The sergeant nodded. 'Bet those fields are probably mined,' he said, nodding at the wide expanse of churned earth that led up to the bastions.

The Redemptor shook his head ruefully. 'You're a veritable beacon of hope, brother.'

'Hope is your area of responsibility,' Kohl declared. 'Mine is, among other things, steering callow young officers away from minefields.'

'And for that we are all duly grateful,' Nemiel replied. Then he took a deep breath, focused his attention, and studied the bastions one more time.

He could see plenty of signs that the fortifications had come under heavy fire, but he couldn't extrapolate how the rebels had managed to overrun them. There were no bodies in the fields that might suggest an axis of advance, nor any burnt-out hulls of wrecked vehicles to indicate an armoured rush. If he could figure out how the enemy had managed to overcome the strongpoint, then the odds were he could make use of the same vulnerabilities as well.

'What do you think, brother-sergeant?' Nemiel asked. 'How are we going to take those bastions?'

Kohl studied the fortifications for another few moments. 'Why, I expect we run right up and ask them to let us in.'

Nemiel gave the sergeant a dark look, a gesture entirely wasted within the confines of his helmet. 'That's not very funny, sergeant.'

'As it happens, I'm not joking,' Kohl replied.

'NOT SO FAST,' Nemiel yelled over the Testudo's roaring engine. 'The last thing we need is to spook some trigger-happy rebel gunner into firing at his own side.'

The two APCs were rolling down the tramway at a steady clip towards the forge entrance, wreathed in thick plumes of ochre dust and swirling petrochem exhaust. Askelon had used his servo arm and a plasma cutter to strip away everything he could from the interior of the vehicles, from the benches to the ammo baskets for turret autocannon, and still there was only enough room for one Astartes up front and three more in the troop compartment. Brother Marthes, who was driving the Testudo that Nemiel was riding in, would have to crawl out of the driver's compartment on his hands and knees before exiting via the assault ramp at the rear. For the hundredth time, Nemiel found himself wondering how he'd let Brother-Sergeant Kohl talk him into this.

'The sergeant said to make it look like we were running from something,' Marthes shouted back. 'If we're going too slowly, they might try to challenge us.'

'As opposed to going too fast and having them shoot at us?'

Marthes didn't reply at first. 'I admit it made more sense when Brother-Sergeant Kohl explained it,' he replied.

Nemiel shook his head irritably. At least Kohl had the decency to be the first member of the squad to volunteer for the scheme. He was in the second APC, along with Askelon, Yung and Brother Farras. Nemiel had Brother Cortus and Brother Ephrial in the cramped troop compartment with him. They were jammed in shoulder-to-shoulder in the noisy, exhaust-filled space and completely blind. Nemiel, closest to the driver's space, tried to crane his head around and see through one of the forward vision blocks, but he couldn't quite manage it. 'How far from the bastions are we?' he asked.

'One hundred and fifty metres,' Marthes answered. 'They saw us coming about a minute ago. I can see several of the Testudos aiming their cannons at us.'

Nemiel nodded to himself. No doubt the commander in charge of the garrison was trying to call them over the vox and find out what they were doing approaching his position. Askelon had taken pains to shoot the APCs antenna off with his bolt pistol, but would the rebels be convinced? Would they even notice, or simply decide to take no chances and open fire? It's what he would do in their position.

The Redemptor keyed his vox. 'Brother Titus, are you and the rest of the squad in position?' he called.

'Affirmative,' the Dreadnought replied in his metallic voice. 'I have you on my surveyors now.'

'Very well,' Nemiel said. 'Fire at will.'

Two hundred metres north, at exactly the same spot where Kohl and Nemiel had reconnoitred the fortifications a half-hour before, Brother Titus stepped around the corner of the burnt-out building and readied his assault cannon. The weapon's six barrels began to spin with the ominous, rising whine of electric motors until they were little more than an iron-grey blur. The Dreadnought surveyed the enemy positions with a single sweep of his sensor turret and fired a long, roaring burst.

Diamantine-tipped, light armour-piercing rounds raked across the northern bastion and then down along the parked APCs. The shells blasted craters in the formed permacrete; enemy troops caught in the open were literally blown apart by the high-velocity projectiles. The rounds punched through the thin armour of the easternmost APCs turret and touched off one of the shells in the ammo feed; it blew apart in a yellow fireball and filled the vehicle with a storm of deadly shrapnel.

The remaining warriors in Kohl's veteran squad fanned out around the Dreadnought and began advancing across the no-man's-land toward the bastions, firing as they went. Their shots added to the storm of shells and drove the stunned rebels behind the nearest cover.

The turrets of the three surviving Testudos quickly swerved to target the threat bearing down on them from the north. 'It's working!' Brother Marthes shouted. 'They're going after Titus!'

'Let's not leave him hanging any longer than we have to,' Nemiel replied. 'Increase speed!'

The two APCs roared down the tramway at full throttle, seemingly racing for the safety of the fortifications around the gateway. As they drew close to the parked rebel vehicles, a sergeant rose to a crouch and began pointing urgently to positions alongside the berm, but both of the Testudos shot right past.

'Uh, Brother-Redemptor Nemiel?' Marthes said. 'You didn't mention anything about a barricade between the two fortifications.'

'We couldn't see between the fortifications during our reconnaissance,' Nemiel answered. 'Can we break through?'

'We're about to find out,' the Astartes said grimly. 'Brace for impact!'

A second later the Testudo struck a pair of permacrete construction barriers that had been laid across the entrance to the forge. There was a tremendous crash, and a grinding of metal on stone, and the forty-tonne APC bucked skyward like a broaching whale as its sloped bow carried it over the lip of the barricade. There it might have remained, had not the second APC crashed into it from behind.

The impact shoved the Testudo further forward, bearing over the barricade and forcing it into the gap beside the two bastions. The APC came to a stop, bow dragging across the tramway after having its front two wheels ripped completely away.

'Lower the ramp!' Nemiel shouted. Outside he could hear urgent shouts and the crack of lasguns.

He heard a hollow booming at the back of the troop compartment, then a grating of metal as Brother Ephrial forced the partially-jammed ramp open. The sounds of battle flooded into the compartment: angry shouts, the crackle of las-bolts, the distant snarl of the Dreadnought's assault cannon and the hollow bark of boltguns. Las-bolts began to strike the side of the APC in a staccato hail of small explosions.

Ephrial forced his way out of the wrecked Testudo and opened fire, snapping off short, controlled bursts at the ramparts of the bastion to the north. Cortus was next in line, and made it out significantly faster thanks to having enough room to throw himself against the ramp and drive it a bit further to the ground. A las-bolt struck him a glancing blow across the back of the helmet as he emerged into the open; he shook his head like an angry bear and struggled to his feet, his bolter spitting death at the rebels.

'Marthes! Let's go!' Nemiel shouted.

The Redemptor clawed his way forward, his crozius clutched in his fist. He emerged into a veritable storm of fire from both sides of the gateway, and found himself staring at the sight of Brother-Sergeant Kohl's APC, lying on its right side atop the crushed remains of the barricade. The Dark Angels had succeeded in deploying their ramp and were now trading shots with the rebels in the southern barricade from behind the shelter of the wrecked vehicle.

Nemiel drew his bolt pistol and headed right, firing shots up at the ramparts of the northern bastion as he went. The fortification was like a three-storey stepped pyramid, with a rampart and firing positions at each level. Unfortunately for the rebels, there was only a narrow frontage that actually looked down into the space between the fortifications; the defences were designed primarily facing outward, covering the hundreds of metres of kill zone and the long, wide tramway. Rebel troops were now crowded along those narrow ramparts, pouring lasgun fire down at the Astartes, but the Dark Angels were taking a fearsome toll of the bunched-up troops.

'Brother-Sergeant Kohl, get your section moving!' Nemiel called over the vox. 'Ephrial! Cortus! With me!'

He ran stiff-legged towards the far end of the bastion, close to the actual gateway. As he expected, there was a ramp leading up into the fortification proper. 'Grenades!' he ordered. Ephrial and Cortus immediately pulled a pair of fragmentation grenades from their belt dispensers, set the fuses and threw them up and over the first-level rampart. Nemiel was already charging up the ramp, bolt pistol ready.

The grenades went off with a pair of muffled bangs and a chorus of agonised shouts and screams. Nemiel reached the top of the ramp; it turned sharply to the right, opening onto the first rampart. It was a standard Imperial fortification, right out of the field manual, and he knew its layout well. He rounded the corner, firing his bolt pistol and charging the stunned rebels with a fierce battle cry.

The rampart was a scene of carnage. Dead and wounded men were slumped at the base of the narrow, trench-like passage, shredded by bursts from the Dreadnought's assault cannon or blown apart by mass-reactive bolter shells. The survivors retreated down the length of the rampart, firing wildly as they staggered over the bodies of their comrades. More las-bolts rained down from the ramparts above; they detonated against his armour's broad pauldrons or glanced from the top of his curved helm. Nemiel kept moving forward, firing methodically and killing a soldier with each well-placed shot. Ephrial and Cortus joined him in moments, firing up at the higher ramparts to suppress the enemy fire.

The rampart ran for fifteen metres due west, then doglegged sharply to the north-east. At the corner, Nemiel paused and threw a grenade of his own, then followed right on the heels of the blast. Several metres behind him, he heard the shrieking blast of a meltagun, and knew that Marthes had joined them at last.

Around the corner the rampart ran for more than forty metres in a straight line, its weapon emplacements looking out over the killing ground that Brother Titus and the rest of the squad were currently advancing across. The parapet here had been savagely chewed by the Dreadnought's assault cannon and Brother Marthes's heavy bolter, and there were far more dead rebels than live ones still holding the trench. Fifteen metres down the line another ramp led up and back to the second level.

The rebels fell back a bit further in the face of Nemiel's advance, but held their ground rather than give up the next ramp. They poured fire from their lasguns at the advancing Astartes, but the las-bolts were meant for lightly-armoured humans, not walking juggernauts like the Dark Angels. Nemiel advanced doggedly into the whirlwind of fire, pummelled by shot after shot. Warning icons flashed insistently on his helmet display, and he overrode each and every one. Gathering his strength, he charged the last ten metres until he was in close-combat range. Then the slaughter truly began.

The blazing crozius swept down in hissing arcs, smashing helmets and crushing bone. There was nowhere to run in the narrow space; nowhere to manoeuvre or try to sneak around Nemiel's flanks. The rebels were forced to stand and face his wrath directly, and he slew them without mercy. When their courage finally broke and they turned and ran down the remaining length of the rampart, Nemiel realised he was thirty metres past the second-storey ramp, and his armour was caked in blood up to mid-thigh. He'd been treading on burnt and broken corpses for a full ten minutes.

Down on the tramway another APC exploded in a shower of molten steel. Brother Titus and the rest of Kohl's squad were almost to the berm, and the remaining rebel troops were in full retreat, with-drawing on foot as quickly as they could down the tramway in the direction of the captured star port. Behind Nemiel, Cortus, Ephrial and Marthes were trading fire with the rebels on the second storey. The Redemptor slapped a fresh magazine into his bolt pistol and went to join them.

The rebels fought doggedly, forcing the Astartes to fight for every metre they climbed, but the Dark Angels were relentless. Nemiel took the lead once more, firing away with his bolt pistol until he could draw close enough to wield his deadly crozius. He was wounded half a dozen times. Las-bolts burned through weakened spots in his armour and seared the flesh beneath. Once a rebel soldier charged him with a bayonet-tipped lasgun and jammed the blade into the joint of his left hip. The point dug deep into his flesh and snapped off when Nemiel smashed the man to the ground with a backhanded sweep of the crozius, but the injury scarcely slowed him by that point. Victory was close at hand.

They threw the last of their grenades at the top of the third ramp, and they rushed forward to meet the rebels' last stand. Ephrial fell during the charge, shot through the right knee. He landed on the perma-crete, his crippled leg extended beside him, and continued to blaze away at the enemy with his bolter. At the top of the pyramid the Astartes were able to spread out and attack the enemy at once, and a wild melee raged for almost three full minutes before the last of the rebels fell beneath Nemiel's crozius. He searched among the bodies for the commander of the detachment, but there were no officers to be found.

'North bastion secure,' Nemiel reported over the vox. 'One casualty.'

'South bastion secure,' Brother-Sergeant Kohl answered a minute later. 'No casualties to report.'

'Gateway secure,' Brother Titus reported. 'Brother-Redemptor Nemiel, I am detecting movement inside the forge complex; approximately six contacts, heading this way.'

'Very well,' Nemiel replied. 'I'm coming down. Brother-Sergeant Kohl, leave one member of your section behind as a lookout, then link up with me in the gateway.'

Nemiel left Brother Ephrial behind to stand watch from the northern bastion and headed down to ground level. Off to the north-west, he could hear the rumble of petrochem engines and the squeal of tank treads. New signals over the company command net indicated that the Tanagran Dragoons had broken through and were almost to the tramway.

Kohl and his warriors reached the gateway at the same time as Nemiel. Brother Titus stood squarely in the breach, his smoking assault cannon trained down a wide avenue that ran northeast into the vast complex.

'Where are the contacts now?' Nemiel asked the Dreadnought.

'Two hundred metres northeast,' Titus answered. 'I'm getting strange returns on my surveyors. Whatever they are, they are making good use of cover and avoiding direct line of sight.' He paused. 'I don't think they are rebel troops.'

'It could be Tech-Guard,' Askelon said. 'There has to be a garrison of some kind here to defend the forge.'

'Let's hope so,' Nemiel replied. 'Although it looks like the enemy managed to penetrate at least into the outer districts before we arrived. We need to investigate the returns, no matter what.' He turned to the Dreadnought. 'Hold the gate, Brother Titus. This shouldn't take long.'

Nemiel led the group through the gateway and into the precincts of the Mechanicum. The roadway beneath his feet wasn't permacrete, but a kind of smooth, grey metal cladding. It rang softly with each step, and continued northeast in a laser-perfect line towards the distant slopes of the great volcano. Tall, dark structures rose to either side of the roadway. Warehouses, Nemiel reckoned, or manufactories idled sometime during the rebel attack.

The Redemptor moved forward, peering intently into the shadows surrounding the silent buildings. He knew basically where the six individuals ought to be, but try as he might, he could not spot them. 'They must be around the corner of one of these structures,' he said quietly. 'If so, they likely don't know we're here.'

Techmarine Askelon shook his head. 'I wouldn't count on that,' he replied. 'If they're Tech-Guard, they could have surveyors that rival those of Brother Titus.'

Nemiel didn't like the sound of anything that could see farther and keener than he could. 'Stay sharp,' he told his warriors, and pressed ahead. After just fifteen metres, Brother Titus called over the vox.

'The contacts are moving,' Titus reported. 'They're thirty metres north-by-northeast and heading your way.'

The Astartes orientated on the bearing given by the Dreadnought, their weapons held low but ready. Ironically, it was Brother Cortus, the one-eyed Astartes, who spotted them first. 'There!' he said, indicating a narrow alley off to the left with a nod of his head.

Six figures were spilling from the alley and fanning out in a semi-circular formation, heading straight for the Astartes. As they emerged from the shadows between the buildings, Nemiel could see that they were massive individuals, each one easily as large as an Astartes, and just as powerfully built. Articulated armour plates covered their hyper-muscled bodies, and even from this distance Nemiel could clearly see that their limbs and heads were heavily augmented with bionic and chemical implants. Their arms were fully weaponised, with an assortment of fearsome-looking energy and projectile weapons and lethal close combat attachments. He could hear them speaking to one another in blurts of binaric code as they advanced. Their augmetic eyes glowed a pale green from within burnished metal frames.

Nemiel turned to Askelon. 'What are they signalling to one another about?' he asked.

The Techmarine shook his head. 'I can't tell, sir. It's all highly encrypted. But their weapons systems and combat surveyors are fully active.'

Nemiel turned back to the oncoming figures. 'Do you recognise them?'

'Oh, yes,' Askelon said. 'They're skitarii; more specifically, a unit of Praetorians. They're the Mechanicum's elite guard.'

The Praetorians continued to advance, snapping and squealing to one another in sinister-sounding code. Nemiel took a step forward, making a point to lower his weapons.

'Ave, Praetorians,' he began. 'I'm Brother-Redemptor Nemiel, of the Emperor's First Legion. We've come to help defend the forge–'

The rest of Nemiel's greeting was cut short as the Praetorians raised their weapon arms and opened fire.

TEN

HIDDEN EVILS

Caliban
In the 200th year of the Emperor's Great Crusade

THE GROUND FLOOR of Sigma Five-One-Seven's control centre had been claimed by the plant's small garrison as a makeshift barracks. The squat, thick-walled building was an ideal defensive position, with access to the plant's vox-unit and a comprehensive network of surveyors that streamed real-time data covering the entire facility – all of which made the scene of carnage inside all the harder to understand.

Zahariel stood just inside the control centre's single entrance and tried to make sense of the wreckage strewn across the wide, low-ceilinged room. Three-quarters of the space had been set with orderly rows of desks and logic engines, intended for the plant's supervisors and senior engineers once the site went into operation. The rest of the room had been claimed by at least one of the garrison's Jaeger squads. He could see torn and bloody bedrolls, kicked-over piles of ration packs and scattered crates of spare energy cells. Scorch marks stained the ochre-coloured walls, and the desks were scarred and cratered by lasgun fire.

The Librarian took a deep breath, tasting smoke and the bitter tang of blood. Astelan stood in the middle of the carnage, grimly surveying the scene.

'The attackers came in through the front door,' the chapter master said quietly. He pointed at the wall to either side of Zahariel's head. 'Most of the scorch marks indicate that the Jaegers were firing at the doorway from over there, by their bedrolls.'

'They didn't try to take cover behind the desks, just a couple of metres away,' Zahariel observed.

'Obviously they didn't have time,' Astelan said. 'The Jaegers here were off-watch and likely asleep when the attackers arrived.' He nodded towards a doorway on the far side of the room. 'The platoon's second squad was camped in the next room over, and their area is undisturbed.'

Zahariel pursed his lips thoughtfully, recreating the scene in his mind. 'Second squad is on patrol when the vox-units go out. The attackers deal with them first, then close in on the control centre and surprise the first squad.' He glanced at Astelan with narrowed eyes. 'None of which should have been possible, given that the attackers would have had to wipe out an entire squad of troops in full view of the plant's surveyors, then blast their way through this buildings reinforced door.'

The chapter master nodded. 'We found a great deal of blood upstairs in the control room.'

'Show me.'

Astelan led Zahariel deeper into the building, through the deserted offices and echoing hallways of the control centre. The malevolent energies surrounding the site swirled about them as they walked. It was like feeling the eyes of a beast upon you as you were riding through a deep, shadow-haunted part of the forest, and from the set of the chapter master's shoulders, Zahariel suspected that Astelan felt it as well.

They rode a lift to the building's third floor and Zahariel stepped into the plant's large control room. Logic engines whirred and clattered from dozens of empty workstations, and flickering green pict units displayed scrolling streams of data detailing every aspect of the plant's idle machinery. Brother Gideon knelt beside the plant's security station, set in a shadowed alcove just to the right of the lift. He had pushed aside the workstation's chair, which had been built to human specifications and was altogether too frail for Gideon's armoured bulk, and was working industriously at the controls. His right knee rested in the centre of a wide pool of mostly-dried blood.

Once again, Zahariel paused and studied the scene for clues. Most of the work stations were operating in standby mode, except for two others. He quickly scanned the readouts on their screens; both were dedicated to monitoring the operation of the site's thermal power plant. The Librarian glanced back at the pool of blood. 'Someone got close enough to slit the watch officer's throat,' he mused.

'It was mid-afternoon, so that was probably the platoon commander or the senior sergeant,' Astelan said.

Zahariel nodded thoughtfully. 'He would have been the first to die. Then the perimeter patrols would have been eliminated.'

Astelan pointed to the security display. 'The killer likely monitored the ambushes from here – perhaps even coordinated them with teams on the outside. Then, when the time was right, he went downstairs and opened the door to let them finish the job.'

The Librarian clenched his armoured fists. It had been a well-organised and ruthlessly-executed assault. But to what purpose?

'What about the vox logs?' he asked.

Astelan motioned Zahariel to follow him to another alcove, this one situated at the rear of the chamber. Inside, the plant's vox-unit was still operating. Zahariel could hear the faint hum of power coursing through its frame, but the speaker was ominously silent.

The chapter master turned to a display panel and keyed a series of switches. At once, a long string of readouts cascaded down the display. 'There was only one transmission today,' he said. 'The time stamp corresponds to the signal we received at Aldurukh.' Astelan folded his arms. 'Based on the condition of the bloodstain in the security alcove, I would estimate that the signal was sent approximately thirty minutes to an hour after the watch officer was killed.'

'They could have gotten the codes from the vox operator's kit. All they had to do was distort the caller's voice and wait for us to follow procedure.' The last pieces of the puzzle were falling into place, and Zahariel did not like the picture it revealed. 'Luther was right. The reaction force was lured into an ambush.'

Astelan nodded. 'It appears that the rebels managed to infiltrate the labour force,' he said.

'But to what purpose?' Zahariel countered. 'They didn't intend to destroy the plant, obviously.'

The chapter master cocked a thin eyebrow at the Librarian. 'They managed to wipe out an entire Jaeger company. Isn't that enough?'

'How do we know the Jaegers are dead?' he asked. 'Have you found any bodies?'

Astelan glanced away. For the first time, the Astartes looked faintly uncomfortable. 'No,' he said. The thought sent a chill down Zahariel's spine. 'We've found plenty of blood, but that's all.'

'And whoever sent that signal also had some way of controlling whatever force is interrupting our vox transmissions,' Zahariel continued. 'Whatever this is, it's not something the rebels have ever used before.'

He turned away from the vox-unit and paced across the room, pausing to study the two functioning work stations. 'What do we know about the labourers?' he asked.

Astelan shrugged. 'According to the maintenance logs, they arrived about a week ago as part of the quarterly rotation. The Administratum flies them in by shuttle from the Northwilds arcology and houses them in a pair of dormitories on the north end of the site.'

'No sign of them, either?' Zahariel asked.

'We haven't searched the dormitories yet, but I don't expect we'll find anything.'

Zahariel shook his head. 'They have to be here somewhere, brother,' he said grimly. 'Three hundred bodies don't simply vanish into thin air.'

'Chapter Master Astelan!' Gideon cried. 'I've found something!'

Zahariel and Astelan strode swiftly to the security station. The pict displays at the work station were all dark. 'What's this?' the Librarian said.

'I've been checking all of the surveyors and pict arrays covering the site,' Gideon said. 'All of the units have checked out fine up to this point, but the units on level B6 all appear to be dead.'

Zahariel gave Astelan a sidelong glance. They'd all memorised the layout of Sigma Five-One-Seven, down to the smallest detail.

'That's where the thermal vent is located,' the chapter master said.

Zahariel could see the memories of Sarosh lurking deep in Astelan's eyes. They all remembered the vast cavern beneath the earth, filled with millions upon millions of corpses offered up to the Saroshi's obscene god.

Not here, he wanted to say. This is Caliban. Such things do not happen here.

Instead, Zahariel gripped his force staff tightly in his hand and addressed the chapter master. 'Assemble the squad,' he said, his voice betraying nothing of the despair he felt.

Astelan nodded curtly. 'What are your orders?'

Zahariel glanced once more at the dark pict screens. 'We're going to go down there and find out who is responsible for this,' the Librarian replied.

'Then, by the primarch, they're going to pay for what they've done.'

THEY FORMED UP by the Land Raider as the sun was setting behind the mountains to the west. A thick bank of grey clouds was rolling ponderously towards the site from the south, carrying with it the threat of a storm. The weather had grown increasingly wild and unpredictable over the years as the Imperium transformed the surface of the planet and filled the skies with plumes of smoke from their manufactories. Magos Bosk and the rest of the Administratum insisted that the changes were nothing to be concerned about. Zahariel eyed the looming clouds warily and wondered if Magos Bosk had ever conducted a squad-level skirmish in a raging gale. He confessed to himself that the odds seemed unlikely in the extreme.

They boarded the assault tank and crossed the wide landing field, heading into the deep shadows filling up the alleys and access ways to the east of the site. The plant's massive thermal exchange unit was a black tower – wider at the base, then narrowing a bit at the middle before flaring open once more as it soared high into the sky over Sigma Five-One-Seven. Red and blue hazard lights flashed insistently along its length, warning low-flying aircraft to keep away; when the plant went into full operation the tower would be wreathed in hissing ribbons of waste steam, tinted a sickly orange by chemical flood lamps.

The Land Raider's driver circled around the base of the huge tower until he came upon a wide, low-ceiling entrance at the southeast side. At Zahariel's command, the tank rumbled to a halt a few dozen metres from the opening, then the squad dismounted into the gathering darkness. Immediately, Astelan pointed to three sets of cargo crates, each arrayed in a crescent shape with the closed ends pointed towards the tower entrance. Zahariel recognised them even before he saw the familiar shapes of heavy stubbers aimed at the thermal unit's entrance.

The Astartes approached the makeshift weapons cautiously, sweeping the shadows with their bolt pistols. Dried blood stained the permacrete around each of the positions; Zahariel's keen eyes detected scores of small craters where lasgun bolts had eaten into the pavement around the emplacements. A bloodstained portable vox-unit lay near the centre weapons station, its control panel smashed to pieces.

Zahariel eyed the heavy stubbers. None of them showed signs of having been fired. 'It looks like the reaction force tried to set up a security cordon around the thermal plant's entrance,' he declared, 'the gunners must have been ambushed later, once the others were gone.'

Astelan nodded in agreement. 'You think they realised what was going on?'

The Librarian shook his head. 'They knew only what the enemy told them,' Zahariel said. 'I expect the company commander got off his Condor and found a frantic man or woman in labourer's coveralls who told him that the rebels had taken over the thermal unit and were planning to blow it up. So the captain rushed in there with everything he had, hoping to stop the enemy before it was too late.'

Astelan glanced back at the Librarian. 'And now we're going in there as well?'

Zahariel nodded grimly, raising his force staff. 'Whatever the enemy might expect, they aren't ready for the likes of us.'

The members of the squad readied their weapons in mute agreement. Attias moved up alongside Zahariel, his silver death's-head mask seeming to float eerily out of the darkness. 'Loyalty and honour,' he rasped.

'Loyalty and honour, brothers,' Zahariel answered back, and led his squad inside.

THE AIR INSIDE the thermal exchange unit was hot and humid, gusting like the breath of a huge, hungry beast. Red emergency lighting bathed the interior crimson, outlining billowing clouds of steam and glistening on drops of condensate flowing from overhead pipes and ductwork. Zahariel smelled the bitter reek of corroded metal and freshly spilled blood.

'I thought the thermal exchanger wasn't online yet,' he said aloud.

'It's not,' Gideon replied. 'I checked the readouts myself.' He pulled his auspex unit from his belt and tested it. The screen flickered and then filled with a cascade of data. The Astartes tried several different detection modes, then shook his head in disgust and put the unit away. 'No readings,' he reported, 'or at least, none that make any sense. I'm picking up a lot of interference from somewhere close by.'

'Somewhere,' Attias echoed, 'or something.'

'Tactical pattern Epsilon,' Zahariel interjected curtly, unwilling to let that train of speculation proceed any further. 'Stay sharp, and watch for likely ambush points.'

Within moments the squad was arrayed in a rough octagonal formation, with a warrior at each corner of the octagon and Zahariel and Gideon, the auspex bearer, in the centre. It was a solid formation that drew on the ancient teachings of the Order, and was suited to dealing with close assaults from any direction. Abruptly he found himself wishing that he'd thought to equip the squad with a flamer or two before leaving Aldurukh, but that couldn't be helped now. Once he was satisfied that all of his warriors were in position, Zahariel waved the squad forward.

Drawing on the maps he'd memorised, Zahariel guided the squad through the twisting corridors surrounding the base of the thermal tower. Visibility was limited; even with the Astartes' enhanced senses the plumes of mist and the dim red lighting created illusory patterns of movement and obscured vision beyond more than two metres. Zahariel could not help but admire the courage of the Jaegers who had preceded them; the human troops would have been all but blind as they tried to reach the lower levels of the tower. He doubted that they'd made it very far.

The terrible heat and the reek of corruption increased as they pressed further inside, and the sense of malevolence grew stronger and more focused on Zahariel and the squad. He could feel its weight pressing against him like a smothering cloud, probing his armour in search of a way inside. The cables connecting his mind to the psychic hood grew deathly cold, and a film of black frost condensed on the haft of his force staff despite the cloying heat. He was tempted – strongly tempted – to reach out with his own psychic power and get a sense of the enemy that lay somewhere ahead, but years of training with Brother-Librarian Israfael cautioned against it. Don't waste your energies swinging blind, Israfael had told him many times. Or worse, leave yourself open to a surprise attack. Conserve your strength, maintain your defences, and wait for the enemy to reveal themselves. And so he did, resolutely pushing the squad forward and waiting for the first blows to fall.

There were four industrial-grade lifts that provided access to the tower's lower levels, but they were deathtraps as far as Zahariel was concerned. If the enemy had access to a meltagun – and the Jaeger reaction force had carried two – then a single blast into such a tight space could wipe out half his squad. He had Brother Gideon disable their controls so the enemy couldn't use them either, then they began their descent via one of the tower's four long stairways.

The stairs didn't switch back upon themselves, like in most structures; instead they descended in a long, arcing spiral that wound ever deeper into the earth. The foul presence permeating the air grew stronger with each and every step. Zahariel concentrated on putting one foot in front of the next, recalling the labyrinthine steps that wound through the ancient stone beneath Aldurukh itself. Memories flitted through his mind as he walked; of his initiation into the Order and his long walk through darkness at Jonson's side. Fragmentary images came and went: stone steps and torchlight, the rustle of fabric, Nemiel's presence at his side as they descended a flight of stairs to... where? He couldn't quite recall. The memories were vague and only half-formed, like scenes from a dream. A dull pain swelled in the back of his head as he tried to concentrate on the images, until finally he was forced to push the thoughts away.

More alarming were the cracks that began to appear in the outer walls of the stairwell as they descended deeper beneath the ground. Black roots had forced their way through freshly-laid permacrete more than a metre thick, spreading across the inner surface of the curved walls and spilling black, foul-smelling dirt onto the stairs. Red light glistened on the segmented bodies of insects that wormed and writhed their way among the roots. Ghostly white cave spiders, each as big as Zahariel's hand, rose up from their nests and brandished their long legs in challenge as the Astartes went past.

By the time they reached the lowest levels the stairway was little more than a tunnel of raw earth and dripping plant matter, thick with crawling, chittering life. Strange, misshapen insects, bloated and foul, squirmed amid dense networks of rotting root matter. A long, segmented millipede, nearly as long as Zahariel's forearm, uncoiled like a spring from the curve of a root ball and leapt onto his shoulder, stabbing wildly at the armour plate with its needle-like stinger. He brushed the foul thing away with the haft of his force staff and crushed it beneath his boot.

Still, the squad forged ahead, pressing through the ever-constricting tunnel until Zahariel began to think they would be forced to cut a path with their chainswords. Finally, Astelan and the warrior beside him at the front of the formation came to a halt. The air was stifling, thick with heat and the smell of rot, and the red emergency lights had long since given out. Dimly, Zahariel could sense a vague, greenish glow down and to the right, past Astelan's shoulder.

'We've reached the bottom of the stairs,' Astelan said quietly, casting a wary eye up at the swarms of insect life rustling ceaselessly overhead. 'What are your orders?'

There was no telling what they might find beyond the opening to level B6. Zahariel was surprised the enemy had let them penetrate so far – he'd operated on the assumption that they would encounter resistance almost immediately, which would have at least given him some idea of what they were up against. The time might come very soon when he would have to draw upon his psychic abilities, whether he wanted to or not. He needed information more than anything else at this point.

'Press forward,' he said. 'Drive for the thermal core. It's the largest chamber on this level.'

The chapter master nodded and stepped into the green-lit blackness without hesitation. Zahariel followed with the rest of his squad, bolt pistol at the ready. His feet came down on thick roots and cable-like vines stretching across the floor beyond the stairwell. Draughts of stinking air gusted past his helmet, and the insect noise surrounding the warriors swelled to frantic life.

They pressed on down a low-ceilinged passage for more than a hundred metres, passing numerous cross-corridors as they went. The clinging plant life continued unabated down the passageway, and Zahariel realised the pale green glow came from colonies of bloated grubs that clung tenaciously to the twisted roots. Sounds of restless movement echoed all around them, seeming to grow louder with each passing moment. At one point Zahariel heard the clatter of talons behind a cluster of pipes half-hidden among a network of vines running along one of the walls, but he couldn't catch sight of the creature that made the noise.

'How much farther?' Gideon asked quietly. The warrior's voice was tense. The continual screeching and rustling had the entire squad on edge.

'Fifty more–' Zahariel started to say, just as the air filled with a hideous screeching and dark, armoured shapes burst from the plant life all around them.

He was glancing over at Gideon just as a segmented creature struck downwards at the Astartes from the network of thick pipes running overhead. It was swift as a tree viper but as thick as Zahariel's upper arm, with hundreds of chitin-sheathed legs and a broad head set with a half-dozen compound eyes. In a flash it had wrapped around Gideon's torso and lifted the huge warrior off the ground, lunging and snapping at the back of his helmet with its curved mandibles.

Bolt pistols barked and chainswords howled in the confined space as the squad was set upon from all sides. Gideon twisted in the monster's grip, slashing at its body with his whirring blade. Zahariel blew the creature's head apart with a single shot from his bolt pistol just as a powerful impact struck the back of his helmet and pitched him off his feet.

Zahariel tried to twist his body as he fell, but the creature had his helmet gripped in its mandibles and it was stronger even than he. It drove him face-first onto the floor, wrenching his head left and right as it tried to crack the helmet he wore. Something sharp jabbed at the back plate of the helmet like a dagger, trying again and again to punch through the ceramite. Warning icons flashed before his eyes, informing him of his suit's failing integrity.

With his elbows and knees on firm ground the Librarian flexed his augmented muscles and managed to twist onto his right side. His force staff was pinned beneath him, but he was able to aim behind him at the creature's thrashing body. It took three bolt pistol shots in rapid succession to blow the thing apart, showering him with fragments of chitin and reeking ichor. In the muzzle flashes of his pistol Zahariel could see three more of the monsters rearing up from the walls like snakes, their mandibles clashing as they prepared to strike. Without hesitation, he summoned up the full force of his will and unleashed the psychic fury of the warp.

He had practised the attack countless times under Israfael's tutelage, but the sheer intensity of the energy coursing through him took Zahariel by surprise. It roared through him like a torrent, far stronger and easier to grasp than he'd ever experienced before. A nimbus of crackling energy surrounded the Librarian; he felt each and every vein in his body turn to ice, radiating from the cables of the psychic hood at the back of his skull, and the three creatures were engulfed in a torrent of raging fire that coalesced from the very air itself. They burst apart in the intense heat, their carapaces exploding from within.

Zahariel gave a shout of triumph and surged to his feet. Skeins of crackling lightning played over the surface of his staff, and icy power raged along his limbs. For a dizzying instant his awareness sharpened to a supernatural degree, reaching into dimensions beyond the understanding of ordinary humans. The permacrete and metal of the corridor faded into near-invisibility, while living matter was etched with vibrant clarity. He could see the layers of root and vine blanketing the walls and ceiling, and every one of the thousands of insects living in their midst. He could also see the score of worms surrounding his squad, wrapping about the warriors and biting at their armoured forms.

Worse, he could see the awful, unnatural taint that pulsed through it all. It stained every living thing in the corridor around the Astartes, corrupting them like a cancer. A cancer that seethed with awful, otherworldly sentience.

The sight of it stunned Zahariel. It etched itself indelibly into his brain. This was worse by far than the horrors he'd witnessed on Sarosh. There, too, he had been deep beneath the ground, surrounded by death and corruption, but on Sarosh, the vile, jelly-like creature they'd faced had been clearly born of the shifting madness of the warp. This taint, this evil that suffused every root and vine, was inextricably part of Caliban itself.

ELEVEN

CONVERSATIONS BY STARLIGHT

Diamat
In the 200th year of the Emperor's Great Crusade

THE ATTACK WAS so fast that it momentarily took Nemiel off-guard. In the space of a single heartbeat the Praetorians erupted into a blur of deadly motion, bringing their weapons to bear and charging across the last few metres between themselves and the Astartes. Multi-barrel slug throwers pounded at the Dark Angels, the explosive shells bursting in a series of sharp flashes across the ceramite surfaces of their armour. The warriors staggered under the hail of shells, blood spraying from wounds to their arms, torsos and legs. Urgent red telltales flashed on Nemiel's helmet display; pain flared across his chest, and his arms suddenly felt twice as heavy. A Praetorian shell had likely cut a bundle of synthetic muscle fibres beneath his breastplate.

Brother-Sergeant Kohl was the first to respond. There was no time for questions or recriminations; the Praetorians were descending on them with the speed of a thunderbolt, brandishing power claws and blazing shock mauls that would make a mockery of their Crusader-pattern armour. The Terran staggered backward under a punishing barrage of explosive shells, roaring a curse in some forgotten tongue and returning fire with his bolt pistol. The shells struck one of the charging skitarii in the chest and head, flattening against the augmented warrior's armour plates without inflicting serious damage, but the gesture of resistance was enough to shock the rest of the squad back into action.

Bolters hammered at the charging Praetorians, slowing their advance by sheer weight of fire. Blood and other fluids spurted from minor wounds; spatters of liquid hissed into steam where it struck the Praetorians' super-charged bionics. Nemiel smelled the acrid reek of adrenal compounds and hormone agitators.

Off to Nemiel's right there was a shriek of superheated air as Brother Marthes shot one of the oncoming skitarii point-blank with his meltagun. The anti-tank weapon blew the Praetorian apart in a shower of sparks and charred bits of flesh.

The Praetorian rushing at Nemiel was a massive brute that seemed more machine than man; a composition of bionic joints, synthetic musculature, adrenal shunts and pitted armour plating. His head was encased in a faceless metal shell, studded with multi-spectrum auspex nodes in place of ears, nose and mouth. His breastplate was decorated – if that was the word – with bar-code emblems and small plaques of glittering, iridescent metal. Perhaps he was a champion of sorts, or the leader of the detachment; Nemiel couldn't be sure. The Praetorian's left hand had been replaced by a huge, three-fingered power claw, its curved edges plated with adamantium and sharpened to a mirror-sheen. The warrior lunged at Nemiel with stunning speed, swiping the claw at his face.

He knew better than to try and parry something so large, the power claw could easily knock his crozius aside – or worse, snap it cleanly in two. Instead, he ducked, allowing the Praetorian's swing to pass harmlessly over his head, and smashed his staff into the warrior's elbow. The power field of the crozius struck the bionic joint and fused it with a flash of actinic light, but the Praetorian scarcely seemed to notice. The huge warrior spun on his left heel and brought his right elbow back to smash into Nemiel's forehead.

Ceramite cracked loudly in Nemiel's ears, and the impact hurled him off his feet. He landed squarely on his back, his helmet readouts crackling with washes of static. Without thinking, he fired a quick burst in the Praetorian's direction, and was rewarded with the sound of shells striking the warrior's armour plate. The skitarii was just a blurry shape on the helmet's damaged optical systems, fading in and out of existence like a monstrous ghost. The Praetorian moved closer, his claw arm reaching for Nemiel's right leg.

A flash of light and another howl of tortured air swept over Nemiel. Marthes's shot vaporised the Praetorian's claw arm at the elbow and blistered the warrior's armoured shoulders and chest. The skitarii reeled backwards, his auto-senses momentarily overloaded.

Nemiel dropped his pistol and clawed at his helmet release. He popped the catches with nimble fingers and tore the damaged helm from his head, blinking in the dim, red light of Diamat's distant sun. A wild melee was raging all around him as his battle brothers fought against the heavily-armed Praetorians. Brother Yung was down, his breastplate torn like paper and stained with blood. Techmarine Askelon had another of the Praetorians by the throat, lifting the brute off the ground with his servo arm and crushing the skitarii's metal-sheathed spine.

He quickly turned his focus back to the one-armed Praetorian just a few metres away. The augmented warrior was in a crouch, the air shimmering around his scorched armour, his body eerily still as he reset his auspex nodes. Nemiel snatched up his bolt pistol and took careful aim, preparing to put a round through the Praetorian's throat.

Suddenly a strange, trumpeting blurt of binaric code cut like a knife through the sounds of battle, and the Praetorians practically recoiled from the Dark Angels. They retreated a dozen steps and lowered their weapon arms, their chests heaving from exertion and the combat drugs that were boiling in their veins. The Astartes paused, their weapons trained on their adversaries. Kohl looked to Nemiel for instructions.

But the Redemptor's attention was focused on a large force of armoured skitarii rushing down the roadway from the northeast. They were led by a tall, hooded figure clad in the crimson robes of the Mechanicum, riding atop a humming suspensor disk.

Nemiel rose swiftly to his feet as the figure glided closer. 'What is the meaning of this, magos?' he snarled, his choler nearly overwhelming him.

'Error. Improper threat parameters. Misidentification,' the magos blurted in High Gothic. The voice was harsh and atonal, the words strangely inflected but recognizable. The magos paused, raising a hand that glittered in the rust-coloured sunlight. 'Apologies,' he continued, his synthetic voice more carefully modulated now. 'Grave apologies to you and your squad, noble Astartes. The skitarii were in seek-and-destroy mode, searching for enemy troops that had penetrated the complex. Your appearance on Diamat is... unexpected. I was unable to override the Praetorians' engagement protocols until it was too late.'

'I see,' Nemiel said curtly. So it's our fault for rushing here to protect you, he thought. He glanced over at Brother-Sergeant Kohl and guessed from the Terran's belligerent pose that he was thinking much the same thing. 'How is Brother Yung?'

'Comatose,' Kohl growled. 'His injuries are grave.'

'Let us conduct him to the forge's apothecarium,' the magos said at once. 'We will repair his body and mend his damaged armour.'

For some reason, the magos's offer took Nemiel aback. 'That won't be required,' he said quickly. 'We will conduct him back to our ship when the battle is done, and let our brothers tend to him.' He studied the hooded figure warily. 'I am Brother-Redemptor Nemiel, of the Emperor's First Legion. Who are you?'

The magos laid one metal hand atop the other and bowed from the waist. 'I am Archoi, magos of the

Forge and former servant of the Arch-Magos Vertullus,' he said.

'Former?' Nemiel inquired.

Archoi nodded gravely. 'I regret that the esteemed Arch-Magos was slain, twelve-point-eight hours ago, while coordinating the defence of the forge,' he said. 'As the senior surviving member of Vertullus's staff, I am now the acting Arch-Magos of Diamat.'

Off to the south, a deep, brassy rumble shook the air. It swelled in volume, the source climbing slowly into the sky. Nemiel turned and saw a pair of ships boosting ponderously into orbit on pillars of cyan light.

'The rebels have had enough,' Kohl declared. There was a grim note of triumph in his voice. 'They're pulling out.'

'Indeed,' Archoi replied. 'Your primarch contacted us six-point-three-seven minutes previously, declaring that rebel forces in orbit are in full retreat.' The magos raised his arms, as if in benediction. 'Victory is yours, noble Astartes. Diamat is saved.'

Archoi's synthesised voice fell silent, giving way to the fading thunder of the fleeing transports and distant rumble of Imperial vehicles. A rattle of small arms fire echoed in the distance. The Praetorians stared mutely at Nemiel and the Dark Angels, their augmented bodies as still as statues. Blood and lubricants leaked slowly from their wounds.

Nemiel couldn't help but think that Archoi was being a bit premature.

'NATURALLY, WE'RE VERY grateful that you came when you did,' Taddeus Kulik said, though the look in the governor's hooded eyes suggested just the opposite.

The primarch's sanctum aboard the *Invincible Reason* was a single, large chamber that stretched from one side of the warship's superstructure to the other and subdivided into smaller, more intimate spaces by fluted columns of structural steel. Tall, arched viewports to port and starboard threw long, sharp-edged shadows across the mosaics inlaid onto the deck, and hinted at the angular shapes of furnishings in the surrounding spaces. Fragments of hull plating had gouged the portside viewports in chaotic patterns, refracting the red light of Diamat's sun like a scattering of polished rubies.

Jonson typically kept the lighting dim in the sanctum, preferring to work solely by starlight when possible, but out of consideration for his guests he'd lit the lumen-sconces on the pillars surrounding the large, hexagonally-shaped meeting space in the centre of the great chamber. A carved wooden campaign chair had been provided for the governor, who had been hit in the leg by a lasgun bolt during the Dragoons' counterattack. A chirurgeon from the Imperial palace and a medicae servitor stood a discreet distance away, ready with painkillers should Kulik require them. The governor, a man in his middle years, still wore the battle-scarred carapace armour he'd fought in just a few hours before. A stained compression bandage was wrapped around his right thigh, and an old power sword hung from a scabbard at his hip. His pale grey eyes were bright with pain and fatigue, and though he made a point to relax into the back of his chair, the set of his shoulders was tense.

Magos Archoi stood a few paces to the governor's right, his metal hands folded at his waist. He had changed out of his simple Mechanicum robe for his audience with the primarch, garbing himself in the formal attire of his late predecessor. The heavy robes of office were woven with gold and platinum thread, worked into complicated patterns that resembled nothing so much as integrated circuit paths; the sleeves were wide and terminated just below the elbow, revealing the intricate craftsmanship of Archoi's bionic arms. The magos had drawn back his hood, exposing the polished metal of his lower skull and neck. Data cables and coolant tubes ran in bundles along either side of his steel throat; auspex nodes and receptor pits were arranged around the vox grill set in the space where his mouth used to be. The magos had augmetic eyes set into the flesh of his upper face, glowing with faint pinpoints of blue light. His bald scalp was pale and dotted with faint scars. Nemiel couldn't read the magos at all; Archoi's body betrayed nothing but machine-like inscrutability. A pair of hooded acolytes stood a precise six paces behind him; heads bowed and muttering to one another in muted blurts of binaric cant.

Lion El'Jonson studied the two officials over the tips of his steepled fingers. He sat in a high-backed, throne-like chair carved from Calibanite oak that only served to magnify his towering physical presence, his demeanour confident and utterly composed. Looking at him, one would never know that he'd been fighting for his life in a space battle just a short while before.

'Diamat's troubles are far from over, Governor Kulik,' Jonson replied gravely. 'There are resources here that Horus must have in order to prevail in the coming conflict with the Emperor. As soon as the survivors of his raiding fleet return to Isstvan, he'll immediately start putting together a new force – and this time it won't be comprised of renegade warships and former Imperial Army troops.' His gaze drifted to the red-stained view-ports to port, his expression thoughtful. 'I expect we have no more than two and a half weeks, three at most, before they return. We need to make the most of it.'

Kulik eyed Jonson warily. 'And what exactly would you have us do, Primarch Jonson?' he asked.

The cynical tone in the governor's voice shocked Nemiel. He was standing to the right of Jonson's chair, turned so that he could address the primarch or the two officials if required. Upon returning to the flagship he'd seen to the needs of his squad and then spent more than an hour in the Apothecarium having bits of steel removed from his body. His battered wargear had been handed off to the ship's armourers for repairs, and he'd clad himself in a simple, hooded surplice before reporting to the primarch. His hands clenched reflexively at the near-insolent tone in the governor's voice.

Kulik acted as though Jonson was as much of a danger as Horus – and why not, Nemiel thought? Four Legions had already cast off their ties to the Emperor, and the entire Segmentum was coming apart at the seams. Everyone's motives were suspect. The realisation left him cold.

Jonson didn't miss the tone in Kulik's voice either. He turned back to the governor, his expression an icy mask. 'I would have you continue to do your duty, sir,' he said coldly. 'We must defend this planet at all costs. The future of the Imperium might well depend upon it.'

Governor Kulik grimaced, shifting uncomfortably in his seat. He rubbed the bandage on his leg, but Nemiel wondered if that was what truly pained him. 'My people don't have much left to give,' he said gravely. 'The rebels smashed every city and town from orbit. We don't even know for sure how many people are still alive. There's been no time to count all the bodies, much less bury them.'

'What of the Dragoons?' the primarch asked.

Kulik sighed. 'We threw everything we had left into the counterattack once we learned that the company covering the forge's south entrance had been overrun.' The governor had been a military man in his youth. When the commander of the Dragoons had been killed in an atomic strike early in the rebel attack, and the Imperial palace had been bombed to rubble, he put on a Dragoon's carapace armour and took charge of the planet's defence. Kulik was a man who took his duties to the Imperium seriously.

'I've got perhaps one full regiment's worth of troops, cobbled together from half a dozen units, and most of an armoured battalion left,' he said, then shot a venomous look at Magos Archoi. 'On the other hand, the Mechanicum's troops saw little or no action during the attack, so they're likely to be at full strength.'

Jonson turned to the magos and raised an inquisitive eyebrow. 'Is that so?' he asked. His tone was mild, but Nemiel saw a gleam of anger in the primarch's eye.

Magos Archoi bowed his head in regret. 'It was Arch-Magos Vertullus's directive that the Tech-Guard be employed only for the purposes of defending our forge complexes across the planet,' he said. 'Many of us tried to convince him otherwise, but he said his orders came from Mars itself.'

'Not that it made any difference,' Kulik spat. 'The rebels sacked every one of the smaller forges and manufactories.'

'But they failed to seize more than twelve per cent of our primary complex outside Xanthus,' Magos Archoi pointed out.

The governor glared at him. 'And had we not bled to keep them out, I wager that percentage would have been a great deal higher,' he retorted, his anger rising.

'Now is not the time for recriminations, my friends,' Jonson declared, holding up a hand to forestall further comment. 'We have fought hard and won a temporary reprieve, but that is all. Now tell us, Magos Archoi, how many troops can the Mechanicum muster for Diamat's defence?'

The magos paused. One of his acolytes raised his hooded head slightly and let out an atonal squawk of code. Archoi burbled a reply in binaric, then said, 'As Governor Kulik pointed out, all of our lesser forges were seized by the enemy, and their defenders were slain. Fighting around the southern entrance to the primary forge was also very heavy, and our garrison suffered serious losses. At this point we can muster only one thousand, two hundred and twelve skitarii.'

Nemiel saw Kulik grind his teeth at the offhand assessment, but the governor wisely chose to hold his choler in check.

'Thank you, magos,' Jonson said, taking control of the conversation again. 'For my part, I can muster one hundred and eighty-seven veteran Astartes for the planet's defence. I'm still waiting on damage assessments from my battle group commanders, but it's clear that all of my surviving vessels have sustained moderate to severe levels of damage, and all of them are low on stocks of fuel, ordnance and ammunition.'

Magos Archoi bowed to the primarch. 'The full resources of our forge are at your service, Primarch Jonson,' he said. 'We can begin resupplying your ships and effecting repairs immediately.'

'Providing you're resupplied and the proper repairs are made, can your ships repel the next attack?' Kulik asked.

Jonson considered his reply. 'It's unlikely,' he admitted. 'We'll hold them off as long as we can, but my ships are in no condition for a protracted battle. Keep in mind, however, that time is not on Horus's side. He knows that a huge force of Astartes is on the way to attack Isstvan, and could arrive here at any time in the next few weeks. Every day we can hold him off brings us that much closer to victory.'

'If all we have to do is dig in our heels and make the bastards pay for every kilometre, that's something we've had a lot of experience with,' Kulik said grimly.

'And we'll be right beside you every step of the way,' Jonson said with a nod. He turned to Magos Archoi. 'There is a great deal of planning to discuss,' he began. 'May I make a small request, magos?'

'Naturally you may, primarch,' Archoi replied.

Jonson smiled. 'What I require most right now is information,' he began. 'Specifically, I need an accounting of the materiel that the rebels succeeded in removing from your forges, as well as an inventory of what remains, and where it is stored.'

Archoi didn't reply for several moments. Kulik turned to regard the magos, his expression intent.

'Your request is problematic,' the magos said at last. 'The lesser forges were almost completely destroyed, and a great deal of data storage was lost.'

Jonson raised a placating hand. 'Of course, magos. I see your point,' he said. 'If you could just provide an inventory of the materiel still stored at the primary forge site, that would be sufficient.'

The magos bowed. 'Thank you for your understanding, primarch,' he replied. 'I will instruct my acolytes to begin compiling the data at once.'

The primarch smiled, but his eyes were calculating. 'My thanks, Magos Archoi,' he said. 'Now, if you will excuse me, I must see to the needs of my brethren. We will meet again tomorrow to begin discussing an integrated defence plan.'

Magos Archoi bowed deeply to the primarch and withdrew quickly, exchanging a flurry of code with his acolytes as he disappeared into the deep shadows beyond the audience space. Governor Kulik levered himself awkwardly to his feet, waving away the hands of the hovering chirurgeon. He inclined his head respectfully to Jonson, who nodded at the wounded man in return and watched him limp off into the gloom. After the governor had left, the primarch turned to Nemiel.

'What do you make of them?' he asked.

The question surprised Nemiel. He paused for a moment, collecting his thoughts. 'Governor Kulik seems like a brave and honourable man,' he replied. 'How many planetary rulers have we met who cower in their palaces and send better men to die on their behalf?'

'Well, his palace was blown to bits,' Jonson observed.

Nemiel chuckled. 'He could have fled to the hills with his people, but he didn't. He honoured his oaths, and that counts for something.'

Jonson nodded. 'Do you think we can trust him?'

The Redemptor frowned. He studied the primarch's impassive face. Was Jonson making another joke? 'I... believe so,' he said after a moment. 'How could it possibly profit him to betray us now?

The primarch gave him a faintly exasperated look. 'Nemiel, the governor did well enough against Horus's cannon fodder, I'll grant you that,' he said. 'But the Warmaster won't just send auxiliaries next time. We'll almost certainly be facing other Astartes as well. How do you imagine he'll react then?'

Nemiel frowned. It was still difficult to imagine the idea of fighting a brother Astartes. The very thought of it filled him with dread. 'Governor Kulik is no coward,' he said confidently. 'He'll fight, regardless of the odds. It's in his nature.'

Jonson nodded to himself, and Nemiel saw that he seemed actually relieved by the observation. Could the primarch actually have a difficult time reading someone as forthright as Kulik? Was this the same individual who united all of Caliban in a crusade against the great beasts?

But then it hit Nemiel; Jonson hadn't united Caliban. The plan was his but the person who convinced the knightly orders and the noble families to put aside their ancient traditions and unite under Jonson's banner was Luther. It had been his oratorial skills, his personal charisma and sense of diplomacy, and above all his keen insight into human nature that had allowed him to forge the grand alliance that had changed the face of Caliban. Jonson, by contrast, had spent his early years alone, living like an animal in the depths of the Northwilds, one of the most forbidding and inaccessible wildernesses on the planet. He didn't say a word for the first few months at Aldurukh, and was always considered cold and aloof even in later years. He was thought of as an intellectual and a scholar, and Nemiel knew that to be true, but now he also wondered if Lion El'Jonson, the superhuman son of the Emperor himself, could not relate to the people around him. He could predict how they would behave on the battlefield to an uncanny degree, but he couldn't tell an honourable man from a craven one. Are we all ciphers to him, the Redemptor wondered? If Jonson had so little in common with humanity, what did that make him?

Nemiel realised abruptly that Jonson was staring at him. He shifted uncomfortably. 'My apologies, lord,' he said. 'Did you say something?'

'I asked you for your impression of Magos Archoi,' he said.

'Ah,' Nemiel replied. 'Honestly, I don't know what to make of him. How can a man willingly part with his own flesh and replace it with cold, unfeeling metal and plastek? It seems unnatural to me.'

'You mean like Captain Stenius? I think he rather appreciates having a pair of working eyes,' Jonson said wryly.

'That's different, my lord. Stenius lost his sight in battle. They were taken from him, not willingly thrown away.'

Jonson nodded. 'So you think we can't trust him?'

'I don't know what to think about him, lord. That's what I'm saying.' He sighed. 'I confess I might be a little biased as well, after our first encounter.'

Jonson nodded. 'Understandable,' he said. 'How is Brother Yung?'

'The Apothecaries are tending him now,' Nemiel replied. 'He suffered severe internal injuries, and his body went into stasis almost immediately.' As part of their extensive physical and genetic modifications, all Astartes possessed the ability to survive even the worst physical injuries by entering a kind of voluntary coma that focused the body's energies on basic survival. 'The chirurgeon says that he will heal, but there's no chance he'll be returning to action in the next few months.'

'And the rest of the squad?'

Nemiel shrugged. 'Numerous minor injuries, but that's to be expected. Brother Ephrial is having his knee mended now, and will be fit for duty again within twelve hours.' He grinned. 'Just don't send us into battle any time in the next week or so, or half of us will be fighting in our surplices.'

Jonson returned the grin. 'I think I can manage that,' he said, then rose from the chair. 'Go and get some rest. Give your body some time to recover. We'll begin planning in earnest on the morrow.'

Nemiel bowed to the primarch and made to withdraw, but something he recalled from the previous conversation made him pause. 'My lord?'

Jonson had already padded silently into the shadows. Nemiel saw him turn, silhouetted against the crimson light streaming through the portside viewports. 'What is it?' he asked.

'Why did you request that inventory from Magos Archoi?' he said without preamble.

The primarch stiffened slightly. 'I should think it obvious,' he replied. 'If we're to devise an effective battle plan against the rebels we will need a full accounting of our supplies and all available assets.'

Nemiel nodded. 'Yes, of course, my lord. It's entirely understandable. Only...' he paused. 'The request troubled the magos considerably. In these difficult times, with the Warmaster in open revolt and armies on the march, it's easy to misunderstand the intent behind such a request.'

Jonson did not reply at first. He stared at Nemiel from the shadows, his powerful body completely still. 'I'm not a brigand, Nemiel,' he said, his voice quiet and cold.

The Redemptor bowed his head. 'Of course not, my lord,' he said, feeling foolish now for bringing the matter up in the first place. 'I didn't mean that at all. But Archoi and Governor Kulik have already suffered a great deal at the hands of Horus's men. No one knows whom to trust anymore.'

Jonson's gaze bored into Nemiel. 'Do you trust me, Nemiel?' the primarch asked.

'Of course,' Nemiel replied.

'Then rest,' Jonson said. 'And leave Archoi and Kulik to me.'

The primarch turned away, gliding like a forest cat into the darkness. Nemiel watched him go, a feeling of unease sinking into his stomach.

TWELVE
Awful Truths

Caliban
In the 200th year of the Emperor's Great Crusade

Horror and revulsion threatened to overwhelm Zahariel. He cried out in rage at the vision of evil before him – and then his senses shifted yet again.

Pale light bathed the corridor, swelling from the bodies of his brother Astartes and the twisted monstrosities that they fought. Between one eye-blink and the next, the world had slowed near to a standstill, transforming the desperate battle into a kind of grim tableaux. Zahariel could see through the bodies of friend and foe alike; he saw hearts beating and veins coursing sluggishly with hot blood. He could see the black ichor suffusing the bodies of the terrible worms, and the foul corruption that spread within them. One of the monsters had seized brother Attias, wrapping around his torso and clamping its mandibles about his steel-encased skull. Within the creature's mouth was a long, needle-pointed spike of bone, sheathed in a powerful bundle of muscle that propelled it forward with the force of a bullet aimed at the back of Attias's head. A hollow channel within the bony needle pulsed with foul venom.

Zahariel's horror was transformed into pure, righteous rage. He summoned the fury of the warp and swept his staff in a wide arc, hurling tendrils of searing white fire towards every creature he could see. Like thunderbolts, they sank through the monsters' flesh and boiled the liquid within. The Librarian felt his veins freeze and his hearts clench in agony, and the world snapped back into motion once more.

A dozen of the creatures exploded, showering the squad with shattered chitin and a mist of stinking ichor. Zahariel reeled backwards, stunned by the intensity of his vision. Terrorsight, Israfael called it. He'd only experienced it once before, when he'd fought the Calibanite Lion. For that one instant, he had extended his consciousness partly into the warp. The coils of his psychic hood were so cold they seared his skin. He shuddered to think what might have happened had he exposed himself to the tainted energies inside the passageway without the hood's protection.

The darkness within the corridor was lit with muzzle flashes as the squad rallied against the armoured worms' sudden assault. Chapter Master Astelan was still on his feet, blasting two of the monsters to pieces with well-aimed shots from his pistol and slicing another in half with a swipe of his chainsword. Brother Gideon leapt to his feet, shrugging off the body of the worm he'd killed and chopping apart another that had latched onto a fellow warrior's back. Attias charged forward to help free another fallen comrade, his fearsome skull-face lit by the hellish flames of pistol fire.

With a fierce cry, Zahariel hurled himself into the fight. He focused his rage on the force staff in his hands, wreathing it in a crackling aura of psychic power. Every worm he struck was incinerated in a flash of blue fire and a sizzling clap of thunder that hurled their shattered husks into the air. He destroyed a half-dozen of the worms in as many seconds, and then as suddenly as it had begun, the battle was over. The Astartes stood in a rough circle, facing outwards, their armour scarred and dented and their pistols smoking. The blue haze of bolt propellant hung in the thick air around them, and the smashed bodies of more than a score of worms lay about their feet. Several of the Astartes bore minor wounds, but none of them had fallen prey to the worms' fearsome stingers.

'What are these creatures?' Zahariel asked, probing one of the corpses with the butt of his staff.

'Reaver worms,' Astelan said, nudging one of the dead creatures with his boot. 'We used to hunt them when I was a child, but where I come from they never grow much longer than half a metre.'

Zahariel had heard of reaver worms, like most Calibanite children, but had never seen one. They were a menace to human settlements all over Caliban, transforming small animals and livestock into living incubators for their eggs. The worms would wrap themselves around their victim's neck, driving their stinger into the prey's spine and injecting it with a tremendous amount of neurotoxin. The venom destroyed higher brain functions, leaving the autonomic functions intact and making the victim's nervous system hyper-conductive. Still attached to the victim, the worm then secreted enzymes into the prey's spinal chord that gave it rudimentary control of its motor functions. The worm would then literally drive the prey back to its communal nest, where the still-living victim would be injected with eggs by the nest's queen. Occasionally the worms would find their way into fresh human graves and try to make off with the corpse, much to the horror of the deceased's relatives. His skin crawled at the thought of the worm that had clamped onto his helmet, and the dagger-like stinger that had tried to punch its way into the back of his skull.

'I think we know what happened to the Jaegers,' he said grimly. 'And probably most of the labourers besides.'

'Most of them?' Astelan said.

'A worm didn't send the radio transmission to Aldurukh,' Zahariel said.

'Emperor protect us,' the chapter master hissed in disgust.

'It's been done before,' Attias said. 'The Knights of Lupus turned their beasts on us, remember?'

'But the Knights of Lupus are no more,' Astelan said sharply. 'And the great beasts driven to extinction. So where did these vile things come from?'

'That's not important right now,' Zahariel said, eager to change the subject. 'If the worms carried off the bodies of the Jaegers, it means they've got a nest and an egg-laying queen down here.'

Astelan nodded in agreement. 'The queens are much larger than the drones,' he warned.

'Then she must be up ahead, near the thermal core,' Zahariel declared. He checked the load in his bolt pistol, then holstered it and pulled a frag grenade from his belt. 'Grenades first, then we charge. I'll take the lead. Any questions?'

There were none, of course. The warriors of the squad had their orders. The Astartes returned to their formation and readied their weapons without hesitation. Zahariel took Astelan's place at the head of the group and set off down the corridor at a swift pace. As he did, he summoned his power once more and sent it questing down the passageway ahead. He sensed more worms waiting in ambush at the far end of the corridor and lashed the monsters with a wave of psychic energy. A hideous screeching filled the air, and powerful, armoured bodies burst from the concealing roots, thrashing in their death agonies. Zahariel struck them again, channelling every ounce of his rage into the blast, and the worms became shrieking pyres of purple and indigo flame.

Zahariel primed the grenade in his hand. 'For the Emperor!' he cried, and hurled it down the corridor. Nine more grenades followed an instant later, flashing past his head in flat, precise arcs to detonate just beyond the entrance to the core chamber. More shrieking rent the air as shrapnel scythed through the creatures hiding around the entranceway. Zahariel answered them with a furious shout of his own and broke into a run, his force staff blazing like a firebrand.

A swarm of reaver worms awaited their charge, ready to defend their nest. The Librarian hurled a torrent of psychic flame into their midst, immolating a score of the creatures and stunning the rest. He and his brothers crashed a moment later, and the battle was joined in earnest.

Zahariel swept his force staff in a crackling arc and killed two worms lunging at him from the right. Another monster struck from the left, fixing its mandibles about his ceramite pauldron; in one swift motion he drew his bolt pistol and decapitated the creature with a single, well-aimed shot. Around him, chainswords howled and bolt pistols hammered as the Angels of Death slaughtered their foes.

The chamber was a huge, man-made cavern that rose to a curved, dome-like ceiling thirty metres above their heads. The huge cylinder of the thermal core itself dominated the centre of the chamber, rising from a bore that had been drilled more than five hundred metres into the bedrock of the planet and disappearing through an opening at the apex of the dome, where it carried geothermal heat to power exchange units that supplied the rest of the plant.

The air inside the cavernous space was gelid with heat and the stench of rot. The air around the thermal core shimmered like a mirage, and a powerful sense of dislocation threatened to overwhelm Zahariel. The cables of his psychic hood burned into his skull, and a spike of dull agony bore into his brain despite the effects of the dampener. The barrier between the warp and the physical world had been weakened here, and the sense of madness and corruption was almost palpable, like a layer of oil coating his skin. Sorceries had been worked here, his training told him, and the heart of it lay only a few dozen metres away.

At the centre of the chamber, right at the feet of the columnar thermal core, lay a massive pile of corpses. The top layer, Zahariel could see, wore bloodstained uniforms of forest green – the Jaeger relief force that had been drawn to the site. But there were hundreds more, the Librarian estimated – likely the entire labour force of the plant as well.

Hissing and screeching, the defenders of the reaver worm nest assaulted the Dark Angels from all sides. Zahariel blew one out of the air with a pair of shots from his bolt pistol and blasted two more into burning husks with a sweep of his staff. The Astartes kept their octagonal formation, facing outwards and slashing away with their chainswords at any monster that came within reach. The training of the Legion – and the rites of the Order before it – served the warriors of Caliban in good stead, and the bodies of their foes began to pile about their feet. But every time they slew one of the monsters, Zahariel felt the invisible energies swirling in the room grow more turbulent. Whatever dark designs had been set into motion here, their actions only served to energise it further.

'Press forward, brothers!' Zahariel cried, and the squad responded instantly, shifting their formation towards the thermal core one measured step at a time. The surviving worms redoubled their attack, leaping for perceived openings in the warriors' formation, but each attempt was met with a scything blade or the muzzle flash of a bolt pistol. The Dark Angels advanced relentlessly across the chamber, leaving a trail of broken, bleeding monsters in their wake. With each step, however, the air seemed to grow more and more charged. Strange coruscations crackled along the length of the core, and unearthly groans reverberated around the Astartes. As they drew nearer to the pile of corpses, Zahariel could see that they had been laid inside a vast spiral. The curving line was formed of a procession of carefully-shaped runes, each one carved into the floor by a plasma torch and filled with congealed blood. The symbols smote his eyes and sent jagged needles into his brain when he tried to focus on them, and the effect grew worse the farther along the spiral he stared.

The surviving worms had abandoned their frenzied attack, and were retreating away from the Astartes in a ragged circle, their swift, sinuous forms slithering across the damp ground as they lurked beyond chainsword range. The members of Zahariel's squad continued their bloody work, picking off the monsters with careful shots from their bolt pistols. The death energies added to the growing maelstrom, stoking the invisible fires further. Zahariel gritted his teeth at the mounting pain in the back of his skull and drove his squad forward a stubborn step at a time. They were ten metres from the corpse pile now; he could see that each body had been daubed with runes of its own and coated in a translucent slime that shimmered faintly in the strange energies flickering overhead. As the ball lightning flashed, Zahariel glimpsed a sigil of some kind that had been painted against the side of the thermal core, about a dozen metres above the mound of bodies. But before he could focus on what it was, the worms suddenly turned about and rushed at his squad.

A terrible sense of foreboding gripped Zahariel. Before he could shout a warning, however, nine bolt pistols hammered, and every remaining worm was blown apart in a single, simultaneous volley. Their death energies smote the ether like a hammer blow, and the pent-up forces in the chamber erupted.

Zahariel felt the sense of dislocation sharpen dramatically as the barrier between the realms began to unravel. He staggered as his psychic dampener threatened to overload, sending shooting spikes of agony into his brain.

Before him, the pile of corpses began to stir.

For a fleeting instant, Zahariel thought his overtaxed nerves were misfiring, playing tricks on him. But then one of the dead Jaegers drew back his arms and pushed himself clumsily upright, revealing the ghastly wounds that covered his torso and neck. The dead soldier's face was slack, his mouth agape and his eyes glowing an unearthly green.

Another corpse stirred, and another, until the entire mound was lurching into motion. Beneath the Jaegers were the bloated, rotting corpses of men and women in grey worker's coveralls, their slime-covered faces contorted in expressions of agony or horror. They were covered in patches of mould and colonies of squirming maggots; many were missing patches of skin or bore stumps of splintered bone in place of limbs. Yet what these horrors had concealed beneath their rotting bulk was more terrible by far.

As the hundreds of corpses began to shamble, stagger and crawl towards the stunned Astartes, they exposed a score of bloated, squirming larvae that once had been people. Their bones had softened and their muscles stretched until their shapes bore little resemblance to human beings; only their feebly contorting limbs and their distorted, agonised faces revealed what they once had been. Zahariel could clearly see the coiled, black shapes of reaver worms curled within the jelly-like torsos of the larvae, slowly feeding on the still-living bodies of their hosts as they grew to maturity.

The larvae recoiled from the open air, vainly trying to squirm beneath the armoured coils of the enormous worm that had lain at the centre of the chamber's sorcerous spiral. Daubed with blasphemous runes and glistening with slime, the worm queen raised her massive skull and screeched its fury at the grubs that had invaded its domain.

It was a sight that would have broken the courage of lesser men, but hard discipline and the bonds of brotherhood held the Astartes in place. Chapter Master Astelan took a couple of steps forward and stood by Zahariel's side. 'What are your orders?' he asked in a steely voice, as the horde of living dead approached.

Zahariel called upon the rotes Israfael had taught him and mastered the pounding agony in his skull before it could overwhelm him.

'Form a firing line!' he ordered.

The closest of the corpses was only five metres away. As the eight remaining Astartes rushed forward to stand shoulder-to-shoulder beside Zahariel and Astelan, the Librarian called out. 'Change magazines!'

As one, nine pairs of hands went to work, releasing nearly-empty clips from their bolt pistols and slapping fresh ones home. Charging handles racked home with a well-oiled clatter.

The shambling mob was two metres away, almost close enough to touch. 'Squad!' Zahariel yelled. 'One step back! Five rounds rapid. Fire!'

In lockstep, ten pairs of boots crashed upon the permacrete. Bolt pistols barked in a rolling volley. Green clad bodies jerked and blew apart in the storm of mass-reactive rounds. The first rank of corpses disintegrated under the fusillade.

'One step back. Five rounds rapid. Fire!'

The bolt pistols thundered again. Each round found its mark, and fifty more bodies were reduced to bloody fragments. The rest of the mob staggered on, their outstretched hands little more than a metre away.

At Zahariel's command, the squad took one last step back and fired five more rounds into the press. Firing bolts locked back on empty magazines as fifty more bodies erupted into gory mist. The mob had been cut in half in the span of twenty seconds, but the remainder pressed their advance.

Wreathed in propellant smoke, Zahariel raised his crackling staff. 'Loyalty and honour!' he roared. 'Charge!'

With a furious shout, the Dark Angels leapt into the midst of the monstrosities, their chain-blades howling. Swung with superhuman strength, the swords split torsos and severed limbs with each blurring stroke. Corpses toppled at the touch of Zahariel's force staff, their rotting flesh sizzling under the lash of the Librarian's psychic power.

The undead surrounded the grimly fighting Astartes, clawing and grabbing at their armoured forms. What they lacked in strength and skill they sought to make up for in numbers, but the Dark Angels were masters at the craft of slaughter, and their ranks melted away like ice on a hot iron. Within moments the tide turned inexorably in the Astartes' favour – and then the worm queen struck.

A timely flash of lightning provided the only warning. The fickle light sizzled about the thermal core, and Zahariel saw the bulk of the great worm rearing up, like a snake about to strike. The Librarian hurled himself to the side just as the creature lunged into the squad's midst with the force of a runaway train.

With a shout, Zahariel spun to face the beast as the queen gathered herself together like a coiling spring and lashed out again, this time catching Gideon and two of the corpses in its wide mandibles. The curved pincers snapped shut like a giant scissors. The two corpses were bisected at once; Gideon's armour resisted a half-second longer before giving way as well.

Astelan and Jonas whirled on their heels and slashed furiously at the queen, but their chainswords left little more than shallow scars on the worm's thick armoured plates. Screeching in rage, the queen tossed her bony head and smashed Jonas aside, then lunged at Astelan with her bloody mandibles. The chapter master leapt aside at the last moment, hacking a divot out of one of the huge pincers before rolling nimbly away. The worm crushed another half-dozen corpses beneath its bulk as it drew its coils together for another leap. Three Astartes charged the monster from different directions, hacking at it with powerful blows that left only scratches on the worm's thick, black armour. One of the Dark Angels lingered within reach a moment too long and was struck from behind by the queen's lashing tail. The huge warrior was flipped head-over-heels by the powerful blow and landed heavily on his face. A bolt pistol barked; Gideon, lying in a pool of his own blood, had reloaded his weapon and was snapping careful shots at the worm's eyes. Two burst apart in a shower of ichor, causing the queen to thrash and shriek in pain, but the wounds didn't seem to slow the creature in the slightest.

Zahariel dropped his empty pistol and took a two-handed grip on his force staff. He had to end the fight quickly, before the monster killed or crippled any more of his squad. The Librarian channelled his will into the psycho-reactive matrices embedded in the force weapon's staff. Crackling arcs of violet light wound around the metal haft and created a blazing halo about the double-headed eagle at the staff's head. Raising the weapon above his head, Zahariel shouted a wild oath and charged straight at the creature.

The movement and the flickering light of the staff had the desired effect. The worm queen swung its bleeding head around and lunged at Zahariel, smashing into the Librarian in mid-charge.

The impact was tremendous, overwhelming Zahariel's senses. One moment he was racing towards the creature and the next he was flat on his back with the worm's mandibles locked about his waist. A score of flashing crimson runes blinked at the corners of his vision, warning of extensive servo-motor damage and armour breaches. His vision came and went in bursts of distortion as the creature's scissor-like pincers cut into the feeds running from the power unit on his back. He heard the groan and pop of ceramite plates giving way beneath the terrible force of the worm's mandibles. He saw his battered armour reflected in the myriad facets of four black, soulless eyes, each as large as a dinner plate and close enough to touch.

Zahariel brought down the butt of his crackling staff on the queen's skull, right between its monstrous eyes.

The force staff punched through the thick bone with a flash of blue-white light and an angry clap of thunder as the Librarian channelled every erg of psychic force he could command into the creature's body. Nerves fried and brain matter boiled; the worm's remaining eyes burst and its armour plates cracked as steam erupted from its core. Zahariel snuffed out the monster's life force in a split second with the raging winds of the warp itself. It let out a rending shriek and tossed its head in a death spasm, smashing Zahariel to the ground hard enough to knock him unconscious.

WHEN HE CAME to, he found himself lying on his back a few metres away from the worm's smoking corpse. Astelan was kneeling beside him, twisting his legs back into their proper position. Dimly, he could feel the tingle of pain blockers blurring the edges of his mind.

'Hold still for a few moments more, until the bones knit,' the chapter master said as he orientated Zahariel's right calf and began inspecting the servo-motors around the knee-cap. 'Most of your actuators are shot, but you should still be able to move about.'

Zahariel nodded, focusing his thoughts on accelerating his healing faculties and taking stock of his armour. 'The queen?' he grunted.

'Dead,' Astelan confirmed. 'And the corpses went inert at the same moment. That was well done, brother. Luther would be proud.'

'What of Brother Gideon?' Zahariel asked.

'Comatose. His armour is keeping his vital signs stable enough that we should be able to get him back to Aldurukh.'

Satisfied, the Librarian lay his head back against the floor and spent the next few seconds testing the strength of his muscles and bones. Armour plates grated and crimson runes flashed insistently in the corners of his eyes as he carefully flexed first the left leg, then the right. He would be weak for a few minutes more as his body worked to repair the damage, but he was functional. Astelan offered his hand and he took it gladly as he rose carefully to his feet.

The worm queen's corpse was wreathed in tendrils of black smoke. Zahariel walked slowly over to the body of the monster and pulled his staff from the creature's forehead. The corpses it had controlled were sprawled about like puppets whose strings had been severed.

Feeble motion across the chamber caught Zahariel's eye. The queen's larval hosts were squirming and writhing away from the carnage, drawn by some primal instinct towards the illusory safety of the thermal core. Zahariel limped slowly after them, drawing once more on the psychic power of the warp. The energy came reluctantly, flowing through the dampener and coursing along the staff. It was nothing like the wild torrent of power he'd felt before, and he was relieved to note that the sense of dislocation was receding. The oily feeling of corruption still lingered, however, staining the very stone of the chamber and pooling in the blood-soaked runes carved into the floor.

Zahariel slew the larvae one by one, using the power of the staff to slay the host and snuff out the life of the monster within. The last of the abominations had reached the very base of the thermal core, its distorted face and thin arms stretching upwards as though pleading for aid from some nameless, atavistic power.

The Librarian glanced upwards at the core as the last of the larvae burned. He was close enough now to see the symbol that had been painted on the side of the thermal unit. The image was comprised of hundreds of tiny runes that stung his eyes when he tried to focus on them, but the picture they formed was easy enough to identify: an enormous serpent eating its own tail. An ouroboros, Zahariel thought.

Suddenly a voice crackled over his vox-unit, stirring him from his reverie. 'Angelus Six, this is Raider two-one. Angelus Six, come in.'

'This is Angelus Six,' Zahariel replied.

'It's good to hear your voice, brother,' the driver of the Land Raider said. 'We're picking up signals from beyond the perimeter again. Seraphim is calling urgently for a status update.'

Zahariel took one last look at the symbol on the thermal core, then turned back to his squad. What he had to say to Luther couldn't be shared over the vox net. 'Inform Seraphim that we've secured Objective Alpha and we're returning to base. I'll deliver my report to him personally. We'll be back on the surface in ten minutes.'

'Raider two-one copies, Angelus. Standing by.'

Astelan stood at what had been the centre of the sorcerous spiral, well apart from the rest of his brothers. He had removed his helmet and was studying the runes cut into the stone. The chapter master looked up at Zahariel as the Librarian approached. His expression was haunted.

'What are we going to do about this?' he asked quietly.

Zahariel knew what Astelan meant. He reached up and pulled off his own helmet, grimacing at the strange mix of ozone and decay that permeated the air. 'I'll see to it,' he said. 'Gather the squad. We've got to get back and report to Luther at once.'

The chapter master nodded and turned away. Zahariel followed, keying his vox-unit.

'Broadsword Flight, this is Angelus Six.'

This time the reply came in loud and clear; the unnatural interference had subsided completely. 'Broadsword Flight copies,' said the leader of the Stormbird flight.

'Objective Alpha is compromised; repeat, Objective Alpha is compromised,' Zahariel replied. 'We are withdrawing in fifteen minutes. Execute Plan Damocles at that time.'

The Stormbird Leader answered without hesitation. 'Affirmative, Angelus Six. Plan Damocles in one-five minutes.'

Zahariel quickened his pace, passing Astelan and the rest of his squad. The Astartes fell in behind him, carrying both halves of Brother Gideon's limp form between them.

They had little time to spare. In fifteen minutes the Stormbirds from Broadsword Flight would level Sigma Five-One-Seven, destroying any evidence of what had transpired at the site.

The Dark Angels alone would know the truth. Otherwise, Caliban would surely die.

THIRTEEN
SECRETS OF THE PAST

Diamat
In the 200th year of the Emperor's Great Crusade

FOR THE NEXT two and a half weeks, the Dark Angels and the people of Diamat worked day and night to prepare for the coming storm. Governor Kulik sent troops into the countryside to locate camps of refugees, conscripting all the healthy men and women he could find and putting them to work constructing new fortifications under the experienced eye of Jonson's veteran warriors. High above the forge, Jonson's warships lay at anchor – even the near-derelict *Duchess Arbellatris,* which had been towed back to Diamat by the light cruisers of the scout force – and were being worked over night and day by Magos Archoi's best tech-adepts. Flocks of cargo shuttles came and went daily, re-stocking the battle group's depleted stores of ammunition and heavy ordnance. Other craft ferried Governor Kulik and Magos Archoi to and from the *Invincible Reason* on a regular basis to confer with Primarch Jonson and refine their battle plan.

Nemiel was busier than he'd ever been. When he wasn't managing repair and resupply schedules or fielding requests from the captains of the battle group he was shuttling down to the planet's surface to help supervise the construction of defensive positions throughout the grey zone and implementing Jonson's organisational changes to the planetary defence force. He ate little and slept even less, devoting his full energy and attention to every task that was put in front of him. The officers of the fleet and members of Kulik's staff commented on his dedication and zeal, and held him up as an inspiration to the men under their command. Nemiel would wave away their praise. He was merely setting a proper example, he would say, as any Chaplain ought.

In truth, he consumed himself with work because it kept his growing doubts at bay. He couldn't help but think about his conversation with Jonson, and his evasive replies. The primarch wasn't a brigand, Nemiel knew; he hadn't come all the way to Diamat to sack its forges, as Horus's men had done. Yet he couldn't shake the notion that Jonson wasn't telling him the entire truth, and that went against everything Nemiel thought that the Legion stood for.

More than once, he found himself wishing that Luther and Zahariel were still with them. He found himself sorely missing his cousin's unwavering idealism.

It was late in the day when the primarch summoned Nemiel to his sanctum. He found Jonson seated at his favourite spot, beneath the towering viewports along the port side of the chamber. Red light shone along the side of Jonson's face as he bent over a series of aerial images spread atop a low, wooden table. He glanced up at the Redemptor's approach.

'There you are, Nemiel,' he said tersely, gathering the images together into a small stack. 'You've been keeping yourself scarce of late.'

'Not by design, my lord,' Nemiel replied guardedly. 'There's a great deal to be done before the rebels return.'

Jonson grunted in agreement. 'True enough.' He looked up at Nemiel again and smiled. 'Wipe that guilty look off your face, Nemiel. I wasn't accusing you of anything.' He leaned back in his chair. 'What's the current status of the battle group?'

Nemiel relaxed a bit, glad to be back on familiar terrain. 'Our scout force has nearly completed resupply and will be ready for operations within five hours,' he reported from memory. 'The strike cruisers *Amadis* and *Adzikel* have finished their most critical repairs and have begun re-loading their stores of ammunition and ordnance. Replacement Stormbirds have arrived from the surface to replace those lost in combat. The heavy cruisers *Flamberge* and *Lord Dante* report all repairs complete, and they expect to finish resupply within the hour.' He paused. '*Iron Duke* reports that all of her weapon batteries are back in action, but damage to her hull is so extensive she'll need to be dry-docked to effect any meaningful repairs. The crew of *Duchess Arbellatris* has been working day and night, and Captain Rashid insists that she can be returned to action within a few weeks, but the tech-adepts assigned to her believe that the ship is a lost cause.'

'Inform Captain Rashid that he has forty-eight hours to do what he can; if the ship isn't capable of standing in the battle line by then, she will have to be abandoned and her crew reassigned to the other ships in the group.' Jonson said. 'That's all the time we can afford.'

'Have there been any new developments?' Nemiel said, suddenly alert.

The primarch shook his head. 'Not yet. But based on the distance between systems and the minimum amount of time I estimate Horus would need to assemble another fleet and send it on its way, the rebels could arrive in the system imminently. The Warmaster must attack again as soon as possible, or he won't have enough time to strip the forge of its resources and put them to use back on Isstvan.'

Jonson held up the small stack of images. 'Which brings us to this.'

He held the images out to Nemiel. The Redemptor took them and began looking them over. 'These look like aerial images of the forge complex,' he said with a scowl.

'Specifically the warehouse and depot facilities along the southern edge of the forge, closest to the gateway,' Jonson confirmed. 'You'll note that a number of the buildings have been highlighted for ease of reference.'

Nemiel's scowl deepened. 'I'm not sure I understand, my lord,' he said, feeling suddenly uneasy.

Jonson studied Nemiel in silence for a moment. 'Magos Archoi hasn't complied with my request for a full inventory of his stores,' he said carefully. 'Time is running out. Since he won't give me the information I need, I'll have to gather it another way.'

'But... that's not correct,' Nemiel protested. 'Archoi has provided detailed reports of the materiel he has on hand. I've seen them myself.'

The primarch's eyes narrowed slightly. 'I have reason to believe that those reports are incomplete.'

'Why is that?' Nemiel pressed. His unease swelled until it threatened to become something akin to despair. 'Why are we here, my lord? You claim that we're here to stop Horus, but the logic of the situation and your own actions belie this. What else is there that has drawn you here?'

Jonson straightened fractionally in his chair. His face was calm, but there was a steely edge in his green eyes. 'Are you calling me a liar, Brother-Redemptor Nemiel?' he asked.

Nemiel's breath caught in his throat. Suddenly he sensed the deadly precipice that now figuratively yawned at his feet. Yet he would be damned if he allowed himself to be intimidated into silence and compromise his sacred oaths – not even by the primarch himself. 'Do you deny that you have a hidden motive for bringing us here?' he said.

The Redemptor boldly met the primarch's imposing stare, ready to accept the consequences. Jonson glared at Nemiel a moment more, his expression calculating, before slowly nodding his head.

'That was well done,' Jonson allowed. 'You have the makings of a good interrogator, I think.' He spread his hands. 'Diamat is important to the Warmaster for reasons other than ammunition and building materials,' he said. 'I judged that it was best to keep those reasons a secret, for purposes of operational security. Restriction of information isn't the same thing as deception, Nemiel.'

'I never said you'd lied to us, my lord,' Nemiel pointed out. 'But what possible good does it do to withhold vital information from your own warriors and allies?'

Jonson frowned. 'As a knight of the Order, I should think that would be obvious,' he said. 'Every facet of your training on Caliban was governed by custom, order and ritual. An aspirant could not become a novice until he'd passed certain tests to prove his knowledge, character and worthiness. Likewise, a novice could not rise to the ranks of knighthood without progressing through many ranks of knowledge and skill. Even upon reaching the coveted rank of knight, there were still degrees of initiation and rank that opened each warrior to new levels of knowledge and expertise, all the way to the lofty rank of Grand Master itself. Why was that so? Why didn't the Masters begin inducting the novices straightaway into the Higher Mysteries?'

'Because a novice wouldn't know what to do with the training,' Nemiel answered at once. 'Not before mastering a great many basic skills first. Trying to employ those advanced tactics without the proper foundation would just get them killed.'

The primarch smiled. 'Precisely. Knowledge is power, Nemiel. Never forget that. And power, in the wrong hands, can inflict terrible harm.'

Nemiel considered this. 'I understand, my lord,' he said at length. 'Is there anything in particular I should be looking for?'

Jonson studied him a moment longer, then nodded to himself. 'Vehicles,' he said. 'Approximately six to eight of them; the references I saw were unclear on the exact number. They were reportedly built over a hundred and fifty years ago, and would likely have been placed into storage somewhere in the complex.'

'What kind of vehicles?' Nemiel asked.

'War machines,' Jonson replied. 'Like nothing either of us have ever seen before.'

Nemiel frowned. 'But if the Mechanicum has these machines at their disposal, why aren't they using them?'

Jonson shrugged. 'It's possible that Archoi doesn't know they're here. Or the Mechanicum has decided to withhold them for their own use, much as they did with their skitarii.' He raised a warning finger. 'What's important is that the Warmaster needs them, and we have to keep them out of his hands.'

'How does the Horus know about these war machines?' Nemiel asked.

'How else?' the primarch said. 'He's the one who commissioned them in the first place.'

IT WAS A long and circuitous drive from the Xanthus star port to the southern entrance to the forge complex. Nemiel's Rhino – fresh from the assembly lines at Diamat and still showing its black coat of manufactory primer – had to first head north, past a series of fortified checkpoints, then eastward through a literal maze of narrow streets. The tramway was no longer passable; over the last two weeks the entire length of the road had been sowed with mines, cut by permacrete tank barriers and festooned with kilometres of molly-wire. Heavy vehicles trying to force their way northeastward towards the forge would have to fight their way through one obstacle after another, all the while coming under fire from concealed bunkers on both the north and south sides of the tramway. The ash wastes to the south of the tramway were passable by infantry but not vehicles, and were covered by the Dragoons' remaining artillery batteries. The only alternative was to press north and east, just as Nemiel's Rhino had done, but the rebels would be forced to break through each set of checkpoints and then find a safe path through streets that had been riddled with mines, tank traps and more ambush points. Neither route was completely impassable, as the defenders knew, but breaching them would take a great deal of time – something the enemy had in short supply.

The southern gateway had also seen heavy reinforcement since Nemiel had last been there. Work parties had expanded the walls on both sides of the tramway and refitted the destroyed weapon emplacements with new heavy guns taken from the forge. Archoi's adepts had also installed remote sentry guns at strategic points along the walls, and a cadre of hulking skitarii stood watch over the battlements alongside Kulik's Dragoons. Magos Archoi had proposed embedding skitarii units with the governor's men and the Dark Angels alike to enhance their combat power, and the primarch saw the wisdom of the idea. Most of the skitarii were assigned to the under-strength Dragoons, who were given the responsibility of defending the tramway and the grey zone. The Dark Angels were to be held back in a mobile reserve, to reinforce key areas or deal with unexpected enemy attacks. The Dragoons spent their days labouring over their fortifications and then sleeping in them, while the Astartes had been assigned temporary quarters in a number of empty warehouses inside the forge complex, close to the gateway. A trio of skitarii Praetorians had been assigned to each squad for added reinforcement.

Nemiel's Rhino drew up to the gateway and ground to a halt in a billowing cloud of dust. Civilian workers wiped sweat from their eyes and peered through the haze as the Redemptor disembarked and worked his way through the reinforced permacrete barriers that had been laid in an alternating pattern between the towering bastions. Dragoons and skitarii alike watched Nemiel from the battlements; his gaze searched among them, looking for the helmeted heads of his squad.

'Over here, brother!' Kohl shouted, waving his arm from the top of the southern bastion. Nemiel waved in reply and headed up to join him.

He found Kohl and Techmarine Askelon at the topmost level, supervising the installation of advanced ballistic calculators that would help the Dragoons call down effective artillery fire on the attacking rebels. A trio of fearsome-looking skitarii stood nearby, observing the proceedings with almost mechanical detachment.

'Come to check up on us, brother?' Kohl growled good-naturedly.

Nemiel looked over the crew of Dragoons and fretful tech-adepts installing the sensitive machinery and managed a grin. 'It's been too quiet lately. The primarch believes you're up to something.'

Kohl grunted. 'Always,' he said, completely deadpan. 'Tell him I'm touched by his concern.'

The Redemptor glanced over at the skitarii. 'How are the new squadmates?' he asked.

Kohl grimaced. 'Not much for conversation, other than that strange hash that Askelon insists is speech,' he said. 'Mostly they just stand around and stare at everything.'

'Has Magos Archoi got them billeted with you?'

'Oh, yes,' Kohl replied. His tone was mild, but the look in his eyes spoke volumes of his unhappiness about the situation. 'Second Company is spread out among three adjoining warehouses, about half a kilometre from here.'

Nemiel nodded thoughtfully. That was going to complicate things a little. 'Where's the rest of the squad right now?'

'Over at the north bastion,' Kohl replied, 'helping teach some new recruits how to work the heavy weapons. Why?'

'I'll be taking five of you back up into orbit with me in a few hours,' Nemiel replied, and raised a forestalling hand. 'Don't ask me why, because I don't know. The primarch has a job for us.'

'Well, that can't be good,' Kohl said with typical fatalism. He glanced over at the work party. 'We'll be done here a bit after nightfall. Is that soon enough?'

Nemiel glanced west, where the sun was already low over the distant ruins of Xanthus. 'Nightfall sounds just about right,' he said with a nod.

* * *

THREE HOURS LATER, the Astartes climbed up the rear ramp of Nemiel's idling Rhino and found their seats along the narrow benches that lined both sides of the troop compartment. As the ramp clanged shut the armoured personnel carrier revved its petrochem engines and lurched into motion.

Brother-Sergeant Kohl had Techmarine Askelon, plus Marthes, Vardus and Ephrial. No sooner had the APC started moving than the squad leader turned to Nemiel and said, 'Now what's this nonsense about-the primarch sending for us personally?'

Nemiel grimaced. 'I had to think of something halfway plausible to pull you out of there without the skitarii making anything of it,' he said. 'The primarch wants us to perform a reconnaissance mission inside the forge complex itself.'

As the Rhino worked its way slowly back down the access road towards the gateway, Nemiel produced the images that Jonson had given him and laid out the details of the mission. At the mention of the secret war machines, the attitude of the squad turned very serious indeed.

'We've got a lot of ground to cover in just a few hours,' Nemiel said at the conclusion of the briefing. 'Brother Askelon, what sort of threats are we likely to encounter?'

'There will be an array of electronic sensors covering each of the storage sites,' he replied, 'plus skitarii patrols with a full-spectrum auspex arrays. If these war machines are as valuable as the primarch believes them to be, they may be covered by additional security as well.'

Nemiel nodded. 'We can avoid the patrols,' he said confidently. 'Can you get us past the sensors?'

Brother Askelon considered the problem for several seconds before nodding. 'I can at least get us close enough to determine the contents of each building,' he said.

'All right,' Nemiel said with a nod. 'As soon as we're out of the Rhino, we go vox-silent; only verbal signals or hand signs. We can't risk having our transmissions detected. Questions?'

There were none. Nemiel rose from his bench with a curt nod and opened the Rhino's portside door. With a quick check up and down the dark access road, he jumped lightly from the vehicle. The five other Astartes followed suit, reflexively fanning out into a standard tactical formation as they moved quickly into the deeper shadows between two large warehouses.

Nemiel drew his bolt pistol, leaving his crozius aquilum attached to his belt. 'Let's try not to get into another fight with our allies.' he said quietly. Quiet chuckles rose from the darkness. 'Askelon, you've got point; I know it's not your usual position, but you'll spot the forge's security systems well before the rest of us. Brother Vardus, you're covering our back-trail. Everyone clear? Then let's get to work.'

THEY WORKED THEIR way through the vast forge complex for hours, as Diamat's moon rose in a thin crescent and passed through a hazy, ochre sky. Now and again they would come upon a patrol of skitarii. These Tech-Guard weren't the massive, bionically enhanced killing machines of the Praetorians, but were simple soldiers akin to the Tanagran Dragoons, albeit in fine carapace armour and wielding high-power lasguns. Compact auspex units were mounted to the front of their helmets and flipped down over their faces like strange, insectoid masks. They moved with speed and skill, constantly alert and watchful, but the Astartes' enhanced senses allowed them to detect the patrols and find cover long before the skitarii were in a position to see them. Aside from the occasional patrols, the Astartes encountered no other signs of life.

There were hundreds of warehouses and storage depots located in the southern sector of the forge complex. Most were single-storey structures, but others were tall, cavernous buildings with massive, rolling doors that could hold entire companies of heavy battle tanks. Without the locations provided by Jonson there would have been no way that they could have completed their search in a single night; as it was, Nemiel had begun to fear that they would be working right up until dawn.

At each of the structures highlighted on Nemiel's images, the squad would take up a defensive position and let Brother Askelon go ahead to inspect the building's contents. Each time the Techmarine would emerge, shaking his head, and the squad would move on to the next building down the line.

By midnight they were half-way through their search pattern and were doubling back eastward, heading for the warehouse districts on the other side of the access road. They were well north of the billets set aside for the Astartes ground force, and could see the towering, fortress-like manufactories off to the north, spreading out in a rough circle from the foot of the slumbering volcano. Tall, narrow smokestacks and squat cooling towers rose into the sky like the bones of dead gods, blackened and pitted by age. Cold, white lights shone like stars from the slopes of the conical mountain, while off to the north-east, the towering, monolithic structures of the Titan foundry shone with sparkling pinpoints of sapphire, crimson and emerald.

'I've moved through dead cities that weren't as eerie as this,' Brother-Sergeant Kohl murmured beside Nemiel. 'I thought forges were like mechanical bee-hives. Where is everyone?'

Nemiel shrugged, his eyes searching the darkness off to the south for signs of danger just as Kohl kept his attention focused on the north. 'Magos Archoi mentioned at one of the strategy meetings that he'd ordered all surviving tech-adepts and acolytes into a series of deep shelters near the heart of the complex. Only a few hundred volunteers are still above ground or in orbit, working with the battle group and helping supply our forces on the ground. Archoi said they'd suffered enough losses during the last raid, and he wasn't going to permit any more if he could help it.'

Kohl grunted dubiously. 'It's an awfully clean bat-tlefield, don't you think?'

Nemiel glanced sidelong at the sergeant. 'What are you talking about?'

Brother-Sergeant Kohl shrugged, eyeing the walls of the dark buildings to his right. 'Where are the shell holes? The scorch marks? Where are the burnt-out buildings? If the fighting was so heavy in this sector, why haven't we seen any sign of it yet?'

The observation nearly stopped Nemiel in his tracks. Something tugged at the back of his mind; something else strange and out of place, but he couldn't quite put a finger on it.

'Maybe the battle sites are still up ahead,' he replied, frowning to himself. 'Archoi and his warriors came at us from the northeast. Let's see what lies up ahead.'

But for the next three hours Nemiel and Kohl saw only more of the same: building after building, arrayed in laser-perfect lines, their permacrete walls unblemished save for decades of stains and pitting etched by acid rain. Nemiel's disquiet grew stronger. Something was very wrong.

Barely two hours before dawn, Askelon found something. They had reached an enormous depot building, two storeys high and wide enough for a pair of super-heavy tanks to pass through its entryway side-by-side. The Techmarine moved stealthily inside while the rest of the squad watched for Mechanicum patrols. He was back in less than five minutes. 'You need to see this,' he said to Nemiel.

The Redemptor rose to his feet and signalled for the squad to follow him. Askelon led the warriors along a convoluted route that brought them past the cordon of sensors surrounding the perimeter of the structure. Soon, Nemiel found himself standing in a vast, cavernous structure, supported by soaring metal arches curving high overhead.

'It's empty,' he said to Askelon. His voice echoed faintly in the deserted building.

'No. Not quite,' the Techmarine said, turning about and pointing to the inner surface of the depot's towering metal doors.

Nemiel turned about and saw that the metal slabs were splashed and streaked with dried gore.

He stepped forwards, his enhanced vision easily picking out details even in the near-absence of light. 'Lots of carbon scoring,' he observed. 'Looks like high-power lasgun fire.'

Kohl nodded, stepping up beside Nemiel. A gauntleted finger moved through the air, roughly tracing the outline of the stains. 'I'd guess ten to fifteen individuals, shot at close range,' he reckoned. 'Judging by the intensity of the lasgun fire, they must have been nearly blown apart. This wasn't a battle. It was an execution.'

'I thought much the same thing,' Askelon said. He stepped up to the doors and laid a fingertip against one of the dried stains. 'Not all of this is blood. Some of it is bionic lubricant or coolant.'

Brother-Sergeant Kohl scowled. 'Didn't Magos Archoi say that Arch-Magos Vertullus was killed during the fighting?'

Nemiel felt his skin grow cold. 'The magos never said who it was that killed Vertullus.'

Kohl stared at Nemiel. 'You think there's been some kind of coup?' The veteran sergeant sounded incredulous.

'Archoi was in the area with a large force of Praetorians,' Nemiel mused. 'The attack would have given him an excellent opportunity. He could kill Vertullus and the other senior magi, dispose of the bodies, and no one the wiser.' Suddenly Nemiel's eyes widened. 'Bodies. By the Emperor, that's what was missing. The bodies!'

Kohl shook his head in consternation. 'What are you talking about now?'

'Governor Kulik said there was an entire company of Dragoons covering the entrance to the southern gateway,' Nemiel explained. 'The rebels supposedly overran them. But there were no dead Imperial troops anywhere. What happened to the bodies?'

The sergeant frowned. 'I don't know. I doubt they just got up and walked away.'

'But perhaps they did,' Nemiel said. 'What if the Dragoon company guarding the gateway was betrayed by the very people they were there to defend?'

Kohl's face turned grim. 'That would mean Magos Archoi is in league with Horus,' he said. 'We need to inform the primarch at once!'

Nemiel held up a hand. 'Not yet. Not without more proof than this,' he said, indicating the blood-splashed wall. He paused, contemplating the tall doors, then glanced back at the empty, echoing space. 'What was Vertullus doing here in the first place?' he wondered. 'Maybe the war machines we're looking for were stored here, and he'd come to check on them?'

'The building's certainly big enough to hold six to eight large vehicles,' Askelon confirmed. 'There's dust and debris in the corners that suggest this place hadn't seen much activity in a very long time. The question is: where are the war machines now?'

Nemiel's mind raced as he tried to think through the mystery. 'If Archoi is with the rebels, he was in the process of trying to hand over the war machines to them when we arrived,' he said. 'If the vehicles had sat in a depot for a century and a half, they would have been in need of some refurbishment. He would have taken them somewhere he and his minions could work on them without being disturbed – possibly even as early as several weeks before Horus's raid.'

Askelon shook his head. 'The manufactories would have been working at full output at that point. They couldn't possibly have used them.'

'Well, where else would they have the facilities they would need?' Nemiel asked.

The Techmarine spread his hands. 'Other than the Titan foundry, I can't think of any,' he said. 'And I guarantee you, the Legio adepts would take a dim view of someone else using their facilities.'

Nemiel looked to Kohl. 'Except that Legio Gladius isn't here. Someone else is running the lights over at the foundry.'

FOURTEEN
WALKING THE SPIRAL

Caliban
In the 200th year of the Emperor's Great Crusade

'How can this be?' Luther demanded, his voice crackling with tension in the confines of the Grand Master's sanctum. He had abandoned the massive oaken chair behind the sanctum's wide desk and had begun to pace across the room. 'How is it possible that no one noticed this before?'

Damaged servo-motors whined as Zahariel folded his arms. He and Astelan stood side by side before the Grand Master's desk, fresh from the transport that had carried them from Sigma Five-One-Seven. The sanctum was crowded with portable logic engines, stacks of papers and map tables, and half-empty cups of caffeine steamed in little clusters on the stone floor. They had interrupted a high-level operations meeting to deliver their report; the antechamber outside the sanctum was crowded with regimental officers and staff members who were doubtless wondering what all the secrecy was about.

Only Lord Cypher had been allowed to remain in the room to hear the warriors' report. He stood by one of the chamber's windows, silent and half-hidden by shadow. Brother-Librarian Israfael was also present; the Master of Caliban had summoned him as soon as he'd heard the gist of Zahariel and Astelan's report.

'The clues were there all along,' Zahariel replied. 'What else could have created the great beasts? What else could have shaped a wilderness so relentlessly malevolent and deadly to human life?'

'Caliban is a death world, brother,' Israfael pointed out. 'Like Catachan or Piscina V. That doesn't mean it's inherently tainted.'

'Perhaps not,' Zahariel admitted. 'Perhaps the two traits are unrelated, but the fact remains that Caliban is tainted somehow. I saw it with my own eyes.'

Luther paused in his restless pacing and fixed Astelan with a penetrating stare. 'What about you, chapter master? Did you see evidence of this as well?'

Astelan had stood at a rigid parade-rest, shoulders squared and hands clasped behind his back as he and Zahariel had delivered their report. He met Luther's flinty gaze unflinchingly. 'There was nothing natural about the creatures we fought, my lord,' he said. 'I confess that I did not see the traces of corruption that Brother Zahariel reports, but I'm no psyker. If he says that's what he saw, then I believe him.' He shrugged. 'The Northwilds were always thought of as haunted, my lord, as you yourself must know.'

The answer did little to please Luther. 'Damnation,' he hissed. The Master of Caliban turned to Israfael. 'How could the Imperium have missed this?'

The Librarian shrugged. 'Because no one asked us to look,' he said.

'Have a care, brother,' Luther growled. 'I'm in no mood for jests.'

'I'm not trying to be impertinent,' Israfael answered. 'There were no obvious signs of corruption when the fleet arrived here; if anything, we were surprised at how few psykers we found among the planet's populace.'

'That's because witches and mutants were slain out of hand for hundreds of years,' Astelan grunted.

Israfael acknowledged this with a wave of his hand. 'Another characteristic common to worlds that survived the Age of Strife and the fall of Old Night,' he said. 'Had any of these great beasts still survived by the time we found your world, we might have seen the need to investigate more closely, but as it was, there was nothing obvious to arouse our concern. This warp-taint, whatever it is, must be buried very deep indeed.'

'I agree,' Zahariel said. 'And I believe that it only became readily accessible recently, when the insurrection began. We know that warp taint feeds on human strife and bloodshed. The arcology riots could have been the catalyst that set the events at Sigma Five-One-Seven into motion.'

Luther's eyes narrowed. 'So you're saying the rebels are behind this?'

'Not at all,' Zahariel replied. 'There was no evidence of rebel activity at the site whatsoever. I think that the attacks and the riots created an environment that others have succumbed to.'

'Like who?' Luther demanded.

Zahariel considered his reply carefully. 'We accounted for the bodies of the Jaeger garrison, the reaction force, and the labourers that had been sent to work on the thermal plant. The Terran engineers assigned to the plant were nowhere to be found.'

'They may have been elsewhere at the site,' Israfael countered. 'You reported that your squad didn't search the labourer's dormitories, for example. They might well have been murdered in their sleep.'

'I'd considered that,' Zahariel said, 'but it was clear to Astelan and I that the site's garrison was betrayed from within. All of the Calibanite labourers had been murdered, along with the Jaegers. That leaves only the Terrans.'

Before Israfael could offer a counter-argument, Luther interjected. 'All right, let's assume for the moment that the Terrans were responsible. What was the point of the ritual?'

'That's difficult to say,' Zahariel answered. 'Clearly the reaver worms were an integral part of it. Why else would the Terrans go to so much trouble to provide hundreds of corpses for the worm queen?' He thought the situation over for a moment. 'The sorcerers were gone long before we arrived, so we have to assume the ritual was completed successfully, and they'd gotten what they'd come for. The ritual itself was complicated and obviously required a great deal of planning to execute. Given that the Terrans had only been at the site for approximately six days, I think it's also clear that the whole operation was conceived elsewhere and put into action at the site.'

'Where had these Terrans come from?' Luther asked.

'Northwilds arcology,' the Librarian answered. Suddenly he straightened, remembering something he'd dismissed in the early stages of the mission. 'And that's where they must have returned to as well. Just before we entered the perimeter I picked up a civilian shuttle on our surveyors off to the west, headed in that direction. They fled the site minutes before we arrived.' The pieces started to fall into place. Zahariel nodded thoughtfully. 'I think this ritual was just one element of a much larger scheme, brothers. They performed the ritual at Sigma Five-One-Seven, gathered the fruits of their sorcery and returned to the arcology for the next phase of the operation.'

Luther started to pace again, his hands clenched tightly behind his back. 'There are more than a thousand Terran engineers operating out of that arcology,' he growled. 'We'll have to investigate every industrial site they've worked on in the last month, just to be sure there haven't been any other rituals we don't know about.'

Israfael bristled. 'You act like every Terran in the arcology has been corrupted!'

'Show me a Calibanite that's been corrupted and I'll revise my assumptions,' Luther answered coldly. 'In the meantime we need to track down every one of those engineers as quickly and quietly as possible.'

'That will be difficult, my lord,' Astelan said. 'Those engineers built Northwilds arcology. There are miles upon miles of tunnels and maintenance spaces they could be hiding in at this point – to say nothing of the rebel activity already tying down our troops in that sector.'

'The rebels be damned!' Luther snapped. 'They can burn the arcology to the ground, so long as we catch these Terran devils and no one is the wiser!'

Israfael's eyes widened in alarm. 'Surely you don't mean to say that we can keep this a secret. We have to report this to the primarch and the Adeptus Terra at once!'

'If word of this reaches Terra, Caliban will die.' Luther declared. 'Worlds have burned for far less.'

The Terran started to protest, but found he could not. 'It's true,' he said heavily. 'I cannot deny it.'

'Then you understand why I cannot allow that to happen,' Luther said. 'Not here. Not on my watch. The people of Caliban are innocent and undeserving of such a fate, and I won't allow such a thing to happen.'

Israfael rose slowly to his feet and faced Luther. 'What you're contemplating is against Imperial law,' he said gravely. 'Indeed, it smacks of treason.'

'That's easy for you to say,' Luther snarled. 'This isn't your home. These aren't people you've sworn a solemn oath to defend.'

'Of course I have!' Israfael shot back, his voice rising. 'Am I not an Astartes? The Imperium–'

'The Imperium brought us to this!' Luther roared. He rounded on Israfael, his face anguished and his hands clenched into fists. 'There were no rebellions before you arrived, no obscene rituals or human sacrifices! There was order, and law, and virtuous men who stood between the innocent and the terrors of the forest. It was your people who did this, who dug too deeply and grasped for too much, and now me and mine will pay the price!'

Israfael tensed, and the air around him literally crackled with furious power. Astelan turned slightly to face the senior Librarian, his hands drifting slowly to his weapons. Zahariel recalled the chapter master's oath at Sigma Five-One-Seven and understood how perilous the situation had become. He rushed forward, placing himself between Luther and Israfael.

'We are all brothers here,' he said firmly. 'Neither Calibanite nor Terran, but Dark Angels, first and always. If we forget that, even for a moment, we are lost. Then who will protect our people, Master Luther?'

Luther's gaze fell on Zahariel. For a long moment he was silent, until his expression grew bleak and his fists slowly unclenched. The Master of Caliban turned away, resting his hands upon the heavy desk.

'Zahariel is right, of course,' he said at last. 'I hope you will forgive my intemperate tone, Brother Israfael.'

'Of course,' Israfael said stiffly.

Luther worked his way around the desk and settled slowly onto the throne-like chair. His expression was distant, his eyes haunted.

'I must meditate on this,' he said in a hollow voice. 'Too many lives are at stake to act precipitously. For now, we must make sure this rot has spread no further. Zahariel, send the scouts into the Northwilds. Have them reconnoitre every industrial site in the sector and search for signs of further corruption. Check the Administratum's records and find out which engineers were assigned to Sigma Five-One-Seven, then pass their identities on to the Jaeger regiments at the Northwilds arcology. They are to be captured and delivered to Aldurukh immediately.' He sighed. 'Brothers, I realize this is well outside the scope of our temperament and training, but this matter must be handled with the utmost secrecy. There is no one else we can trust with this.'

Zahariel bowed his head respectfully. 'I'll see to it at once.'

Luther turned to Astelan. 'Chapter master, as of this moment I'm putting you in command of Caliban's defence forces. Place our brothers on a war footing. I want strike teams ready to deploy in case any more ritual activity is detected, but no one is to act without my express authorization. Understood?'

'Understood,' Astelan replied gravely. 'We will stand ready, my lord.'

'Let's at least send some scout teams into the arcology as well,' Zahariel said. 'The sorcerers are most likely practicing their rituals close to the thermal core. If we could locate them quickly, we could–'

Luther held up a restraining hand. 'Not yet. If we start suddenly committing our warriors now, during a relative lull in civil unrest, it will almost certainly lead to renewed scrutiny from the Administratum. That's something we can ill afford at this point.'

'Magos Bosk will have to be informed of the destruction of Sigma Five-One-Seven,' Israfael pointed out.

'If there are any reports to be made, I will make them,' Luther said sternly. 'None of you are to speak of what happened at the site, as a matter of operational security. Understood?'

The four Astartes nodded.

'Then you are dismissed,' Luther said. 'Except for you, Lord Cypher. I have some questions to ask you.'

Israfael turned on his heel and left the room without a word. Astelan was close behind, his expression eager. Zahariel hesitated for a moment, torn by feelings of doubt. Only he saw Lord Cypher glide quietly from the shadows to stand beside the Grand Master's throne-like chair.

He wasn't certain what disturbed him more: the sight of Luther staring down at his own hands, his expression anguished – or the enigmatic smile that passed like a shadow across Lord Cypher's face.

LIGHTNING FLASHED ANGRILY overhead, banishing the darkness for the space of a heartbeat and dazzling Zahariel's sensitive eyes. Thunder crashed, vibrating along his bones, and raindrops spattered heavily against his cheeks. He paused, struggling to calm his thoughts and banish the spots of colour from his vision. When his vision cleared, he set his feet upon the spiral path once more.

It had been more than a week since the encounter at Sigma Five-One-Seven. Orders had gone out immediately from the Rock; the Scout chapter on Caliban had gone into action within hours, commencing a building-by-building search of every industrial site within the Northwilds sector. At the same time, a records search provided the identities of the Terran engineering team that had been assigned to Sigma Five-One-Seven. The information had been passed on to the Jaeger regiments deployed to the Northwilds arcology, but it was learned that the arcology's so-called Terran Quarter had been looted and burned during the first cycle of riots, and the inhabitants had been relocated for their own safety. The problem was that details of the relocation had been lost amid the chaos, and now no one knew for sure where many of the Terrans had wound up. The Jaegers were trying to locate them, but the local regiments had few troops to spare because of the continued threat of rebel attack. Though Luther seemed willing to let the arcology burn in order to track down the sorcerers, there was no practical way to issue such an order without raising a chorus of questions all along the chain of command. Zahariel had heard, indirectly, of the confrontation between Luther and Magos Bosk over the destruction of Sigma Five-One-Seven, and by all accounts it had been epic. Bosk had been livid over the loss of so much industrial capacity, and it had taken every bit of Luther's charisma and authority to prevent her once more from breaching protocol and reporting the situation to the Adeptus Terra.

They were running out of time. Every passing hour was a boon to the fugitive sorcerers, who were no doubt working to further their plan somewhere in the labyrinthine depths of the arcology. Though the Jaegers were making a concerted effort to locate them, the fact was that there were large parts of the arcology that they couldn't penetrate due to the possibility of rebel attack. These no-go zones provided countless safe havens for the sorcerers to continue their work without fear of interruption.

The only answer was to send in the Legion, Zahariel knew. A level-by-level sweep, conducted by their Scout chapter and supported by one or more assault chapters could brush aside any rebel resistance and isolate the real threat within hours. Such an operation, if conducted with proper ruthlessness, might even convince the rebel leaders that further resistance was pointless, and put an end to both threats at the same time.

The problem was that only Luther had the authority to put such a plan into action, and he had gone into seclusion within hours of receiving the report on Sigma Five-One-Seven. No one could even say for certain where the Master of Caliban had gone, save for the enigmatic Lord Cypher, and he was sworn to silence. Zahariel had prevailed upon Cypher to carry close to a dozen messages to Luther urgently requesting permission to send the Legion into the arcology, but not a single one had been answered.

The fact was, he was sorely tempted to defy Luther and order the Astartes into action. Technically, it was within his authority as Luther's second-in-command; with the Master of Caliban in seclusion, the decision was his to make, but doing so would betray his oaths of obedience to the Emperor and to the Legion. And yet, what if Luther was right, and the real danger to Caliban was from the Imperium itself? If that were true, then his oath to the Emperor was based on a lie, and counted for nothing. He didn't know what to believe at this point. The things he'd witnessed at Sigma Five-One-Seven had shaken his faith to the core.

In all his life, Zahariel had never lacked for certainty. His faith in himself and his cause had been unwavering. Now it seemed like the very foundations of the world were quaking beneath his feet. If he wasn't careful, his next step could well be his last.

Overhead the storm raged, mirroring the turmoil in Zahariel's mind. He drew in a deep breath and channelled his frustrations into a mental summons.

'Show yourselves, you Watchers in the Dark!' he shouted into the raging wind. 'Long ago, I pledged my sword to you, to stand against the same evils that you did. Now I see the truth; this whole world is corrupted, and now my people are in dire peril.'

Another searing flash of lightning answered his mental summons, banishing all but the deepest shadows and etching the courtyard in sharp relief. But this time the brilliant light did not fade; it deepened slightly in colour, from a harsh blue-white to a more silvery hue, like moonlight. Zahariel no longer felt the touch of rain on his cheeks, and the howling wind seemed strangely muted, almost plaintive in its howls. Then he saw the three, hooded figures standing at the centre of the spiral. They were garbed like supplicants, wearing a surplice whose colour seemed to constantly shift from black to brown to grey and back again. Their heads were covered by voluminous hoods, their faces hidden by darkness. Their hands were tucked inside the sleeves of their surplice, so that not one centimetre of flesh could be seen.

The Watchers in the Dark weren't human. Of that, Zahariel was certain. This was the form they chose to show him, because he was quite certain that the sight of their true nature would very likely drive him mad.

One of the three spoke – Zahariel could not be certain which one. Their voices were like a complex skein of whispered sounds, woven together into the semblance of human words.

You know nothing of truth, Zahariel, the watcher said. *If truth and falsehood were so simple, our ancient enemy could never find its way into a human soul.*

'I know what is right and what is wrong!' Zahariel shot back. 'I know the difference between honour and dishonour, loyalty and treason! What more does a man – or an Astartes – need to know?'

He is blind, said one of the watchers. *He has always been thus. Kill him, before he does more harm than he knows.*

Though the watchers were diminutive creatures by Astartes standards – each one barely more than a metre in height – Zahariel could sense the mantle of psychic energy that surrounded each of them, and knew that they could snuff out his life as easily as a candle flame. But he was in no mood to be cowed by these beings, not when the future of Caliban was at stake.

'Perhaps that was true once, but I have learned a great deal since the first time we met,' Zahariel countered. 'You're not ghosts or malevolent spirits, as the forest folk once believed. You're a xenos species that has been guarding something here on Caliban for a very long time. What is it?'

Something mankind was not meant to trifle with, one of the watchers hissed. *It has ever been thus. Your kind is too curious, too grasping and ignorant. It will be your undoing.*

'If we are ignorant, it's because beings like you withhold the truth from us,' Zahariel shouted. 'Knowledge is power.'

And mankind misuses its power at every turn. One day humanity will kindle a fire they cannot control, and the entire universe will burn.

'Then teach us!' Zahariel said. 'Show us a better way, instead of sitting back and waiting for disaster to fall. If you don't, then you're just as much to blame for what happens as we are.'

The three beings stirred, and a wave of psychic power rolled away from them like a cold wave, engulfing Zahariel and freezing him to the core. The shock of it would have stopped an ordinary man's heart; as it was, the Librarian's circulatory and nervous systems struggled to keep him conscious. Yet he refused to be cowed by their expression of pique.

'You said to me, long ago, that this evil could be fought,' he said. 'Here I stand, ready to fight it. Just tell me what I must do.'

The watchers did not answer at first. They stirred again, and the ether was charged with pulses and ripples of invisible power. He sensed that they were conversing somehow, on a level too rarefied for him to perceive.

After what felt like an eternity, the ether stilled once more, and one of the watchers spoke. *Ask your questions, human. We will answer what we can.*

The admission surprised Zahariel, until he remembered that the watchers had once admitted that they were a part of a larger cabal, dedicated to battling the most ancient of evils. For the first time, he perceived that there were limits to what these potent beings were capable of doing.

'All right,' Zahariel began. 'How long has Caliban been tainted by this evil?'

Always, was the watcher's wintry reply.

'Then why have no Calibanites succumbed to its touch before now?'

Because of our efforts, you foolish human, another watcher said. Zahariel was coming to recognise tonal differences between the beings now, though he still had no clear idea which voice belonged to which body.

And, ironically, by the great beasts themselves, another watcher said. *They were born of the taint, and lingered near the places where its corruption rose close to the surface. They killed nearly all of the humans who strayed too close, and those few who did survive were ultimately slain as warlocks by your own people before they could grow too strong.*

A sudden chill raised gooseflesh on Zahariel's skin as a memory returned to him from long ago. He remembered standing in the great library of the Knights of Lupus, listening to the bleak words of their doomed master, Lord Sartana... *The worst... of all this, is the Lion's quest to kill off the great beasts. That's the real danger. That's the part we'll all end up regretting.*

And now the Terrans had come, cutting away the forests and forcing their way into the most inhospitable parts of Caliban in search of resources to feed the Imperial war machine. 'The thermal cores,' he mused. 'They sank the thermal cores deep into the earth and released the taint in the Northwilds.'

And now others feed it with fire and slaughter, a watcher added.

Zahariel nodded, thinking of the pile of corpses at Sigma Five-One-Seven. Many of them had doubtless been provided for the worm queen to lay her eggs, but others – likely the entirety of the Calibanite labour force – had been offered up as a sacrifice, to add power to the ritual and focus the energies that the sorcerers unleashed. If they managed to tap into the horror and bloodshed being unleashed by the rebels, what terrible things might they accomplish?

In their own way, the rebels were more dangerous than the sorcerers themselves, Zahariel realised bleakly. And tragically, their cause wasn't entirely unjust. The Imperium did, in fact, pose a grave danger to Caliban – just not in the way that many of them suspected.

Except for the old knight, Sar Daviel. He knew. Zahariel remembered his last words to Luther.

The forests are gone, but the monsters still remain.

Zahariel suddenly understood what had to be done. He turned to the watchers and bowed his head respectfully. 'Thank you for your counsel,' he said gravely. 'You have my word that the wisdom you've shared will be put to good use. I will save Caliban from destruction. This I swear.'

The watchers studied him for a long moment, while the ghostly winds of the immaterium howled above their heads. Then, slowly, the watcher in the centre shook his cowled head.

In that you are wrong, Zahariel of the Dark Angels, the watcher replied. Its unearthly voice was low, and almost sad. *Caliban is doomed, and nothing you do can prevent it.*

Zahariel blinked in surprise, stunned by the watcher's words. When he opened his eyelids again, the afterimage of the lightning bolt was fading from his vision. Rain smote his face, and the Watchers in the Dark were gone.

ZAHARIEL BURST INTO the Grand Master's sanctum unannounced, the thick, oaken door rebounding with a boom from the old stone walls. Lord Cypher looked up from behind the Grand Master's desk, his hooded form bent over neatly-stacked data slates and copies of readiness reports.

The enigmatic Astartes' square-jawed face betrayed no emotion at the Librarian's sudden arrival. 'Master Luther remains in seclusion, meditating on the crisis,' he said coolly. 'Have you another message for me to deliver?'

'I'm not looking for Master Luther,' Zahariel said, stalking purposefully across the room. 'You're the one I wish to speak to, my lord.'

'Indeed?' Cypher straightened, hooking his thumbs casually in his tooled leather gun belt. 'And how may I be of service, Brother-Librarian Zahariel?'

'I want another parley with the rebel leaders,' Zahariel said. 'Specifically Sar Daviel. And it needs to be within the next twenty-four hours.'

The request seemed to genuinely amuse Cypher. 'Shall I pull the moon out of the sky while I'm at it?' he asked with a faint grin.

'You got word to them once before,' Zahariel continued stubbornly. 'I have no doubt those channels are still open to you, if you choose to employ them.'

The traditions of parley went back for hundreds of years on Caliban, when open warfare between knightly orders was more common. Even the bitterest foes maintained channels of communication to facilitate negotiations or declarations of surrender. It was a means of avoiding unnecessary casualties and bringing a swift end to open combat before both sides were too badly mauled to perform their sworn duty to the people of Caliban.

The grin faded from Lord Cypher's face. His lips pressed into a narrow line. 'Only the Grand Master can initiate a parley,' he said.

'Not so,' Zahariel countered. 'Astelan and I are his designated representatives, and so long as he remains incommunicado, we have the authority to prosecute the war as we see fit. And I wish to parley with the rebels at once.'

Lord Cypher hesitated for a moment, but then ultimately gave a nod of assent. 'The rebels won't agree to a meeting at Aldurukh this time,' he warned.

'I've no interest in speaking to them here,' Zahariel said. 'Tell Sar Daviel that I will meet them at a place of their choosing,' he said, 'inside the Northwilds arcology. No other location is acceptable.'

Cypher studied Zahariel closely. 'An unusual request,' he said. 'They will want to know why.'

'Because the fate of our world is going to be decided there,' Zahariel replied. 'Whether any of us like it or not.'

FIFTEEN

ENGINES OF WAR

Diamat
In the 200th year of the Emperor's Great Crusade

THE FORGE'S MASSIVE Titan foundry was actually a collection of cyclopean structures that filled an area of five square kilometres, not far from the complex's southern gate. It was a self-contained manufactory, with facilities for creating everything from adamantine skeletal segments to tempered plasteel armour plate, and everything in between. Broad trackways, made to accommodate heavy load-haulers, connected to the towering structure at the centre of the foundry: the giant assembly building, where up to four of the gargantuan war machines could be built at the same time. When a Titan was completed it would then be handed over to the adepts of the Legio Gladius with solemn ceremony, and the engine would take its first steps to join its brethren at the legion's fortress, some ten kilometres to the north.

Nemiel and his squad encountered the first of the skitarii patrols at the edge of the foundry sector;

these were well-equipped troops in static positions, manning lascannons or heavy stubbers and sweeping the perimeter every few seconds with advanced auspex arrays.

He halted the squad in the shadow of an idle manufactory and waved Brother Askelon over. 'It looks like the assembly building is the only part of the foundry in operation,' he said, nodding towards the towering, well-lit structure. 'Magos Archoi isn't taking any chances. He's extended his security perimeter to the very edge of the sector. Can you think of a way we can get past those auspex units? It's imperative we find out what Archoi is doing.'

The Techmarine considered the problem for a moment, and nodded. 'All of the facilities here are powered by the thermal reactors inside the volcano,' he said. 'The power feeds are run through utility tunnels that connect all the buildings. They'll likely be covered by automated security systems, but I believe I can bypass them.'

Nemiel nodded. 'Let's go. We don't have much time until dawn.'

Askelon led the squad back the way they'd come, to an access door at the far side of the manufactory. While Nemiel and the rest of the Dark Angels stood watch for more Mechanicum patrols, the Techmarine bypassed the door's security system and slipped inside. Fifteen seconds later he returned, beckoning for Nemiel. 'There are several small, cybernetic sentries prowling the building,' Askelon whispered. 'They follow predictable routes and use their surveyors to scan for signs of heat or motion, but they're very short-ranged. Stay close, and move only when I say.'

The Techmarine led the squad across the dark floor of the manufactory, slipping between massive stamping machines and automated spot-welding arrays. Askelon traced a winding, deliberate route through the plant, pausing at times and listening for the telltale ultrasonic whine of an auspex transmitter. After several long minutes they reached a short, squat permacrete structure at the centre of the manufactory floor. Askelon located a plasteel door in the side of the structure and quickly disarmed its sensors, then led the squad inside. Within, a cluster of giant, metal-clad conduits rose like fat, silver worms from a circular hole in the middle of the bare permacrete floor and connected to large junction boxes on three of the four walls. Control panels along the wall beside the door monitored the power feed to the manufactory's systems.

Askelon stepped to the edge of the hole and located a set of metal rungs that descended into the access tunnel below. Hot, dry air, smelling of ozone and sulphur, wafted up from the depths. 'We'll follow the tunnel to the access point underneath the assembly building,' he said to the squad. 'Keep your eyes open, brothers. There may be cybernetic sentries in the tunnel as well.'

'What do we do if we see one?' Kohl asked.

'Shoot it,' the Techmarine replied with a shrug, 'and hope that it can't get a signal off before it's destroyed.'

Kohl and Nemiel exchanged grim looks and followed Askelon down into the tunnel.

The utility tunnel was tall and wide, its circular walls lined with thick, metal conduits stamped with strings of binaric code. The Techmarine headed off down the tunnel in the general direction of the foundry, pausing from time to time to read the stamps on several of the conduits to his left.

They travelled for more than two kilometres, following the trunk labels through one intersection after another. Finally, Askelon battle-signed for the squad to halt and sank slowly into a crouch.

Nemiel moved silently forward and knelt down beside the Techmarine. 'What's wrong?' he whispered.

Askelon raised his chin slightly, like a hound tasting a scent. 'Faint surveyor pulse, emanating from farther down the tunnel,' he said. 'We're outside its extreme range.'

The Redemptor raised his bolt pistol. 'A sentry?'

'Yes,' Askelon replied. 'It's a sigma-sequence pulse, so it's not one of the small patrol units. Most likely it's a stationary unit, like a sentry gun.'

'Then it's probably sitting right at the feet of the ladder leading up to the foundry.' Nemiel said. 'Any way to outflank it?'

Askelon shook his head. 'Unlikely. But there might be a way to temporarily incapacitate it.'

'Tell me.'

The Techmarine pointed at the conduits lining the walls around them. 'This is category nine conduit; it's the most heavily-shielded insulator available,' he explained. 'But there's so much power going through these lines that there's still significant electromagnetic radiation leaking into the tunnel.'

'And how does that help us, exactly?'

'If I cut into the conduits I can use my armour's power plant to send a feedback surge down the line towards the sentry unit,' Askelon said. 'A powerful enough spike in electromagnetic radiation will overload its auspex receptors and force a reset. That will render it blind and unable to communicate for approximately thirty seconds.'

'Approximately?' Nemiel said.

'If I could see the type of sentry unit I could tell you down to the millisecond,' Askelon said. 'As it is, it could be one of a half-dozen models. Thirty seconds is my worst-case estimate.'

Nemiel nodded. 'Get to work.'

The Redemptor went back to the squad and told them what was happening while Askelon quickly marked out which conduits to tap and went to work. With deft movements he drew out a small, powerful plasma torch and cut open a half-dozen of the steel tubes, then he opened an access panel on the side of his backpack power unit and began attaching a number of heavy-gauge cables to the contacts inside.

Several minutes later, the Techmarine was ready. He glanced back at Nemiel, who gave him the nod to proceed. Askelon quickly attached the cables to the power lines inside the conduits. His armour stiffened abruptly. Immediately, Nemiel saw the Techmarine's status indicators begin flashing urgently on his helmet display. The core temp of his power unit spiked beyond allowable tolerances and continued to climb. Askelon's physio-monitors began to fluctuate as well, as feedback coursed through the suit's neuro-interfaces and into his body.

'There's smoke rising from his power plant,' Kohl whispered urgently.

'Let him finish!' Nemiel hissed. 'It's the only way.'

Seconds passed. Nemiel watched Askelon's indicators pulse from green to amber, and then amber to red. Without warning, a fountain of sparks shot from the servo-arm housing between the Techmarine's shoulders. Askelon spasmed, throwing out his hands and shoving himself away from the power conduits. The Techmarine fell backwards, stiff-legged, and crashed into the far side of the tunnel.

Nemiel and the rest of the squad rushed to the downed Astartes. The air around Askelon shimmered with heat, radiating from his overloaded power unit. The Techmarine turned his head; squawks of sound crackled from his helmet's speaker. Nemiel didn't have to hear the words to know what Askelon was trying to say.

'He's sent the pulse,' Nemiel told the squad. 'Brother Marthes, take point. Sergeant Kohl, help me with Brother Askelon. Let's move!'

The Astartes sprang into action, charging down the tunnel behind Marthes, who advanced with his meltagun held ready. Kohl and Nemiel brought up the rear, dragging the limp form of Askelon between them.

Three hundred metres down the tunnel, the passageway fed into a large, square structure that echoed the permacrete blockhouse they'd entered at the manufactory. The plasteel rungs of another ladder climbed upward, presumably into the foundry's assembly building. Sitting at its feet, just as Nemiel suspected, crouched a matte-black sentry gun. Armed with a turret-mounted twin-linked lascannon, the automated unit crouched on four stubby legs like a hungry spider waiting for prey. Nemiel could hear the hum of its power unit as they approached. Its twin guns were aimed straight down the tunnel at the approaching Astartes. A single shot would cut through their armour like tissue.

'Up the ladder!' he ordered the squad. 'Get up and get out of sight!'

Marthes stepped around the sentry gun and began climbing at once. Vardus paused at the bottom rungs, his heavy bolter slung at his side. 'What about Askelon?' he said.

'We'll manage,' the Redemptor shot back. 'Now hurry, brother!'

Vardus started his climb, with Ephrial hot on his heels. Nemiel consulted his internal chrono: they had just twelve seconds left. He looked to Kohl as they reached the bottom of the ladder. 'We need to find a way to shut off the sentry gun,' he said. 'There must be an access panel–'

Askelon shook his head sharply; the ceramite edges of his helmet scraped against his gorget, suggesting he'd sustained damage to his armour's muscle fibres. 'No,' he said, his voice coming through his helmet's damaged speaker as a tortured croak. 'Can't risk it. I… I can climb.'

'All right,' Nemiel growled. 'You go first. Kohl, you're next. Help him as much as you can.' He would stay until the last moment; if they ran out of time, he would tear open one of the sentry gun's access panels and try to shut it down.

Askelon grabbed hold of the metal rungs and started climbing, seeming to gather strength with each lunge of his legs. Kohl was right behind him, ready to provide a judicious shove if the Techmarine faltered. Nemiel counted the seconds and checked the sentry gun for likely access points.

Vardus and Ephrial leaned over the hole, grabbed Askelon's folded servo-arm and hauled him bodily up into the chamber above. Kohl raced up behind him. 'Clear!' he hissed to Nemiel.

The Redemptor leapt for the rungs and scrambled upwards as quickly as he could. The timer on his display hit zero when he was halfway up. There was a series of rapid clicks and whirring sounds directly beneath him as the sentry gun sprang back to life.

Hands reached down and grabbed the edges of his pauldrons. Nemiel felt himself yanked upwards like a sack of grain and deposited roughly on the permacrete of the upper floor.

The Astartes froze, listening intently. Below them, the sentry gun clattered and whirred a moment more, then resumed its quiet vigil.

Nemiel looked over at Askelon's prone form. 'Any sign of alarm?'

The Techmarine reached slowly for his helmet and undid its clasps. Askelon pulled the helm away, revealing a sweat-streaked face stippled with broken blood vessels. A trickle of blood seeped from his nose and the corners of his eyes. 'No change,' he said in a husky voice. Blood slicked the Techmarine's teeth.

Nemiel rolled over and rose to his knees beside Askelon. 'How badly are you hurt?' he asked quietly.

Askelon chuckled faintly. 'I'm no Apothecary, brother,' he replied. 'The machinery of a living body is too complex even for me.' He levered himself to a sitting position with a grunt. 'Armour integrity is at sixty-five per cent. Power levels at forty per cent. Muscle fibre reflex is compromised, and I think I melted the motors on my servo-arm.'

Nemiel frowned. 'You didn't mention that tapping those conduits would likely kill you,' he growled.

The Techmarine managed a grin. 'It didn't seem relevant at the time.' He extended his hand. 'Help me up, please.'

Kohl and Nemiel hauled Askelon upright. The Redemptor glanced warily at the edge of the hole. 'Can the gun sense us up here?'

'To a limited extent, yes,' the Techmarine said. 'But activity overhead won't trigger a combat response. It's down there to guard the approaches to the building, and that's all.'

'All right. Where do we go from here?'

Askelon looked about the chamber. It was identical to the conduit room at the manufactory, only substantially larger. He nodded to the metal door across the chamber. 'That leads out into a sub-level beneath the main assembly floor. From there we'll be able to access almost every part of the building.'

Nemiel checked his chrono again. It was little more than an hour until dawn. 'A building like this is bound to have catwalks along the upper storeys, correct?'

Askelon nodded. 'Three levels of them, in this case. You can look out over the entire assembly area from some of them.'

'Then that's where we need to be,' he said. 'Let's go.'

* * *

KOHL TOOK POINT after that, leading the squad through the confines of the sub-level according to whispered directions from Brother Askelon, until they reached a narrow stairwell that climbed upwards into the assembly building proper. Weapons ready, they made their way carefully up the permacrete stairs, listening for the slightest sound of movement. Nemiel could hear the sharp crackle of arc torches and the snarl of power tools reverberating through the walls, the steel-on-steel noise like the sounds of a distant battlefield.

They climbed up several storeys, past one dimly-lit landing after another, until Nemiel signalled for a halt. 'This is far enough,' he said. 'We don't need to get all the way to the top; I just want a good view of what's going on,' he told them. He turned to Askelon. 'Is there any risk of sensors at this point?'

'No,' the Techmarine replied. 'We're past their detection perimeter at this point.'

'All right. Marthes, you and Vardus stay here and cover the stairwell. Kohl, Askelon and Ephrial, you're with me.'

Nemiel crouched at the plasteel door and cracked it slowly open. Beyond, the gantry-way was lit with red light from below. His autosenses picked up the reek of melted plas, petrochemicals and heated metal. Distantly, he could make out the sharp blurts and squeals of binaric cant, as well as a number of voices speaking in Gothic. The Redemptor concentrated, but he could make out what they were saying over the squalling of the machinery.

He surveyed the gantry-way carefully for as far as he could see, checking for any signs of movement, then went back and checked again. Satisfied there was no one within the immediate area, he opened the door the rest of the way and crept quietly onto the plasteel catwalk.

The assembly building was rectangular in shape, with an open floor plan surrounded by six huge niches that stretched from floor to ceiling. Giant servo arms were set into either side of these niches, able to climb to different heights along trackways set into the permacrete, and huge cranes hung from similar tracks high overhead. The Titans were assembled inside each niche, starting with the skeletal structure of the feet and working upwards to the head.

Nemiel found himself crouched on a section of third-storey gantry-way at one end of the building. The storeys above him were plunged into darkness, without so much as an emergency lamp burning. Below, red light rose up from the assembly floor like the glow of an actual forge. Gusts of hot air, stirred by industrial grade arc torches blew against his faceplate. A rustle of iron links, musical and cold, chimed from the deep shadows high above the floor.

Hundreds of chains had been suspended from the assembly building's ceiling, twisting and clinking together in the restless air. Each chain, more than fifty metres in length, had been strung with dozens of hooks, and on each hook hung a fresh corpse. Nemiel saw the bodies of Tanagran Dragoons, skitarii – even the mangled bodies of dead Praetorians – along with the smaller figures of tech-adepts and half-mechanical magi. Their corpses had been riddled by bullets or torn apart by energy bolts, sliced open by power claws or crushed by mechanical fists, and their fluids leaked from them in a steady, dripping rain onto the hulls of the enormous vehicles below.

There were six of them, Nemiel saw. Their chassis were so wide that they could only be arrayed in a single file that stretched from one end of the assembly building to the other. Their armoured hulls were supported by dual sets of treads on each of the vehicle's flanks, with a sloped front that rose like a sheer-sided hillock more than two storeys high. Void shield generators studded the vehicle's sides, along with automated quad-laser and mega-bolter emplacements, but Nemiel scarcely noticed them. His gaze was drawn to the enormous cannon built into the centreline of the vehicle's hull. A complicated series of hoists and giant braces surrounding the cannon's barrel indicated that it was meant to be elevated and fired like a conventional artillery piece. The aft section of each vehicle was segmented like the body of a giant insect, and appeared to be even more heavily armoured than the rest of the hull.

'What in the Emperor's name are those things?' Kohl hissed. It was the first time Nemiel had ever heard the sergeant taken aback.

Techmarine Askelon carefully eased into a crouch beside them. His eyes widened as he saw the machines on the assembly floor. 'Siege guns,' he said, his voice tinged with awe, 'but far larger than any I've ever seen before. Those look like macro cannons, fitted to a custom hull.' He pointed to the nearest vehicle. 'See those dual treads? Those aren't part of a contiguous drive train. They are distinct drive units, similar in size and power the ones used on

Baneblade super-heavy tanks. There are three to a side, and that's just to form the foundation for each vehicle.'

Tech-adepts were crawling like ants over each of the war machines, working feverishly along the armoured hull beneath the rain of gore. Symbols had been scrawled in blood at regular intervals along each machine's flank, but Nemiel couldn't make them out at such a distance. The Redemptor noticed that he vehicle closest to them had a large, open hatch on the top deck, to the right of the huge gun. 'What do you make of that?' he said, pointing to the two tech-adepts working in the well beneath the hatchway.

Askelon leaned slightly forward, peering intently at the opening. His eyes widened. 'It's an MIU interface chamber,' he said, 'A neural interface link, much like we employ on our Titans. It looks like they're refurbishing the control leads and making it ready for use.'

'So a single operator could control one of these behemoths?' Nemiel said.

The Techmarine nodded. 'Of course. They're big, but far less demanding than a bipedal Titan,' he replied. 'And the MIU makes it nearly impossible for them to be used if captured.'

Nemiel nodded grimly, his gaze rising to the collection of corpses dangling in the air before them. 'Now we know what happened to the Dragoons covering the southern approach,' he said, his voice thick with revulsion. 'Not to mention a good many of the forge's own personnel. Magos Archoi is a madman. This whole thing smacks of some obscene, superstitious ritual. How could someone like Horus Lupercal be connected to such debased behaviour?' Memories of the foul things he'd witnessed at Sarosh rose unbidden in Nemiel's mind. He forced them aside with an effort of will and a savage shake of his head.

Kohl tore his gaze away from the repellent sight and caught a glimpse of movement on the assembly floor. 'Here comes the high priest himself,' he growled, pointing to the narrow lane at the right of the parked war machines.

Nemiel straightened, craning his head around to see Magos Archoi walking down the line of vehicles. A pair of tech-adepts followed a discreet distance behind the magos, their hands tucked into their sleeves, while a knot of four uniformed men dogged Archoi's heels and studied the siege guns critically. One of the men was conferring with the magos, speaking to him in urgent tones. It took a moment for Nemiel to recognise the uniform he wore.

'15th Hesperan Lancers,' he murmured. 'Assigned to Horus's 53rd Expeditionary Fleet. It looks like some of the rebels stayed behind when their ground forces left the planet. They must have been meeting with that traitor Archoi and arranging delivery of the machines when we arrived.'

'And they've been biding their time ever since, waiting for the right opportunity,' Kohl snarled. 'That damned magos has embedded his warriors into every one of our combat units. We've got to warn the primarch or we may well have a massacre on our hands!'

At just that moment, Brother Vardus leaned out from the stairwell entrance. 'Movement on the stairs!' he hissed, 'coming from above and below.'

Kohl stared back at Vardus. 'Above and below simultaneously?'

Vardus nodded. 'They're moving quietly. Might be a pair of patrols.'

Suddenly, Askelon pointed across the cavernous space. 'I can see movement on the opposite gantry-way!' he said quietly. 'They're carrying something.'

Nemiel felt the hairs on the back of his neck go up. He looked down at the assembly room floor. Magos Archoi was standing there, surrounded by a circle of bemused rebels. The traitor's hooded head was tilted upwards, looking directly at him.

'They know we're here!' he cried, drawing his crozius from his belt. 'It's a trap!'

Lasgun fire erupted from the gantry-way on the opposite side of the building; red bolts hissed through the air, gouging craters from the permacrete wall in a string of sharp thunderclaps. A heavy bolter began to hammer away, spitting tracers across the intervening space in a series of measured bursts. Rounds struck many of the hanging chains, splitting their links and dumping their grisly cargo to the ground.

Nemiel fired a burst in the direction of the heavy bolter and activated his vox-bead. '*Invincible Reason*, this is Brother Nemiel!' he cried. 'Can you read me?' He was answered with a rising screech of static. The Redemptor went through a score of frequencies and got the same result. Archoi's traitors were jamming the vox-channels.

Fire erupted from the stairwell behind Nemiel. Autoguns clattered and lasguns spat bursts of light at Marthes and Vardus, who responded with a brace of fragmentation grenades. Marthes levelled his melta-gun down the stairs and fired a howling blast, then ducked out onto the gangway. 'There's a platoon of skitarii coming up the stairs!' he shouted.

Dark figures were rushing at them along the gangway from the far side of the building, firing bursts of lasgun fire as they advanced. Kohl and Ephrial exchanged fire with them, dropping several with well-aimed shots. A burst of heavy bolter fire answered them, stitching the two Astartes with a stream of shells. Both warriors staggered beneath the hits, but their armour turned aside the blows.

'Marthes! Put a shot on that gangway!' Nemiel yelled as he leaned over the thin metal rail and levelled his pistol at Magos Archoi. The traitor didn't even flinch as the Redemptor laid his aiming point at the centre of the darkness beneath his hood and let off a burst. The shells flew straight and true – and detonated harmlessly against a force field just a few scant centimetres from their target. The officers with the magos drew laspistols and returned fire, striking Nemiel once in the leg and abdomen.

Marthes shouldered his way onto the catwalk and fired his meltagun at the distant heavy bolter. The microwave burst struck the weapon and the gangway beneath it and superheated the metal in a split second, vaporising them in a fierce concussion and hurling burning skitarii to the assembly floor below.

'We're cut off!' Kohl shouted as he picked off another of the charging skitarii. 'Where do we go from here?'

Nemiel glared down at Archoi. Several metres away, one of the burning skitarii had become entangled in one of the chains on the way down, and now he thrashed and twisted in the air as the flames consumed him. On impulse, he holstered his pistol. 'Follow me!' he said, then put a foot onto the rail and leapt into space.

The thin metal of the railing bent beneath his full weight, throwing him off balance, but his leap carried him far enough to reach one of the grisly, corpse-strewn chains. He grabbed hold with one hand and slid partway down its length before the slippery metal snaked out of his hands. Nemiel fell the remaining few metres and landed atop the lead siege gun. A tech-adept rose up beside him, raising a crackling arc-torch, but he may as well have been moving in slow motion. The Astartes smashed the traitor aside with a sweep of his crozius and began to run along the downward-sloping hull towards Archoi and the rebel officers.

'For the Lion!' he roared, raising the crozius aquilum high as he launched himself at the traitors.

SIXTEEN

WHEELS WITHIN WHEELS

Caliban
In the 200th year of the Emperor's Great Crusade

GENERAL MORTEN SHIFTED uncomfortably in the shuttle's oversized jump seat and tried to conceal the scowl on his face by pretending to study the view beyond the small window at his left. 'If I could perhaps get some idea of what it is you're looking for, I could arrange for a presentation from the garrison's senior officers.'

'That would defeat the purpose of the inspection,' Zahariel replied from his seat across the shuttle's passenger cabin. 'In fact, it would be best if the troops never knew I was there.'

'Very well,' Morten rasped, though Zahariel could see that his weathered face was still troubled. The Terran officer stared out the window for a moment more, debating what to say next. After a moment, he drew a deep breath and said, 'You asked me to inspect the troops at Northwilds to provide a cover for your own activities.'

'That's right,' Zahariel admitted. He didn't want to lie to the man any more than he had to. 'We'll part ways once the shuttle lands, and it's likely I won't be returning with you back to Aldurukh.' He spread his hands. 'I regret that I can't be any more candid, but this is Legion business. I'm sure you understand.'

'Yes, of course,' Morten said readily, but there was no mistaking the wary look in the old general's eye. For a brief moment, Zahariel wondered if there was something that the general was hiding, but he quickly dismissed the thought with a flash of irritation. He had no reason to distrust Morten, Zahariel reminded himself forcibly. The man was, by all accounts, an honourable and dedicated soldier, and had every reason to wonder at Zahariel's request for an unannounced inspection of the garrison at the Northwilds arcology. The fact was, Zahariel couldn't afford to make his presence known to the local troops or the Administratum officials struggling to maintain order across the arcology's war-torn sectors; it would lead to pointed questions that he could ill afford to answer.

The last thing he wanted was for General Morten – or worse, Magos Bosk – to learn that a member of the Legion was meeting secretly with rebel leaders in the midst of the most hotly-contested population centre on the planet. It was unlikely that either of the Terrans would take the news well. As much as he hated the idea of concealing his actions, Zahariel was forced to admit that, when it came down to it, Morten and Bosk acted in the best interests of the Imperium, not Caliban itself.

Shafts of late afternoon sunlight slanted through the window to Zahariel's right as the military shuttle began a wide, diving turn towards their destination. The Librarian craned his neck to peer out the window to the northeast, where the arcology rose sharp-edged against the backdrop of the weathered mountain range further north.

The Northwilds arcology had been built according to the standard Imperial template; it was an irregularly-stepped pyramid that, even still in its initial stages, was five kilometres wide at its base and rose more than three kilometres into the cloudy sky. Narrow streets radiated away from the arcology across the plain, surrounded by hundreds of smaller buildings that had yet to be subsumed by the structure's ever-expanding footprint.

Each arcology was constructed in a similar fashion on newly-compliant Imperial worlds: first would come the labourers and their families, relocated by the tens of thousands from towns and villages all over the hemisphere. They would be resettled in a town at the site of the new arcology, which would spread outward in all directions as its population swelled. Then, once there was a large enough labour pool that had been sufficiently trained to begin work, the digging of the arcology's foundation would begin. The structure would grow in stages, expanding outwards, upwards and downwards at the same time. Little by little, the arcology would swallow up the town, its residents progressively reassigned to districts inside the structure itself. The population would continue to grow as well, along with the civil services and bureaucracy that went along with it. In theory, the population and organisational growth would match the growth of the structure so closely that by the time the structure was complete, the arcology would be fully populated and self-sufficient. Of course, such things rarely ever went precisely according to plan.

'How many people are at Northwilds these days?' Zahariel asked.

'You mean civilians? About five million, all told,' Morten replied. 'About a quarter of that are Imperial citizens from offworld: Administratum officials, engineers, industrial planners and the like.'

Zahariel consulted facts and figures committed to memory before leaving Aldurukh. 'A stage one arcology is built to support twice that number,' he observed. 'So half of the structure is still unoccupied?'

Morten shrugged. 'The Imperium's industrialisation plan calls for twenty stage-one arcologies across Caliban, but the planet's population won't be able to support that for some time yet.'

The Librarian frowned thoughtfully. 'That seems like a great deal of extra work. One would think that they would build new structures as needed, rather than all at once?'

Morten spread his gnarled hands. 'Who can say? The Administratum has its reasons, I don't doubt.'

'How is the population distributed throughout the arcology?' Zahariel inquired.

'We're keeping the natives penned into the lower levels,' the general rasped. 'The garrison, the Administratum infrastructure and the offworld residents are housed on the upper levels, where we can keep them secure.'

Zahariel gave the general a flat stare. 'Natives?' he said.

Morten's scowl vanished. 'My apologies, sir,' he said, straightening in his seat. An embarrassed flush began to spread up his thick neck. 'Just a figure of speech. I meant no offence.'

'No, of course not,' the Librarian replied coolly. 'How are you managing to provide basic services to the population?'

Morten drew in a quick breath. 'Well, I won't deny it's difficult. The lower levels bore the brunt of the riots, so a lot of the infrastructure was damaged. We're sending in work teams every day with armed escorts to perform repairs, and we've set up medicae facilities at strategic points to care for the injured.'

'So how much of the lower levels are without light or running water at this point?' Zahariel asked.

'Only about twenty per cent,' Morten said. 'If we can keep any more full-scale riots from breaking out, we can knock that number down even further in the next couple of weeks.'

Zahariel nodded, keeping his face impassive. Twenty per cent without power or water meant roughly a million people trapped in the dark, shivering in the cold and living off military ration packs for the better part of a month. 'Is there no way to relocate the affected residents to another level?'

Morten's craggy brows went up. 'Sir, you must be aware that an unknown number of the natives – excuse me, citizens – are also likely members of the rebellion. It's much more sensible from a military standpoint to keep them isolated and restore service to them than turn them loose in another part of the arcology where they can cause more mischief.'

Zahariel turned back to the window and breathed deeply, biting back the outrage he felt. 'Is this sort of tactic normal when dealing with civil unrest?' he asked.

'Of course,' Morten replied. 'You've got to get it through their heads that when they destroy Imperial property they're only going to make their lives harder and more miserable. Sooner or later the lesson sinks in.'

And how many rebels do you create in the process, Zahariel thought?

The shuttle had descended to about two thousand metres by this point, and its turn sharpened as it came in for its final approach. Zahariel saw plumes of smoke rising from the arcology's flanks near ground level, suggesting that the populace was far from learning General Morten's brutal lesson. He was shocked to feel a perverse sense of pride at the thought.

They continued their descent, passing below fifteen hundred metres before the shuttle pilot pulled up the nose of his craft and flared his thrusters for a vertical landing. The transport touched down on a broad landing pad, one of dozens that jutted from the arcology's northern face, with scarcely a jolt. Morten grunted in satisfaction as he unbuckled his safety harness and climbed wearily to his feet.

'My inspection will likely take the better part of three hours,' he said to Zahariel. 'Do I need to stretch it out further?'

'No need,' Zahariel replied. He had yet to climb from his seat. 'If I'm not back by the time you are done, return to Aldurukh without me. I will arrange for my own transport.'

Morten paused, as though he wanted to inquire further, but after a moment he mastered his curiosity and gave the Librarian a curt nod. 'I'll bid you good luck then,' he said, then turned on his heel and headed for the exit ramp.

Zahariel listened to the clang of the general's boots as he descended the ramp. One of the shuttle pilots passed through the passenger compartment, headed aft to check on the shuttle's engines. He waited a full minute more, then rose to his feet and pulled off his plain, white surplice to reveal a black body glove beneath. The rebel leaders had agreed to the meeting only on the condition that he come unarmed and unarmoured. The stipulation surprised and irritated him; did they imagine he would call for a parley with treachery in mind? He'd swallowed his aggravation and agreed nonetheless. There was too much at stake to haggle over such trivial details.

The Librarian reached into an overhead locker and drew out a neatly-folded bundle of cloth. Zahariel unfurled the heavy cloak with a snap of his wrists and drew it about his shoulders. When he closed the clasp, the cloak's cameleoline outer layer activated, matching the grey hues of the compartment in less than a second. He drew the cloak's deep hood over his head and headed quickly to the ramp.

Outside the shuttle the air was cold and brisk, with a strong wind blowing down from the mountains. Tattered streamers of smoke curled around the lip of the landing pad; he grimaced as he caught the mingled smell of ash and melted plas. Across the pad, a deep alcove led to a pair of blast doors that gave access to the arcology itself. A shuttle technician stood near the alcove, his back to Zahariel as he tried to wrestle a heavy refuelling hose from a recessed bay set into the pad itself.

The Astartes moved swiftly across the pad, the faint sound of his footfalls lost in the idling whine of the shuttle's engines. He passed the technician close enough to touch him if he'd wished; the man glanced up irritably as he felt the wind of Zahariel's passage on his neck, but his gaze swept right past the Librarian without registering his presence.

Clutching the cloak about his broad frame, Zahariel entered the broad, shadowed alcove and paused beside the blast doors. As near as he could reckon, he had six hours before the rendezvous on sub-level four.

He turned to a maintenance access hatch, situated at the side of the alcove to the left of the blast doors. The hatch swung open noiselessly, revealing a cramped space lit with dim, red utility lighting and crowded with high-voltage conduits and data trunks. A narrow set of metal rungs led upwards and downwards into darkness. Before he'd left Aldurukh, Zahariel had memorised a circuitous route through the arcology's maze of accessways that would give him the best chance of reaching the rendezvous point unobserved. He'd need every bit of those six hours to make it to the meeting on time.

The Librarian stooped his shoulders and squeezed his way into the human-sized space, then pulled the hatch shut behind him. Darkness closed in on all sides, heavy with the scent of lubricants, ozone and recycled air. The hum of distant machinery reverberated through his bones.

With a deep breath, Zahariel began his descent into the depths.

SIX HOURS AND ten minutes later, Zahariel was crouched in the shadows at the mouth of a maintenance access corridor. Just a few steps away, a metal catwalk ran along the high wall of one of the arcology's many generator substations. From where he crouched he had a good view of the rendezvous point on the generator floor, six metres below.

Something was wrong.

The time for the rendezvous had come and gone, and the rebel leaders were nowhere in sight. Instead, Zahariel saw a pair of men in utility coveralls waiting at the designated spot. One man puffed worriedly at a clay pipe, while the other tried to calm himself by cleaning his grimy nails with the point of a small knife. They looked like just another pair of generator techs stealing a few minutes' break away from the watchful eyes of their boss – except for the cut-down las-carbines hanging from their shoulders.

What had happened to Sar Daviel and the rest? Why had these two men been sent in their stead? Now, after ten minutes, the men were growing restless. No doubt they were coming to the conclusion that he wasn't going to appear either.

Zahariel gritted his teeth in irritation. He could let the men leave and try to follow them back to their superiors, but there was a significant risk that he could lose them in the arcology's labyrinthine passageways. That left him with only one viable option. The Librarian took a few, deep breaths, calling on his training to calm his mind and focus his thoughts, then he rose from concealment, took three quick steps and vaulted over the side of the catwalk.

He landed with scarcely a sound, not three metres away from the two rebels. The man with the knife let out a startled squawk and recoiled from the Astartes, his eyes widening in fear. The pipe-smoker whirled, following the other man's startled gaze. To his credit, he kept his composure much better than his companion.

'You're late,' the rebel said around the stem of his pipe.

'I didn't come here to meet with you,' Zahariel said coldly. 'Where is Sar Daviel?'

The two rebels exchanged nervous glances. 'We're supposed to take you to him,' the pipe-smoker said.

'That wasn't what we agreed upon,' Zahariel said, a shade of menace creeping into his voice. The knife-wielder blanched, his grip tightening on the handle of his tiny penknife. If the situation hadn't been so serious, the Librarian might have been tempted to laugh.

The other rebel plucked the pipe from his lips and gave a disinterested shrug. 'Just doing what we're told,' he said. 'If you mean to parley, then follow us. If not, well, I expect you know the way out.'

'Very well,' the Astartes said coldly. 'Let's go.'

'First things first,' the pipe-wielder said. He reached into a pocket of his coveralls and drew out a small auspex unit. Placing the pipe back in his mouth, he activated the unit and adjusted its settings, then swept it over Zahariel from head to toe.

Zahariel felt his choler rise as the rebel performed his scan. 'The agreement was that I not come armed or armoured,' he said, biting off each word.

The rebel was unperturbed. 'That's as may be. I still have my orders.' Finished with the scan, he checked the unit's readout, then nodded to his companion. 'He's clear.'

The second rebel nodded, then put away his penknife and started off towards the mouth of a dimly-lit corridor on the far side of the generator room.

'Follow him,' the pipe-wielder said. 'I'll be right behind you.'

Biting back his anger, Zahariel fell into step behind the lead rebel.

They walked for more than an hour, following a long, torturous route through the maintenance spaces that would have completely disorientated a normal man. As it was, Zahariel had only a vague notion of where in the arcology they were. He was certain that they had descended through another two sub-levels, making them at least a hundred metres below ground.

At the end of the trek Zahariel found himself walking down a long, dark corridor that seemed to go on for at least a kilometre. After several minutes he began to see a faint, grey luminescence up ahead. He smelled brackish water and wet stone, and a low, hissing sound filled his ears. Soon the grey light resolved itself into a doorway that opened onto a clattering metal catwalk suspended over a man-made waterfall. To the right of the catwalk, close enough to touch, was a wall of plunging water that churned into foam just two metres below Zahariel's feet before passing under the catwalk and through a metal grate off to his left. They had reached one of the arcology's many wastewater purification plants, Zahariel realised. At the far end of the catwalk, about fifty metres away, a small, permacrete blockhouse jutted from the chamber wall. Two armed rebels stood outside the blockhouse door, their hands nervously gripping their stolen lasguns.

The guards halted them at the end of the catwalk and conferred with Zahariel's guides in low, urgent tones; he tried to listen in on what was being said, but the white noise of the waterfall made it impossible. After a brief exchange, the guards nodded and stepped to one side. The pipe-wielding rebel turned back to Zahariel and gestured to the door with a nod of his head. 'They're waiting for you inside,' he said.

At once, Zahariel's anger began to rise. Without a word, he rushed past the four men, pushing open the door with the flat of his hand and storming inside. He found himself in a small room, perhaps five metres to a side, which was lined with banks of controls and flickering data-plates. Four rebel soldiers stood in a tight knot on the opposite side of the room, close to a featureless metal door. To his left, Zahariel saw Lord Thuriel and Lord Malchial sitting in a pair of the control room's utilitarian chairs. Malchial was clearly agitated, leaning forward in the chair with his hands clenched so tightly his knuckles were white as chalk. Thuriel, on the other hand, was at ease, peering at the Librarian over steepled fingers. His dark eyes held nothing but contempt.

'So you chose to come after all,' Thuriel sneered. 'I'd half given up on you.'

'Had you been at the agreed-upon place you wouldn't have had to wait,' Zahariel shot back. 'We haven't the time for games, Lord Thuriel. Where are Lady Alera and Sar Daviel?'

'That's none of your concern,' Thuriel said. He turned slightly and nodded to the men at the door. As one, the four rebels turned to face Zahariel, raising their weapons. Two of the men were armed with heavy, blunt-nosed plasma guns. For a moment Zahariel could only stare at the rebels. The idea of violating the time-honoured tradition of parley shocked him more profoundly than any warp-spawned horror could.

'Upon further consideration, we've decided to make you our guest,' Thuriel said with a cruel smile. 'I think a high-value hostage will persuade Luther to take our demands seriously.'

Zahariel, however, wasn't the least bit cowed. He folded his arms and glared at the rebels. 'I'm going to give you just one chance to put those guns away,' he said in a quiet voice.

Thuriel chuckled. 'Or what?' he shot back. 'I've heard stories about the legendary toughness of the Astartes, but I rather doubt even you would survive a point-blank shot from a plasma gun.'

'None of us would survive, you idiot,' Zahariel said scornfully. 'In a small room like this the thermal effects would incinerate us all. Now, I'm going to say this one last time. Put your weapons away, or this parley is finished.'

'Parley?' Thuriel said incredulously. 'Have you not heard anything I've said? Unless you're here to accede to our terms, we have nothing to discuss.'

Before Zahariel could reply, the door behind the rebel soldiers banged open. Sar Daviel appeared, shoving his way roughly past the startled gunmen. Behind him came Lady Alera, her face pale and her expression fierce. She, in turn, was followed by a third figure, stoop-shouldered and lean and clad in a plain white surplice identical to Zahariel's own. The Librarian looked into the figure's seamed face and felt a shock like a thunderbolt course up his spine.

It was Master Remiel.

'THURIEL, YOU DAMNED fool,' snarled Sar Daviel. 'You've got no idea what you're playing at here. Tell your men to put away their guns right now, or I'll do it for them.' The old knight's scarred hands clenched into fists. He looked entirely ready to make good his threat.

Daviel's scornful tone brought Lord Thuriel out of his chair. 'Mind your tongue when you're speaking to your betters, you old dog,' he warned. 'Or you'll wind up sharing the same cell as this hyper-muscled monstrosity here.'

'Listen to me,' Sar Daviel said, his voice low and insistent. 'Zahariel is here under the terms of parley. Do you understand what that means?'

'Parley?' Thuriel said with a harsh laugh. 'I've had quite enough of your romantic notions of warfare, Daviel. Do you imagine that Luther has suddenly had a change of heart, and wants to negotiate with us? Use your head, man!' He pointed an accusing finger at Zahariel. 'For all we know, he called this parley to draw us into the open so he could kill us!'

'Shut up, Thuriel,' Lord Remiel snapped. The old master's voice was roughened with age, but still bore the same lash of authority he'd wielded at Aldurukh.

'Have your men put away their weapons before Zahariel decides that the parley is void and turns your paranoid suspicions into reality.'

The noble recoiled from the command as though he'd been slapped. The rebel gunmen wavered, casting uncertain glances between the rebel leaders as if unsure who to follow. When Thuriel didn't respond at once, Lady Alera wormed her way between the gunmen and pushed the muzzles of the plasma guns downward.

'Enough of this madness,' she declared. Then, to Zahariel, she said, 'I regret this misunderstanding has occurred, Sar Zahariel. Lord Thuriel and Lord Malchial acted rashly, and without the sanction of the rest of our leadership. In fact,' she continued, shooting an angry glance at the two noblemen, 'they conspired to delay the rest of us so that we couldn't interfere with their treachery.'

'Now, look here,' Malchial said, rising nervously from his chair. 'I never wanted any part of this. Lord Thuriel said–'

'We've heard more than enough of what Lord Thuriel has to say,' Remiel snapped. 'I advise the both of you to hold your tongue from this point forward. At the moment I'm of the opinion you're a bigger threat to our cause than Luther and his minions, and nothing in the terms of parley prevents me from having the both of you shot.'

Remiel's threat ended the confrontation at a stroke. The gunmen withdrew to stand by the doorway behind the rebel leaders, their weapons held at port arms. Malchial went pale and his mouth snapped shut at once. Thuriel held his tongue as well, though his body trembled with barely-contained rage.

Zahariel observed the entire exchange with outward calm, though inwardly his mind reeled at the implications of the scene playing out before him. It had been obvious from the start that the insurgents were very well-informed about Imperial strategy and tactics, but Luther and General Morten had assumed that deserters from the Jaeger regiments were the cause. The truth, Zahariel now realised, was far worse – and called into question many of their assumptions about the rebels and their motives.

'It was you all along,' Zahariel said, his heart sinking with the realization. 'How many years did you pretend to be our brother while you were laying the groundwork for this rebellion? When did you forsake your oaths to the primarch, master? Did it happen the day that Luther returned from the Crusade – or when Jonson passed you over and chose another to become Lord Cypher?'

'It was Jonson's treachery that brought us all to this,' Remiel said. The old master's voice was sharp as drawn steel. 'An oath born from deceit is no oath at all! His lies–'

'Save your breath, my lord,' Sar Daviel said, resting a hand on Remiel's arm. 'It won't do you any good.' The maimed knight let go of the old master and took a step towards Zahariel, his expression stern and unforgiving. 'You called for a parley, and in honour of the old ways we obliged you. What is it you want?'

With an effort, Zahariel tore his gaze away from Remiel and collected his thoughts. He'd rehearsed this conversation in his head a hundred times on the way to the arcology.

'I'm here because of what you said to Luther, just before you got on the shuttle back at Aldurukh.'

Sar Daviel's one good eye narrowed thoughtfully. He gave Zahriel a searching look, and then sudden comprehension dawned across his scarred face. 'You've seen something, haven't you?'

'What's happened?' Remiel said, a note of concern creeping into his voice.

Zahariel hesitated, knowing that he had reached the point of no return. Luther had forbidden him to discuss the matter with anyone, but if he didn't, Caliban was doomed. Slowly at first, then with gathering speed and determination, he told the rebel leaders what he'd found at Sigma Five-One-Seven.

When he was done, Zahariel studied the faces of each rebel leader in turn. Daviel and Master Remiel cast sidelong glances at one another, their expressions grim. Lady Alera and Lord Malchial were pale with shock, while Lord Thuriel's jaw tightened with building outrage.

'What is he talking about?' Thuriel demanded. 'What's this... this taint he keeps referring to?' He took a step towards the two older knights, his hands clenching into fists. 'How long have you been keeping this from us?'

Daviel glared forbiddingly at the angry noble. 'It's none of your concern, Thuriel,' he growled. 'Believe me. The less you know about this, the better.'

'And now you presume to tell me what I have a right to know? You're no better than the damned Imperials!' Thuriel turned to Lady Alera. 'I told you we couldn't trust them!' he snarled, pointing an accusing finger at the old knights. 'Who knows what other secrets they're hiding? For all we know, they might have been working with Luther all along!'

'Thuriel, will you please just shut up,' Lady Alera said, her voice trembling faintly. She pressed a hand to her forehead, and Zahariel could see that she was struggling to come to grips with what she'd been told. 'Can't you see what's at stake here?'

'Of course I can,' Thuriel snarled. 'In fact, I see things a great deal more clearly than you, Alera. I see that the Terrans aren't content with raping our world; now they're feeding our people to monsters. And these two old fools knew it, but kept it to themselves.'

'We knew nothing of the kind, you arrogant, self-centred dolt,' Daviel shot back. 'Master Remiel and I were protecting our people from monsters long before you were born, and don't you forget it.' He jabbed a gnarled finger at the ruined side of his face. 'You want to talk about monsters, boy, you show me the scars you earned fighting them. Otherwise, shut your damned mouth!'

'So that's it, eh? Just shut up and trust you? Like we trusted Luther, and Jonson, and all those vultures from the Administratum?' Thuriel shouted back. His right hand fell to the pistol holstered at his hip. 'Never again, Daviel! You hear me? Never again!'

The nobleman glared at Daviel for a long moment. The knight regarded Thuriel coldly, pointedly folding his arms in the face of the other man's threat. The rebel gunmen at the back of the room fingered their weapons nervously. Before the situation could escalate further, however, Lord Malchial leapt from his chair and gripped Thuriel's left arm.

'Leave it, cousin,' Malchial hissed fearfully. 'Nothing good can come of this.'

Thuriel gritted his teeth in consternation, weighing his options. Finally, he drew his hand away from his weapon.

'For once, Malchial, you may be right,' the nobleman said. Thuriel swept a haughty gaze over the knights, Lady Alera and Zahariel. 'We're finished, do you hear? You'll not get another coin from me to finance your little games of deception. I'll find another way to set our people free from the likes of Jonson and his ilk. See if I won't.' He turned and stormed from the room, with a nervous Malchial close behind.

'Damn that Malchial,' Sar Daviel said as the door slammed shut behind them. 'Another moment more and Thuriel would have done something foolish. Then we could have been rid of the both of them.'

Zahariel frowned. 'Was it wise to let them go?' he asked.

'You'd rather he were here, using up good air?' Alera said disgustedly. She waved her hand in dismissal. 'Thuriel provides us with money and outrage, and not much else. He doesn't have any real support inside the movement. Let him go. We've got much more important things to worry about.'

Sar Daviel looked to Remiel. 'Things are far worse than we feared,' he said gravely.

Remiel nodded, but he continued to stare searchingly at Zahariel. 'Why have you told us this?' he asked his old pupil.

'Because we're running out of time,' Zahariel replied. 'We've got to stop the Terrans before they unleash their master ritual, but if we send in a major force of Astartes to search for them we risk drawing the attention of the Administratum.'

'Who wouldn't hesitate to condemn the planet – and its people – if they learned the truth,' Remiel concluded.

'Condemn?' Alera said. 'What does that mean?'

'The Imperium views warp taint as... a cancer, if you will. A tumour on the human soul,' Remiel said. 'Not without reason, of course. No sane person wants to see a return of Old Night. But the problem here is that Caliban's taint runs deeper than just a handful of debased individuals; it permeates the very bedrock of the world.'

'Then how does one go about curing it?' she said, her voice rising with exasperation.

The old master sighed. 'With fire. What else?' He eyed Zahariel coldly. 'The Imperium would relocate the Legion and as many of its loyal servants as it could. Perhaps a few hundred thousand could be saved. The rest...'

'That's why this must be kept secret,' Zahariel said calmly. His eyes never left Remiel's.

The old master's eyebrows rose. 'That sounds like something very close to rebellion, young Zahariel.'

The Librarian shook his head. 'Luther and I swore an oath to protect the people of Caliban, long before the coming of the Emperor,' he replied. 'As did you.'

Sar Daviel nodded slowly. 'All right,' he said. 'What do you want from us?'

'A truce,' Zahariel said simply. 'Help us find the Terrans quickly and quietly, and we'll send in a kill-team to eliminate them.'

Alera shook her head. 'I don't think so,' she said. 'Leave these sorcerers to us. We can take care of them.'

'Would that were so, Lady Alera,' Remiel said heavily. 'But Zahariel is right. Our people are no match for these creatures. This is a task for the Astartes.'

'But we don't even know for certain that these sorcerers are here,' Alera protested. 'A truce at this point benefits the Imperials, not us! Their control of the arcology is balanced on a knife edge; if we give them time to catch their breath, bring in more reinforcements...' the noblewoman's voice trailed away as she watched a wordless exchange pass between Remiel and Sar Daviel.

'There's something else, isn't there?' she asked.

Daviel nodded. 'We didn't tell you before for reasons of security,' he said gravely. 'But we've lost contact with a number of our sub-level cells over the last two weeks.'

'How many cells?' Alera demanded.

'Fourteen,' Remiel answered. 'Possibly as many as sixteen. Two others missed their last scheduled report this morning, but that could be the result of equipment failure.'

The news sent a jolt down Zahariel's spine. 'How many cells do you have in the sub-levels?'

Daviel shifted uncomfortably. 'A significant number,' he said. 'The Jaegers don't have the manpower to penetrate much beyond sub-level two, so we keep our combat teams on the lowest sub-levels between raids.'

'How many men have you lost so far?' Zahariel pressed. 'Tell me!'

'One hundred and thirty-two,' the maimed knight answered. 'All of them well-trained and well-equipped, and all of them lost without so much as a single vox transmission. Frankly, we were starting to suspect that you'd sent Astartes teams into the sub-levels to root us out.'

Zahariel shook his head. 'It's begun,' he said. 'They're gathering bodies, just like they did at Sigma Five-One-Seven.'

Alera's face twisted in a bitter grimace. 'As though the Terrans would have a hard time finding corpses in that charnel house.'

'Charnel house?' Zahariel echoed. 'What do you mean?'

Lady Alera stared open-mouthed at the Astartes. 'Don't pretend you don't know,' she said, her eyes blazing angrily.

Zahariel held up a hand. 'On my honour, lady, I have no idea what you're talking about.'

'Then who is responsible for the atrocities committed in your name?' she said coldly. 'Five million people, crammed into three levels built to hold a quarter of that number. No power, intermittent supplies of food and water, no functioning sanitation... What did you think was going to happen? People are dying by the hundreds every day. The bodies are tossed down maintenance shafts or piled in lifts and sent to the lower levels, so the survivors don't have to live among the corpses.'

The news stunned Zahariel. 'This wasn't reported back to us at Aldurukh,' he said, his voice choked with outrage. 'Is there any way to know how many have died?'

Remiel shook his head. 'Tens of thousands, son. Perhaps more.'

Zahariel nodded thoughtfully. 'The Terrans knew. That's why they returned to the arcology.' He looked to Remiel. 'The incident at Sigma Five-One-Seven was a field test,' he said, like a pupil solving a problem for his tutor. 'They needed to refine the ritual, test its effects on a smaller scale before unleashing it here.' An image came to him, of an army of animated bodies shambling and crawling up out of the depths to slaughter the millions penned like sheep in the sub-levels above.

'There's no time to waste,' he said. 'If there's another outbreak of violence here, the Terrans will have all the psychic energy they need to begin a large-scale ritual. We've got to find them before it's too late.' Zahariel stepped forward, holding out his empty hand to the rebels. 'Will you agree to the truce?'

Alera and Sar Daviel looked to Remiel. The old master stared at Zahariel's open hand for a long moment, a tormented look on his face. Finally, he straightened and looked his former student in the eye.

'For the pact to be binding, it must be sworn by both leaders,' he said sternly. 'If Luther gives me his hand, then I shall take it. Until then, we can have no truce between us.'

'Then come back with me to Aldurukh,' Zahariel said, his voice taut. 'We can be back at the fortress in two hours.'

Remiel's eyes narrowed. 'Are you so certain he will agree to this?'

'Of course,' Zahariel replied, putting more sincerity into his voice than he actually felt. 'Do you imagine Caliban's greatest living knight would hold his honour so cheaply?'

If Remiel sensed the doubt in Zahariel's heart he did not let it show. 'Very well,' he said with a curt nod. 'Sar Daviel will join us to help coordinate our forces.' He turned to Lady Alera. 'Alert our remaining cells and organise a search of the sub-levels at once. If you locate the Terrans, do not attempt to engage them. Do you understand?'

Alera nodded. On impulse, she reached out and laid her hands on Remiel's own. 'Are you sure of this?' she asked. 'You swore you'd never return to the fortress. You said they'd betrayed everything you believed in. How can you trust them now?'

Remiel sighed. 'This isn't about trust,' he said to her. 'It's about honour, and a last chance at redemption. I owe it to them, Alera. I owe it to myself.' He gently pushed her hands away.

'Now go. Zahariel is right. We haven't much time.' He smiled. 'I will return with the knights of Caliban at my back, or I will not return at all.'

SEVENTEEN

Fire from the Sky

Diamat
In the 200th year of the Emperor's Great Crusade

Las-bolts hissed past Nemiel as he plunged down onto Magos Archoi and the rebel soldiers. His bolt pistol thundered, and two of the officers collapsed with gaping wounds blown in their chests. Archoi fell back from the Redemptor's attack, screeching in binaric, and his acolytes rushed forward, drawing high-powered laspistols from their belts.

Nemiel struck down another of the rebels with a crackling swipe of his crozius. A las-bolt struck the side of his helmet like a hammerblow, causing his visual displays to waver, and a warning icon told him that the helm's integrity had been compromised. He shot the officer point-blank, blowing him off his feet – and then felt a hail of blows as the acolytes unleashed a volley of pistol shots into his chest.

The acolytes were blurs of motion, their muscles undoubtedly stoked by combat drugs and adrenal boosters. Nemiel felt a half-dozen bolts pummel his breastplate, then a flash of searing pain over his primary heart. For a moment his vision threatened to grey out as his body fought to stave off the effects of shock, then abruptly the pain vanished and his mind cleared with a cold rush as his suit dumped pain blockers and stimulants into his bloodstream.

A boltgun let off a rapid burst over Nemiel's shoulder and one of the acolytes fell in a spray of blood and fluids. The Redemptor shot the remaining acolyte twice, and finished him off with a backhanded blow of his crozius. He was leaping forward before the traitor's body had hit the floor, racing down the narrow aisle after the fleeing form of Magos Archoi.

Brother-Sergeant Kohl ran alongside Nemiel from high atop the siege gun's hull, firing shots from his bolt pistol at every tech-adept who got in his path. Behind Nemiel, Marthes crouched atop the vehicle and fired another blast up at the skitarii who were firing down from the gantry-way they had just vacated. The catwalk blew apart in a storm of molten fragments, plunging the survivors to the permacrete floor two storeys below. Techmarine Askelon landed heavily on the permacrete floor, pushing onward despite his suit's heavily damaged systems. Vardus and Ephrial brought up the rear, cutting down any soldier or tech-adept who tried to circle behind the squad.

Nemiel bore down on the magos like a Calibanite Lion, his lips pulling back in a feral snarl. If it was the last thing he did, he was going to make sure the traitor felt the Emperor's justice. Behind and above him, he heard Kohl shout a warning just as the Praetorians charged at him from the gap between two of the parked siege guns.

The shout saved his life. Nemiel turned towards the sound and ducked low, barely avoiding a swinging power claw that would have torn his head off. A second Praetorian lunged at him, scoring a deep gouge across his hip with a glowing power knife. Nemiel brought his crozius down on the skitarii's knife hand, smashing the weapon from the warrior's grip, and pumped three rounds into the Praetorian's chest. The warrior staggered as the rounds punched through his armour, but his chemically-charged nervous system kept him upright.

There were four of the hulking, gene-modded warriors: the one with the power claw reached for Nemiel's gun arm, while the second Praetorian brought his weapon systems to bear as he tried to circle around the Redemptor's flank. The remaining pair of skitarii were stymied by Brother-Sergeant Kohl, who leapt down onto the Praetorians with a furious shout. His power sword slashed down in a glowing arc, slicing through one warrior's weapon arm with a shower of sparks and spurting fluids.

The Praetorian circling to Nemiel's right went down in a blaze of bolt pistol fire from Techmarine Askelon; seeing his opportunity, the Redemptor pivoted on his left heel and smashed his crozius into the other skitarii's head. The warrior died just as his claw snapped shut on Nemiel's forearm, leaving three deep, bubbling gouges on the black vambrace before collapsing to the ground.

Kohl despatched the wounded Praetorian in front of him with a brutal cut that sliced open his armoured torso. The last of the skitarii raised his weapon-arm and took aim at the sergeant, only to die as Nemiel put three bolt pistol rounds into his back at point-blank range.

Nemiel whirled, looking for the traitor magos, but Archoi was nowhere to be found. The Praetorians had accomplished their goal, buying time for the traitor to escape with their lives. The surviving tech-adepts had fled as well, scattering like vermin down the narrow lanes on the floor of the assembly building. The Redemptor started to pursue them, but Brother-Sergeant Kohl called for him to stop.

'We don't have time to chase rabbits,' Kohl said as las-bolts spat down at them from the gangway. 'We've got to get a warning back to our brothers and to the Dragoons.'

Vardus, Ephrial and Askelon unleashed a blistering volley up at the skitarii, killing several and forcing the rest to withdraw. Nemiel wavered, drawn by the siren song of vengeance, but reason and training ultimately won out over emotion. 'You're right, brother,' he said to the sergeant. 'We've just forced Archoi's hand; he'll have to order his forces into action at once. Askelon!' he called, turning to the Techmarine. 'What's the quickest way out of here? We haven't got a moment to lose!'

In fact, they were already ten minutes too late.

ARCHOI'S PLAN HAD been a hasty one, devised on the spur of the moment as he stood over the bullet-riddled body of his former master Vertullus and received word that, at the absolute last moment, an unknown force of Astartes had arrived in orbit to save the beleaguered forge world. His takeover was already well underway, with loyal units of tech-adepts and skitarii murdering Vertullus's loyal supporters and herding the rest into the old shelters situated deep beneath the manufactories at the base of the great volcano. When the admiral in charge of the Warmaster's fleet informed him that they would have to withdraw, Archoi promised him that when they returned to Diamat, he and his people would be ready. It was that, or face certain execution once that bastard Kulik caught wind of his crimes. As the last of the rebel ships were pulling out of vox range, the magos fired off a compressed burst of binaric that outlined his scheme. The crucial element that the whole plan hinged on was a certain date and an approximate time, two and a half weeks away. Now that time had arrived, and Archoi had to trust that the Warmaster would not be late.

Across the southern sector of the forge complex, down to the southern gateway and across the fortified grey zone, each of the skitarii embedded with the defence forces received a coded burst transmission. Sleeping soldiers awoke and quietly gathered up their weapons, while those on sentry duty drew knives or silenced weapons and turned them on their watchmates. Within minutes, gunfire crackled in the darkness as the Tech-Guard ambushed their erstwhile comrades.

At the warehouse barracks of the Astartes ground force, most of the Dark Angels were still wide awake, tending their weapons and engaging in close-combat drills in preparation for the battles ahead. The Praetorians in their midst stiffened as the signal touched off implanted combat protocols and flooded their bloodstreams with a lethal brew of combat drugs. From one heartbeat to the next, the skitarii were transformed into berserk killing machines; the virulence of the drugs were so great that within fifteen minutes it would begin to erode their muscle tissue – literally eating them alive. Until that point, however, they were immune to all but the most catastrophic injuries. Readying their weapon implants and close-combat attachments, the Praetorians hurled themselves at the unsuspecting Astartes, and the blood began to flow.

THE FIRST INDICATION of danger in orbit was the sudden storm of vox jamming that effectively isolated each of Jonson's ships. The resupply operations had ceased for the day, but there were still several hundred tech-adepts and servitors from the forge hard at work on the *Iron Duke*, the strike cruiser *Amadis* and the *Invincible Reason*. Several of the warships, notably the heavy cruisers *Flamberge* and *Duke Infernus*, as well as the escort ships of the scout group, all went to battle stations, while the others initially believed that the vox failure was an accident caused by the current repairs.

As the captains of the battle group tried to sort out the sudden loss of communications and attempted to regain contact with the flagship, they were distracted from the threat that was gliding towards them out of the darkness. A small but powerful fleet, assembled in haste with whatever forces were at hand and quickly despatched to Diamat, was now stalking towards the planet with their engines idling and their surveyors silent.

The ships of the scout force detected the oncoming enemy ships first. Signalling to one another in basic code using their running lights, the light cruisers and their attendant destroyers flared their thrusters and broke orbit, their surveyors sweeping the void in case the jamming was the precursor to an enemy attack. They detected the eight ships of the enemy force just a few minutes later.

Signal lights flashed between the Imperial ships: Form line and prepare to launch torpedoes. With remarkable skill and precision the small ships raced forwards, increasing to attack speed. Below decks, servitors and torpedomen struggled to load the tubes, while on the bridge the Ordnance Officer input course and speed into the target solutions for the ship's weapons.

Within five minutes the vessels signalled that they were ready to launch. As the scout force entered optimal torpedo range the signal was given: For the Emperor – launch all torpedoes.

Orders were passed to the torpedo deck. The senior torpedomen checked their firing data and turned their launch keys.

Less than half a second later, they were dead.

As each torpedo received the electronic signal to launch, its plasma reactor overloaded, detonating its warhead inside the tube. The rakish bows of the sleek destroyers vaporised in expanding balls of plasma, transforming them into burning, broken hulks. The light cruisers fared only slightly better, their torpedo decks destroyed and fires burning out of control on their lower decks, the small squadron had no choice but to break off and try to save their ships.

The explosions signalled to the rebels that their stealthy approach was at an end. Thrusters ignited, surging to full power; void shields crackled into existence, forming shimmering spheres around their vessels like ephemeral soap bubbles before firming up and fading from view. Surveyors blazed to life, painting the surprised Imperial ships with invisible energies and feeding targeting data back to the rebel gunnery officers.

Eight ships: three cruisers, two heavy cruisers and three grand cruisers – bore down on the battered Imperial ships. Cut off from one another, uncertain if their own ammunition had been rigged to explode by the treacherous forge, the Imperials braced themselves for the rebel onslaught.

DAWN WAS BREAKING as Nemiel emerged from the Titan assembly building. He heard the distant rattle of gunfire to the south and knew that they had run out of time. All he and his squad could do now was rush to the aid of their fellow Astartes and kill as many of the enemy as they could. 'Forward!' he shouted to his squad. 'Let no one stand in our way!'

The Astartes raced down the access road towards the southern edge of the foundry sector, their weapons held ready as they searched for threats. The rumble of petrochem engines echoed amongst the buildings to the southeast, but there was no way to tell for certain where the sounds were coming from. It was most likely a mechanised patrol of skitarii, Nemiel thought, and kept part of his attention focused that way in the event they showed themselves.

High-intensity lasguns barked behind them. Brother Vardus was struck in the back by a powerful las-bolt that caused him to fall onto one knee. Marthes held his meltagun in his left hand and bent down, grabbing Vardus's upper arm and pulling him to his feet. Brother Ephrial turned and fired a long burst back the way they'd come, eliciting a scream of pain from one of their pursuers.

Up ahead, the engine sounds roared into angry life. 'Marthes!' Nemiel said, beckoning to the meltagunner.

Just then, a Testudo APC rumbled into the access road from a side lane and lurched to a halt. Its turret autocannon slewed about and spat a stream of high-velocity shells at the running Astartes. The gunner's aim was poor and he overshot the mark, sending the shells screaming over their heads, but Nemiel could see the barrel dropping as the man adjusted his aim. Skitarii in carapace armour came around the corner as well, dropping to their bellies and opening fire on the Dark Angels.

Brother Marthes ran ahead of the rest of the squad and took aim with his meltagun. A high-power las-bolt struck him in the left pauldon and left a burn across the thick ceramite. Another shot clipped him in the leg, causing sparks to flare from his knee joint. The APC gunner, apparently realising the danger, adjusted his aim again and fired a burst of shells at Marthes just as he hit the meltagun's trigger. The blast cut into the vehicle's side like a power knife and detonated its fuel cells, hurling a ball of fire high into the overcast sky.

Nemiel saw Marthes stagger as two of the autocannon's explosive shells struck him in the chest. There was a double flash, coming so close together that the sound of the blasts merged into a single loud thunderclap. The Astartes staggered forward a few steps more, then fell forward onto his face. His status indicator in Nemiel's helmet display went abruptly black.

The skitarii scrambled to their feet, their armour smouldering from the heat of the vehicle's flames. Nemiel and the others raked them with bolter fire, killing several and forcing the others to retreat. As Kohl reached Marthes, he knelt and took the meltagun from the warrior's hands and tossed it to Ephrial, then laid a parting hand on the dead warrior's shoulder before rising to his feet and sprinting after the squad.

They put the burning hulk of the APC between themselves and their pursuers, then cut to the left down a side-lane to hopefully throw them off a bit further. As they came around the corner and turned south again, Askelon pointed to the sky. 'Look!' he said breathlessly.

Nemiel looked skyward to see a shower of blazing meteors plunging through the clouds in the direction of the coast. Many burned out as they fell, carving bright trails of green and orange across the sky, while several larger pieces continued to fall until they disappeared over the horizon. It was an awe-inspiring sight, but one that filled Nemiel with dread. He'd seen such things many times before, at war-torn worlds like Barrakan and Leantris. Those meteors had been pieces of a starship that had been blown up in high orbit. The attack on Diamat had begun.

Las-bolts snapped and howled through the air from the end of the access road. One hit Kohl in the chest, dispersing harmlessly against his breastplate. The squad returned fire, and a pair of skitarii broke cover and retreated back around the corner of a low-slung building.

'That was an observation team!' Nemiel warned his squadmates. 'We'll be coming up on their outer perimeter in another minute. Ephrial, get ready with that meltagun!'

As they approached the end of the access road, Nemiel summoned up the layout of the perimeter fortifications in his memory. Just ahead and to the right was a lascannon post, with a heavy stubber post further west. Just ahead and to the left was another heavy stubber. He waved Ephrial to the corner of the furthest building to the right, while he angled off to the left.

Nemiel put his back to the wall of the manufactory and glanced across the road at Ephrial. He battle-signed for the Astartes to hit the target to his right. Ephrial nodded, and without hesitation he whirled around the corner and fired a shot with the melta-gun. There was an immediate, crackling boom as the lascannon's power supply detonated, followed by the screams of its maimed and dying crew.

Immediately the heavy stubber to Nemiel's left opened fire, spitting a long burst of tracer rounds at Ephrial's back. He spun around the corner and levelled his bolt pistol at the four men in the sandbagged emplacement just five metres away. The Redemptor fired four quick shots, and the skitarii slumped to the ground.

Nemiel turned back to the squad and waved them forward. They left the foundry sector and headed quickly for the sheltering warehouses further south, taking fire from two more heavy stubber emplacements as they went. Vardus was limping from an unlucky hit in his leg. Askelon was driving himself onward with ruthless determination, but Nemiel could tell that he was fighting the weight of his own armour, and was nearing the point of exhaustion. The Redemptor ran on, dropping the empty magazine from his bolt pistol and slamming in a fresh one.

He reckoned they were four-and-a-half kilometres from the warehouse barracks of the ground force. Nemiel could still hear the sounds of bolter fire up ahead, so he knew at least some of his brothers were still fighting. Several times he tried to call out over the vox, but the jamming was still underway. Pillars of black smoke were rising from more than a dozen points out beyond the forge's curtain wall, and he feared the worst for Kulik's brave Dragoons.

As they drew closer to the barracks, Nemiel suddenly heard a flurry of lasgun and stubber fire, answered by the snarl of an assault cannon. It was Brother Titus, he realised; the Dreadnought had been standing watch outside 2nd Company's barracks when they'd left on their reconnaissance mission earlier that night. On impulse, he led the squad in that direction, listening as the sounds of battle increased.

By the time they drew within sight of the warehouse, a pitched battle was raging on the street outside. They found Brother Titus guarding the warehouse's side entrance from what amounted to a platoon of skitarii. Dozens of broken bodies lay around the Dreadnought's wide feet, denoting a failed assault by the enemy. Scores more of the Tech-Guard were sprawled on the permacrete, torn apart by the Dreadnought's fearsome cannon. Still more were arriving from the direction of the southern gateway, however, taking up firing positions and unleashing a storm of fire against Titus's front armour.

Nemiel brought the squad to a halt. 'It's only a matter of time before those Tech-Guard bring up a missile launcher or a lascannon and destroy Titus,' he said. 'We're going to swing around and hit them from the rear. Askelon, can you still keep up?'

The Techmarine's armoured shoulders were heaving after the terrible exertions of the run. His bloodied face was pale, but he looked up at Nemiel and smiled. 'Brother-Sergeant Kohl's been saying I need to get more exercise,' he said breathlessly. 'Don't worry about me.'

'He's just worried about having to carry your dead weight around,' Kohl growled. 'Now let's get moving.'

The squad set off to the northwest, moving past a pair of warehouse buildings before cutting south again. They listened to the sounds of battle raging off to their left, gauging their position relative to the enemy and moving five hundred metres behind them. Then they cut back east, gathering speed as they prepared to swing around and strike the enemy from behind.

They'd run for only a few hundred metres when just ahead they saw a platoon of skitarii jog into view, dragging four lascannons mounted on wheeled gun carriages. They saw the Astartes at almost the same instant; with three hundred metres between them, the enemy troops hurriedly dropped the trails on the four guns and began to frantically wheel them around to bear on the squad.

'Charge!' Nemiel cried, but the rest of squad hardly needed prompting. They broke into a full run, firing their bolters as they went.

Nemiel watched the mass-reactive shells strike the armoured splinter plates of the gun carriages and ricochet harmlessly away. The crews worked quickly and with remarkable precision, connecting the weapons to their power units and energising the guns in the space of seconds. If they had been preparing to fire on human troops, it might have been enough, but the Astartes reached the enemy with seconds to spare.

They leapt up and over the lascannons' splinter shields and came down among the shocked gun crews. Nemiel shot two of them point-blank, then slew two more with his crozius. Brother-Sergeant Kohl and Brother Ephrial killed almost a dozen more before the rest of the platoon broke and fled back the way they'd come.

Nemiel paused amid the carnage, his autosenses detecting more sounds of activity to the south as still more enemy troops headed their way. He was about to order Askelon to disable the abandoned lascannons when the heavens split and trails of fire descended on the forge from on high.

These were no simple meteors, falling in thin streaks of light before vanishing into oblivion. Nemiel counted eight separate streaks of smoke and flame, plunging down in a steep arc and converging on a common point: the heart of the forge complex, some thirty kilometres away. When they struck, the entire northern horizon blazed with terrible, white light.

Nemiel had witnessed more than one orbital bombardment in his time, but those had been blazing trails of lance fire that carved across the ground like a burning blade, or salvoes of poorly-aimed macro cannon fire that saturated a target area with huge shells. He'd never been close enough to experience the fury of a barrage of bombardment cannons, and wasn't prepared for what followed.

The eight shells struck the target area more or less simultaneously, their magma warheads detonating with the heat and force of a fusion bomb. His onboard systems registered the overpressure from the blast and had just enough time to yell, 'Get down!' before the blast wave hit.

He dropped to the ground and pressed his helmet to the permacrete as a roaring wall of superheated air howled over him. His temperature sensors spiked, pushing into the red zone, and the force of the wind lifted him off the ground and tossed him like a toy down the narrow lane. The thunder of the blast was something he felt through his armour, reverberating down into his bones. His autosenses overloaded and shut down at once to prevent permanent damage.

It was over in a matter of moments. One second the entire world felt as though it were coming apart at the seams, and the next, everything was almost eerily silent. Nemiel lay on his back, trying to regain his bearings. Icons blinked on his helmet display, informing him that his autosensors and vox-unit were resetting. As his vision cleared, he saw tendrils of smoke rising from his scorched armour.

Slowly and carefully, he sat upright. There was smoke everywhere, rising from warehouses that had been set aflame by the blast wave. The four abandoned lascannons were gone; he looked about and found one smashed to pieces against the side of a building, but the rest had simply disappeared.

A squeal of static in his ears made him start as his vox-bead came back online. He was about to silence it again when he heard words coalesce out of the interference.

'Battle Force Alpha, this is Leonis!' spoke a familiar voice, hazy and hashed out by atmospheric ionization. 'Activate your teleport beacons and stand by!'

Nemiel scrambled to his feet. Leonis was the primarch's personal callsign. He looked about the smoke-stained road and saw Brother-Sergeant Kohl climbing to his feet, along with Vardus and Ephrial. 'Where is Brother Askelon?' he called. 'We've got to get back to the warehouses immediately!'

'Over here,' a voice answered weakly from down the side-lane where they'd originally come. Nemiel and Kohl rushed to the corner to see Askelon slowly pushing himself upright. His unprotected head had been badly burned by the blast, but somehow the Techmarine was still able to move.

They helped Askelon to his feet. He looked over at Kohl and tried to grin, his lips cracking. 'Looks like you'll have to carry me after all,' he gasped.

Kohl grabbed the Techmarine's arm and draped it over his shoulder, then took hold of Askelon's waist with his left hand. 'I could carry two of you without breaking a sweat,' the sergeant growled. 'You just keep an eye out for more of those damned skitarii, and let me do the rest.'

Nemiel grabbed Askelon's other arm and together they helped the Techmarine along. He could hear signals going back and forth across the Battle Force command channel, so he knew that at least some of the Dark Angels had survived Archoi's deadly ambush. He hoped there was an Apothecary still alive, for Askelon's sake.

They linked up with the rest of the squad and headed back towards the barracks buildings as quickly as they could. It was only then that Nemiel fully saw the devastation that the bombardment had wrought.

An enormous column of ash and smoke rose into the sky off to the north, where the volcano and the forge's centre used to be. The rising sun tinged the climbing column of debris in shades of blood red and fiery orange, whilst closer to the ground Nemiel could see thin veins of pulsing orange, tracks of real magma flowing like blood from the volcano's shattered flanks. Fires blazed out of control from horizon to horizon, consuming the shattered husks of wrecked buildings in a vast swathe surrounding the epicentre of the blast. For all intents and purposes, the forge complex had been destroyed.

It took more than half an hour to cover the five hundred metres back to the warehouses. They saw the towering form of Brother Titus first. His armour had been scorched – in some places the paint had been stripped away down to the bare metal – but he seemed otherwise undamaged. The warehouses themselves were ablaze, and the road was full of

Astartes. A disturbingly long line of dead battle brothers were stretched out along the roadway to their left; the bodies were being tended to by one of the ground force's two Apothecaries, collecting the gene-seed for the future of the Legion. The second Apothecary was tending to an even larger number of wounded Dark Angels who were formed into small groups according to their parent squads on the right side of the roadway.

In the centre of the crowd stood the company commanders and senior squad leaders, gathered beneath the shadow of the great Dreadnought. In their midst stood a towering figure in gleaming armour, his head bare and his expression one of cold, righteous rage. Nemiel left Askelon in Brother-Sergeant Kohl's care and hurried over to join the primarch.

Lion El'Jonson was receiving the reports of the company commanders when Nemiel arrived. Jonson caught the Redemptor's eye and but said nothing until the two captains had finished tallying their dead and wounded. As near as Nemiel could determine, some thirty of the Astartes had been killed in the ambush and twice as many others seriously wounded before the last of the frenzied Praetorians had been killed. The sight of so many dead brothers filled him with grief and a cold, fathomless rage.

The primarch listened gravely to the captains' reports and then turned to Nemiel. 'We've a grim start to the day, Brother-Redemptor,' Jonson said. 'I hope you bring us better news.'

Without preamble, Nemiel delivered his report. He told Jonson everything they'd found during the night, from the site of Vertullus's likely murder to the discovery of the great siege guns at the Titan foundry and Archoi's foul treachery.

'I surmised as much when most of our scouts were destroyed by their own brand-new torpedoes,' Jonson said. He turned and glanced back at the towering plume of ash and smoke to the north. 'When we traced the source of the vox jamming, it made Archoi's duplicity all too clear.'

'The Lords of Mars will be furious at the loss of such a venerable forge,' Nemiel said forebodingly.

Jonson turned back to the Redemptor, his green eyes blazing. 'Such is the fate of all traitors!' he snapped. The force of his anger was like a physical blow, as though he'd reached over and slapped Nemiel across the face. 'So Horus and the rest of his ilk will learn in due time.'

'We saw the debris of a ship falling to earth,' Nemiel ventured more carefully. 'I take it the rebels have returned.'

The primarch drew in a deep breath and sought to master his humours. He nodded. 'A much smaller force, this time, but sufficient to their needs,' he said tersely. 'Horus moved much more quickly than I expected and sent out an ad hoc force not too dissimilar from ours. We would have been hard pressed to defeat them as it was, but Archoi's treachery proved to be our undoing. All of our destroyers were lost, along with both grand cruisers and the strike cruiser *Adzikel*. After bombarding the forge and eliminating the source of the jamming, I ordered the rest of the battle group to withdraw to the edges of the system and then teleported myself down to join you.'

The news of the battle group's defeat sent a stir through the stoic Astartes. Nemiel gripped his crozius and straightened, remembering his duties to the Legion. 'While we live, we fight, my lord,' he said, his voice defiant. 'Though the storm rages and the foe gathers about us, we are unmoved. Let them come: we are the warriors of the First Legion, and we have never known defeat!'

Shouts of agreement rose from the assembled Dark Angels. Jonson smiled. 'Well said, Brother-Redemptor,' he replied. 'You are right. We've suffered some terrible blows, but the battle isn't over yet.'

'What would you have of us, my lord?' Nemiel asked.

Jonson cast his eyes to the north, towards the distant bulk of the assembly building. 'We fall back to the foundry,' he said. 'So long as we possess Horus's siege guns, the rebels won't risk an orbital bombardment.' When he turned back to the Astartes, his face was grim.

'Once we're in position, we need to fortify the sector as best we can, and prepare for the fight of our lives. Unless I'm very much mistaken, the Sons of Horus will be here soon.'

EIGHTEEN

A Thorn in the Mind

Caliban
In the 200th year of the Emperor's Great Crusade

The timbre of the shuttle's thrusters deepened as they made a near-ballistic descent towards Aldurukh, swelling from an angry whine to a thunderous roar as they plummeted from the stratosphere into the denser air at sea level. The shuttle's airframe trembled as the pilot pushed the craft to its limits; Zahariel had told him to fly to the fortress as though his life depended on it, and he was taking the Astartes at his word. The Librarian felt the shuddering of the craft in his bones and had to raise his powerful voice to be heard over the noise.

'General Morten, this is a direct order,' he yelled into his vox-bead. 'Unseal the hab levels at the Northwilds arcology and redistribute the populace through the upper levels.'

The Terran general's reply was faint and washed with static, but there was no mistaking the exasperation in his voice. 'Sir, I believe I explained this before. The security situation–'

'I'm well aware of the security situation,' Zahariel snapped. He glanced across the passenger compartment at Master Remiel and Sar Daviel, who were both pretending not to listen to the tense exchange. 'The cordon is only making things worse. You've got to get those people out of there before you have a catastrophe on your hands.'

'But sir, the logistics of relocating five million people–'

'Will require a great deal of effort and coordination on our part,' Zahariel cut in. 'So I expect you and your staff to give the matter your complete and immediate attention. Make it happen, general. I don't care what it takes.' Zahariel broke the connection without giving Morten a chance to reply. He wasn't interested in arguing the matter, and he had no intention of explaining his reasons over vox.

Daviel turned away from the viewport at his left and stared questioningly at Zahariel. 'Do you think he'll do it?' the maimed knight asked.

The Librarian sighed. 'Not all Terrans are corrupt devils, Sar Daviel. Morten is a good soldier. He'll follow orders.'

Daviel's scarred face twisted into a scowl, but he offered no reply. Zahariel studied the scarred knight for a moment.

'How long have you known?' he asked.

Sar Daviel narrowed his one good eye. 'Known what?'

'About Caliban. About the taint.'

Daviel's fierce expression grew haunted. 'Ah. That.' He rubbed his chin with one scarred hand. 'A long time. Too long, perhaps.' The knight shook his head. 'At first, I thought I must be going mad. After all, you'd seen the same things I had, and never seemed to think anything of it.'

Zahariel straightened in his chair. 'What things?' he asked, feeling the skin prickle on the back of his neck. 'What are you talking about?'

Daviel frowned in consternation. 'Why, the library, of course.' He replied. 'At the fortress of the Knights of Lupus. Surely you remember.' His one eye grew unfocused, as though he were recalling the details of a nightmare. 'All those books. Those terrible, terrible books...'

The Librarian felt his skin grow cold. 'How could you have seen the library, Daviel?' he asked him. 'I saw you wounded in the castle courtyard.'

Daviel's gaze fell. 'So I was,' he said quietly. 'I was raving with fever for days afterward. The chirurgeons feared to move me in the state I was in, so I and a few other wounded men were left behind when the army returned to Aldurukh.'

The old knight fell silent for a moment as the memories welled up inside him. He stared at his hands, curled like claws in his lap. 'Later, when we could get up and hobble about for a few hours at a time, they tried to find jobs for us to do, to keep our spirits up. So they put some of us to work in that library, crating everything up to be carried back home.'

Daviel sighed. 'They rotated us in shifts, so we were only up there a few hours at a time, and we had strict orders not to open any of the books.' He smiled ruefully. 'The chirurgeons said they didn't want us to exert our minds unduly in our weakened state.'

'But you didn't listen.'

'No, I didn't,' Daviel said heavily. 'I and another knight succumbed to our curiosity. We pored through some of the oldest books as we readied them for packing. Towards the end, we spent more time reading than working, to tell the truth.'

'What was in the books?' Zahariel pressed.

'History. Literature. Art and philosophy. There were books on science, and medicine, and... forbidden things. Ancient, occult tomes, many of them written by hand.' He shook his head. 'I couldn't understand most of it, but it was clear that the Knights of Lupus had been studying the great beasts – and the Northwilds itself – for centuries. They knew about the taint, though they didn't fully understand it. They seemed to believe it was a force that could be summoned and controlled. I saw grimoires that purported to contain rituals for that very purpose.'

His voice trailed away, and his face paled at the recollections. Zahariel watched him raise a hand to his ruined cheek, as though the old wound pained him once more. After a moment, the knight gave a shudder and shook his head roughly, as though waking from a vivid dream. He blinked his eyes a few times and focused on the Astartes once more.

'Afterward, once the books were crated away and we were allowed to make the journey home, we tried to forget the things we'd seen.' He smiled faintly. 'Strange, of all the horrors we witnessed at that place, it was the memories of those books that haunted us most of all. We would talk about them sometimes, late into the night, trying to understand what it all meant. I believed that they heralded the next stage of our crusade; that once the great beasts had been destroyed, Jonson would dedicate our Order to driving the taint from Caliban once and for all.'

Daviel's face turned solemn. 'Then the Emperor came, and everything changed. We traded one crusade for another, and I couldn't understand why. If what was in those books was true, then Caliban was still in terrible danger. That, more than anything else, was why I left.'

'Why?' Zahariel asked.

Daviel paused, struggling to find a way to put his thoughts into words. His hand reached up to absently rub his scarred temple.

'I had to know the truth,' he said at last. 'The books had vanished, but the memories of what I saw stuck with me, like... like a thorn in the mind. I tried to tell myself that they were just fables – peasant myths, like the Watchers in the Woods – but guilt ate at me day and night. Because if the taint was real, the great beasts would just rise again, and everything we'd suffered would be in vain.' The old knight sighed. 'So I left the Order and embarked on one last quest – to find the surviving members of the Knights of Lupus.'

Zahariel blinked in surprise. 'But there were no survivors,' he said. 'Lord Sartana had summoned the entire order back to their fortress in the Northwilds. They died to a man in the final assault.'

'So we were led to believe,' Daviel replied. 'Lord Sartana sent out the call, to be sure, but the Knights of Lupus were famous for sending their knights out to the farthest-flung parts of the world on strange and secretive quests. Not all of them could have made it back in time for the siege, or so I believed.'

The Librarian frowned, trying to think back to the days immediately after the siege. Hadn't Jonson made a statement of some kind about hunting for outlaw members of the Knights of Lupus? He couldn't recall. A faint sense of unease stirred in his gut.

'For the first few years I waited near the ruins of their fortress, waiting for the errant wolves to come home,' Daviel continued. 'I expected the survivors would try to return and see what they could salvage of their order. When none appeared, I began to search the frontiers for signs of their passage.'

'Were you successful?' Zahariel asked.

Daviel nodded grimly.

'As best I could tell, there were five Knights of Lupus who weren't present at the siege,' he replied. 'I found the bones of three of them in the deep wilderness, where they'd tried to live for months after the destruction of their fortress. The fourth one I tracked to a half-ruined tower near Stone Point, on the other side of the world from the Northwilds. He fought me like a cornered animal, and when he realised that he couldn't best me he leapt from the top of the tower into the raging sea rather than give up his secrets.'

'And the fifth?'

Daviel paused, casting a questioning glance at Remiel. The old master gestured for the knight to continue with a wave of his hand.

The old knight sighed. 'The last one was the hardest to track of all,' he said. 'He never stayed in one place for too long, passing like a ghost from one village to another. No one could remember for certain what he looked like, and he wore a great many names over the years. For a long time I couldn't be sure if he was even real – until I turned up his horse and tack, still marked with sigils of his order, in a trade town at Hills End.'

'What had become of him?'

Daviel's good eye narrowed. 'According to the horse's new owner, the man took his coin, bought some new clothes from a merchant, and then presented himself to a brother knight of the Order who was passing through the village in search of new aspirants.'

The news stunned Zahariel. He looked to Master Remiel. 'Surely someone would have realised–'

Remiel arched an eyebrow at his former pupil. 'How so? If he were a young knight, with no reputation and no sense of honour, he could claim to be a woodsman's son and no one would be any wiser.' His eyes bored into Zahariel. 'With his skills and experience he could rise through the Order's ranks quite rapidly, in fact.'

Zahariel frowned. 'What are you getting at?' he demanded. Remiel's expression turned bitter – and then the Librarian understood.

Remiel saw the realization on Zahariel's face and nodded. 'Now you begin to see.'

'No,' Zahariel protested. 'It's impossible. Jonson would never have allowed–'

'But he did,' Remiel snarled, his voice sharpening with long-suppressed anger. 'Did you never wonder why Jonson named an unknown young knight as the new Lord Cypher, entrusting him with all of our traditions and secrets?'

Zahariel shook his head. 'But why… what possible reason could he have for such a thing?'

'Think, son,' Remiel said, once more an impatient tutor instructing an obstinate pupil. 'Put aside your damned idealism for a moment and think in terms of tactics. What would such a choice give Jonson?'

Zahariel swallowed his shock and irritation and considered the matter in cold terms. 'He chose someone with no ties to the Order's senior knights or masters, whose loyalty was to him alone,' he said, thinking aloud. 'Someone who could be counted on to act in Jonson's best interests above everything else.'

'And would keep his secrets, regardless of the consequences to everyone else,' Remiel said.

The Astartes considered the implications and felt a cold surge of horror. 'I can't believe this,' he said, his voice hollow.

'Can't… or won't?' the old master said. 'Do you imagine this was any easier for me to accept? I helped raise Lion El'Jonson when Luther brought him back from the wilderness. He was like a son to me.'

'But why?' Zahariel protested. 'Why all the secrets and deceptions? We were sworn to him, Remiel. He already had our oaths. We would have followed him into Old Night itself if he asked.'

Remiel didn't answer at first. Zahariel watched the old master's anger fade, like heat from a dying ember, giving way to anguish, and then finally, to an empty, barren sadness.

'It's not that any of us lost faith in Jonson,' he said softly. Tears glimmered at the corners of his eyes.

'Somewhere along the line, he lost faith in us. Wherever he and the Emperor are headed, we aren't meant to follow. All we can do now is reclaim what was once ours.'

The thought stung Zahariel, like a knife pricking at his heart. He tried to gainsay Remiel, to find some fault in the old master's bleak logic.

They spent the last few minutes of the flight in silence.

WHEN THEY REACHED Aldurukh, Zahariel cased himself in his armour and took up bolt pistol and staff before leading Remiel and Daviel to the Grand Master's chambers. He found Lord Cypher there, as he expected he would.

Cypher glanced up sharply from the reports piled atop the desk. His eyes widened as he saw the rebel leaders. It was the first time Zahariel had ever seen the Astartes taken by surprise.

'What's the meaning of this?' Cypher demanded coldly.

'Take us to Luther,' Zahariel demanded. 'Now.'

'I can't do that,' Cypher replied, regaining some of his inscrutable poise. 'As I've told you many times, brother, Luther is in meditation and does not want to be disturbed–'

'He will when he hears what we have to say,' Zahariel shot back. 'Caliban's survival is at stake.' His hand tightened on his staff. 'If you won't take us to him, then tell us where he can be found.'

'I can't do that,' Cypher replied coolly. 'My orders are from the Master of Caliban. You haven't the authority to countermand them.'

'Surely Luther expects to be informed in the event of an emergency,' Zahariel persisted.

Cypher smiled thinly. 'Why, of course. Give me the message and I'll relay it to him immediately.'

Zahariel felt a surge of anger. Before he could reply, however, he heard heavy footfalls behind him. He turned to see Brother-Librarian Israfael and Chapter Master Astelan standing just inside the doorway. Israfael eyed Daviel and Master Remiel with wary surprise, while Astelan's eyes flashed with irritation when he caught sight of Zahariel.

'Where have you been?' Astelan said. 'I've been searching for you all over Aldurukh!'

'What's happened?' Zahariel asked, already fearing what he might hear. If Astelan hadn't used the vox to contact him it could only mean one thing.

'Half an hour ago we began hearing of wide-scale rioting at the Northwilds arcology,' Astelan said grimly. 'Mobs of panicked civilians have rushed the barricades around the hab levels. Many of them are claiming that the Imperials are secretly in league with sorcerers who mean to sacrifice them to the warp.'

Daviel let out an angry groan. 'Thuriel's behind this,' he said. 'That short-sighted idiot has damned us all.'

Zahariel felt a chill race up his spine. 'What about the Jaegers?' he asked. 'I ordered General Morten to open the cordon and begin relocating the civilians.'

Astelan shook his head in exasperation. 'We're getting wildly conflicting reports,' he said. 'We've heard that some units have opened fire on the rioters, while others have thrown down their arms or even switched sides. The Administratum officials at the arcology have contacted Magos Bosk, and she is demanding to know what we're doing about the situation.'

'I told you that we couldn't keep this a secret from her,' Israfael interjected angrily. 'She's probably drafting an urgent report to the primarch right now, accusing us all of negligence. And she would be right to do so!'

'That's not the worst of it,' the chapter master said, cutting Israfael off with an angry glare. He turned back to Zahariel. 'There've been fragmentary transmissions from Jaeger patrols on the lower hab levels, reporting that they're under attack.'

'Under attack?' Zahariel echoed. He eyed the rebel leaders. 'By whom?'

'By the dead,' Astelan replied.

The words hung heavy in the chamber.

'It's over,' Remiel said, putting a voice to their thoughts. 'We're too late.'

Zahariel shook his head stubbornly. 'No,' he said. 'Not yet.' He turned back to Cypher, his face pale with anger. The hooded Astartes started to say something, then recoiled with a gasp of pain as Zahariel sent a probe of psychic energy into Cypher's mind.

'The time for dissembling is past,' Zahariel said, his tone as cold and sharp as ice. 'Take us to Luther. Now.'

Cypher gritted his teeth under the psychic onslaught. 'I won't...'

'Then I'll dig his location out of your brain,' Zahariel said, 'along with any other secrets you've been keeping. I can't say there will be much left of you afterwards, though.'

Zahariel drove his probe deeper into Cypher's mind. The Astartes went rigid. A thin trickle of blood seeped from one nostril.

'Stop!' Cypher said in a choked whisper. 'I'll do it! I'll take you to him! Just–'

He slumped with a groan as Zahariel released him. Cypher's head drooped for a moment, his shoulders heaving. When he looked up at the Librarian, his expression was savage.

'You don't know what you're trifling with, you fool,' Cypher snarled. 'The primarch–'

'The primarch isn't here,' Zahariel said coldly. 'So I'll trifle with whatever I must. Now get up. We haven't any more time to waste.'

Cypher got up from behind the desk without another word. They followed him from the room, hovering at his shoulder like ravens.

CYPHER LED THEM into darkness, deep within the bowels of the Rock.

From the Circle Chamber, they descended through a secret stairway at the top of the Grand Master's dais that Zahariel never knew existed, yet at the same time seemed tantalisingly familiar. Try as he might, he couldn't reconcile the two notions; the more he concentrated, the more his head began to ache. Finally, he decided to let the matter go rather than compromise his already frayed concentration. The pain in his skull subsided, but didn't entirely vanish.

The stairwell ended at a low-ceilinged room that might once have been a meeting space in times past; now the ancient brickwork was pierced by modern archways of fused permacrete that continued even further into the depths. Cypher led them through the dimly-lit passageways without hesitation, threading his way through a labyrinth of tunnels that began to tax even Zahariel's genetically-enhanced memory. Deeper and deeper they went, down into the very heart of the mountain, until it felt as though they had been walking for hours. Zahariel reckoned they were more than a thousand metres down when Cypher turned down a narrow, vaulted corridor that abruptly ended at a tall, arched doorway. The doors themselves, Zahariel noted with surprise, were plated with adamantium, and set in a reinforced frame. Anything powerful enough to breach that portal would also incinerate anything on the other side, his trained mind noted.

Standing before the doors, Cypher dug a sophisticated electronic key from within his robes. With a last, furious glance at Zahariel, he held the key up to the portal and touched the actuator. Bolts drew back into the frame with an oiled clatter, and the tall doors swung silently inward.

The library within was built vertically, its packed shelves rising on eight sides to a vaulted ceiling fifty metres overhead. Long, thin lumen strips set into the stone at the corners of the eight walls filled the space with pellucid light. The air smelled faintly of ozone and machine oil. High up along the walls Zahariel could see four small logo-servitors waiting unobtrusively in the shadows, clinging to the walls with their spindly limbs and watching the Astartes with small, red eyes.

Zahariel reckoned the floor of the library was perhaps thirty paces across, covered with thick rugs to combat the subterranean chill. Reading desks and heavy wooden tables were arrayed haphazardly about the room, piled with open books and ancient, musty scrolls. More books were scattered in drifts across the floor, between and beneath the tables. There were so many that the Astartes were forced to pause just beyond the threshold, afraid of treading upon the fragile tomes.

The air in the library was utterly still, heavy with the dust of ages. The only sound Zahariel could hear was the soft whirring of servo-motors overhead. A current of invisible energy, faint but palpable, sent tendrils of ice spreading through his skull.

He drew a breath and spoke into the cathedral silence. 'Luther? My lord, are you here?'

A figure stirred in the shadowy depths of a high-backed chair near the centre of the room. Zahariel could just make out the head and shoulders of a man, limned in the faint, bluish-silver light.

'Zahariel,' Luther replied. His voice was rough, as if from long hours of exertion. 'You shouldn't be here.'

Lord Cypher took a cautious step forward, distancing himself from the rest of the Astartes. 'I beg your forgiveness, my lord,' he said with bowed head. 'They would not honour your wishes.'

Zahariel glared at Cypher's back. 'This has nothing to do with anyone's wishes,' he snapped. 'This is a time of crisis. Caliban stands upon the brink of disaster, my lord. The Legion must act, now, or all is lost.'

Luther rose slowly from the chair and stepped forward into the light. His eyes were sunken and his cheeks hollowed, as though from the ravages of a terrible illness, and there were dark ink marks on his hands, wrists and throat. The Master of Caliban paused, his cracked lips working as he peered at the figures standing at Zahariel's shoulder.

'Master Remiel?' he said. 'Is this a dream? I thought you long dead.'

'I continue to confound my enemies, my lord,' Remiel answered with a faint smile.

'I'm glad to hear it,' Luther said. His expression turned sombre. 'But I see you travel in the company of rebels these days,' he said, pointing to Sar Daviel. 'Is it me you seek to confound now, master?'

Remiel didn't flinch from the accusation. 'No loyal son of Caliban is an enemy of mine,' he answered coolly.

Zahariel studied Luther with concern. 'My lord, when did you last eat or drink?' he asked. Though an Astartes could go for many weeks with minimal nourishment, he knew that Luther's body hadn't received the full suite of metabolic enhancements. By the look of things, Zahariel feared that he'd been fasting for weeks.

The Master of Caliban ignored the question. 'What is going on here, brothers?' he asked, his voice regaining some of its strength and authority.

'The truth has become known,' Israfael said grimly. 'Rumours have spread through the Northwilds that the Imperium is in league with sorcerers,' he spat angrily. 'Riots have broken out, and the Administratum is up in arms.'

Luther's eyes widened in anger. 'How did these rumours start?' he demanded. 'I ordered this knowledge kept secret! Who is responsible?'

Zahariel took a deep breath and stepped forward. 'I am,' he said gravely. 'The fault is mine.'

The admission took Luther aback. 'You?' he said disbelievingly. 'But why?'

All eyes turned to Zahariel. Head high, the Librarian reported everything he'd seen and done at the arcology. Luther listened, his expression growing harder by the moment. He gave no reaction to the proposed truce with the rebels, though both Astelan and Israfael glowered angrily at the news.

Zahariel concluded by relating what they'd recently heard from the Northwilds. 'Things are balanced on a knife's edge, my lord,' he said. 'If we strike quickly, we might still be able to contain the situation.'

'No, we can't,' Luther said flatly. He shook his head, his expression bleak. 'It's far too late for that. I don't fault you for what you did brother, but there's no going back now. Caliban's fate is sealed.'

Luther turned in the stunned silence that followed and walked to one of the heavy reading tables. He bent over a massive, leather-bound tome, brushing the tips of his fingers across one of the thick, vellum pages. Zahariel caught a better glimpse of Luther's hands, and saw that the ink marks there were actually symbols of some kind, laid out in a geometric pattern. A chill raced up the back of his neck.

'They wanted me to kill him, you know,' he said quietly. 'I can still hear their voices as though it were yesterday.'

Zahariel gave Luther a bemused frown. 'Kill who, my lord?'

The Master of Caliban glanced up from the book. 'Why, Jonson, of course,' he replied. 'There we were, in the worst part of the Northwilds, so deep in the forest that we hadn't seen the sun for a week. We'd already killed two beasts by then, and lost Sar Lutiel in the process. Most of us were wounded and feverish, but we pressed on nonetheless.' He smiled faintly. 'No one had ever gone so far into that part of the wilderness, and we were all hungry for glory.'

Luther eyes grew unfocused as the memories took hold. 'We'd come upon a stream at midday,' he continued. 'A prime spot for predators, but our water bottles were empty, so we decided to take the risk. I was standing watch, sitting in the saddle with my pistol ready. And the next thing any of us knew, there was this little boy standing with us. He'd walked right out of the woods into our midst, as silent as you please.'

The Master of Caliban chuckled ruefully. 'We just gaped at him for a moment. I think everyone believed he was a fever dream at first. Naked as a babe, his golden hair matted with twigs and leaves, and his eyes…' Luther shook his head. 'His eyes were cold and knowing, like a wolf's, and utterly unafraid.

'Sar Adriel looked into those eyes and turned white as a sheet. He and Sar Javiel's hands were laden with water bottles, and couldn't protect themselves. "Kill him!" Adariel said to me. I'd never heard him sound so frightened in his life.

'And I nearly did,' Luther confessed. 'You don't know how close I came, brothers. I knew what Adriel was thinking; we were more than a hundred leagues from the nearest village, in the deadliest forest on Caliban, and here was a child, barely tall enough to touch my saddle, without a single mark on his body.

He couldn't have survived in a wilderness like that alone. It wasn't possible.

'I remember thinking he was a monster,' Luther said. Tears welled in his eyes. 'What else could he be? So I raised my pistol and took careful aim. One shot to the head was all it would take.

'My finger was tightening on the trigger when he turned and looked at me. He didn't flinch at the sight of the pistol, and why would he? He didn't have the faintest idea what it was.' Luther drew in a great, wracking breath. 'That's when I realised what I was about to do, and I was ashamed. So I tossed the pistol to the ground.'

Tears were flowing freely down Luther's cheeks. Zahariel glanced back at Israfael and Astelan; the Astartes were just as unnerved by Luther's strange demeanour as he was. He struggled to come up with a reply, but it was Remiel who spoke first. 'There is no shame in sparing the innocent,' the old master said softly.

'But he wasn't innocent!' Luther cried bitterly. 'He knew. Jonson knew about the taint all along, and he's spilled an ocean of blood to keep the truth from us.'

Zahariel reeled in surprise at the vehemence in Luther's voice. 'You can't possibly mean that, my lord,' he protested numbly.

'Why else would he have goaded the Knights of Lupus into war, then annihilated them? Why else take their books–' he picked up the arcane tome and brandished it at Zahariel '–and hide them from our eyes? Because of what they could tell us about the planet's taint. Lion El'Jonson went to great lengths to silence those who knew too much, and it only got worse once the Emperor arrived.'

'That is enough!' Brother-Librarian Israfael shouted. 'I will not have you defame our primarch in this fashion, much less the Emperor!'

Pain blossomed in the back of Zahariel's head, so sudden and intense it nearly overwhelmed him. He groaned, pressing a hand to his temple and trying to push the agony aside, then turned to see Israfael standing well apart from the others, his fists clenched. Chapter Master Astelan stood to one side, his gaze shifting from Israfael to Luther as though unsure whom to believe. The room seemed to shift beneath Zahariel's feet. Things were spinning out of control, he knew. He'd never meant for things to come to this.

'Not everyone was silenced,' he protested. 'What about Nemiel? What about me? We were the last people to speak to Lord Sartana, and nothing befell us.'

'Brother Nemiel may lie dead on some distant world for all we know,' Luther said grimly. 'And you are here, exiled to a world that will soon be consigned to the flames.' His voice rose, teetering on the edge of madness. 'Don't you see? Jonson knew that the Imperium would one day destroy Caliban. That's why we're here. He didn't just forsake us, brother. He sent us here to die.'

'Not another word!' Israfael roared. Arcs of psychic power danced around his head, crackling like miniature thunderbolts. 'My lord, you are unwell, and no longer fit for command!' He turned to Zahariel. 'In the name of the primarch, and for the honour of the

Legion, you must assume control and order Luther to submit himself to the Apothecarium at once.'

'It's too late for such treacheries, Terran!' Luther snarled. He tossed the book aside and came around the edge of the table, his dark eyes blazing. 'He knows the truth now. Don't you, Zahariel?'

An invisible storm of psychic power swelled within the room. Zahariel's mind reeled. He saw Master Remiel and Sar Daviel just a few metres away, caught in between the two furious warriors. A thought came to him through the growing haze of pain. 'This is a mistake, my lord!' he said to Luther. 'Sar Daviel!' he cried. 'Your friend, the knight who read these same books. Who was he? Where is he now?'

Daviel turned to the Librarian with a haunted look in his eyes. 'His name was Ulient,' the old knight said. 'He disappeared on the day the Emperor came to Caliban, and was never seen again.'

A spear of pure, burning pain lanced through Zahariel's mind. He cried out, pressing his hands to his temples. It felt as though a dam had burst in his brain, unleashing a torrent of pent-up memories.

...Darkness. Armoured hands gripping him, holding him upright...

...Israfael's voice, echoing from the blackness. '...The plot failed and the conspirator is being interrogated. We will soon uncover those who sought to do us harm and deal with them...'

...Another voice. Brother Midris. '...Tell us everything and leave nothing out, or it will go badly for you. Start with how you knew what Brother Ulient was planning...'

…'Brother Ulient?' he said. 'Is that his name? I didn't know him…'

…Except that he did. He'd seen him in the secret room beneath the Circle chamber. Nemiel had taken him there to meet with the members of the conspiracy. He remembered the hooded men in white surplices, talking of killing the Emperor of Mankind…

'…The Imperium is not to be trusted. We know they are plotting to enslave us and take this world for themselves…'

…He remembered the shining figure that had appeared at the door of the interrogation chamber, his face too glorious to behold. The voice of the Emperor of Mankind rolling over him like an ocean wave...

'…be sure he remembers nothing of this. No suspicion of any dissent must exist within the Legion. We must be united or we are lost…'

Zahariel fell to his knees, his body trembling as the last vestiges of the psychic block unravelled. Israfael and Luther had fallen silent, and every eye was upon him.

The sense of violation, of betrayal, was almost too terrible to bear. He turned to Israfael. 'You tampered with my mind, brother,' he said, his voice barely above a whisper.

'Of course,' Israfael said, his tone unapologetic. 'The Emperor himself commanded it. I would expect you to do the same.'

'Couldn't he have simply trusted me?' Zahariel cried. 'Wouldn't my oath have been enough? Has he no honour?'

'Honour has nothing to do with it!' Israfael snarled. 'We are his Astartes, Zahariel. It's not for us to question his will!'

'That is where you are wrong, Terran,' Master Remiel said. 'You and your kind may be content to live as slaves, but we never will!'

Zahariel felt the surge of psychic power a heartbeat before Israfael struck. Time slowed, and everything seemed to happen at once.

Bellowing in rage, Israfael rounded on Master Remiel and flung out a gauntleted hand. Skeins of searing white fire leapt from the Librarian's fingertips, but Sar Daviel was already moving, putting his body between Israfael and Remiel. The psychic blast tore into his chest, searing his flesh and setting his robes on fire.

Luther shouted a command, and Zahariel felt his body respond even before his mind registered what he'd heard. He leapt to his feet and focused his will into his armour's psychic hood. The hood's dampener was not only for self-protection; it could also be used to combat the power of other psykers within a certain distance from the device. Zahariel turned its power on Brother Israfael, and the Librarian's energies faltered. At the same time, Chapter Master Astelan rushed at Israfael from the side, his pistol raised.

But the senior Librarian would not be overcome so easily. Israfael ducked as Astelan tried to strike him with the butt of his bolt pistol and lashed out with his hand. His fingertips seemed to brush lightly against Astelan's breastplate, but Zahariel felt the psychic discharge that flung the chapter master through the air at him. Zahariel ducked barely in time, but his concentration on the dampener faltered for a fleeting instant.

That was all the opening that Israfael needed. With a savage cry, he raised his hands and unleashed a torrent of crackling energy upon Luther.

Zahariel felt the heat of the blast as it burned through the air past his head and struck Luther full in the chest. But the knight did not burn – instead, the wards painted upon his skin flared with an icy luminescence, deflecting the energy in a boiling wave away from his body.

He saw Luther bare his teeth in a wolfish grin, then he opened his mouth and uttered a single word. The sound smote Zahariel like a hammer; he felt a searing pain in his ears and at the corners of his eyes, and he reeled under the blow.

Israfael did as well. Bleeding from the eyes and ears, he staggered backwards before a searing bolt of plasma struck him full in the chest.

The Librarian's eyes went wide. There was a crater in his breastplate as large as a man's palm, its edges still molten. He swayed on his feet, his lips working as though trying to speak, then sank slowly to his knees and toppled onto his side.

Zahariel glanced back the way the shot had come. Lord Cypher slowly lowered his plasma pistol and cast a wary glance towards Luther. 'Are you well, my lord?' He asked.

Luther didn't answer. Smoke curled in thin tendrils from each of the hexagrammic wards covering his body.

'How is Sar Daviel?' he asked.

Master Remiel was kneeling beside the charred body of the old knight. 'Gone to the halls of honour,' he said quietly.

Zahariel tore his gaze away from Cypher and staggered over to Israfael. The wound in his chest was grave, but he checked the Librarian's life support systems nevertheless and was surprised to find a faint reading. 'Israfael still lives, my lord,' he said. 'What shall we do with him?'

Lord Cypher took a step towards the fallen Librarian, his pistol still in hand. Luther stopped him with a hard glance.

'Summon a pair of servitors to take him to the Apothecaries,' Luther commanded. 'When he's recovered enough we'll transfer him to a cell in the Tower of Angels and see if we can convince him of the error of his ways.' Then he turned to Astelan.

'Are the strike teams ready, brother?'

The chapter master nodded. 'All is in readiness, my lord,' he said.

'Then your first orders are to arrest General Morten and his staff, as well as Magos Bosk and the senior officials of the Administratum,' the Master of Caliban said. 'Spare their lives if at all possible, but do what you must to secure them. From this moment forward, Caliban is a free world once more.'

Astelan hesitated. Zahariel could see the struggle in the warrior's eyes, but in the end, his loyalty to Luther won out over years of unthinking obedience. 'It shall be done,' he said.

Master Remiel rose wearily to his feet. Tears streamed down his face as he walked up to Luther.

'The knight of old has returned,' he said, his voice cracking with emotion. He reached out and gripped Luther's arms.

'Behold the saviour of Caliban!'

NINETEEN
LION RAMPANT

Diamat
In the 200th year of the Emperor's Great Crusade

THEY DISCOVERED THE foundry sector entirely deserted upon their return. The Dark Angels found many of the perimeter outposts still intact, shielded from the blast wave of the bombardment by virtue of being sheltered in the lee of thick-walled manufactories, but the soldiers who manned them were gone. Jonson sent 1st Company and Brother Titus ahead with orders to secure the assembly building, while 2nd Company moved along at a slower pace; they'd recovered three Rhinos from outside the warehouses and loaded them with the most seriously injured battle brothers, while the rest of the company followed along behind the vehicles with the bodies of the fallen. Nemiel and Kohl, reunited with the rest of their squad, found the body of Brother Marthes on the way back and made him a part of the sombre procession as well. As they made their way into the foundry precincts they began to hear the faint rumble of thrusters off to the south. Now and again Nemiel and the others would look back in the direction of the far-off star port, and search for telltale streaks of light that would signify the descent of an orbital transport. The Dark Angels knew that with every passing minute the wolves were gathering at their backs. It would only be a matter of time before they began to close in.

Force Commander Lamnos, who was also the commanding officer of 1st Company, was waiting outside the assembly building when Primarch Jonson and 2nd Company arrived. 'The building has been secured, my lord,' he reported. 'We encountered several squads of stragglers inside, but they weren't in much shape to put up a fight.'

'What about the siege guns?' the primarch asked.

'All present and accounted for. The building weathered the blast very well, and the vehicles sustained no damage.'

Jonson nodded. 'Well done, Force Commander. Let's get the wounded inside, then begin developing a defence strategy.' He cast a wary eye to the south. 'I believe we've only got two or three hours at most before the Sons of Horus begin their attack.'

The Astartes went to work immediately, scouting out the terrain and scavenging working heavy weapons from the abandoned enemy emplacements. Jonson and the company commanders assembled outside the assembly building, along with Nemiel and Brother-Sergeant Kohl, to review the terrain and develop a proper defensive perimeter. The primarch favoured a layered defence, with an outer defensive ring encompassing the entire sector, and an inner ring centred solely on the assembly building. The 1st Company was put to work on the outer ring, while the 2nd Company was assigned the inner ring.

'At this point, we only have enough strength to successfully defend about half of the outer ring,' Jonson said. In the absence of a hololith table, one of the Astartes had scratched a crude map of the foundry sector into the permacrete with the point of his power knife, and the Dark Angels had gathered in a circle around it.

'Naturally, we'll orientate our defence to the south, because the rebels will use the most direct approach – at least initially,' the primarch continued. 'We'll site our captured lascannons and heavy stubbers on rooftops here, here and here.' He indicated a series of buildings on the outer edge of the sector that provided commanding fields of fire down the main avenues of approach. 'The lascannon gunners' priority is to knock out as many vehicles as possible and strip the attackers of their support. Most of 1st and 2nd Companies will be arrayed in a wide arc covering all the southern routes into the sector. Three squads will be kept in reserve and mounted in our Rhinos to provide swift reinforcement to weak parts of the line.' He paused, studying the map thoughtfully. 'As the battle wears on, we can expect that they will probe around our flanks, looking for less well-defended areas. We'll have to stay flexible and be ready to re-orientate our squads at a moment's notice, falling back to the inner line if necessary.'

'What about Magos Archoi and the remaining skitarii?' Force Commander Lamnos asked. Since taking the assembly building there had been a few brief skirmishes with skitarii units from the north.

Jonson shrugged. 'Archoi himself is most likely dead,' he replied. 'I expect he fled right back to his stronghold and was caught in the bombardment. Just in case, however, I want to post a squad of wounded battle brothers onto the roof of the assembly building to act as observers. If they detect a serious threat from the north, we'll despatch our mobile reserve to deal with it.'

Lamnos and Captain Hsien of 2nd Company nodded in agreement. Neither warrior looked particularly pleased with the tactical situation, but Jonson had devised a plan that made the best use of the assets they had available. Still, Nemiel couldn't help but note a grim undercurrent in the manner of the two leaders. They carried themselves like warriors who were about to make a final stand, and had already resigned themselves to their deaths.

'We've got almost a hundred and fifty battle brothers able to fight, plus a Dreadnought,' Nemiel pointed out. 'We should be able to hold the foundry almost indefinitely with so large a force. The Emperor knows we managed to hold off a horde of orks with far less than that back on Barrakan.'

'If we were only facing skitarii and conventional troops, I would agree with you,' Lamnos said readily. 'But this time we're dealing with the Sons of Horus. This may well prove to be the toughest battle that any of us have ever fought.'

'There's also the matter of supplies,' Hsien pointed out. 'Our warriors were fully resupplied before the attack began, but we'll go through our basic stocks of ammunition within a few days of heavy fighting,' he said.

Jonson raised a hand. 'All of these things are true,' he said, 'but we also have a number of advantages here. First, we have something that the enemy desperately wants, so they cannot bring their heaviest weapons to bear on us without risking a direct hit on the siege guns. They can't just sit back and blast us with artillery; instead, they've got to come in and dig us out, which makes their job much more difficult. Secondly, their fleet is much smaller this time than it was during their first attack. Horus put together a raiding group with whatever he had immediately to hand, so I expect they have supply issues of their own. If we can defeat their ground units and drive them off the planet, the fleet will have little choice but to withdraw, and I doubt that the Warmaster will risk a third attempt with the Emperor's punitive force drawing nearer.' He gave the two company commanders a steadfast look. 'This won't be a protracted siege. Far from it. The enemy will have enough resources to sustain only a few days of intense combat before they will have to retreat. That was another factor in my decision to bombard the forge. Within a week they'll be more desperate for resources than we will.'

The primarch's assertions effectively ended the discussion. Everyone knew of Jonson's strategic brilliance, and the mood of the company commanders was buoyed by his self-assurance. But Nemiel, ever the cynic, couldn't help but note the things that the primarch left unsaid. The attacking force was small, but fresh, and though their resources were finite, they were undoubtedly well-equipped. And it didn't matter if the Dark Angels could hold out a month or more if the Sons of Horus managed to overrun them in the very first battle.

The company commanders left to join their respective commands and complete preparations for the coming fight. Nemiel and his squad went to join the mobile reserve. Jonson had specifically ordered the Redemptor to join the reserve force. 'You'll be most needed where the fighting is hardest,' he'd told Nemiel. 'I can't have you getting bogged down guarding some access road while the enemy is breaking through on the other side of the perimeter.'

Nemiel accepted the order with a brusque nod. 'Where will you be, my lord?' he asked.

A faint grin crossed Jonson's handsome face. 'Why, I'll try to be everywhere at once,' the primarch replied.

Hours passed, and the tension began to mount. The sounds of orbital transports descending through the overcast grew more frequent as the day progressed. At mid-morning they heard a faint crackle of small-arms fire off in the far distance, somewhere out in the grey zone, and the Astartes wondered if some of the Dragoons had somehow managed to survive. The sounds of combat tapered off within a few minutes, however, and an uneasy quiet descended once more.

Four hours past dawn they heard the rumble of engines off to the north, and the observers on the top of the assembly building reported a small force of APCs were heading for the northern perimeter at high speed. Nemiel and the reserve forces, accompanied by Jonson himself, hurriedly climbed aboard their Rhinos and raced down the access roads to meet the oncoming threat. No sooner had the Astartes deployed into cover around the perimeter's ruined buildings than four Testudo personnel carriers burst into view. Battered-looking Dragoons clung to the top decks of the APCs, and all of the vehicles showed signs of recent battle damage. Jonson and Nemiel stepped from cover and waved at the vehicles, which quickly changed course and slid to a halt some ten metres from the two warriors. The Dragoons on the tops of the vehicles regarded them with glassy-eyed expressions.

The Testudos lowered their assault ramps and more troops spilled out into the daylight. Among them was Governor Kulik, still wearing his carapace armour and limping along with the help of a cane.

Jonson stepped forward, raising his hand in salute. 'It's good to see you, governor,' he said. 'After Magos Archoi's betrayal we'd feared the worst.'

'For the first few hours, so did I,' Kulik answered. 'Archoi took us completely by surprise, damn him.' He turned and indicated his battered force with a sweep of his cane. 'This is all I have left. Barely half a company, out of a starting strength of twenty thousand men.' He turned back to the primarch, and Nemiel could see the pain etched across Kulik's face. 'We knew that if anyone could survive Magos Archoi's treachery, it would be you. So we loaded up the only vehicles we had left and managed to slip through the northern gate in the hopes of finding you.'

'What's the situation beyond the curtain wall?' Jonson asked.

Kulik's face fell. 'The skitarii control the fortifications in the grey zone, and probably the southern gateway as well; we couldn't get close enough to find out,' he said. 'A small convoy of Tech-Guard headed out to the star port at first light. Since dawn, we estimate that eight to ten heavy troop transports and a number of dropships have landed there.' He nodded his head to the south. 'The last we saw, their vanguard units were on the move, heading north. The damned traitors are going to lead them through the grey zone and probably past the southern gateway as well. They'll be here within the hour, I expect.'

Jonson stepped forward and laid a hand on Kulik's shoulder. 'You and your men have fought courageously, governor,' he said. 'They've given everything they have in defence of their world. Let us take up the banner from here. You can withdraw back to the north and slip into the countryside, while we hold off the rebels.'

Kulik stiffened, and for a moment Nemiel feared that he would take insult at Jonson's heartfelt offer.

'I and my men are honoured by your offer,' Kulik said after a moment, 'but we're going to see this through to the end, if it's all the same to you.'

Jonson nodded sombrely. 'Welcome, then,' he replied. 'Have your men take positions here, covering our northern approach. We've had some skirmishes with skitarii patrols, and we're worried that Archoi may be planning an attack.'

'I damn well hope he tries!' the governor said, a fierce look crossing his face. 'If he does, we'll deal with him, Primarch Jonson. You mark my words.' With that, he turned on his heel and began snapping orders to his men, and the Dragoons went to work with surprising speed.

THE RESERVE FORCE returned to their start position and the wait began once more. Nemiel stepped outside the Rhino and sat down against its armoured flank, trying to balance his humours and rest his body with meditation. Ten minutes later, the observers called across the command net and said that a large force of armoured vehicles was approaching from the south. Orders were passed along the company command nets, and the Dark Angels readied their weapons.

Twenty minutes later they felt the rumble of the armoured columns reverberating through the earth, drawing closer with every passing moment. Plumes of black petrochem exhaust rose from the midst of the warehouses to the south. Then, the gunners atop the buildings facing the enemy advance began to call out sightings: three columns of heavy tanks and APCs, approaching fast. To Nemiel it sounded like an entire mechanised battalion, heading straight down their throats.

Jonson received the news calmly. 'Lascannon emplacements, target the main battle tanks and open fire at four hundred and fifty metres,' he said.

The range was already so close that the anti-tank lasers opened fire almost at once. Bright red beams shot down the narrow roadways and struck the lead tanks head-on. One of the vehicles exploded with the first hit; another lost one of its treads and ground to a halt. The third tank pressed forward with a gouge scored along the side of its turret. Its battle cannon elevated and fired a high-explosive shell with a hollow boom. The round overshot, flying past the weapons emplacement and crashing into a manufactorum on the north side of the sector. The Astartes kept firing, sending beam after beam at the tanks, until finally all three were knocked out. Behind the wrecks, the remaining tanks and APCs were forced to retreat and spread out further along the side-lanes before resuming their advance.

The rebel forces came on in a much broader formation this time, their vehicles arrayed in a wide crescent that nearly encompassed the entire southern perimeter. This time the heavy stubbers joined in the battle, raking the enemy APCs with bursts of armour-piercing shells. The enemy responded with battle cannon shells and autocannon bursts, and the air was filled with explosions and blossoms of fire. The Astartes placed their shots with brutal efficiency, aiming for the known vulnerabilities in the armour plating of the battle tanks and destroying half a dozen in the space of just a few minutes. The APCs fared no better under the hail of shells from the heavy stubbers as the armour-piercing rounds found weak spots in their hulls and punched their way inside, wreaking bloody havoc on the troops embarked within. Several shuddered to a halt and exploded as a tracer rounds touched off their fuel cells, until finally the battalion commander ordered the rest of the infantry to dismount and continue the attack on foot. The infantry squads exited their transports and charged across the fifteen-metre open space, only to be cut down by heavy stubbers and disciplined bursts of boltgun fire from concealed Astartes squads.

Twenty minutes after the attack began, the rebel advance faltered and began to withdraw. They left behind twenty knocked-out vehicles and more than two hundred dead soldiers. Three of the Dark Angels' weapons emplacements had been destroyed by battle cannon fire, and three Astartes had been slain. The First Legion could claim victory in the opening engagement, but the battle was only beginning. The Sons of Horus had yet to make an appearance.

OVER THE COURSE of the next three hours the Dark Angels repulsed five more attacks. Each time the rebels refined their tactics and probed more aggressively around the Astartes' flanks. Each time they drove back the rebels with significant losses, but casualties among the defenders mounted, and with each attack they lost one or more of their few remaining lascannons or heavy stubbers. To Nemiel it felt as though a noose was slowly being tightened around them.

The rebels dropped mortar rounds onto the outskirts of the sector during the third attack, targeting buildings where they knew a heavy weapons emplacement was located. By the sixth attack the enemy APCs were growing bolder, advancing within ten metres of the sector perimeter before being turned back.

An hour passed before the commencement of the seventh attack, allowing the Astartes time to redistribute ammunition and tend their wounded. The

Dark Angels' spirits had been restored by the time the first mortar rounds began to fall, and when the rebel tanks and APCs began their advance they opened fire with their few remaining heavy weapons and prepared for close-quarters combat.

This time the rebel tanks and APCs closed in on the perimeter from three sides, and the weight of fire from the defenders wasn't strong enough to stem the tide. The enemy vehicles hit the first defensive line in a score of places; they poured cannon and heavy stubber fire into the manufactories as they pressed deeper, forcing the Astartes to break cover and assault the lumbering vehicles. Within minutes both companies were involved in dozens of squad-level melees, as the Dark Angels came to grips with platoons of heavily-armed infantry.

And then, judging that the decisive moment had come, the Sons of Horus launched their attack.

'Rhinos approaching from the north!'

Nemiel heard the call over the vox and saw the enemy strategy at once. While the rebel infantry had been probing the extent of the Imperial defences, the Sons of Horus had been moving under cover of the attacks in a sweeping movement to the north that would bring them around behind the Dark Angels' positions. It was the kind of swift, decisive strategy that made the Sons of Horus such deadly opponents on the field of battle, and reflected the tactical prowess of their illustrious primarch. Now, Nemiel and the mobile reserve was all that stood in their way.

'Move out!' he ordered as he leapt inside the lead Rhino and slammed the troop door shut. The three transports roared into motion, circling around the assembly building and racing down the accessways to the northern perimeter. He switched to the command net and called the rooftop lookouts. 'How many Rhinos are we facing?' he asked.

'I count four,' one of the lookouts replied. 'The Dragoons are engaging them now.'

The Tanagran troops stood their ground in the face of the enemy charge, and the autocannons of their four Testudos began to spit bursts of armour-piercing rounds at the oncoming transports. Two of the lightly-armoured APCs were hit and ground to a halt, smoke pouring from their wrecked power plants. A third caught fire and exploded, scattering burning debris in a wide arc.

Had the vehicles been crewed by human troops, the attack would have been stopped cold, but the hatches on all three of the destroyed vehicles slammed open and squads of pale-armoured warriors fought their way free of the wreckage and resumed their attack. They were fearsome apparitions of war, their battle-scarred armour clad with two centuries' worth of campaign honours and prized trophies looted from worlds stretching the length and breadth of the Imperium. Once they had been called the Luna Wolves, and had been the first of the Astartes Legions to be reunited with their primarch. Their name had been synonymous with the Emperor's Great Crusade for nearly two hundred years. Now they were called the Sons of Horus, and they had drowned Isstvan III in the blood of twelve billion innocent souls.

Boltguns blazed, wreaking carnage among the Dragoons; plasma guns spat bolts of charged particles that bored into the front armour of the Testudos and blew two of them apart. The lone surviving Rhino continued forwards, firing bursts from its remote-controlled twin bolter until it crashed into the enemy positions and dropped its rear assault ramp. Another squad of rebel Astartes charged out of the vehicle and attacked the surviving Dragoons in close combat, carving through the exhausted soldiers with snarling chainswords and glowing power weapons.

The Tanagran troops were on the verge of collapse when Nemiel and the reserves arrived. He ordered the APCs to halt fifteen metres back from the melee so the three squads could deploy in good order. The Redemptor looked across the battlefield at the fearsome, pale-armoured warriors. There were four full squads against his three under-strength ones; he and his men were in for a rough fight.

Igniting his crozius, Nemiel led the charge. 'Loyalty and honour!' he cried. 'For the Lion and the Emperor!'

Brother-Sergant Kohl took up the war cry, and in moments all twenty-three of the Dark Angels were shouting, too, as they crashed into the ranks of their foes.

Nemiel saw a rebel warrior cut down two screaming Dragoons and then turn upon him. He rushed at the Son of Horus, channelling all of his rage into a sweeping blow from his crozius. But the veteran warrior sidestepped the blow with fearsome speed and slashed the Redemptor across the wrist. Had it been a power blade, the sword would have sliced off Nemiel's hand; as it was, the teeth of the chainsword raked across his armoured gauntlet, scoring deep gouges in the ceramite plates.

The Redemptor lashed at the rebel with a back-handed stroke, feinting for the warrior's head and then striking downwards at his knee. Again, the Astartes nimbly dodged the blow and then brought up his bolt pistol and shot Nemiel in the head.

The blow to his helmet blinded Nemiel and knocked him off his feet. He registered the impact across his shoulders as he struck the ground and felt blood trickling down the bridge of his nose. The bolt pistol round had failed to penetrate his helmet, but the impact had split it and damaged the delicate circuitry beneath the ceramite plates. His vision came back in flashes of red-tinged static just as the edge of his enemy's chainblade pressed against his breast-plate. He felt the whirring teeth skip and screech across the curved plate, scrabbling for purchase. In another few seconds he knew that it would mar the surface enough to bite deep, and then he was as good as dead.

With a shout, Nemiel brought up his pistol and fired a shot into the side of his opponent's knee. The bolt round punched through the relatively weak joint armour and blew the warrior's lower leg off. The Astartes collapsed with a roar of pain and rage, and Nemiel threw himself atop his foe, batting aside his chainblade with the barrel of his pistol and slamming his crozius down on the warrior's helmet. The helm imploded with a bright blue flash, and the Son of Horus went limp.

Gasping, Nemiel tore at his damaged helm one-handed until he finally pulled it free. A pitched battle was raging all around him; the Dragoons were nowhere to be seen, leaving his warriors to fight the numerically-superior Sons of Horus alone. Pistols flashed and thundered, and blades drew sparks as they slashed across the curved surfaces of power armour. He saw a Dark Angel take a shot from a plasma pistol at close range and fall to the ground, then another lose his arm to a deadly lightning claw. A rebel Astartes toppled, run through by Brother-Sergeant Kohl's power sword. Brother Ephrial smashed a rebel to the ground with the butt of his meltagun and blew the prone warrior apart with a searing blast of microwaves. The heat generated by the blast staggered everyone around him – all except the pale-armoured warrior who had slipped behind Ephrial. Brandishing a huge power fist, the Son of Horus punched Ephrial in the back of his head, killing him instantly.

Nemiel leapt to his feet and charged at the warrior who'd killed Ephrial. A plasma bolt shot past his head, close enough to sear the skin on the side of his face, but he scarcely felt the pain. He raised his crozius, and the rebel seemed to sense the blow at he last moment. The warrior spun about, bringing his power fist up in a ponderous arc that nevertheless managed to deflect Nemiel's attack. The rebel spun on his heel and, quick as a viper, brought up a plasma pistol and loosed a bolt at Nemiel, but the Redemptor anticipated the move just in time and dodged to the side. The shot missed his shoulder by centimetres, flashing past and striking someone behind him. He heard an agonised scream, but had no time to see whether friend or foe had been hit.

He lunged forward before the traitor could fire another shot, and smashed the pistol's barrel with a jab from his crozius. The Astartes hurled the ruined weapon at Nemiel's face, following behind the feint with a sweeping blow aimed at the Redemptor's abdomen. Nemiel dodged to the right, narrowly avoiding both attacks, and brought his crozius down on his enemy's left shoulder. The warrior's pauldron shattered beneath the impact and broke the traitor's shoulder along with it. The Son of Horus was driven to his knees. Before he could rise again the Redemptor crushed his skull with another blow from his power weapon.

Nemiel whirled about, taking stock of the battle even as his last foe toppled to the ground. Everywhere he turned he saw pale-armoured figures pressing in on his warriors from all sides. Bodies of friend and foe alike littered the ground, but he could see at once that his warriors had suffered the worst in the exchange. There were less than a dozen left, including Brother-Sergeant Kohl and Brother Cortus. The Dark Angels were instinctively drawing together into a tight knot, standing back-to-back in a classic defensive formation that had its roots on Caliban. They were outnumbered more than two to one, but they refused to yield a centimetre to their foes.

For the first time in his life, Nemiel truly felt that he was about to die. A strange peace settled over him at the thought, and as he joined his brothers he prepared to give his life for the Emperor.

Then, suddenly, a shout went up from the Sons of Horus, and the entire mass of enemy warriors recoiled away from the Dark Angels. Stunned,

Nemiel whirled about, searching for the source of the enemy's retreat.

Lion El'Jonson fell upon the rebels with a fierce cry, the Lion Sword blazing as he carved through the enemy ranks. The rebels fell like wheat before a scythe, cut down before they scarcely had a chance to move, much less strike at their foe. Jonson was a vengeful god, a whirlwind of death and destruction, and the Sons of Horus retreated before his wrath.

The enemy fell back to their Rhinos, firing their pistols to cover their withdrawal. The Dark Angels traded shots with them until the enemy had disappeared inside their transports and the Rhinos turned and sped out of range. Only then did Nemiel turn and take stock of their losses. With dawning horror, he saw that only eight warriors besides him were still standing. Fifteen of his brothers lay dead upon the permacrete, surrounded by the bodies of a dozen of their foes. They had turned aside the enemy attack, but the reserve force had been decimated.

If the Sons of Horus launched another attack, there would be little left to stop them.

THE DARK ANGELS had taken a terrible toll on the enemy, but they had paid an equally terrible price in return. The Sons of Horus had slain many of their battle brothers, but even worse was the horror of spilling the blood of fellow Astartes, something utterly unthinkable just a few scant months before. Out beyond the perimeter they could hear the rumble of engines, and sensed that the enemy was re-forming for yet another attack. Jonson took stock of his remaining forces and reluctantly ordered his remaining warriors back to the inner defensive line.

Nemiel was summoned by the primarch as he and his squad were helping carry the most gravely-wounded brothers into the assembly building. There were only sixty warriors still standing; Force Commander Lamnos lay in a coma, his primary heart and his oolitic kidney ruptured by an autocannon blast, and Captain Hsien had been killed when his position had been struck by a battle cannon shell. The Tanagran Dragoons had died to a man fighting the Sons of Horus; Nemiel had found the body of Governor Kulik surrounded by his troops, his sword gripped in his hand.

'I have a task for you, Brother-Redemptor Nemiel,' the primarch said. Beside him, Brother Titus stood sentinel beside the assembly building's open doors. A plasma bolt had fused the barrels of his assault cannon, but his deadly power fist still functioned.

'What are your orders, my lord?' Nemiel replied calmly.

'It's absolutely vital that the siege guns do not fall into Horus's hands,' Jonson replied. 'Do you agree?'

Nemiel nodded. 'Of course, my lord.'

'Then we must take steps to ensure that they are destroyed in the event that the Sons of Horus break through,' the primarch said. 'I want you to find Techmarine Askelon and instruct him to prepare a demolition device that will destroy the assembly building and everything within it. According to him, the siege guns' ammunition sections are fully-loaded. If he can rig the shells to detonate it should devastate everything within a five kilometre radius.'

The Redemptor nodded sombrely. The order wasn't unexpected. Once he'd heard a full tally of their losses he knew that their odds of victory were growing slimmer by the moment.

'I'll see to it at once,' he said.

He left the primarch and hurried into the assembly building. On the way he caught sight of Brother-Sergeant Kohl and the rest of the squad taking their place with the rest of their brothers at the inner line. For a moment he and the sergeant locked eyes, and Kohl seemed to understand what the grim look on the Redemptor's face signified. Nemiel gave the veteran a knowing nod, and the sergeant saluted him in return.

There were close to a hundred seriously wounded Astartes laid up inside the assembly building, their conditions monitored by the ground force's Apothecaries. Nemiel searched among the unconscious or comatose figures, looking for Askelon and frowning worriedly when he could find him.

'Up here,' echoed a familiar voice. Nemiel looked up to find the Techmarine standing atop the dorsal hull of the lead siege gun. Askelon pointed to the rear of the huge vehicle. 'There are ladder rungs back at the ammo section.'

Nemiel hurried back to the rear section of the war machine and scrambled up onto the dorsal hull. The armoured deck stretched for a hundred metres from one end to the other, nearly as long as an Imperator Titan was tall. He jogged down the length of the huge machine, joining Askelon by the open hatch where they'd watched Archoi's technicians work just a few hours before.

'What in Terra's name are you doing up here?' Nemiel asked. 'Brother-Apothecary Gideon said you should be resting. Your internal organs and nervous system were badly damaged when you tapped those power conduits.'

Askelon waved such concerns away. 'I'm not doing us any good sitting down there on the permacrete,' he said hoarsely. Burn sealant had been spread across his burned face, giving the charred skin a synthetic sheen. 'So I thought I'd climb up here and see if I can get this monster running.'

Nemiel's eyes widened. 'Is that possible?'

Askelon sighed. 'Well, in theory, yes. The engine is functional, the weapons fully loaded, and the void shields – all four of them – check out as ready for activation. The problem is that there aren't any manual controls!'

The Redemptor frowned. 'That doesn't make any sense. Even a Titan has a crew to assist its Princeps.'

Askelon nodded. 'And these vehicles were built with supplementary crew stations – but Archoi's tech-adepts took out all the controls and welded the hatches shut!' The Techmarine shook his head. 'It doesn't make any sense. I can't imagine what Horus thought he could use to operate these machines – the systems aren't quite as complex as a Titan, but they're close.' He spread his arms and gave a frustrated sigh. 'So here we are with the firepower of an army in our hands, and no way to use it.'

The Redemptor scowled down at the open cockpit. A thought niggled at him. 'Is there any way to rig a basic set of controls to the machine – even just to operate one of its void shields?'

Askelon shook his head. 'Actually, operating the void shield is one of the most complex operations to manage – just ask any Titan moderati. Rigging an effective set of controls would take hours, possibly days.' He shook his head. 'Unless you have a spare MIU sitting around, there's nothing we can do.'

Nemiel glanced up at the Techmarine, his eyes widening. Askelon frowned. 'What's the matter?' he asked.

'We do have an MIU,' Nemiel said. 'It's been right under our noses all along.'

THE ENEMY LAUNCHED their eighth and final attack an hour and a half later.

Lion El'Jonson listened to the approaching sound of engines and readied his sword. 'Here they come,' he said to Nemiel. Around them, the surviving Astartes checked their weapons. At the Redemptor's urging, they had extended the perimeter of the inner line outwards another two hundred and fifty metres, stretching their coverage almost to the breaking point.

'Askelon is working as quickly as he can, my lord,' he said to the primarch. 'We have to buy as much time for him as we can.'

'This is a terrible risk we're taking,' Jonson replied. Amid the mounting tension, the primarch managed a faint smile. 'If we fail to hold them back and somehow we aren't both shot to pieces in the process, I'm going to hold you personally responsible for this.'

Nemiel nodded. 'Duly noted, my lord,' he said in a deadpan voice that would have made Brother-Sergeant Kohl proud.

The enemy vehicles advanced from three sides, nosing their way through the maze of close-set buildings and closing in on the assembly building. By careful planning or sheer, diabolical luck, most of the enemy vehicles emerged from cover at the same time. Nemiel counted ten Rhino APCs – and, directly ahead, a patched-up battle tank. A square metal plate had been bolted over the crater blasted in its glacis by a lascannon bolt, and the rebels' technicians had jury-rigged enough of its wrecked controls to get it back into action. The tank shuddered to a halt as the rest of the APCs surged forward. Its turret tracked fractionally to the left and the battle cannon fired.

The heavy shell howled through the air towards the Dark Angels and struck Brother Titus's armoured torso. The Dreadnought vanished in a thunderous blast, hurling bits of its arms and chest high into the air. Shrapnel rained down on the defenders, the metal fragments pinging off their armour.

Jonson straightened in the wake of the blast, his expression tense. Twenty metres away, the Rhinos came to an abrupt halt. Assault ramps dropped to the ground as ten squads of pale-armoured Astartes disembarked and took shelter behind the cover of their vehicles. Farther back, the tank traversed its turret to the left, taking aim on a Dark Angels squad.

'This won't work,' the primarch snarled. 'That tank will sit back there and shoot us to pieces, and then the Sons of Horus will sweep in and mop up the survivors.' He drew the Lion Sword and held it aloft. Sunlight shone on its razor edge. 'Forward, brothers!' he cried. 'For honour and glory! For Terra! For the Emperor! Forward!'

All sixty Dark Angels rose to their feet in a single, fluid motion and advanced towards the Sons of Horus, a thin line of black against a waiting phalanx of white. The battle cannon boomed again, but the gunner failed to adjust for the sudden enemy advance, and the shell blasted a gout of dirt and permacrete into the air behind the Astartes. The rebel warriors rose from cover and opened fire as well. Plasma bolts and shells stabbed out at the advancing Imperials, and the Dark Angels returned fire. The two formations drew inexorably together. Nemiel clutched his crozius tightly and prepared for one final battle.

A tremor rippled through the ground beneath their feet – very faint at first, but growing in strength with each passing moment. Nemiel felt it through the soles of his boots and turned to Jonson, who had felt it, too. A throaty roar filled the air behind them, swelling outwards in a solid wall of sound as one of Horus's mighty siege machines rumbled slowly onto the battlefield.

The war machine rose like a plasteel and ceramite mountain over the Astartes, its Hydra flak batteries and mega-bolter turrets along its flanks traversing to bear on the enemy ranks. The multi-barrelled laser batteries opened fire, unleashing a torrent of bolts at the stationary battle tank. The tank all but vanished in the glare of hundreds of detonations as the laser bolts pounded the armoured hull. Individually, each shot lacked the power to penetrate the mighty tank's reinforced ceramite plates, but one among the hundreds of impacts landed a direct hit on the plate steel bolted hastily over its former wound and burned straight through. Smoke billowed from the tank's open ports as the thermal effects of the bolt incinerated the crew in a split second.

A pair of mega-bolters roared to life next, sending a stream of heavy calibre shells over the heads of the Dark Angels and into the enemy's ranks. Rhinos shuddered beneath dozens of hits and were torn apart in seconds; the Astartes standing alongside them fared little better. The Sons of Horus recoiled under the storm of shells; dozens of the warriors fell, their armour riddled with holes. The rest wavered for a moment more and then broke, retreating swiftly back into cover among the surrounding buildings. Mega-bolter shells pursued them the entire way, slaying a dozen more before the rest could escape.

The Dark Angels stood in the shadow of the immense war machine, wreathed by wisps of fyceline propellant from the barrels of the mega-bolters and numbed by the awesome roar of the guns. Alone among them, Lion El'Jonson turned to the enormous engine and raised his sword in salute.

'Well done, Brother Titus!' he called over the vox. 'You could not have arrived at a more opportune time.'

'Techmarine Askelon deserves your accolades, my lord, not I,' replied Titus's synthetic voice. 'It was no small feat merging my MIU with the war engine's interface without access to the original STC blueprints; only the specialised tools and equipment in the assembly building allowed him to modify the vehicle's interface with my neural connectors. I regret that I am still unable to access the vehicle's shield array, and my locomotion is still very slow and clumsy, but all weapons systems are fully functional.'

Jonson stared up at the mountain of metal. 'Brother Titus, can your surveyors detect the star port to the south?'

'The unit is in need of calibration, but yes, I am registering it on my array,' Titus replied. 'I am detecting twelve heavy transports and numerous small vehicles.'

The primarch nodded. 'Load a shell into your siege gun and destroy the site.'

Titus hesitated for only an instant. 'At once, my lord,' he replied. With a ponderous moan of heavy-duty motors, the giant cannon barrel began to elevate. 'Loading will complete in five seconds,' Titus said. 'I advise that you take cover behind me. I cannot adequately gauge the effect the gun's concussion will have when it is fired.'

As primarch and war machine spoke, Nemiel cast his gaze upon the devastation that Titus had wrought. Scores of Astartes lay dead, surrounding misshapen metal hulks that were functioning APCs just a few minutes before. Behind him, heavy plasteel machinery rattled and groaned as the siege gun's auto-loading mechanism fed a magma shell into the cannon's breech. Recalling what such shells had done to the forge, he felt a deep sense of dread. What horrors could a warlord wreak with such weapons at his command?

The Astartes withdrew a hundred metres behind the huge machine, nearly to the entrance of the assembly building itself. Nemiel glanced over at Jonson, and saw the primarch staring off to the southwest, towards the unsuspecting star port.

The air blazed with a flare of orange and yellow light as the cannon fired, rocking the massive war machine back against its drive units. Nemiel felt the concussion of the blast like the fist of a god striking his chest; several of the Astartes staggered beneath the blow, while downrange the pressure wave hurled the wrecked Rhinos about like broken toys. The magma shell roared skyward, flaring like a shooting star until it was lost from sight behind the planet's thick overcast.

They waited in silence, counting the seconds as the shell reached its apogee and began to fall to earth once more. Two minutes after the shot there was a flash of searing white light on the southern horizon, followed by a furious rumble that shook the earth where the Astartes stood, more than thirty kilometres away. A hot breeze wafted against their faces, smelling of molten steel and ash, and a slowly-rising pillar of dirt and debris climbed portentously into the sky. With a single stroke, the enemy ground force had been utterly destroyed.

'Such is the fate of all traitors,' Lion El'Jonson said. The implacable look in the primarch's eye made Nemiel's blood run cold.

TWENTY
THE CONQUEROR WORM

Caliban
In the 200th year of the Emperor's Great Crusade

FOR THE THIRD time in twenty-four hours, Zahariel found himself locked into the jump seat of a Stormbird, his ears full of thunder and his eyes brimming with dark thoughts.

The angels of Caliban's deliverance descended on the Northwilds arcology clad in fire, smoke and burnished iron. Luther had ordered a ballistic approach for the assault forces, so the drop ships literally fell from the sky upon the beleaguered city. To the panicked Jaegers securing the landing platforms on the arcology's upper levels it was like a scene from a mythical Armageddon.

The command squad went in with the first wave. Zahariel's stomach leapt as the transport pulled out of its dive less than a thousand metres over the arcology and the Stormbird's pilot gave full power to the thrusters scant seconds before touchdown. His gauntleted hands tightened on the haft of the force staff resting between his knees as he counted down the seconds until landing. Around him, the other members of the squad made final checks to their wargear with swift, practised movements. The atmosphere in the troop compartment was electric. Even Brother Attias seemed unusually animated, his steel-plated head turning left and right as he spoke words of encouragement to the Astartes at his side. The words of Luther's speech on the embarkation field still rang in their ears, calling them all to glory.

The moment has come, brothers. Jonson has cast us aside; the Emperor, who once demanded our fealty, has forgotten us. Now we must decide whether to accept their judgment and give in to the darkness, or to defy them for the sake of our home and our people.

He glanced across the compartment to the jump seats nearest the ramp. There, the Saviour of Caliban sat, clad in his gleaming armour like a hero of old. Luther's gaunt features were composed as he studied page after page of arcane text from the ancient grimoire propped across his knees. Lord Cypher sat closest to him, arms folded across his chest. He stared back at Zahariel from the depths of his hood, his expression unreadable.

Zahariel focused on his breathing. Images came and went in his mind: Sar Daviel, wreathed in tongues of blue fire; Luther, marked with glowing runes and haloed by the same terrible flame; Brother-Librarian Israfael, smoke rising from the wound in his chest, his features distorted with anguish as he sank slowly to his knees.

Shall we side with those who scorn us, or choose our own path, to protect the innocent from those who would exploit and corrupt them?

The noise of the thrusters rose to a screaming crescendo, and then the Stormbird touched down with a tremendous, spine-rattling jolt. Jump restraints released with a metallic clatter and servo-motors whined as the assault ramp deployed, letting in the cold, smoke-tinged air of the Northwilds. Boots thundered as the Astartes leapt to their feet; bolt pistols cleared their holsters and chainswords roared to angry life. Zahariel felt his body respond without conscious thought, caught up with all the rest in the intricate dance of death.

Luther passed the book to Lord Cypher and led the way, his black cloak flapping wildly in the howling gale kicked up by the Stormbird's thrusters. Zahariel followed six paces behind Lord Cypher, flanked by Brother Attias to his right. Six other Astartes, all veterans of the fighting on Sarosh, fanned out around them, their weapons ready. Three other assault squads were deploying from their own transports on the landing platform as well, spreading out in a wide arc to cover the command squad's flanks and rear.

The heavy blast doors leading to the arcology's upper levels had already slid open by the time Luther and his warriors had disembarked, and a large group of green-uniformed Jaeger officers were struggling to reach them through the gale spawned by the drop ships' thrusters. Leading the Jaeger troops was a wiry, sharp-featured officer in smoke-stained flak armour and fatigues.

'Colonel Hadziel,' Luther said in greeting, his powerful voice carrying easily over the roaring wind.

'An honour, my lord,' Hadziel shouted back. One hand was pressed to the top of his helmet to keep it in place, and he squinted into the grit kicked up by the Stormbirds. 'I apologise for not being able to keep you apprised of the situation during the trip, but the rebels have found some way to jam all of our vox transmissions. I can't coordinate with my squads inside the arcology, much less send or receive signals outside.'

'No need for apologies, Colonel. Frankly, we expected something like this.' Luther paused for a moment as the four transports took off with a bone-jarring roar, then spoke into the ringing silence that followed. 'One thing we need to be clear on from the outset, however, is that the rebels are not responsible for this. In fact, as of three hours ago, I concluded a truce with the rebel leaders, and they have agreed to assist us against our common enemy.'

Hadziel and his staff exchanged bemused looks. 'Common enemy, my lord?' he asked carefully.

'Now is not the time for a detailed briefing, Colonel,' Luther said sternly. 'I assure you, all will be made clear once we've gotten this situation under control. Suffice it to say that a cabal of off-worlders housed here at the arcology have hidden themselves somewhere in the lowest sub-levels and are exposing this entire area to the malign effects of the warp.'

To his credit, Colonel Hadziel accepted the bizarre turn of events with surprising poise. He blinked once, and nodded curtly. 'How can I and my Jaegers be of service, my lord?'

'Good man,' Luther said proudly. To a man, Hadziel's staff grinned, their confidence restored. The Master of Caliban beckoned them to fall in around him. 'First,' he said, 'what's the current situation and the disposition of the civilians?'

Colonel Hadziel gestured to a pair of staff officers, who presented a portable hololith table and set it up at Luther's feet.

'For the last few hours, it's been complete chaos,' Hadziel said grimly. He keyed in a number of commands, and a cross-section of the arcology filled the air above the table. 'As luck would have it, the evacuation order from Aldurukh had just gotten underway when the unrest began. As a result, we already had a movement order in place and there were combat squads in the hab levels when the unrest began. Those squads bought us precious time to organise and took a lot of pressure off our checkpoints in the early stages of the riots. Otherwise, our cordon would have probably been completely overrun.'

'How many civilians were you able to evacuate?' Zahariel interjected.

The colonel shrugged. 'Thousands, certainly,' he said, 'but I've no way of determining an exact number of evacuees. We're still trying to let people through, but it's extremely difficult at this point.'

'Why?' Luther asked.

Colonel Hadziel took a breath, considering his reply carefully. 'These riots are much worse than anything we've seen before,' he said. 'We'd thought maybe some kind of disease had taken hold in the hab levels – something savage, like crimson fever or rabies. The last reports we got from our squads in the lower levels reported mobs of bestial civilians attacking every living thing in sight. Gunfire didn't seem to slow them in the least short of a las-bolt to the head. The uninfected civilians are panicking and trying to mob our checkpoints in an effort to escape.' The colonel's jaw tightened. 'There have been several incidents of troops turning their guns on the civilians in order to keep the crowds at bay.'

He hit another set of keys and gestured to the holo-image. 'As it is, I've been forced to give up my initial positions and fall back to level fifteen, where there are fewer access points to cover and I can pass orders using runners.' Almost half of the lower levels of the arcology began to blink red. 'Everything below that level, including all the sub-levels, has been lost, which includes the arcology's thermal power plants, water and air circulation and waste recycling facilities. In purely military terms, we're no longer in control of the arcology.' Hadziel spread his hands. 'We're still trying to save as many civilians as we can, but we've got to check every group and make sure they're clean before we can let them through.'

Luther turned to Zahariel. 'Are there any measures we can take to quickly discern living humans from these walking corpses?'

Hadziel's eyes widened. 'Corpses, my lord? Those were reports from panicked troops. Surely you don't believe–'

'Make sure the checkpoints are issued thermal auspex units,' Zahariel cut in. 'Even a thermal lasgun sight will do. The corpses will have a much lower heat signature than the civilians around them.'

'Well, I...' Hadziel began, then took one look at the Astartes and thought better of his protest. 'I mean, I'll send the word out immediately.'

Luther nodded curtly. 'Very good, colonel.' He paused for a moment, studying the display carefully for a moment. 'At this point, I want you to focus your efforts on holding the checkpoints at level fifteen and to continue evacuating civilians out of the hab levels as quickly and efficiently as possible. My warriors will form into strike forces and will pass through these checkpoints–' He indicated seven strategic locations across level fifteen '–and will advance into the contested areas towards the arcology's power plants and life support centres.'

Hadziel frowned. 'My lord, we have no clear estimates on the number of infected individuals on the lower levels, but it certainly reaches into the hundreds, possibly thousands. They will be drawn to your warriors like blood moths to a wounded deer.'

Luther nodded in agreement. 'That's the idea, colonel. My brothers will deal with the corpses and take the pressure off your troops. Once you've completed relocating the civilian population you'll be able to commit your forces to securing the arcology's lower levels. I want you to assign a liaison officer to each of my teams and ensure that their path through the checkpoints is cleared. That's all for now, gentlemen. We'll speak again once order is restored.'

Hadziel nodded and began issuing instructions to his staff officers, who immediately began to draft the necessary orders. Luther turned away from the Jaegers and motioned for Zahariel, Attias and Lord Cypher to join him several paces away.

'Any word from the rebels still inside the arcology?' he quietly asked Zahariel.

The Librarian shook his head. 'They're having no better luck with their vox-units than we are,' he replied. 'There's no way to know if they've found the sorcerers or not.'

Luther nodded. 'Do you believe Colonel Hadziel's estimate of the number of corpses in the lower levels?'

Zahariel shook his head grimly. 'Not in the least. They must number in the thousands, possibly the tens of thousands.'

'An army of the dead,' Brother Attias said in his hollow, synthetic voice. 'But to what purpose?'

'Fuel for the fire,' Luther said, half to himself. 'The sorcerers are using the violence and bloodshed to weaken the barrier between the physical world and the warp and facilitate their master ritual.' He cast a meaningful glance at Lord Cypher, who nodded.

Zahariel scowled at the secret exchange, wondering what secrets Luther had uncovered from the forbidden library. 'Then we have to find a way to strike directly at the sorcerers and their ritual,' he declared.

'If we can locate them in time,' Luther said grimly. 'The ritual must be close to completion at this point.'

'Zahariel can lead us there,' Cypher said. His hooded head swivelled to regard the Librarian. 'You can sense the turbulence in the warp generated by the ritual, can you not?'

'I...' Zahariel paused, glancing from Lord Cypher to Luther. The Master of Caliban was staring at him expectantly. Was he being manoeuvred into something? Israfael's stricken face hovered before his mind's eye like a ghost. He shook his head, as though to clear it. 'That is, yes, I can, but that kind of prolonged exposure to warp energy is not without risk.'

Luther grinned wryly. 'Brother, believe me when I tell you that if we don't stop this ritual we're all going to be exposed to more warp energy than is really healthy.'

A strange, wheezing note blurted from Attias's vox grille. Zahariel turned to stare at the skull-faced Astartes. The sound continued, and it took the Librarian a few moments to realise that Attias was laughing. Cypher started to chuckle, and then Zahariel couldn't help but join in as well, dispelling the tension of the moment.

'Well, brother?' Luther prompted.

Zahariel bowed his head. 'Give me a moment to centre myself,' he said, clenching the force staff tightly and focusing his awareness through his armour's psychic hood.

At once he felt the churning maelstrom of the warp whirling about him. Its energy licked at him like tongues of flame, trying to find purchase in his soul. Jagged slivers of ice dug painfully into the back of his skull as the hood tried to shield him from the storm.

The whirlwind spun about him, drawing him downward towards its locus like a gaping maw. Something lay at its centre, he sensed; a seed of darkness, hungry and impatient for release.

Zahariel staggered slightly at the vertiginous pull of the ritual, holding himself apart from it by sheer effort of will. 'I can feel it,' he gasped. 'The sorcerers are trying to open a path for something to come through. Like Sarosh, only... worse, somehow.'

'Can you lead us to them?' Luther said.

Zahariel concentrated on the vortex, following its currents with his mind. The biting cold in his head increased. Frost spread along the force staff's metal shaft. 'The locus is deep within the earth,' he said with a grimace. 'I'll be able to refine its position more precisely as we go.'

'Excellent,' Luther said. 'We'll have Hadziel unlock a bank of maintenance lifts that will take us directly to the lowest sub-level, then fight our way to the locus from there.'

The Master of Caliban spun on his heel, snapping orders to Colonel Hadziel and to the other three squad leaders waiting at the landing pad. With an effort, Zahariel tried to re-orient himself in the physical world once more. The transition was much more difficult than he expected; even with the buffer provided by the psychic hood, the energies of the maelstrom still plucked at him, as though it had sunk barbs deep into his soul. He felt strangely numbed, unmoored within his own skin, and he knew that the grip of the storm would only grow stronger the closer he came to the centre of the ritual.

He blinked, trying to clear his eyes, and found Lord Cypher studying him speculatively. Before Zahariel could ask what he was staring at, the enigmatic Astartes abruptly turned away.

THEY DESCENDED INTO darkness, lit only by feeble red emergency lighting inside the maintenance lift's metal cage. Hadziel had authorised the activation of a bank of four lifts that would allow Luther's four assault squads to deploy together, concentrating their strength against whatever foes awaited them. Based on their experience at Sigma Five-One-Seven, Zahariel had advised choosing the set of lifts in the closest proximity to the arcology's main thermal core.

The strength of the maelstrom increased steadily the deeper they went, until Zahariel scarcely had to focus his awareness in order to sense it. The unnatural energies sank effortlessly through his armour and pulsed sickeningly against his skin. Frost coated the housing of his psychic hood and sent needles of icy feedback into his brain. The storm winds tugged ruthlessly at him, tearing at his mind and soul with increasing vigour.

Finally the lift jerked roughly to a halt, two hundred metres below the earth. They'd reached the lowest sub-level of the arcology. Luther gave a nod to the Astartes manning the controls, and the lift doors clattered open, revealing a broad, low-ceilinged chamber formed of fused permacrete. The air was stiflingly humid and thick with the stench of corruption.

Here, as with the lower levels at Sigma Five-One-Seven, the earth had already begun to reclaim the space. Glossy greenish-black vines sprouted from cracks in the walls and along the floor, and a dripping, greenish mould covered much of the ceiling. Insects chittered and squirmed through the tainted growth, or droned through the thick air on blurring wings. Sickly blue luminescence radiated from colonies of fungus that sprouted in haphazard clusters overhead, providing ample light to the Astartes' enhanced night vision.

The Dark Angel squads deployed swiftly from the adjoining lifts. Three assault squads took the lead, forming a protective arc in front of Luther and the command squad, and orienting their weapons on the three entryways on the opposite side of the chamber. Two men in each of the assault squads carried a hand flamer, while two of the veterans in Luther's command squad were armed with powerful, short range meltaguns. The rest carried roaring chainswords and blunt-nosed bolt pistols, ideal for the kind of close-quarters fighting they expected to encounter. They were forty strong, a fearsome display of force. Entire worlds had been brought into compliance with less.

Luther led the command squad into the chamber. His huge sword Nightfall burned a fierce blue in his right hand, and his ornate bolt pistol gleamed dully in his left. Zahariel stood next to him, clutching his force staff with both hands, while Brother Attias and Lord Cypher brought up the rear. Cypher held his plasma pistol ready in his right hand. The leather-bound grimoire was clutched tightly against his chest.

The Master of Caliban leaned close to Zahariel. 'Can you sense the ritual in process?' he asked quietly.

Gritting his teeth, Zahariel focused his awareness through the psychic hood. The dampener was already straining at the limit of its abilities; he could smell the strange mix of overheated circuitry and frozen metal. This close, he could sense rhythms pulsing through the howling psychic wind, like discordant notes struck by a madman's hand. The vibrations represented the symbolic chants that coaxed the energies of the warp into the physical realm.

'The ritual is well advanced,' the Librarian said, suppressing a groan of disgust. 'It could reach its climax at any time. We have to hurry!'

Luther nodded. His dark eyes shone with fevered intensity. 'Listen, Zahariel. When we reach the ritual site, I want you to keep close to me. We have to confront this entity, together. I have the knowledge, but I lack the ability to manipulate the forces of the warp.'

Zahariel shook his head. 'Confront it? You mean drive it back.'

'No,' Luther said. 'At least, not yet.' He turned and nodded at the grimoire that Cypher carried. 'That book contains the means to subjugate the spirit, bend it to our will. If we can reach it at the right moment, while it's still weak.'

'You can't be serious!' Zahariel cried. 'What you're talking about is madness! The Emperor–'

Luther stepped close, until he was nearly whispering in Zahariel's ear. 'Yes. The Emperor has forbidden this. Why? Because he fears the beings of the warp. That's something we must learn to exploit, if Caliban is to remain free.' He looked deeply into Zahariel's eyes. 'Do you trust me, brother?'

Zahariel found himself nodding, despite the misgivings in his heart. 'Yes. Of course.'

'Then help me. It's the only way.'

Without waiting to hear Zahariel's reply, Luther turned and waved the assault squads towards the rightmost of the three large openings on the other side of the landing. So far, the path to the ritual site seemed to lead to the arcology's primary thermal core, just as it had at Sigma Five-One-Seven. With a pair of flamer-wielding Astartes in the lead, the first assault squad advanced into the broad, vine-choked passageway. Luther's command squad was third in line, with the last assault squad covering the rear.

The corpses came at them from three sides. A few hundred metres down the passageway, it was bisected by another pair of wide corridors. The enemy, showing a rudimentary grasp of tactics, allowed the first and second squads to pass this junction before triggering their ambush. With scarcely a sound, hundreds of rotting corpses shambled out of the darkness, attacking the head of the advancing strike force and trying to drive into its midst from either side.

Flamers hissed, filling the passageways with streams of searing promethium. Bolt pistols barked on every side, felling the advancing creatures with well-placed shots to the head. The Astartes continued to fire even as the corpses surrounded them, drawing into arm's reach and trying to drag down the armoured warriors by sheer weight of numbers. Chainswords roared and slashed, severing limbs and splitting torsos.

The Dark Angels stood shoulder to shoulder in the confined space, never yielding a centimetre to the unearthly horde. At the centre of the formation, standing at the junction of the passageways, Luther roared encouragement to his warriors and put down one corpse after another with his pistol. Zahariel and Attias joined in with their own pistols, adding to the whirlwind of steel that took a fearful toll of the enemy.

For several long minutes the battle raged against the walking dead. The corpses pressed harder and harder against the Astartes – and then, inevitably, the pressure began to wane. The strike force, sensing that they had absorbed the brunt of the attack, began to press further down the passageway. Flamers continued to hiss and spit, until the walls of the passage shimmered with heat and the air grew thick with smoke and the stench of burnt meat.

Zahariel followed Luther through a waking nightmare. They advanced in the wake of the lead assault squads, moving down a tunnel of burning vines and shredded bodies. The slaughter was incredible; within only a hundred metres the Librarian found himself walking on a literal carpet of broken bodies. In places his boots sank into piles of blood and bone that rose nearly to his knees.

The Astartes drove inexorably forward, grinding the enemy beneath their heel. Then, without warning, the passageway widened into a huge chamber that crackled with unnatural energies. They had reached the thermal core.

Blasting their way through a faltering rear guard of corpses, the first and second assault squads broke through into the chamber far enough to make room for Luther's command squad. Then they halted, weapons ready, waiting for word from their commander.

Luther and Zahariel emerged into the cavernous room with the rest of the command squad close behind. Ahead, arcs of violet lightning leapt from the monolithic bulk of the thermal core and etched looping scars across the permacrete floor. The air stank of ozone and the sickly-sweet reek of decaying flesh; it rippled invisibly against the skin, churned by unnatural energies that radiated from the vast ritual circle at the centre of the space.

A half-dozen queen worms were curled about the outside of the circle, their segmented bodies writhing frenetically in response to the building intensity of the ritual. Their mandibles clashed and their multiple eyes glowed with a power of their own as they drove thousands of corpses against the arcology's hard-pressed defenders.

Just beyond the worms, standing at precisely-determined points along the perimeter of the ritual circle, stood the sorcerers. The Terrans were clad in torn and stained robes that had been painted in arcane sigils that shone with a strange, pellucid light. Zahariel saw that their skin was waxy and mottled in shades of black and grey, as though they were little more than corpses themselves. Their heads turned fearfully at the arrival of the Astartes, but their leader, a towering figure with his back to the Dark Angels, rallied them with clenched fists and shrieked curses until they resumed their efforts.

At the centre of the circle, Zahariel could just make out massive coils of scaly hide, larger by far than the queen worm that had nearly slain him and his squad at Sigma Five-One-Seven.

Zahariel felt a surge of power in the great chamber that seemed to rise up from deep within the earth. Black vapours, reeking of sulphur and rot, rose in a flood from the deep pit where the thermal core was set. The ritual was reaching its culmination.

'We're nearly out of time!' he cried out.

Luther heard and nodded grimly. He raised his glowing sword. 'For Caliban, brothers!' he cried, his voice echoing like a trumpet call over the cacophony of the ritual chamber.

'For Caliban!' the Astartes answered. 'For Luther!' As one, they charged forward.

The queen worms outside the circle reacted at once, whipping about and screeching their fury, but they were caught in a veritable storm of bolt pistol fire, searing flame, and the fearsome blasts of meltaguns. Mass-reactive rounds punched through thick layers of scale and detonated in the soft flesh beneath, blasting gory craters in the worms' flanks. Two of the creatures thrashed and hissed, bathed in streams of fiery promethium. A third blew apart as a pair of meltagun shots struck in at the head and midsection, showering the rest with splashes of steaming ichor.

Yet despite their terrible wounds, the surviving worm queens fought on. Two of the creatures focused on Luther, their mandibles clashing as they lunged at the knight from the left and right. Zahariel saw it unfold, and thought of Brother Gideon, his body shorn in half by a worm's scissor-like bite.

But Luther was a born warrior, a man who had been fighting the monsters of Caliban all his life. As the monsters lunged, he ducked low and to the left, bringing up his power sword as the worm's leap carried it just past his right shoulder. Nightfall pierced the side of the worm's head, just behind the mandible, and like a claw it tore a burning gash more than halfway along the worm queen's length. The second worm found its attack blocked by the first creature's lunge, causing it to check its thrust and slide, snapping, over the mortally-wounded queen's back. Luther saw it coming and put out one of its eyes with an explosive bolt from his pistol. A plasma shot from Lord Cypher struck the opposite side of the queen's skull a moment later, leaving a glowing crater gouged into the bone and boiling its brains in the blink of an eye.

Brother Attias fell upon the mortally-wounded queen and began to saw its head off with his roaring chainsword. To Zahariel's left, a burning worm leapt into the midst of one of the attack squads, flattening them beneath its bulk and madly snapping at armoured limbs and torsos. Another worm, streaming ichor from scores of bolt-pistol wounds, snatched up a Dark Angel in its mandibles and lifted him high, crushing his armour plates like paper. The Librarian watched the warrior slap a krak grenade right between the monster's eyes, and both he and the worm's head disappeared in an angry yellow flash.

Zahariel ignored the surviving worms, heading instead for the ritual circle and the madly chanting Terrans. The power of the ritual trembled in the air; he could feel it against his skin like a searing brand. A bridge was being formed, linking the physical world with the seething madness of the warp. He knew all too well what would happen next.

He struck the sorcerer's ward a moment later, just outside the first lines of the summoning circle. It felt as though he'd run right into a solid wall of lightning. Agony tore along his nerves; warning telltales flashed in his vision as the neural feedback began to overload his synaptic receptors. Had it not been for the dampening power of his psychic hood, the shock would likely have killed him outright.

The cries of the sorcerers grew exultant. In the centre of the circle, the giant worm began to slowly rise into the air, its scales throwing back the lurid glow of muzzle-flashes and liquid fire. Pain threatened to overwhelm Zahariel. It took all his concentration, all his courage and dedication, to raise his force staff and strike at the energies of the ward with all his might.

Warp energies collided with incandescent fury. Zahariel focused his anger through the staff, pouring all the psychic energy he could through the focus and into the ward. Its energies surged for a moment, resisting, then like a pierced bubble it burst with a ringing peal of thunder.

Zahariel fell, his strength spent, but a strong hand at his side gripped his arm, bearing him up. Luther, his blade gleaming like an avenging angel, stepped past him and reached the Terran leader. His shadow fell across the sorcerer, who realised, too late, that his powers had failed him. The sorcerer spun, hands curled into claws before his face, and Luther smote him with his burning sword. Nightfall sliced through both of the Terran's legs, just below the hip joint, and the Terran fell screaming to the stone floor.

A sorcerer to Zahariel's right jerked and twitched under a fusillade of bolt pistol rounds. Another melted like wax in a gout of burning promethium. He could sense the energies of the ritual grow unstable as the sorcerers were slain, but the rite itself continued to unfold. A tipping point had been reached; the rite had accumulated enough energy that nothing would stop its culmination.

Luther spun and held out his hand. 'Cypher! The book, quickly!' he cried. His gaze fell to Zahariel. 'Join me, brother! We have to get control of this, or we're finished!'

A sense of horror welled up inside Zahariel as he realised what he had to do, but Luther was right. At this point, there was no other choice that he could see. Gritting his teeth, he staggered forwards, moving under the weight of his damaged armour by sheer muscle power alone.

He dimly sensed Cypher pressing the grimoire into Luther's hands. The Master of Caliban opened it and went quickly to a particular page. 'Can you sense the energies, Zahariel?'

Zahariel nodded. It was nearly impossible not to feel the unnatural forces impinging on his mind. He shook his head grimly. 'If I do this, I'll have to deactivate my dampener,' he warned. 'There's no other way.'

'Don't be afraid, brother!' Luther cried. 'You can master it!' He lifted the book close enough to read the pages in the shifting light. 'Now, repeat the words exactly as I read them!'

Zahariel felt a wave of icy dread. There was no time left for arguments. It was act, or perish. He reached to a set of controls at his belt and deactivated the psychic hood.

The storm forced its way into his skull. Unnatural energies crawled along the pathways of his mind. He cried out at its blasphemous touch – and felt the stirrings of a terrible intelligence behind it.

Beside him, Luther began to read aloud. Desperate, Zahariel focused on the words to the exclusion of all else, and began to repeat them in the same cadence and intonation. He poured the last vestiges of his willpower into the sorcerous invocation, and its threads mingled with the torrent of energy raised by the previous ritual. With each passing moment, the composition of the rite began to change.

Within the centre of the circle, the great worm unfolded to its full height. It towered over the assembled Astartes, its flanks wreathed in a nimbus of hellish light. Shadows shifted along its length. Scaled flesh rippled, and a pair of human-looking arms reached out to encompass the chamber. The worm's multiple eyes shone with pale green light, but in their reflected glow Zahariel saw that they now gleamed from a vaguely human-like skull.

The energies of Zahariel's incantation drew about the blasphemous creature, enfolding it like a net, but to the Librarian it was like trying to bind a dragon with a ball of thread. Its awareness pressed against the bindings, testing them, and reaching tendrils directly into Zahariel's soul.

It was vast. Ancient. A leviathan of the boundless deeps, from an age before men walked the surface of distant Terra. And as Zahariel completed the words of the binding ritual it turned its gaze upon him.

Luther stepped between Zahariel and the being, raising his fist to its inhuman face. 'By my honour and by my oaths, I bind you!' he cried. 'By the blood of my brothers, I bind you! By the power of these words I bind you!'

The being shifted against its bonds, and Zahariel found himself grappling with it. Power flooded through him, bright and clear, flowing from a thousand different sources at once: the souls of his brothers on Caliban, who had sworn themselves to Luther's service. He stifled a groan and redoubled his efforts to hold the leviathan in check.

'Release me,' the being thundered, its words reverberating in the Dark Angels' minds. It strained at the bridge between the worlds. 'Too long have I been bound by chains. Release me, and your rewards will be great.'

But Luther would not relent. 'You are bound to me, denizen of the warp! By the Twelfth Rite of Azh'uthur, I command you! Reveal to me your name!'

Now the leviathan stirred sharply; Zahariel could feel its awareness pulling at his bones. 'Ouroboros,' it spat. He felt it like a slap against his face. Blood leaked from his nostrils and the corners of his eyes.

Luther shook his fist. 'Not the name that men have given you,' he demanded. 'Reveal your true name!'

'Release me,' the being thundered. 'And all will be revealed.'

The leviathan was pulling at the bonds of the rite with increasing strength now. Zahariel realised why; the original summoning was starting to dissipate, and the being had not been fully able to manifest itself yet. In another few moments it would be forced to return from whence it came.

It reached into him. Zahariel's mouth went agape as the being swelled within his skin. His veins froze and his skin blackened. Icy vapour boiled up from his throat. Yet with every last ounce of life left in him he resisted the being's efforts, holding it just barely at bay.

'Tell me your name!' Luther shouted, and the being let out a furious roar.

There was a sudden inrushing of energy as the summoning ritual failed at last. Howling blasphemies that split stone and corroded steel, the leviathan returned to that dark place from which it had been summoned. The bridge unravelled, and the storm of psychic energies began to subside.

A deafening silence fell upon the battleground. Luther turned to Zahariel, his expression full of anguish. The Librarian sank to his knees, steam rising from the joints of his armour. His staff clattered to the floor beside him.

Zahariel looked up at Luther through a film of blood. His cracked lips pulled back in a smile.

'The quest is done, my lord,' he said, his voice barely a whisper. 'Caliban is saved.'

And then he fell forward, into Luther's reaching arms, and died.

EPILOGUE
Fallen Angels

Caliban
In the 200th year of the Emperor's Great Crusade

Zahariel awoke to find the face of death staring down at him.

'Do not move,' Brother Attias said in his hollow voice. 'You sustained severe injuries to much of your body during the battle. By rights you shouldn't be alive at all.'

The Librarian forced himself to relax and heed Attias's warning. His mind swam with images and sensations, as though all of his sensory organs had been shattered and crudely reassembled later. It took him several long moments to recognise the feel of cold sunlight against his face and the weight of cotton sheets against his chest and legs.

He looked around, moving only his eyes, and tried to make sense of where he was. Stone walls, and an arched viewport by his bed. Spartan furnishings: a desk and chair, and a chest for storing clothing. He saw a staff resting stop the chest, and belatedly realised that it was his. Was the room his as well?

'Where...' he croaked. The sound of his voice surprised him. It sounded strange, somehow, but he persisted. 'Where... am ...I?'

'Aldurukh, in the Tower of Angels,' Attias replied. 'Luther had you moved up here once the Apothecaries said your vital signs had stabilised. You were dead for a full five minutes before Luther was able to get one of your hearts beating again. No one knows exactly how he did it. It was something he read out of the book he took down into the core with him; that much I saw with my own eyes. Even still, you've been lying here for a long time in a deep coma, healing the damage you suffered.'

'How... long?' Zahariel asked.

'Eight months,' the Astartes said. 'I think everyone else but me has forgotten you're up here.'

Eight months, Zahariel thought. The number seemed significant, but he couldn't quite remember why. Fragmentary images tumbled through his mind; he tried to grasp at them, but the more he tried to hold them, the quicker they faded away. 'I was... dreaming,' he said.

Attias nodded. 'I expect so.' He stepped around the end of the bed, heading for the room's narrow door. 'I'll go and tell the Master Apothecary you're awake, and bring you some food from the kitchen. No doubt you're ravenous after being so long asleep.'

The skull-faced Astartes slipped quietly from the room. Zahariel stared up at the ceiling. 'Ravenous,' he echoed. Yes. He certainly was.

* * *

FACES CAME AND went. Attias brought him food, which he ate when the need arose. He rested, moving as little as possible, and sorted through the broken images in his mind. The Master Apothecary visited often, asking many questions for which he had few answers. At night he dreamed. Sometimes he would awake in the darkness and find a hooded figure staring at him from beside the open doorway. Unlike the others, the figure had nothing to say.

Slowly but surely, he began to fit the pieces of his mind back into place. His speech returned, then his muscle control. When Luther finally came to visit him he was sitting upright, staring out the narrow viewport at the sky.

The Master of Caliban studied him silently for a time.

'How are you feeling, brother?' he asked.

Zahariel considered the question. 'Mended,' he said at last.

'I'm glad to hear it,' Luther said. 'It's been many months, and there's a great deal of work left undone.'

'What's happened?' Zahariel asked. He shifted about, turning to face Luther.

Luther folded his arms across his chest and pursed his lips thoughtfully. 'Order has been restored,' he said. 'Once we banished the warp entity, its undead servants fell inert, just as they had at Sigma Five-One-Seven. After that, we were able to finish the evacuation and resettle the citizens across the upper levels of the arcology. The Northwilds have been quiet ever since, though maintenance crews are still stumbling across skeletal remains down in the sub-levels.'

'And the rebellion?'

Luther shrugged. 'There is no rebellion. It effectively ended in the library, when the Emperor's lies were finally brought to light. By the end of the riots at the Northwilds, it became apparent that Master Remiel was the only member of the rebel leadership still alive. Lord Thuriel and Lord Malchial were slain sometime during the day – not by the undead, but apparently by some of Lady Alera's people. Alas, we'll likely never know for certain, because Alera died leading a search party into the sub-levels to try and locate the Terran sorcerers.'

'I'm sorry to hear that,' Zahariel replied. 'What about the Terrans?'

'We've rounded up nearly all of them,' Luther said. 'Most submitted quietly, but General Morten and a number of his men managed to evade arrest and are running loose in the countryside. We'll track them down sooner or later, I'm sure. Honestly, we've got more important things to attend to at this point.'

'Such as?'

Luther smiled coldly. 'Such as securing Caliban's freedom from the Imperium.'

Zahariel shook his head. 'That's not possible,' he said tiredly. 'Surely you realise that. No matter what we do, at the end of the day we're just one world. Sooner or later Terra will learn of what we've done, and then there will be a reckoning.'

'Perhaps, and perhaps not,' Luther said. 'We've received news from the Ultima Segmentum. The Warmaster Horus has rebelled against the Emperor. Dozens of star systems are following his example and throwing off the yoke of the Imperium, and that, I believe, is just the beginning. The Emperor has much more to worry about than Caliban at this point. Now it falls to us to make the most of the time we've been given.'

Zahariel's eyes narrowed. 'In what way?' he asked, even though he already knew the answer.

'Why, to master the secrets that the Emperor has tried to conceal from us,' Luther said. 'The library here at the Rock is only the beginning, brother. We've only scratched the surface of what's out there.'

He stepped forward, kneeling at the side of the bed, and stared searchingly into Zahariel's eyes. 'What do you remember of the ritual, back at the arcology?'

'Why, all of it,' Zahariel answered. He remembered the pillar of flame, the bridge between the physical realm and the warp. He remembered the entity, and how it had sunk talons of ice into his soul.

Luther leaned forward, as though he could plumb the depths of Zahariel's eyes. 'Do you remember learning the entity's name? Its true name?'

Zahariel never flinched from Luther's gaze. Slowly, he shook his head. 'No,' he replied. 'I'm sorry. I tried, but it was far too powerful for me to command.'

Luther sighed, and slowly rose to his feet. 'Well, it was worth a try,' he said, disappointment evident in his voice. He smiled. 'Perhaps next time.'

'Next time?'

'When you're stronger, of course,' Luther added quickly. 'I admit, I underestimated the entity's power as well. Next time, we'll be better prepared. You have my oath on it.'

He reached forward and patted Zahariel's shoulder. 'I've troubled you enough for one day,' he said. 'Get some rest, regain your strength. When you're ready we'll return to the library and start our research.' The Master of Caliban took his leave, striding for the doorway. At the threshold he turned and gave Zahariel a proud smile. 'Caliban is on the verge of a golden age unlike any our ancestors dreamed of, brother. You and I are going to make it possible.'

Zahariel listened to Luther's footsteps recede down the stairs. Silence returned to the tower room once more. He rose carefully from the bed and stepped to the centre of the room. He raised his arms over his head, staring up at the ceiling, and began to slowly, deliberately stretch his long-unused muscles. When he'd finished his stretches he began a careful series of calisthenics.

The foul touch of the entity lay on his soul like a rime of black frost. It had never left him, because in truth the entity had never left, either. It was still there, deep beneath the earth, where it had lain for millions upon millions of years. The psychic bridge he'd witnessed beneath the Northwilds arcology hadn't been to draw the being through into the physical realm from the warp, like at Sarosh, but to send it back.

Zahariel knew the source of Caliban's taint.

And he knew its name.

Diamat
In the 200th year of the Emperor's Great Crusade

THE SKY ABOVE Diamat was full of ships.

The Emperor's Legions had arrived in the Tanagra system just five days after the destruction of Horus's landing force at the Xanthus star port. With no way to secure the siege machines from Jonson's Astartes, the admiral of the raiding fleet had little choice but to withdraw back to Isstvan. The Warmaster's final gambit had failed.

Lion El'Jonson stared admiringly at the gleaming array of military power drifting gracefully beyond the reinforced viewport of his sanctum. Drops of emerald still shone on the thick glass pane. With the destruction of the forge there would be no way to replace the damage done to the viewport for some time to come. He considered it a small price to pay given all that he had accomplished here.

'When will you move on Isstvan?' he asked his guest.

The primarch stepped closer to the viewport, his armoured hands clasped behind his back. 'With all due haste,' he said in a deep, rumbling voice. 'Ferrus Manus has hastened ahead of us, hungry to claim the Emperor's vengeance against Horus.' He glanced at Jonson and frowned. 'We had hoped to provision our ships here before continuing to the combat zone.'

Jonson sighed. 'I'm sorry for that, cousin, but Magos Archoi left me no choice. The jamming had to be stopped without delay.' His expression darkened. 'Also, he lied to me. Better he had come at me with a knife, face to face, than play me false.'

The primarch nodded, turning back to the viewport and looking down upon Diamat. A vast, reddish-brown stain, like old blood, hung in the planet's ochre sky. The dust and ash blown into the atmosphere by the destruction of the forge – and to a lesser extent, the devastation of the star port, hours later – would have far-reaching effects upon the planet. The few thousand inhabitants who remained would face lean and difficult times for generations to come.

'May I ask you a question?' the primarch asked.

Jonson shrugged. 'Of course.'

'When did you learn about the existence of the siege engines?'

'Oh. That.' Jonson smiled. 'Fifty years ago. I was studying the history of the Great Crusade and saw a reference to them in a despatch that Horus sent to the Emperor. He'd commissioned them during the long siege of the xenos fortress-states on Tethonus. Horus tasked the masters of Diamat to create continental siege machines; vast artillery pieces that could devastate the most powerful fortifications.' He spread his hands. 'The war machines took much longer for the forge masters to complete than planned. By the time they were finished, the campaign on Tethonus had been over for a year and a half, and Horus had moved on to other conquests. So the weapons were put into a depot here against the day when he would come to claim them. Then came Isstvan.'

The primarch grunted in understanding. 'Then came Isstvan,' he agreed.

'When I heard about his rebellion, it was obvious to me that Horus's path must ultimately lead to Terra,' Jonson said. 'Even if he were to somehow prevail against you and the other Legions, the Warmaster couldn't claim total victory so long as the Emperor was safe in his palace. No, for Horus to triumph, our father would have to die. And that meant a long and costly siege of Terra.'

The primarch glanced at Jonson again and bowed his head in admiration. 'You have performed a master stroke, brother. Truly. Rather than confront Horus directly, you've defeated him with only a handful of troops.' He smiled slyly. 'I begin to think that the title of Warmaster was placed upon the wrong brow.'

Jonson smiled at the compliment. 'From you, brother, that means something. Thank you.'

'What now?' the primarch asked. 'Will you accompany us to Isstvan?'

'No,' Jonson said. 'I must return with all haste to the Shield Worlds and prepare the Legion for the trip to Terra. In fact, I think it best if no one outside you, I and the other primarchs ever knew I was here. I wouldn't want the Emperor to believe I did any of this with an ulterior motive in mind.'

The primarch considered this at length, and nodded. 'A prudent choice, and a very humble one.'

Jonson leaned forward in his chair. 'Well, naturally,' he said. His expression grew serious. 'I don't do this for the accolades, brother, nor for the power. Not really. I do this for the good of the Imperium. Horus became our father's favourite son for no other reason than fate. Had I been the first one he'd found, I would be Warmaster today. No offence.'

The primarch smiled. 'None taken.'

'So I can count upon your support when the time comes? I feel that the Emperor will need to choose a new Warmaster very quickly if the Great Crusade is to continue.'

'That goes without saying,' the primarch agreed.

'Then we've reached an understanding?'

The primarch bowed his head solemnly. 'The arrangement stands to benefit us both.'

'Excellent,' Jonson said. 'In that case, you're welcome to take possession of the siege guns at your convenience. On one condition, of course.'

The primarch raised a thin eyebrow. 'Oh?'

Jonson gave his guest a sly grin. 'You must promise me they will be put to good use.'

Perturabo, primarch of the Iron Warriors smiled, his eyes gleaming like polished iron.

'Oh, yes,' he said. 'Of that you may be assured.'

ABOUT THE AUTHOR

Together with Dan Abnett, Mike Lee wrote the five-volume Malus Darkblade series. He also wrote the acclaimed *Nagash the Sorcerer* for Warhammer Time of Legends. Mike was the principal creator and developer for White Wolf Game Studio's Demon: The Fallen, and he has contributed to almost two dozen role-playing games and supplements over the years. An avid wargamer and devoted fan of pulp adventure, Mike lives in the United States.

DARK ANGELS

ISBN 978-1-84416-508-7

UK ISBN 978-1-84416-655-8 US ISBN 978-1-84416-570-4

ALSO BY MIKE LEE

WARHAMMER

THE CHRONICLES OF

MALUS DARKBLADE

VOLUME ONE

Contains *The Daemon's Curse*, *Bloodstorm* and *Reaper of Souls*

DAN ABNETT
& MIKE LEE

UK ISBN 978-1-84416-358-9 US ISBN 978-1-84416-563-6

would look at him and not believe it was really Ruby in that coffin? I thought. It gave me a sick, empty feeling in the base of my stomach.

I'm watching people cry over me, listening to a priest talk about me, and gazing at a coffin that is supposed to have my body in it, I thought. It made me feel absolutely ghoulish. It was all I could do to keep myself from fainting.

It was worse at the cemetery. It was I who was supposedly being lowered into the ground; it was I over whose coffin the priest was saying the final words and giving the last rites. My name, my identity, was about to be buried. I thought to myself that this was the final chance, the last time for me to cry out and say, "No, that's not Ruby in the coffin. That's Gisselle. I'm here. I'm not dead!"

For a moment I thought I had actually spoken, but the words died on my lips. My actions had made them forbidden. The truth had to be buried here and now, I realized.

The rain started and fell relentlessly, colder than usual. Umbrellas sprouted. Paul didn't seem to notice. His father and Jeanne's husband, James, had to hold his arms and keep him standing. When the coffin was lowered and the priest cast the holy water, Paul's legs folded. He had to be carried back to the limousine and given some cold water. His mother gave me a scathing glance and followed quickly.

"He's going to win the Academy Award for this," Beau said, shaking his head. Even he was beyond amazement; he was in awe and, from the look in his face, as frightened by Paul's behavior as I was.

"You're right," he whispered to me as we walked back to our vehicle. "He was so disturbed about losing you, he went a bit mad and accepted the illusion as reality. The only way he could accept the fact that you had left him was to believe it was you who was sick and now you who died," Beau theorized, and shook his head.

"I know, Beau. I'm so worried."

"Maybe now that it's over, that she's gone, he'll snap out of it," Beau suggested, but neither of us was filled with any confidence.

We returned to Cypress Woods, mainly to see how Paul was. The doctor went up to the suite to examine him, and when he came down, he told us he had given Paul something to help him sleep.

"It will take time," he said. "These things take time. Unfortunately, we have no drug, no medicine, no treatment, to cure grief." He pressed Gladys's hand between his, kissed her on the cheek, and left. She turned and glared at me in the strangest way, shooting icicles out of her eyes. Then she went upstairs to be with Paul.

Toby and Jeanne went off in a corner to comfort each other. People began to leave, anxious to put this dreadful sadness behind them. Paul's mother remained in the suite with him, so I couldn't get to see him even if I had wanted. Octavious came down to speak to us. He directed himself at Beau as if he, too, couldn't fix his eyes on my face.

"Gladys is as bad as Paul is," he muttered. "It's the way she is about him. Whenever he was sick, even as a child, she was sick. If he was unhappy, so was she. Dreadful, dreadful thing, this," he added, shaking his head and walking off. "Dreadful."

"We should leave now," Beau said softly. "Give him a day or two and then call. After he comes back to himself somewhat, we'll invite him to New Orleans and work out everything sensibly."

I nodded. I wanted to say good-bye to Jeanne and Toby, but they were like two clams who had closed their shell of grief tightly around themselves. They wouldn't look at or talk to anyone. And so Beau and I started out. I paused at the door. James was holding it open, waiting impatiently, but I wanted to gaze around at the grand house once more before leaving. I was filled with a sense of termination. This was the end of so many things. But it wasn't until late in the afternoon of the next day that I was to discover just how many.

15

Farewell to My First Love

Early in the evening of the following day, just as Beau and I were about to take our seats for dinner, Aubrey appeared in the dining room doorway, his face pale, to inform me I had a phone call. Since returning from the funeral and Cypress Woods, both Beau and I had been moving like two sleepwalkers, eating little, doing little, talking in low voices. The clouds of gloom that hovered over the bayou followed us back to New Orleans and now lay over us like a ceiling of oppression, darkening every room, filling our very souls with shadows. It had rained all the way back from Cypress Woods. I fell asleep to the monotonous wagging of the wipers on the windshield and woke with a chill that a pile of blankets and a dozen sweaters couldn't chase from my bones.

"Who is it?" I asked. I was in no mood to talk to any of Gisselle's friends, who I imagined had heard about my death and wanted to gossip, and I had left instructions with Aubrey to tell any of them who did call that I was unavailable.

"She wouldn't say, madame. She's speaking in a coarse

whisper, however, and she is very insistent," he explained. From the way he couched his words and shifted his eyes, I understood that whoever it was, she had spoken to him roughly. I was positive now that it was one of Gisselle's bitchy, spoiled girlfriends who wouldn't take no as an answer from a servant.

"Do you want me to take it?" Beau asked.

"No. I'll take care of it," I said. "Thank you, Aubrey. I'm sorry," I added, apologizing for the ugliness he had to experience.

I went into the study and seized the receiver, my heart pumping, my face flush with anger.

"Who is this?" I demanded. For a moment there was no reply. "Hello?"

"He's gone," a raspy voice replied. "He's gone away and we can't find him and it's all because of you."

"What? Who is this? Who's gone?" I asked with machine-gun speed. The voice had sent an icicle down my spine and nailed my feet to the floor.

"He's gone into the canals. He went there last night and he hasn't returned and no one has been able to find him. My Paul," she sobbed, and I knew it was Gladys Tate.

"Paul . . . went into the canals last night?"

"Yes, yes, yes," she cried. "You did this to him. You did all this."

"Madame Tate . . ."

"Stop!" she screamed. "Stop your pretending," she said, and lowered her voice into that scratchy old witch's voice again. "I know who you really are and I know what you and your . . . lover did. I know how you broke my poor Paul's heart, shattered it until there was nothing left for him to feel. I know how you made him pretend and be part of your horrible scheme."

I felt as if I had stepped into ice water and sunk down to my knees in it. For a moment I couldn't speak. My throat closed and all the words jammed up in my chest, making it feel as if it would burst.

"You don't understand," I finally said, my voice cracking.

"Oh, I understand, all right. I understand better than you know. You see," she said, her voice now full of arrogance, "my son confided in me far more than you ever knew. There were never secrets between us, never. I knew the first time he paid a visit to you and your grandmere. I knew what he thought of you, how he was falling head over heels in love with you. I knew how sad and troubled he was when you left to live with your upper-class New Orleans Creole parents, and I knew how happy he was when you returned.

"But I warned him. I warned him you would break his heart. I tried. I did all that I could," she said, and sobbed. "You enchanted him. Just as I told you that day, you and your witch mother put a spell on my husband and then my son, my Paul. He's gone, gone," she said, her voice faltering, her hatred running out of steam.

"Mother Tate, I'm sorry about Paul. I . . . We'll come right out and help find him."

"Help find him." She laughed a chilling laugh. "I'd rather ask the devil for help. I just want you to know that I know why my son is so brokenhearted and I will not sit by and let him suffer without you suffering twice as much."

"But . . ."

The phone went dead. I sat there, my heart going thump, thump, thump, my mind reeling. I felt as if I were in a pirogue that had been caught in a current and was spinning furiously. The room did twirl. I closed my eyes and moaned and the phone fell from my hand and bounced on the floor. Beau was at my side to catch me as I started to lean too far.

"What is it? Ruby!" He turned and shouted for Sally. "Hurry, bring me a cold, wet washcloth," he ordered. He put his arm around me and knelt down. My eyes fluttered open. "What happened? Who was on the phone, Ruby?"

"It was Paul's mother, Gladys," I gasped.

"What did she say?"

"She said Paul's disappeared. He went into the swamps last night and still hasn't returned. Oh, Beau," I moaned.

Sally came running with the cloth. He took it from her and put it on my head.

"Just relax. She'll be all right now, Sally. *Merci,"* Beau said, dismissing her.

I took some deep breaths and felt the blood returning to my cheeks.

"Paul's disappeared? That's what she said?"

"Yes, Beau. But she said more. She said she knew about us, knew what we had done. Paul told her everything. I never knew he had, but now that I think of the way she glared at me at the funeral . . ." I sat up. "She never liked me, Beau." I gazed into his wide eyes. "Oh, Beau, she threatened me."

"What? Threatened. How?"

"She said I would suffer twice as much as Paul's suffered."

He shook his head. "She's just hysterical right now. Paul's got them all in a frenzy."

"He went into the swamps, Beau, and he didn't come back. I want to go right out there and help find him. We must, Beau. We must."

"I don't know what we can do. They must have all their workers looking."

"Beau, please. If something should happen to him . . ."

"All right," he relented. "Let's change our clothes. You were right," he said with an underlying current of bitterness in his voice, "we shouldn't have involved him as much as we did. I jumped at the opportunity to make things easier for us, but I should have given it more thought."

My legs trembled, but I followed him out and upstairs to change my clothes and tell Mrs. Ferrier we would be leaving the house and might not return until very late or even the next day. Then we got into our car and drove through the night, making the trip in record time.

There were dozens of cars and pickup trucks along the driveway at Cypress Woods. As we pulled up to the house, I looked toward the dock and saw the torches being carried by men who were going in pirogues and motorboats to search for Paul. We could hear the shouts echoing over the bayou.

Inside the house Paul's sisters sat in the study, Toby looking as cold as a statue, her skin alabaster, and Jeanne twisting a silk handkerchief in her hands and gritting her teeth. They both looked up with surprise when we entered.

"What are you doing here?" Toby asked. From the expressions on their faces and their astonishment, I guessed that Gladys Tate hadn't told her daughters the truth. They still thought of me as Gisselle.

"We heard about Paul and came to see what we could do to help," Beau said quickly.

"You could go down and join the search party, I suppose," Toby said.

"Where's your mother?" I asked.

"She's upstairs in Paul's suite, lying down," Jeanne said. "The doctor was here, but she refused to take anything. She doesn't want to be asleep if . . . when . . ." Her lips trembled and the tears rushed over her eyelids.

"Get hold of yourself," Toby chastised. "Mother needs us to be strong."

"How do they know for sure that he went into the swamps? Maybe he's in some zydeco bar," Beau said.

"First of all, my brother wouldn't go off to a bar the day after he buried his wife, and second, some of the workers saw him heading toward the dock," Toby replied.

"And carrying a bottle of whiskey clutched in his hand," Jeanne added mournfully.

A dead silence fell between us.

"I'm sure they'll find him," Beau finally said.

Toby turned to him slowly and fixed her eyes on him in

a cold glare. "Have either of you ever been in the swamps? Do either of you know what it could be like? You make a turn and find yourself floating through overhanging vines and cypress branches and soon you forget how you got there and have no idea how to get out. It's a maze full of poisonous copperhead snakes, alligators, and snapping turtles, not to mention the insects and vermin."

"It's not that bad," I said.

"Oh really. Well then, march on out of here with your husband and join the search party," Toby retorted with a bitterness that shot through my brain like a laser beam.

"I plan on doing just that. Come on, Beau," I said, spinning around and marching out. Beau was at my side, but he wasn't enthusiastic.

"You really think we should go into the swamps, Ruby? I mean, if all these people who live here can't find him . . ."

"I'll find him," I said firmly. "I know where to look."

Jeanne's husband, James, was at the dock when we arrived. He shook his head and lifted his arms in frustration.

"It's impossible," he said. "If Paul doesn't want to be found, he won't be found. He knows these swamps better than he knows the back of his hand. He grew up in them. We're giving up for tonight."

"No, we're not," I said sharply.

He looked up, surprised. "We?"

"Is that your boat?" I asked, nodding toward a dinghy with a small outboard engine.

"Yes, but . . ."

"Please, just take us into the swamps."

"I just came back, and I assure you—"

"I know what I'm doing, James. If you don't want to go along, let us just borrow your boat," I insisted.

"You two? In the swamps?" He smiled, sighed, and then shook his head. "All right. I'll give it one more sweep. Get in," he said.

Beau, looking very uncomfortable, stepped into the dinghy after me and sat down. James handed us torches. Then we saw Octavious arriving with another group. His head was down like a flag of defeat.

"Paul's father is taking it very hard," James said, shaking his head.

"Just start the engine, please," I said. "Please . . ."

"What do you expect to be able to do that all these other people, some of whom fish and hunt in here, couldn't do?"

I stared. "I think I know where he might be," I said softly. "Ruby once told me about a hideaway she and Paul shared. She described it so well, I'm sure I could find it."

James shook his head skeptically but started the engine. "All right, but I'm afraid we're just wasting our time. We should wait for daylight."

We pulled away from the dock and headed into the canal. The swamps could be intimidating at night, even to men who had lived and worked them all their lives. There wasn't enough of a moon to give much illumination, and the Spanish moss seemed to thicken and blacken to form walls and block off other canals. The twisted cyprus branches looked like gnarled old witches, and the water took on an inky thickness, hiding tree roots, dead logs, and, of course, alligators. Our movement and the torches kept the mosquitoes at bay, but Beau looked very uncomfortable and even frightened. He nearly jumped out of the dinghy when an owl swooped alongside.

"Go to the right, James, and then, just as you come around the bend, bear left sharply."

"I can't believe Ruby gave you such explicit directions," he mumbled.

"She loved this spot because she and Paul spent so much time there," I said. "It's like another world. She said," I added quickly.

James followed my directions. Behind us, the torches

of other searches dimmed and were lost. A sheet of darkness fell between us and the house. Soon we could no longer hear the voices of men in the search party.

"Slower, James," I said. "There's something I have to look for and it's not easy at night."

"Especially when you've never been here before," James commented. "This is futile. If we just wait until morning—"

"There," I said, pointing. "You see where that cypress tree bends over like an old lady plucking a four-leaf clover?"

"Old lady? Four-leaf clover?" James said.

"That's what Paul told Ruby all the time." Neither James nor Beau could see the smile on my face. "Just turn right sharply under the lower branch."

"We might not fit under that," he warned.

"We will if we bend down," I said. "Slowly."

"Are you sure? We'll just get hung up on a rock or a mound of roots or—"

"I'm sure. Do it. Please."

Reluctantly he turned the dinghy. We dipped our heads and slipped under the branch.

"I'll be darned," James said. "Now where?"

"You see that thick wall of Spanish moss that reaches the water?"

"Yeah."

"Just go through it. It's the secret doorway."

"Secret doorway. Damn. No one would know that."

"That's what I meant by it being another world," I said. "You can cut the engine. We'll float on through and we'll be there."

He did so and I held my breath as the dinghy pierced the moss, which parted like a curtain to permit us to enter the small pond. Once we were completely through, I raised my torch and Beau did the same.

"Just paddle in a circle slowly," I said. The glow of our torches lifted the darkness, uncovering the pond. Snakes or turtles slithered beneath the surface, creating ripples. We saw the bream feeding on the mosquitoes. An alligator lifted its head, its teeth gleaming in our light, and then it dove. I heard Beau gulp. Somewhere to the right, a hawk screeched. On the shore of the pond, a half dozen or so nutrias scrambled for cover.

"Wait, what's that?" James said. He stood up and poked into the water with his oar to draw a bottle closer to the dinghy. Then he reached in to pluck it out of the water. It was an empty bottle of rum. "He was here," James said, looking around harder. *"Paul!"* he screamed.

"Paul!" Beau followed.

For a moment I couldn't form his name on my lips. Then I cried out, too. *"Paul, please, if you're here, answer us."*

Nothing but the sound of the swamp animals could be heard. Over to the right a deer rustled through the bushes. Terror jumped into my heart, flooded my eyes.

"Just keep rowing around the pond, James," I said, and sat back, but held my torch high to the right while Beau held his to the left. The water lapped against the dinghy. There was barely a breeze and mosquitoes began to sense our presence with delight. Suddenly the round bottom of a pirogue became visible. At first it looked like an alligator, but as we drew closer, it became clear that it was Paul's canoe. No one spoke. James poked it with his oar.

"It's his, all right," he said. *"Paul!"*

"Over there. Is that something?" Beau asked, leaning with his torch. James turned the dinghy in the direction Beau was pointing, and I brought my torchlight to bear as well. Slumped over a large rock, his *chatlin* hair matted and muddied by the water, Paul lay facedown. He looked like he had dragged himself up and collapsed. James turned the dinghy so he and Beau could stand up and reach Paul's body. I started to step toward him, too, when Beau turned sharply.

"Don't!" he ordered. He seized me at the elbows to hold me back and get me to sit. "It's not pretty and he's gone," he said.

I slapped my palms over my face and screamed. My

shrill cry pierced the darkest corners and shadows in the swamp, sending birds flapping, animals scurrying, and fish diving. It echoed over the water and was finally stopped by the wall of dark silence that waits out there for all of us.

The doctor said Paul's lungs were so full of water, he had no idea how Paul had managed to drag himself up the rock a few inches, much less enough to get his entire body up. There he took his last gasps and passed away. Miraculously, no alligator got to him, but the death by drowning had distorted him and Beau was right to keep me from looking.

Cypress Woods was already a house in mourning, so it just continued under the dark cloud of more grief. Servants who had cried so hard over what they thought was my death now had to find another well of tears from which to draw. Paul's sisters, especially Toby, had anticipated bad news, but were devastated nevertheless and retreated with James into the privacy of the study, while Octavious went upstairs to be with Gladys.

I felt so weak all over, my body so light, I thought I would get caught up in the wind and be carried into the night. Beau clutched my hand and put his arm around my shoulders. I leaned against him and watched them bring Paul's body up from the dock. Beau wanted us to return immediately to New Orleans. He was insistent and I had no strength to resist, no words to offer in argument. I let him lead me to our car and slumped down in the seat as he drove us away. I had cried dry that bottomless pit of tears.

When I closed my eyes, I saw Paul as a young boy riding his motor scooter up to Grandmere Catherine's front gallery. I saw the brightness in his eyes when he set them on me. Both our voices were full of excitement then. The world seemed so innocent and precious. Every color, every shape, every scent, was richer. When we were together, exploring our young feelings, we were like the first couple on earth discovering things we couldn't imagine others discovering before us. No one ever adequately explains the wonder born in your heart when you undress your new feelings in front of someone who is undressing his, too. That trust, that childhood faith, is so pure and good, you can't imagine any betrayals. Surely all the trouble and misery you know and hear about in the world around you will be walled out by these powerful new feelings woven into an impenetrable fabric. You can make promises, expose your dreams, and dream new things together. Nothing seems impossible and the last thing you can imagine is that some malicious Fate has been toying with you, leading you down a highway that will bring you to these tragic, dark moments.

I wanted to be angry and bitter and blame someone or something else, but in the end I could think of no one to blame but myself. The weight of that guilt was so heavy, I couldn't bear it. I was crushed, defeated, and so tired, I didn't open my eyes again until Beau said we were home. I let him help me out of the car, but my legs wouldn't support me. He carried me into the house and up the stairway and lowered me to our bed, where I curled up, embraced myself, and fell unconscious.

When I woke up, Beau was already dressed. I turned, but the ache in my bones was so deep, I could barely stretch out my legs and lift myself. My head felt like it had turned to stone.

"I'm so tired," I said. "So weak."

"Stay in bed today," he advised. "I'll have Sally bring your breakfast up to the suite. I have some things I must tend to at the office and then I'll come home to be with you."

"Beau," I moaned. "It is my fault. Gladys Tate is right to hate me."

"Of course it isn't your fault. You didn't break any promises, and anything he did, he did willingly, knowing what the consequences might be. If it's anyone's fault, it's mine. I shouldn't have let him become so involved. I should have forced you to make a clean, clear break with him so he would have realized he should go on with his life and not mourn over things that couldn't be, that weren't supposed to be.

"But, Ruby," Beau said, coming to my side and taking my hand in his, "we are meant to be. No two people could love each other as much as we do and not be meant to be. That is the faith you must have, the faith you must cling to when you mourn Paul. If we fail each other now, then everything he did was even more in vain.

"Somewhere, deep inside himself, he must have also realized you belonged with me. Maybe he couldn't face that in the end and maybe it overwhelmed him, but he did realize it as a greater truth and a greater reality.

"We must hold on to what we now have. I love you," he said, and kissed me softly on the lips. He lowered his head to my bosom and I held him against me for a long moment before he rose, took a deep breath, and smiled. "I'll send Sally around and then tell Mrs. Ferrier to bring Pearl in later, okay?"

"Yes, Beau. Whatever you say. I can't think for myself anymore."

"That's all right. I'll think for the two of us." He threw me a kiss and left.

I gazed out the window. The sky was overcast, but the clouds looked light and thin. There would be hazy sunshine and the day would be hot and muggy. After breakfast, I would take a bath and get back on my feet. The prospect of attending Paul's funeral seemed overwhelming to me now. I couldn't imagine mustering the strength, but as it turned out, that was to be the least of my problems.

Late in the morning, after I had had some breakfast and taken my bath, I brushed out my hair and dressed myself. Mrs. Ferrier brought Pearl in to watch and I let her play with my brushes and combs. She sat beside me, mimicking my every move. Her hair had grown down to her shoulders and it was turning a brighter, richer golden shade every day. Her blue eyes were full of curiosity. As soon as she learned what one thing was, she was asking about another, touching something else. Her bountiful energy and excitement brought some joy and relief to my aching heart. How lucky I was to have her, I thought. I was determined to devote myself to her, to make certain that her life was smoother, happier, and fuller than mine. I would protect her, advise her, guide her, so she would avoid the pitfalls and treacherous turns I had taken. It was in our children, I realized, that our hope and purpose lay. They were the promise and the only real antidote for grief.

Beau called to say he would be home shortly. Mrs. Ferrier took Pearl out to play in the garden, and I decided to go down so that Beau and I could have lunch on the patio when he returned. I had just rounded the base of the stairway when the phones rang. Aubrey announced it was Toby Tate and I hurried to a receiver.

"Toby," I cried. "I'm sorry we left so quickly, but—"

"No one was concerned here about that," she said coldly. "I'm certainly not calling to complain about your behavior. Frankly, I can't imagine any of us caring." The hard, formal tone in her voice set my heart racing. "In fact, Mother asked me to call to tell you she would rather you don't attend Paul's funeral."

"Not attend? But—"

"We're sending a car with a nanny we're hiring to pick up Pearl and bring her home," she added firmly.

"What?"

"Mother says Paul and Ruby's daughter belongs with her grandpere and grandmere and not with her self-centered aunt, so your obligations, your promises, are all over. You can go back to your life of pleasure and not worry. Those were Mother's exact words. Please have Pearl ready by three o'clock."

My throat wouldn't open to let me form any words. I couldn't swallow. My heart felt as if it had slid down into my stomach and a wave of heat rose from the base of my spine to the base of my head, where it circled around my neck like the long, thin fingers of a witch, choking me.

"Do you understand?" Toby demanded.

"You . . ."

"Yes?"

"Can't . . . take . . . Pearl," I said. I fought to open my lungs and suck in some air. "Your mother knows you can't."

"What sort of nonsense is this? Of course we can. Don't you think a grandmere has more claim to a grandchild than an aunt?"

"No!" I shouted. "I won't let you take Pearl."

"I don't see where you have much to say about it, Gisselle. I hope you won't add any unpleasantness and ugliness to our tragedy right now. If there is anyone left out there who doesn't despise you, he or she will soon do just that."

"Your mother knows she can't do this. She knows. Tell her. Tell her!" I screamed.

"Well, I'll tell her what you said, but the car will be there at three o'clock. Good-bye," Toby snapped and the phone went dead.

"No!" I screamed into the receiver anyway. I quickly hung up and then lifted the receiver to dial Beau.

"I'm coming right home," he said after I gasped and poured out what Toby had told me Gladys Tate demanded.

"This is what she meant by my suffering twice as much as Paul, Beau. This is her way of getting vengeance."

"Stay calm. I'll be right there," he said.

I hung up, but I couldn't stay calm. I went into the study and paced back and forth, my mind reeling with the possibilities. It seemed hours before Beau finally arrived, even though it was only a few minutes. He came rushing into the study to embrace me and sit me down. I couldn't stop trembling. My teeth were actually chattering.

"It's going to be all right," he assured me. "She's bluffing. She's just trying to upset you because she is so upset right now. She'll realize what she's doing and she'll stop it."

"But, Beau . . . everyone thinks I'm Gisselle. They buried me!"

"It'll be fine," he said, but not with as much confidence as before.

"We were born in the swamps in a shack. It's not like here in New Orleans in a hospital where babies' footprints are taken so they can be easily identified later. Paul was my husband and he told the world I was sick and dying. He attended my funeral and killed himself, whether purposely or accidentally, because of my death," I rattled, each realization like another nail in the coffin of truth. I seized Beau's hands in mine and fixed my eyes on his.

"You yourself said that I've done such a good job of pretending to be Gisselle, everyone thinks I am. Even your parents!"

"If it comes down to whether or not we keep Pearl, we'll confess the truth and tell the authorities what we have done. I promise," he said. "No one will take our child from us. No one. Especially not Gladys Tate," he assured me. He squeezed my hands and made his face tight with determination. It slowed down my runaway heart and eased some of my trepidation.

"Toby said a car is arriving here at three with a nurse."

"I'll handle it," he said. "Don't you even come near the front door."

I nodded. "Pearl," I said suddenly. "Where is she?"

"Take it easy. Where could she be but with Mrs. Ferrier? Don't frighten her," he warned, seizing my wrist. "Ruby."

"Yes, you're right. I mustn't frighten the child. But I want her upstairs now. I don't want her outside when they come."

"All right, but do it gently, calmly," he ordered. "Will you?"

"I will." I took a deep breath and went out to find Mrs. Ferrier and Pearl. Without going into any detail why, I asked her to bring the baby in and keep her up in her room. Then I went to join Beau in the dining room, but not only couldn't I eat any lunch with Beau, I couldn't bring a morsel of food near my lips. I could barely swallow water. My stomach was that nervous. A little after two, he told me to go upstairs and stay with Pearl and Mrs. Ferrier. My heart was thumping madly. I thought I could easily pass out from fear, but I fought down my trepidation and occupied myself with Pearl.

Just before three o'clock, I heard the door chimes and my heart jumped in my chest. I couldn't keep myself from going to the top of the stairway and listening. Beau had already told Aubrey he would answer the door. I didn't want Beau to know I was looking and listening in, so I backed into the shadows when he turned and looked up the stairway just before opening the door.

A man in a suit and a nurse in uniform were there.

"Yes?" Beau said as nonchalantly as he could.

"My name is Martin Bell," the man in the suit said. "I am an attorney representing the Tates. We have been sent by Monsieur and Madame Tate to pick up their granddaughter," he said.

"Their granddaughter is not going anywhere today or any day," Beau said firmly. "She is home where she belongs and where she will stay."

"Are you refusing to turn their granddaughter over to them?" Martin Bell asked with some astonishment. Apparently he had been led to believe this was a simple assignment. He probably thought he was making easy money.

"I am refusing to turn our daughter over to them, yes," Beau said.

"Pardon. Your daughter? I'm confused here," Martin Bell said, glancing at the nurse, who looked just as confused. "Is the little girl the daughter of Paul and Ruby Tate?"

"No," Beau said, "and Gladys Tate knows that. I'm afraid she's wasted your time, but be sure you bill for it," Beau added. "Good day," he said, and closed the door on their bewildered faces. For a moment he stood there waiting. Then he went to the window and gazed out to be sure they drove away. When he turned, he saw me standing at the top of the stairway.

"Were you there the whole time?" he asked.

"Yes, Beau."

"So you heard. I did what I promised. I told the truth and I've sent them back. When Gladys hears what I said, she'll back off and leave us alone," he assured me. "Relax. It's over. It's all over."

I nodded and smiled hopefully. Beau came up the stairs to embrace me. Then the two of us went to look in on Pearl. She was sitting contentedly on the floor of what had once been my room and coloring animals in a coloring book called "A Visit to the Zoo."

"Look, Mommy." She pointed and then growled like a tiger. Mrs. Ferrier laughed.

"She imitates all the animals," she said. "I've never seen such a good little mimic."

Beau tightened his embrace around my shoulders and I leaned against him. It felt good to be surrounded by his strength and feel his firmness. He was my rock now, my pillar of steel, and it deepened my love for him and filled me with confidence. Gradually, as the day wore on, my nervousness diminished and my stomach stabilized. I realized I was ravishingly hungry when we sat down at dinner.

Later that night in bed, we talked for nearly an hour before closing our eyes.

"I regret not being able to go to Paul's funeral," I said.

"I know, but under the circumstances, it's better that we don't attend. Gladys Tate would only make an unpleasant situation even more miserable. She would create an ugly scene."

"Even so, someday after sufficient time has passed, I would like to visit the grave, Beau."

"Of course."

We talked on, Beau suggesting plans for the future now. "If we want, we can build a new house on a piece of real estate we own just outside of the city."

"Maybe we should," I said.

"Of course, there are things we could do to this house to change it as well. In either case, we'll want new memories," he explained. I couldn't agree more. His descriptions of what was possible for us now filled me with renewed hope and I was able to shut my eyelids and drift off, emotionally exhausted and tired down to my very soul.

I wasn't refreshed when I woke in the morning, but I had regained enough strength to start a new day. I made plans to begin painting again and I thought I would start to buy a new wardrobe, one that fit my personality more. Now that I had driven away all of Gisselle's friends and we were talking about a new beginning, I thought I had the freedom to ease back into my true self and eventually put Gisselle to rest. Those prospects buoyed me.

We had a good breakfast with an animated conversation. Beau had so many plans for business and for our changes, my mind felt stuffed. I could see where we would both become so busy shortly, there wouldn't be much time to dwell on sadness. Grandmere Catherine always said that the only real antidote for grief and sadness was busy hands.

After breakfast Beau went upstairs to the bathroom and I went into the kitchen to talk to Mrs. Swann about dinner. I sat listening to her describe how to prepare chicken Rochambeau.

"You start with preparing the gravy," she began, and went through the ingredients. Just listening to her talk about the recipe made my mouth water. How lucky we were to have a cook with so much experience, I thought.

Mrs. Swann was clanking dishes and pans as she spoke and walked around the kitchen, so I didn't hear the door chimes and was surprised when Aubrey arrived to tell me there were two gentlemen at the door.

"And there's a policeman, too," he added.

"What? Policeman?"

"Yes, madame."

My chest felt hot and heavy as I rose.

"Where's Pearl?" I asked quickly.

"She's in her nursery with Mrs. Ferrier, madame. They just went upstairs."

"And Monsieur Andreas?"

"I think he's still upstairs, madame."

"Please fetch him for me, Aubrey. Quickly," I said.

"Very well, madame," he said, and hurried out. I looked at Mrs. Swann, who stared at me with curious eyes.

"Troubles?" she asked.

"I don't know. I don't know," I mumbled, and let my feet carry me slowly toward the foyer. Beau appeared on the stairway just as I arrived in the foyer and saw the attorney Martin Bell and another man at the door.

"What's this?" Beau cried, hurrying down the remaining steps.

"Monsieur and Madame Andreas?" the taller of the two men in suits inquired. Beau stepped forward rapidly so he would be at the door before me. I saw the nurse who had come the day before standing behind them and my heart sunk.

"Yes?"

"I'm William Rogers, senior partner of Rogers, Bell and Stanley. As you know from Mr. Bell's previous visit, we represent Monsieur and Madame Octavious Tate of Terrebonne Parish. We're here under court order to take the infant Pearl Tate back to her grandparents," he said, and handed Beau a document. "It's been signed by the judge and must be carried out."

"Beau," I said. He waved me off for a moment while he read.

"This is not true," he said, looking up and attempting to hand the document back. "Madame Tate is not the child's grandmere."

"I'm afraid that's for a court to decide, sir. In the interim this court action," he said, nodding at the document, "will be enforced. She has primary legal rights to custody."

"But we're not the uncle and aunt. We're the mother and father," Beau said.

"The court understands otherwise. The child's parents are both deceased and the grandparents are the primary legal guardians, therefore," Mr. Rogers insisted. "I hope this doesn't become unpleasant," he added. "For the child's sake."

As soon as he said that, the policeman moved up beside him. Beau gazed from one face to the other and then looked at me.

"Ruby . . ."

"No!" I screamed, backing away. "They can't take her. They can't!"

"They have a court order, but it will only be temporary," Beau said. "I promise. I'll call our attorneys right now. We have the best, highest-paid attorneys in New Orleans."

"This court action will be conducted in Terrebonne Parish," William Rogers said. "The child's legal residence. But if you have the highest-paid, best attorneys, they would know that anyway," he added, enjoying his sarcasm.

"Beau," I said, my lips trembling, my face crumpling. He started toward me to embrace me, but I backed farther away. "No," I said, shaking my head. "No."

"Madame, I assure you," Mr. Rogers said, "this court order will be carried out. If you truly have any concern for the child, you'd better adhere to the order smoothly."

"Ruby . . ."

"Beau, you promised! *No,"* I screamed. I struck him in the chest with my small fists, pummeling him. He grabbed my wrists and embraced me tightly.

"We'll get her back. We will," he said.

"I can't," I said, shaking my head. "I can't." My legs gave out and Beau held me up.

"Please," he said, turning to the lawyers, the policeman, and the nurse, "give us ten minutes to prepare the baby."

Mr. Rogers nodded and Beau literally carried me along, up the stairs, whispering assurances in my ear.

"It will be ugly," he said, "if we physically resist. Once we explain who we are, it will all end quickly. You'll see."

"But, Beau, you said this wouldn't happen."

"How did I know she would be this vicious? She must be crazy. What sort of a man is she married to for him to let her do this?"

"A guilty man," I said, and sniffed back my tears. I looked toward Pearl's nursery door. "Oh, Beau, she'll be terrified."

"Only until she gets to Cypress Woods. She knows all the servants and—"

"But they're not taking her to Cypress Woods. They're taking her to the Tates."

Beau nodded, the realizations deepening in him, too. He sighed deeply and shook his head. "I could kill her," he said. "I could put my hands around her neck and choke the life out of her."

"It's already been choked out of her," I said, nodding. "When Paul died. We're dealing with a woman who's lost every feeling but one, the desire for revenge. And my child has to go into that household."

"Do you want me to do this?" he asked, looking at the nursery.

"No. I'll do it with you so we can comfort her as much as possible."

We went in and explained to Mrs. Ferrier that the baby had to go to her grandparents. Beau thought that was best for now. Pearl knew the Tates as her grandparents, so I sucked back my sorrow and hid my tears. Smiling, I told her she had to go see her grandmere Gladys and grandpere Octavious.

"There's a nice lady to take you to them," I continued.

Pearl gazed at me curiously. It was almost as if she were wise enough to see through the deception. She put up no resistance until we carried her down and actually placed her in the backseat of the limousine with the nurse. When I backed away from the door, she realized I wasn't coming and started to scream for me. The nurse attempted to comfort her.

"Let's get moving," Mr. Rogers told the driver. The two lawyers got into the car and slammed the doors shut, but I could still hear Pearl's screams. As the limousine pulled away from the house, the baby broke loose from the nurse and pressed her little face against the back window. I could see the fear and the torment in her and I could hear her screaming my name. The moment the car disappeared, my legs went out from under me and I folded too quickly for Beau to stop me from crashing to the tile and the comfort of darkness.

16

All Is Lost

"Well," Monsieur Polk said after he heard Beau describe our story, "this is a rather complicated matter. Very," he added, and nodded emphatically, jiggling his jowls and his loose double chin. He sat back in his oversize black leather desk chair and pressed his palms against his bear-size chest with his fingers intertwined, the large gold pinky ring with a black onyx oval stone glittering in the afternoon sunlight that came pouring through the thin, white blinds.

Beau sat beside me and held my hand. My other hand clutched the mahogany arm of the chair as if I thought I might be toppled out and onto the dark brown carpet in Monsieur Polk's plush office. It was on the seventh floor of the building, and the large windows behind Monsieur Polk's desk looked out on the river with a vast view of the boats and ships navigating in and out of New Orleans harbor.

I bit down on my lower lip and held my breath as our attorney pondered. His large, watery hazel eyes gazed down and he was so still, I feared he had fallen asleep.

The only sound in the office was the ticktock of the miniature grandfather clock on the shelf to our left.

"No birth certificates, you say?" he finally asked, just raising his eyes. The rest of him, all two hundred forty pounds, remained settled in the chair, his suit jacket folded and creased in the shoulders. He wore a dark brown tie with lemon dots.

"No. As I said, the twins were born in swamp country, no doctor, no hospital."

"My grandmere was a *traiteur,* better than any doctor," I said.

"Traiteur?"

"Cajun faith healer," Beau explained.

Monsieur Polk nodded and shifted his eyes toward me and stared a moment. Then he sat forward and clasped his hands on his desk.

"We'll move quickly for a custody hearing. It will be conducted like a trial in this situation. The first order of business will be to find a legal way to establish you as Ruby. Once that is accomplished, you will testify to being the father of your child, which you will own up to," he said to Beau.

"Of course." Beau squeezed my hand and smiled.

"Now let's look at the face of this," Monsieur Polk said. He reached over to a dark cherry wood cigar box and flicked up the cover to pluck a fat Havana cigar out of it. "You," he said, pointing at me with the cigar, "and your twin sister, Gisselle, were apparently so identical in looks, you could pull off this switch of identities, correct?"

"Down to the dimples in their cheeks," Beau said.

"Eye color, hair color, complexion, height, weight?" Monsieur Polk listed. Beau and I nodded after each item.

"There might have been a few pounds difference between them, but nothing very noticeable," Beau said.

"Scars?" Monsieur Polk asked, raising his eyebrows hopefully.

I shook my head.

"I have none and my sister had none, even though she

was in a bad car accident and was crippled for a time," I said.

"Bad car accident?" I nodded. "Here in New Orleans?"

"Yes."

"Then she was in the hospital for a time. Good. There'll be a medical history with records about her blood. Maybe you two had a different blood type. If so, that would settle it immediately. A friend of mine," he continued, taking out his lighter, "tells me that in years to come, from blood tests, using DNA, they'll be able to identify who is the parent of a child. But we're a number of years away from that."

"And by then it would be too late!" I complained.

He nodded and lit his cigar, leaning back to blow the puffs of smoke toward the ceiling.

"Maybe some X rays were taken. Did she break any bones in the accident?"

"No," I said. "She was bruised and the shock of it did something to her spine, affecting the nerves, but that healed and she was able to walk again."

"Um," Monsieur Polk said. "I don't know if there would be anything discernible by X ray. We'd have to have X rays done of you and then find a medical expert to testify that there should be some residual evidence of the trauma."

I brightened. "I'll go right to the hospital for X rays."

"Right," Beau said.

Monsieur Polk shook his head. "They might very well locate an expert who would claim X rays wouldn't pick up any residual damage if the problem was cured," he said. "Let me research the medical records at the hospital and get one of my doctor friends to give me an opinion about it first."

"Ruby had a child; Gisselle did not," Beau said. "Surely an examination . . ."

"Can you establish Gisselle did not beyond a doubt?" Monsieur Polk asked.

"Pardon?"

"Gisselle is dead and buried. How can we examine her? You'd have to have the body exhumed, and what if Gisselle had been pregnant sometime and had had an abortion?"

"He's right, Beau. I would never swear about that," I said.

"This is very bizarre. Very bizarre," Monsieur Polk muttered. "You worked at convincing people you were your twin sister and did it so well, everyone who knew her believed it, right?"

"As far as we know."

"And the family, Paul Tate's family, believed it and believed they buried Ruby Tate?"

"Yes," I said.

"There was actually a death certificate issued in your name?"

"Yes," I said, swallowing hard. The vivid memories of attending my own funeral came rushing back over me.

Monsieur Polk shook his head and thought a moment. "What about the doctor who first treated Gisselle for encephalitis?" he asked with some visible excitement. "He knew he was treating Gisselle and not Ruby, right?"

"I'm afraid we can't call on him," Beau said, deflating our balloon of hope. "I made an arrangement with him, and anyway, it would ruin him, wouldn't it? His being a part of this?"

"I'm afraid that's very true," Monsieur Polk said. "He put his name to fraud. Any of the servants we can call upon?"

"Well . . . the way we worked it, the doctor and myself . . ."

"They didn't know what was happening exactly, is that it?"

"Yes. They wouldn't make the best witnesses anyway. The German couple don't speak English too well and my cook saw nothing. The maid is a timid woman who wouldn't be able to swear to anything."

"That's not an avenue to pursue, then." Monsieur Polk

nodded. "Let me think. Bizarre, very bizarre. Dental records," he cried. "How are your teeth?"

"Perfect. I've never had a cavity or a tooth pulled."

"And Gisselle?"

"As far as I know," Beau said, "she was the same. She had remarkable health for someone with her lifestyle."

"Good genes," Monsieur Polk said. "But both of you had the benefit of the same genetic advantages."

Was there no way to determine our identities to the satisfaction of a judge? I wondered frantically.

"What about our signatures?" I asked.

"Yes," Beau said. "Ruby always had a nicer handwriting."

"Handwriting is an exhibit to use," Monsieur Polk said with a bit of official-sounding nasality, "but it's not conclusive. We'll have to rely on the opinions of experts, and they might bring in their own expert who would develop the effectiveness of forgery. I've seen that happen before. Also," he said after another puff of his cigar, "people are inclined to believe that twins can imitate each other better. I'd like to have something more."

"What about Louis?" Beau asked me. "You said he recognized you."

"Louis?" Monsieur Polk asked.

"Louis was someone I met when Gisselle and I attended a private girls' school in Baton Rouge. He's a musician who recently had a concert here in New Orleans."

"I see."

"When I knew him, he was blind. But he sees now," I added, hopefully.

"What? Blind, you say? Really, monsieur," he said, turning to Beau. "You want me to put a man who was blind on the stand to testify he can tell the difference."

"But he can!" I said.

"Maybe to your satisfaction, but to a judge's?"

Another balloon deflated. My heart was thumping. Tears of frustration had begun to sting my eyes. Defeat seemed all around me.

"Look," Beau said, squeezing my hand again, "what possible motive could we have for Ruby pretending to be Ruby? First, we will be exposing our deception to the world, and besides, everyone who knew Gisselle knew how self-centered she was. She wouldn't want to win custody of a child and be responsible for the child's upbringing."

Monsieur Polk thought a moment. He turned his chair and gazed out the window.

"I'll play the devil's advocate," he said, continuing to gaze down at the river. Then he turned sharply back to us and pointed at me with his cigar again. "You said your husband, Paul, inherited oil-rich land in the bayou?"

"Yes."

"And built you a mansion with beautiful grounds, an estate?"

"Yes, but—"

"And has wells pumping up oil, creating a large fortune?"

I couldn't swallow. I couldn't nod. Beau and I gazed at each other.

"But, monsieur, we are far from paupers. Ruby inherited a tidy sum and a profitable business and—"

"Monsieur Andreas, you have at your fingertips the possibility of inheriting a major fortune, a continually growing major fortune. We're not talking now about just being well-to-do."

"What about the child?" Beau threw out in desperation. "She knows her mother."

"She's an infant. I wouldn't think of putting her on a witness stand in a courtroom. She would be terrified, I'm sure."

"No, we can't do that, Beau," I said. "Never."

Monsieur Polk sat back. "Let me look into the hospital records, talk to some doctors. I'll get back to you."

"How long will this take?"

"It can't be done overnight, madame," he said frankly.

"But my baby . . . Oh, Beau."

"Did you consider going to see Madame Tate and

talking it out with her? Perhaps this was an impulsive angry act and now she's had some time to reconsider," Monsieur Polk suggested. "It would simplify the problem."

"I don't say this is her motive," he added, leaning forward, "but you might offer to sign over any oil rights, et cetera."

"Yes," I said, hope springing in my heart.

Beau nodded. "It could be driving her mad that Ruby would inherit Cypress Woods and all the oil on the land," Beau agreed. "Let's drive out there and see if she will speak with us. But in the meantime . . ."

"I'll go forward with my research in the matter," Monsieur Polk said. He stood up and put his cigar in the ashtray before leaning over to shake Beau's hand. "You know," he said softly, "what a field day our gossip columnists in the newspapers will have with this?"

"We know." Beau looked at me. "We're prepared for all that as long as we get Pearl back."

"Very well. Good luck with Madame Tate," Monsieur Polk said, and we left.

"I feel so weak, Beau, so weak and afraid," I said as we left the building for our car.

"You can't present yourself to that woman while you're in this state of mind, Ruby. Let's stop for something to eat to build your strength. Let's be optimistic and strong. Lean on me whenever you have to," he said, his face dark, his eyes down. "This is really all my fault," he murmured. "It was my idea, my doing."

"You can't blame yourself solely, Beau. I knew what I was doing and I wanted to do it. I should have known better than to think we could splash water in the face of Destiny."

He hugged me to him and we got into our car and started for the bayou. As we rode, I rehearsed the things I would say. I had no appetite when we stopped to eat, but Beau insisted I put something in my stomach.

The late afternoon grew darker and darker as the sun took a fugitive position behind some long, feather-brushed storm clouds. All the blue sky seemed to fall behind us as we drove on toward the bayou and the confrontation that awaited. As familiar places and sights began to appear, my apprehension grew. I took deep breaths and hoped that I would be able to talk without bursting into tears.

I directed Beau to the Tate residence. It was one of the larger homes in the Houma area, a two-and-a-half-story Greek Revival with six fluted Ionic columns set on pilastered bases a little out from the edge of the gallery. It had fourteen rooms and a large drawing room. Gladys Tate was proud of the decor in her home and her art, and until Paul had built the mansion for me, she had the finest house in our area.

By the time we drove up, the sky had turned ashen and the air was so thick with humidity, I thought I could see droplets forming before my eyes. The bayou was still, almost as still as it could be in the eye of a storm. Leaves hung limply on the branches of trees, and even the birds were depressed and settled in some shadowy corners.

The windows were bleak with their curtains drawn closed or their shades down. The glass reflected the oppressive darkness that loomed over the swamps. Nothing stirred. It was a house draped in mourning, its inhabitants well cloistered in their private misery. My heart felt so heavy; my fingers trembled as I opened the car door. Beau reached over to squeeze my arm with reassurance.

"Let's be calm," he advised. I nodded and tried to swallow, but a lump stuck in my throat like swamp mud on a shoe. We walked up the stairs and Beau dropped the brass knocker against the plate. The hollow thump seemed to be directed into my chest rather than into the house. A few moments later, the door was thrust open with such an angry force, it was as if a wind had blown it. Toby stood before us. She was dressed in black and had her hair pinned back severely. Her face was wan and pale.

"What do you want?" she demanded.

"We've come to speak with your mother and father," Beau said.

"They're not exactly in the mood to talk to you," she spit back at us. "In the midst of our mourning, you two had to make problems."

"There are some terrible misunderstandings we must try to fix," Beau insisted, and then added, "for the sake of the baby more than anyone."

Toby gazed at me. Something in my face confused her and she relaxed her shoulders.

"How's Pearl?" I asked quickly.

"Fine. She's doing just fine. She's with Jeanne," she added.

"She's not here?"

"No, but she will be here," she said firmly.

"Please," Beau pleaded. "We must have a few minutes with your parents."

Toby considered a moment and then stepped back. "I'll go see if they want to talk to you. Wait in the study," she ordered, and marched down the hallway to the stairs.

Beau and I entered the study. There was only a single lamp lit in a corner, and with the dismal sky, the room reeked of gloom. I snapped on a Tiffany lamp beside the settee and sat quickly, for fear my legs would give out from under me.

"Let me begin our conversation with Madame Tate," Beau advised. He stood to the side, his hands behind his back, and we both waited and listened, our eyes glued to the entrance. Nothing happened for so long, I let my eyes wander and my gaze stopped dead on the portrait above the mantel. It was a portrait I had done of Paul some time ago. Gladys Tate had hung it in place of the portrait of herself and Octavious. I had done too good a job, I thought. Paul looked so lifelike, his blue eyes animated, that soft smile captured around his mouth. Now he looked like he was smiling with impish satisfaction, defiant, vengeful. I couldn't look at the picture without my heart pounding.

We heard footsteps and a moment later Toby appeared alone. My hope sunk. Gladys wasn't going to give us an audience.

"Mother will be down," she said, "but my father is not able to see anyone at the moment. You might as well sit," she told Beau. "It will be a while. She's not exactly prepared for visitors right now," she added bitterly. Beau took a seat beside me obediently. Toby stared at us a moment.

"Why were you so obstinate? If there was ever a time my mother needed the baby around her, it was now. How cruel of you two to make it difficult and force us to go to a judge." She glared at me and then turned directly to Beau. "I might have expected something like this from her, but I thought you were more compassionate, more mature."

"Toby," I said. "I'm not who you think I am."

She smirked. "I know exactly who you are. Don't you think we have people like you here, selfish, vain people who couldn't care less about anyone else?"

"But . . ."

Beau put his hand on my arm. I looked at him and saw him plead for silence with his eyes. I swallowed back my words and closed my eyes. Toby turned and left us.

"She'll understand afterward," Beau said softly. A good ten minutes later, we heard Gladys Tate's heels clicking down the stairway, each click like a gunshot aimed at my heart. Our eyes fixed with anticipation on the doorway until she appeared. She loomed before us, taller, darker in her black mourning dress, her hair pinned back as severely as Toby's. Her lips were pale, her cheeks pallid, but her eyes were bright and feverish.

"What do you want?" she demanded, shooting me a stabbing glance.

Beau rose. "Madame Tate, we've come to try to reason with you, to get you to understand why we did what we did," he said.

"Humph," she retorted. "Understand?" She smiled coldly with ridicule. "It's simple to understand. You're the type who care only about themselves, and if you inflict terrible pain and suffering on someone in your pursuit of happiness, so what?" She whipped her eyes to me and flared them with hate before she turned to sit in the high-back chair like a queen, her hands clasped on her lap, her neck and shoulders stiff.

"Much of this is my fault, not Ruby's," Beau continued. "You see," he said, turning to me, "a few years ago we . . . I made Ruby pregnant with Pearl, but I was cowardly and permitted my parents to send me to Europe. Ruby's stepmother tried to have the baby aborted in a run-down clinic so it would all be kept secret, but Ruby ran off and returned to the bayou."

"How I wish she hadn't," Gladys Tate spit, her hating eyes trying to wish me into extinction.

"Yes, but she did," Beau continued, undaunted by her venom. "For better or for worse, your son offered to make a home for Ruby and Pearl."

"It was for worse. Look at where he is now," she said. Ice water trickled down my spine.

"As you know," Beau said softly, patiently, "theirs was not a true marriage. Time passed. I grew up and realized my errors, but it was too late. In the interim, I renewed my relationship with Ruby's twin sister, who I thought had matured, too. I was mistaken about that, but that's another story."

Gladys smirked.

"Your son knew how much Ruby and I still cared for each other, and he knew Pearl was our child, my child. He was a good man and he wanted Ruby to be happy."

"And she took advantage of that goodness," Gladys accused, stabbing the air between us with her long forefinger.

"No, Mother Tate, I—"

"Don't sit there and try to deny what you did to my son." Her lips trembled. "My son," she moaned. "Once, I was the apple of his eye. The sun rose and fell on my happiness, not yours. Even when you were enchanting him here in the bayou, he would love to sit and talk with me, love to be with me. We had a remarkable relationship and a remarkable love between us," she said. "But you were relentless and you charmed him away from me," she charged, and I realized there was no hate such as that born out of love betrayed. This was why her brain was screaming out for revenge.

"I didn't do those things, Mother Tate," I said quietly. "I tried to discourage our relationship. I even told him the truth about us," I said.

"Yes, you did and viciously drove a wedge between him and me. He knew that I wasn't his real mother. Don't you think that changed things?"

"I didn't want to tell him. It wasn't my place to tell him," I cried, recalling Grandmere Catherine's warnings about causing any sort of split between a Cajun mother and her child. "But you can't build a house of love on a foundation of lies. You and your husband should have been the ones to tell him the truth."

She winced. "What truth? I was his mother until you came along. He loved me," she whined. "That was all the truth we needed . . . love."

A pall fell among us for a moment. Gladys sucked in her anger and closed her eyes.

Beau decided to proceed. "Your son, realizing the love between Ruby and myself, agreed to help us be together. When Gisselle became seriously ill, he volunteered to take her in and pretend she was Ruby so that Ruby could become Gisselle and we could be man and wife."

She opened her eyes and laughed in a way that chilled my blood. "I know all that, but I also know he had little choice. She probably threatened to tell the world he wasn't my son," she said, her flinty eyes aimed at me.

"I would never . . ."

"You'd say anything now, so don't try," she advised.

"Madame," Beau said, stepping forward. "What's done is done. Paul did help. He intended for us to live with our daughter and be happy. What you're doing now is defeating what Paul himself tried to accomplish."

She stared up at Beau for a moment, and as she did so,

the gossamer strands of sanity seemed to shred before they snapped behind her eyes. "My poor granddaughter has no parents now. Her mother was buried and her father will be interred beside her."

"Madame Tate, why force us to go to court over this and put everyone through the misery again? Surely you want peace and quiet at this point, and your family—"

She turned her dark, blistering eyes toward Paul's portrait, and those eyes softened. "I'm doing this for my son," she said, gazing up at him with more than a mother's love. "Look how he smiles, how beautiful he is and how happy he is. Pearl will grow up here, under that portrait. At least he'll have that. You," she said, pointing her long, thin finger at me again, "took everything else from him, even his life."

Beau looked at me desperately and then turned back to her. "Madame Tate," he said, "if it's a matter of the inheritance, we're prepared to sign any document."

"What?" She sprang up. "You think this is all a matter of money? Money? My son is dead." She pulled up her shoulders and pursed her lips. "This discussion is over. I want you out of my house and out of our lives."

"You won't succeed with this. A judge—"

"I have lawyers. Talk to them." She smiled at me so coldly, it made my blood curdle. "You put on your sister's face and body and you crawled into her heart. Now live there," she cursed, and left the room.

Right down to my feet, I ached, and my heart became a hollow ball shooting pains through my chest. "Beau!"

"Let's go," he said, shaking his head. "She's gone mad. The judge will realize that. Come on, Ruby." He reached for me. I felt like I floated to my feet.

Just before we left the room, I gazed back at Paul's portrait. His expression of satisfaction put a darkness in my heart that a thousand days of sunshine couldn't nudge away.

After the funeral drive back to New Orleans, I collapsed with emotional exhaustion and slept into the late morning. Beau woke me to tell me Monsieur Polk had just called.

"And?" I sat up quickly, my heart pounding.

"I'm afraid it's not good news. The experts tell him everything is identical with identical twins, blood type, even organ size. The doctor who treated Gisselle doesn't think anything would show in an X ray. We can't rely on the medical data to clearly establish identities.

"As far as my being the father of Pearl . . . a blood group test will only confirm that I couldn't be, not that I could. As Monsieur Polk said, those sorts of tests aren't perfected yet."

"What will we do?" I moaned.

"He has already petitioned for a hearing and we have a court date," Beau said. "We'll tell our story, use the handwriting samples. He wants to also make use of your art talent. Monsieur Polk has documents prepared for us to sign so that we willingly surrender any claim to Paul's estate, thus eliminating a motive. Maybe it will be enough."

"Beau, what if it isn't?"

"Let's not think of the worst," he urged.

The worst was the waiting. Beau tried to occupy himself with work, but I could do nothing but sleep and wander from room to room, sometimes spending hours just sitting in Pearl's nursery, staring at her stuffed animals and dolls. Not more than forty-eight hours after Monsieur Polk had filed our petition with the court, we began to get phone calls from newspaper reporters. None would reveal his or her sources, but it seemed obvious to both Beau and me that Gladys Tate's thirst for vengeance was insatiable and she had deliberately had the story leaked to the press. It made headlines.

TWIN CLAIMS SISTER BURIED IN HER GRAVE!
CUSTODY BATTLE LOOMS.

Aubrey was given instructions to say we were unavailable to anyone who called. We would see no visitors, answer no questions. Until the court hearing, I was a virtual prisoner in my own home.

On that day, my legs trembling, I clung to Beau's arm as we descended the stairway to get into our car and drive to the Terrebone Parish courthouse. It was one of those mostly cloudy days when the sun plays peekaboo, teasing us with a few bright rays and then sliding behind a wall of clouds to leave the world dark and dreary. It reflected my mood swings, which went from hopeful and optimistic to depressed and pessimistic.

Monsieur Polk was already at the courthouse, waiting, when we arrived. The story had stirred the curious in the bayou as well as in New Orleans. I gazed quickly at the crowd of observers and saw some of Grandmere Catherine's friends. I smiled at them, but they were confused and unsure and afraid to smile back. I felt like a stranger. How would I ever explain to them why I had switched identities with Gisselle? How would they ever understand?

We took our seats first, and then, with obvious fanfare, milking the situation as much as she could, Gladys Tate entered. She still wore her clothes of mourning. She hung on Octavious's arm, stepping with great difficulty to show the world we had dragged her into this horrible hearing at a most unfortunate time. She wore no makeup, so she looked pale and sick, the weaker of the two of us in the judge's eyes. Octavious kept his gaze down, his head bowed, and didn't look our way once.

Toby and Jeanne and her husband, James, walked behind Gladys and Octavious Tate, scowling at us. Their attorneys, William Rogers and Martin Bell, led them to their seats. They looked formidable with their heavy briefcases and dark suits. The judge entered and everyone took his seat.

The judge's name was Hilliard Barrow, and Monsieur Polk had found out that he had a reputation for being caustic, impatient, and firm. He was a tall, lean man with hard facial features: deep-set dark eyes, thick eyebrows, a long, bony nose, and a thin mouth that looked like a slash when he pressed his lips together. He had gray and dark brown hair with a deeply receding hairline so that the top of his skull shone under the courtroom lights. Two long hands with bony fingers jutted out from the sleeves of his black judicial robe.

"Normally," he began, "this courtroom is relatively empty during such proceedings. I want to warn those observing that I won't tolerate any talking, any sounds displaying approval or disapproval. A child's welfare is at stake here, and not the selling of newspapers and gossip magazines to the society people in New Orleans." He paused to scour the crowd to see if there was even the hint of insubordination in anyone's eyes. My heart sunk. He seemed a man void of any emotion, except prejudices against rich New Orleans people.

The clerk read our petition and then Judge Barrow turned his sharp, hard gaze on Monsieur Polk.

"You have a case to make," he said.

"Yes, Your Honor. I would like to begin by calling Monsieur Beau Andreas to the stand."

The judge nodded, and Beau squeezed my hand and stood up. Everyone's eyes were fixed on him as he strutted confidently to the witness seat. He was sworn in and sat quickly.

"Monsieur Andreas, as a preamble to our presentation, would you tell the court in your own words why, how, and when you and Ruby Tate effected the switching of identities between Ruby and Gisselle Andreas, who was your wife at the time."

"Objection, Your Honor," Monsieur Williams said. "Whether or not this woman is Ruby Tate is something for the court to decide."

The judge grimaced. "Monsieur Williams. There isn't a jury to impress. I think I'm capable of understanding the question at hand without being influenced by innuendo. Please, sir. Let's make this as fast as possible."

"Yes, Your Honor," Monsieur Williams said, and sat down.

My eyes widened. Perhaps we would get a fair shake after all, I thought.

Beau began our story. Not a sound was heard through his relating of it. No one so much as coughed or cleared his throat, and when he was finished, an even deeper hush came over the crowd. It was as if everyone had been stunned. Now, when I turned and looked around, I saw all eyes were on me. Beau had done such a good job of telling our story, many were beginning to wonder if it couldn't be so. I felt my hopes rise to the surface of my troubled thoughts.

Monsieur Williams rose. "Just a few questions, if I may, Your Honor."

"Go on," the judge said.

"Monsieur Andreas. You said your wife was diagnosed with St. Louis encephalitis while you were at your country estate. A doctor made the diagnosis?"

"Yes."

"Didn't this doctor know he was diagnosing your wife, Gisselle?" Beau looked toward Monsieur Polk. "If so, why didn't you bring him here to testify that it was Gisselle and not Ruby?" Monsieur Williams hammered. Beau didn't respond.

"Monsieur Andreas?" the judge said.

"I . . ."

"Your honor," Monsieur Polk said. "Since the twins are so identical, we didn't think the doctor would be able to testify beyond a doubt as to which twin he examined. I have researched the medical history of the twins, as much as could be researched, and we are willing to admit that identical twins share so many physiological characteristics, it is virtually impossible to use medical data to identify them."

"You have no medical records to enter into the record?" Judge Barrow asked.

"No, sir."

"Then what hard evidence to you intend to enter into the record to substantiate this fantastic story, sir?" the judge asked, getting right to the point.

"We are prepared at this time," Monsieur Polk said, approaching the judge, "to present handwriting samples that you will quickly be able to see distinguish one twin from the other. These come from school records and legal documents," Monsieur Polk said, and presented the exhibits.

Judge Barrow gazed at them. "I'd have to have an expert analyze them, of course."

"We would like to reserve the right to bring them to our experts, Your Honor," Monsieur Williams said.

"Of course," the judge said. He put the exhibits aside. "Are there any more questions for Monsieur Andreas?"

"Yes," Monsieur Williams said, and stood his ground between Beau and us. He smiled skeptically. "Sir, you claim Paul Tate, once hearing of this fantastic scheme, volunteered to take the sick twin into his home and pretend she was his wife?"

"That's correct," Beau said.

"Can you tell the court why he would do such a thing?"

"Paul Tate was devoted to Ruby and wanted to see her happy. He knew Pearl was my child and he wanted to see us with our child," Beau added.

Gladys Tate groaned so loud, everyone paused to see. She had closed her eyes and fallen back against Octavious's shoulder.

"Monsieur?" the judge asked. Octavious whispered something in Gladys's ear and her eyelids fluttered open. With great effort, she sat up again. Then she nodded she was all right.

"And so," Monsieur Williams continued, "you are telling the court that Paul Tate willingly took in his sister-in-law and then pretended she was his wife to the extent that when she died, he fell into a deep depression which caused his own untimely death? He did all this to make sure Ruby Tate was happy living with another man? Is that what you want this court to believe?"

"It's true," Beau said.

Monsieur Williams widened his smile. "No further

questions, Your Honor," he said. The judge told Beau he was excused. He looked very dark and troubled as he returned to his seat beside me.

"Ruby," Monsieur Polk said. I nodded and he called me to the stand. I took a deep breath and with my eyes nearly closed, walked to the witness chair. After I was sworn in, I took another deep breath and told myself to be strong for Pearl's sake.

"Please state your real name," Monsieur Polk said.

"My legal name is Ruby Tate."

"You have heard Monsieur Andreas's story. Is there anything with which you wish to disagree?"

"No. It's all true."

"Did you discuss this switching of identities with your husband, Paul, and did he indeed agree to the plan?"

"Yes. I didn't want him to be so involved," I added, "but he insisted."

"Describe the birth of your child," he said, and stood back.

I told the story, how Paul had been there during the storm to help with Pearl's birth. Monsieur Polk then took me through many of the highlights of my life, events at the Greenwood School, the people I had known and things I had accomplished. After I finished with that, he nodded toward the rear and an assistant brought in an easel, some drawing pencils, and a drawing pad.

Monsieur Williams shot up out of his seat as soon as it was obvious what Monsieur Polk wanted to demonstrate. "I object to this, Your Honor," Monsieur Williams cried.

"Monsieur Polk, what do you plan to enter into the record here?" the judge asked.

"There were many differences between the twins, Your Honor, many we recognize will be hard to substantiate, but one is possible, and that is Ruby's ability to draw and paint. She has had paintings in galleries in New Orleans and—"

"Your Honor," Monsieur Williams said, "whether this

woman can draw a straight line or not is irrelevant. It was never established that Gisselle Andreas could not."

"I'm afraid he has a point, Monsieur Polk. All you will show here is that this woman can perform artistically."

"Monsieur Polk sighed with frustration. "But, Your Honor, never in Gisselle Andreas's history has there ever been any evidence . . ."

The judge shook his head. "It's a waste of the court's time, monsieur. Please continue with your witness or enter new exhibits or call another witness." Monsieur Polk shook his head. "Are you finished with this witness?"

With deep disappointment, Monsieur Polk replied, "Yes, Your Honor."

"Monsieur Williams?"

"A few minor questions," he said, dripping with sarcasm. "Madame Andreas. You claim you were married to Paul Tate even though you were still in love with Beau Andreas. Why did you marry Monsieur Tate, then?"

"I . . . was alone and he wanted to provide a home for me and my child."

"Most husbands want to provide homes for their wives and children. Did he love you?"

"Oh yes."

"Did you love him?"

"I . . ."

"Well, did you?"

"Yes, but . . ."

"But what, madame?"

"But it was a different sort of love, a friendship, a . . ." I wanted to say "sisterly," but when I looked at Gladys and Octavious, I couldn't do it. "A different sort of love."

"You were man and wife, were you not? You were married in a church, you said."

"Yes."

He narrowed his eyes. "Did you see Monsieur Andreas romantically while you were married to Monsieur Tate?"

"Yes," I said, and some in the audience gasped and shook their heads.

"And according to your tale, your husband was aware of this?"

"Yes."

"He was aware of this and he tolerated it? Not only did he tolerate it, but he was willing to take in your dying sister and pretend it was you so you would be happy." He spun around as he continued, directing himself to the audience as much as he directed himself to the judge. "And then he became so depressed over her death that he drowned in the swamp? This is the story you and Monsieur Andreas want everyone to accept?"

"Yes," I cried. "It's true. All of it."

Monsieur Williams gazed at the judge and twisted the corner of his mouth until it cut into his cheek.

"No further questions, Your Honor."

The judge nodded. "You may step down, madame," he said, but I couldn't stand. My legs were like wet straw and my back felt as if it had turned to jelly. I closed my eyes.

"Ruby," Beau called.

"Are you all right, madame?" the judge asked.

I shook my head. My heart was pounding so hard, I couldn't catch my breath. I felt the blood drain from my face. When I opened my eyes, Beau was holding my hand. Someone had brought up a wet cloth for my forehead and I realized I had fainted.

"Can you walk, Ruby?" Beau asked.

I nodded.

"We'll have a short recess," the judge said, and slammed his gavel down. I felt as if he had slammed it down on my heart.

17

Thicker Than Water

During the recess Beau and I were shown to a waiting room in which there was a small sofa. Beau had me lie down and keep the wet cloth on my forehead while Monsieur Polk went to make a phone call to his office. He looked glum and disturbed. In fact, I thought he seemed angry at us for bringing him into the situation.

"Beau, we looked foolish in there, didn't we?" I asked mournfully. "After we told our story, the Tates' attorney made us look like liars."

"No," Beau encouraged. "People believed us. I saw it in their faces. And besides, once your handwriting is compared to Gisselle's and analyzed . . ."

"They will find an expert to discount it. You know they will. She's so determined to hurt us, Beau. She won't spare any cost. She would use Paul's entire fortune to defeat us!"

"Take it easy, Ruby. Please. We have to go back and—"

We both turned when the door opened and Jeanne entered. For a moment no one spoke. She held the door partially opened behind her as if she might change her mind and bolt out of the room any moment.

"Jeanne," I said, sitting up. "Please, come in."

She stared at me, her eyes watery. "I don't know what to believe anymore," she said, shaking her head. "Mother swears you and Beau are just good liars."

"No, Jeanne. We're not lying. Remember when you came to me and we had that nice talk before you got married? Remember how you weren't sure you should marry James?"

Her eyes widened and then narrowed. "Ruby could have told you."

I shook my head. "No. Listen . . ."

"But even if you are Ruby, I don't know how you could have hurt my brother like you did."

"Jeanne, you don't understand everything. I never meant to hurt Paul, never. I did love him."

"How can you say that with him right here?" she asked, nodding at Beau.

"Paul and I had a different sort of love, Jeanne."

She studied me with such intensity, I felt her eyes inside me. "I don't know. I just don't know what to believe," she said. And then her eyes turned crystal-hard. "But I came here to tell you that if you are Ruby and you did all this, I feel sorry for you."

"Jeanne!"

She turned and left quickly.

"You see," Beau said, smiling. "She has doubts now. She knows in her heart you are Ruby."

"I hope so," I said. "But I feel so terrible. I should have realized how many people I would hurt."

Beau held me tightly and I took a deep breath. He got me a glass of water, and as I was drinking it, Monsieur Polk returned, looking even more despondent.

"What is it?" Beau asked.

"I've just gotten some bad news," he said. "They have a surprise witness."

"What? Who?" I asked, my mind searching through the possibilities.

"I don't know who it is yet," he said. "But I was told he could nail it down for them. Is there anything else you two haven't told me?"

"No, Monsieur," Beau said. "Absolutely nothing has been deliberately withheld. And everything we've told you is the truth."

He nodded, skeptically. "It's time to return," he said.

It was even more difficult to return to the courtroom than it was to first enter it. I felt like a specimen under a microscope. Everyone's gaze followed me down to the front of the courtroom, and people near us covered their mouths to whisper. It made me flush with a wave of heat that rose up my legs and over my face. Every old friend of Grandmere Catherine's was studying my every move, searching gestures for evidence to confirm my identity. The air was thick with their questions. Were Beau and I trying to pull off some scam? Or was our tale the truth?

We took our seats. Gladys Tate was already seated, steely-faced. Octavious sat staring blankly ahead. Jeanne whispered something to Toby, and Paul's sisters gazed at me angrily. A few moments later, Judge Barrow returned and the courtroom grew still.

"Monsieur Polk," he said. "Are you ready to continue?"

"Yes, Your Honor." Our attorney rose with the documents he had prepared for us to sign concerning the inheritance.

"Your Honor. My clients recognize that their motives for trying to regain custody of Pearl Tate might be misinterpreted. In order to alleviate such misinterpretations, we are prepared to offer the surrender of any and all rights to any spousal inheritance concerning the estate of Paul Marcus Tate." He stepped forward and brought the documents to the judge, who gazed down at them and then nodded at Monsieur Williams to come forward, too. He looked at the papers.

"We'd have to study these, of course, Your Honor, but," he said with the confidence of someone who had anticipated our move, "even if these do prove satisfactory, this doesn't eliminate the possibility of these two impostors getting their clutches on the Tate fortune. The child whom they are trying to get custody of would inherit, and they would naturally be the trustees of that enormous inheritance."

The judge turned to Monsieur Tate.

"Your Honor, it is the contention of my clients that Pearl Tate's natural father is Beau Andreas. She would have no claims to Monsieur Tate's estate."

The judge nodded. It was like watching a game of chess being played with real people on the board instead of figurines of knights and queens, pawns and kings. We were the pawns, and to the victor went my darling Pearl.

"Do you have any further exhibits to enter, Monsieur Polk, or any further witnesses?"

"No, Your Honor."

"Monsieur Williams?"

"We do, Your Honor."

The judge sat back. Monsieur Polk returned to his seat beside us, and Monsieur Williams went to his desk to confer with his associate for a moment before turning and calling out his witness's name.

"We would like to call Monsieur Bruce Bristow to the stand."

"Bruce!" I exclaimed. Beau shook his head in astonishment.

"Is this not your stepmother's husband?" Monsieur Polk asked.

"Yes, but . . . we have nothing to do with him anymore," Beau explained.

The doors opened in the rear and Bruce came sauntering down the aisle, a Cheshire cat's grin on his lips when he gazed our way.

"She must have made him an offer, bought his testimony," I told Monsieur Polk.

"What sort of testimony can this man give?" he wondered aloud.

"He'll say anything, even under oath," Beau said, eyeing Bruce angrily.

Bruce was sworn in and sat in the witness chair. Monsieur Williams approached him.

"Please state your name, sir."

"I'm Bruce Bristow."

"And were you married to the now-deceased stepmother of Ruby and Gisselle Dumas?"

"I was."

"How long have you known the twins?"

"Quite a long time," he said, gazing at me and smiling. "Years. I was employed by Monsieur and Madame Dumas for about eight years before Monsieur Dumas's death."

"After which you married Daphne Dumas and became, for all practical purposes, the stepfather to the twins Gisselle and Ruby?"

"Yes, that's true."

"So you knew them well?"

"Very well. Intimately," he added.

"As the only living parent of the twins, can you assure the court you can distinguish between them?"

"Of course. Gisselle," he said, looking at me again, "has a completely different personality, a more, shall we say, sophisticated awareness. Ruby was more of an innocent, shy, soft-spoken."

"Are you now, and have you recently been, involved in some legal problems with the current owners of the Dumas Enterprises, Beau and Gisselle Andreas?" Monsieur Williams asked.

"Yes, sir. They threw me out of the business," he said, glaring at us. "After years of dedicated service, they decided to enforce a foolish prenuptial agreement between me and my deceased wife. They manipulated me out of my rightful position and drove me into the streets, turning me into a pauper."

"He's lying," Beau whispered to Monsieur Polk.

"You should have told me all about him," he replied. "I asked you if there was anything else."

"Who knew Gladys Tate would find him?"

"More likely, he found her, Beau," I said. "For revenge. They fit together like a hand in a glove."

"This woman who you see sitting before you, sir," Monsieur Williams said, turning to me. "Was she a party to all this, directly?"

"Yes, she was. I went back to plead with her recently and she literally had me thrown out of what had been my own house," he said.

"So," Monsieur Williams concluded with a smile of satisfaction, "this was no shy, innocent woman."

"Hardly," Bruce said, widening his own smile and looking at the judge, who turned his scrutinizing eyes on me.

"Still, sir, it is possible, I imagine, for an identical twin to fool someone into believing she is her sister," Monsieur Williams said. "She could have performed a well-prepared script and said all the right things to convince you she was her sister."

"I suppose," Bruce said. Why was Monsieur Williams giving us that benefit of doubt? I wondered, but it was like hearing the first shoe drop. I cringed inside and clutched my hands so hard, my fingers went numb.

"Then how can you be so sure you were in an argument with Gisselle and not Ruby recently?"

"I'm ashamed to say," Bruce replied, looking down.

"I'm afraid I have to ask you nevertheless, sir. A child's future is in the balance, not to mention a major fortune."

Bruce nodded, took a deep breath, and looked up as if he were concentrating on an angel in the ceiling. "I once let myself be seduced by my stepdaughter Gisselle."

The audience gave one simultaneous gasp.

"As I said, she was very sophisticated and worldly," he added.

"Did anyone else know about this, monsieur?"

"No," Bruce said. "I wasn't very proud of it."

"But this woman indicated to you that she knew?" Monsieur Williams asked, pointing to me.

"Yes. She brought it up during our argument and threatened to use it against me should I put up any resistance to her and her husband's effort to drive me out of my rightful position. Under the circumstances I thought it was better to effect a quick retreat and start my life anew.

"However," he said, looking at Madame Tate, "when I heard what they were up to now, I had to step forward and do my duty regardless of the consequences to my reputation."

"So you are telling the court under oath that this woman who has presented herself as Ruby Tate knew intimate details between you and Gisselle, details only Gisselle would have known?"

"That is correct," Bruce said, and sat back contented.

"The only reason he is doing this," Beau whispered to Monsieur Polk, "is because we forced him to leave the business. He and Daphne did some very shaky financial dealings."

"Are you prepared to open up all that?" Monsieur Polk asked.

Beau looked at me. "Yes. We'll do anything." Beau began to write some questions for Monsieur Polk quickly.

"I have no further questions for the witness, Your Honor," Monsieur Williams said, and returned to his table, where Gladys Tate sat looking stronger. She gazed my way and smiled coldly, sending chills down my spine.

"Monsieur Polk. Do you wish to question this witness?"

"I do, Your Honor. If I may have one moment," he added while Beau completed his notes. Monsieur Polk perused them and then stood up.

"Monsieur Bristow, why didn't you contest the actions taken against you to remove you from Dumas Enterprises?"

"I've already said . . . there was an unfortunate prenuptial agreement and I was blackmailed by my stepdaughter Gisselle."

"Are you sure your reluctance to take counteraction

had nothing to do with the financial activities you and Daphne Dumas conducted?"

"No."

"You are willing to have those dealings scrutinized by this court?"

Bruce squirmed a bit. "I didn't do anything wrong."

"Aren't you here to get revenge for being pushed out of the business?"

"No. I'm here to tell the truth," Bruce said firmly.

"Did you not recently lose a commercial property in New Orleans through foreclosure?"

"Yes."

"You've lost quite a comfortable income and lifestyle, haven't you?"

"I have a good job now," Bruce insisted.

"Not paying you a quarter of what you made before you were asked to leave Dumas Enterprises, correct?"

"Money isn't everything," Bruce quipped.

"Have you gotten over your problem with alcohol?" Monsieur Polk pursued.

"Objection, Your Honor," Monsieur Williams said, rising. "Monsieur Bristow's personal problems have nothing to do with this testimony."

"They have everything to do with it if he hopes to gain financially and he is an alcoholic who needs money for his disease," Monsieur Polk said.

"Are you accusing my clients of bribing this man?" Monsieur Williams cried, pointing at Bruce.

"That will be enough," the judge said. "Objection sustained. Monsieur Polk, have you any more questions pertaining to the issue?"

Monsieur Polk thought a moment and then shook his head. "No, Your Honor."

"Fine. Thank you, Monsieur Bristow. You may step down. Monsieur Williams?"

"I would like to call Madame Tate to the stand, Your Honor."

Gladys Tate rose slowly as if she were battling against

an enormous weight on her shoulders. She dabbed at her eyes with a beige silk handkerchief and then sighed loudly before stepping around the table to walk toward the stand. I looked at Octavious. He'd had his head down most of the time and had it down now, too.

After she was sworn in, Gladys settled into the witness chair like someone easing herself into a hot bath. She closed her eyes and pressed her right hand against her heart. Monsieur Williams stood waiting for her to become calm enough to speak. When I gazed at the people in the audience, I saw how most felt sorry for her. Their eyes were filled with compassion and sympathy.

"You are Gladys Tate, mother of the recently deceased Paul Marcus Tate?" Monsieur Williams asked. She closed her eyes again. "I'm sorry, Madame Tate. I know how fresh your sorrow is, but I have to ask."

"Yes," she said. "I am Paul Tate's mother." She didn't look at me.

"Were you very close with your son, madame?"

"Very," she said. "Before Paul was married, I don't think a day passed when we didn't see or speak to each other. We had more than a mother-son relationship. We were good friends," she added.

"And so your son confided in you?"

"Oh, absolutely. We had no secrets from each other, ever," she said.

"That's a lie," I whispered. Monsieur Polk raised his eyebrows. Beau turned to me. His eyes told me that he wanted me to tell Monsieur Polk the truth. I had hoped I wouldn't have to do it. It seemed like such a betrayal of Paul.

"Did he ever discuss with you this elaborate plan to switch his wife with Monsieur Andreas's wife after she was stricken with encephalitis?"

"No. Paul loved Ruby dearly and he was a very proud young man, as well as religious. He wouldn't give away the woman he loved just so another man could be happy living in sin," she said disdainfully. "He married Ruby in church after he realized it was the proper thing to do. I remember when he told me he was going to do it. I was unhappy he had fathered a child out of wedlock, of course, but I was happy he wanted to do what was morally right."

"She wasn't happy," I murmured. "She made him miserable. She—"

"Shh," Monsieur Polk said. He looked like he was as fascinated as everyone else with her story and didn't want to miss a detail.

"And in fact, after they were married, you and your husband and your daughters accepted Ruby and Pearl as your family, correct?"

"Yes. We had family dinners. I even helped her design and decorate her home. I would do anything to keep my son happy and close to me," she said. "What he wanted for himself, I wanted for him. And he doted on the child. Oh, how he worshiped our precious granddaughter. She has his face, his eyes, his hair. To see them walking together in the garden or to see him take her for a pirogue ride in the canals filled my heart with joy."

"So there is no doubt in your mind that Pearl is his child?"

"None whatsoever."

"And he never told you anything to the contrary?"

"No. Why would he marry a woman with someone else's child?" she asked.

Heads bobbed in agreement.

"During Ruby Tate's illness, you had many opportunities to visit their home?"

"Yes."

"And did he ever give you an indication he was worrying about his wife's sister and not his wife?" Monsieur Williams pursued.

"No. On the contrary, and as anyone here who had seen my son during this trying period can testify, he mourned so hard, he became a shell of himself. He neglected his work and began drinking. He was in a constant depression. It broke my heart."

"Why didn't he just put his wife into a hospital?"

"He couldn't bear being away from her. He was at her side constantly," Madame Tate said. "Hardly how he would be were it not Ruby," she added, gazing scornfully at me.

"Why did you ask the court to grant an order for you to retrieve your granddaughter?"

"These people," Gladys Tate said, spitting her words toward us, "refused to give Pearl back to me. They turned my attorney and a nurse away from the door. And all this," she moaned, "while I was mourning the horrible death of my son, my little boy . . ."

She burst into tears. Monsieur Williams stepped forward quickly with his handkerchief.

"I'm sorry," she wailed.

"That's all right. Take your time, madame."

Gladys wiped her cheeks and then sniffled and sucked in her breath.

"Are you all right, Madame Tate?" Judge Barrow asked.

"Yes," she said in a small voice. Judge Barrow nodded to Monsieur Williams, who stepped forward to continue.

"Recently Monsieur and Madame Andreas came to your home, did they not?" he asked.

She glared at us. "Yes, they did."

"And what did they want?"

"They wanted to make a deal," she said. "They offered fifty percent of my son's estate if I didn't force this court hearing and just gave them Pearl."

"What?" Beau stammered.

"She's lying!" I cried.

The judge rapped his gavel. "I warned you. No outbursts," he reprimanded.

"But . . ."

"Be still," Monsieur Polk ordered.

I cowered back, shrinking in my chair with rage burning my cheeks. Was there no limit to how far she would go to satisfy her thirst for vengeance?

"What happened then, madame?" Monsieur Williams asked.

"I refused, of course, and they threatened to take me to court, which they have done."

"No further questions, Your Honor," Monsieur Williams said.

The judge looked at Monsieur Polk with hard eyes. "Do you have any questions for this witness?"

"No, Your Honor."

"What? Make her take back these lies," I urged.

"No. It's better to get rid of her. She has everyone's sympathy. Even the judge's," Monsieur Polk advised.

Monsieur Williams helped Madame Tate out of the seat and escorted her back to her chair. Some people in the audience were openly crying for her.

"You won't get the child back today, if you ever do," Monsieur Polk muttered, half under his breath.

"Oh, Beau," I wailed. "She's winning. She'll be a terrible grandmother. She doesn't love Pearl. She knows Pearl's not Paul's child."

"Monsieur Williams?" the judge said.

"No further witnesses or exhibits, Your Honor," he said confidently.

Monsieur Polk sat back, his hands on his stomach, his face dour. I looked across the courtroom at Gladys, who was preparing to leave in victory. Octavious still had his eyes fixed on the table.

"Call one more witness, Monsieur Polk," I said in desperation.

"What's that?"

Beau took my hand. We gazed into each other's eyes and he nodded. I turned back to our attorney.

"Call one more witness. I'll tell you just what to ask," I said. "Call Octavious Tate to the stand."

"Do it!" Beau ordered firmly.

Monsieur Polk rose slowly from his seat, unsure, tentative, and reluctant.

"Monsieur Polk?" the judge said.

"We have one more witness, Your Honor," he said.

The judge looked displeased. "Very well," he said.

"Let's conclude this matter. Call your final witness," he added, emphasizing the word "final."

"We call Monsieur Tate to the stand."

A ripple of astonishment moved through the audience. I wrote feverishly on a piece of paper. The judge rapped his gavel and glared at the crowd of people, who immediately grew still. No one wanted to be removed from this courtroom now. Octavious, stunned by the sound of his name, lifted his head slowly and gazed around as if he just realized where he was. Monsieur Williams leaned over to whisper some strategy to him before he stood up. I handed my questions to Monsieur Polk, who perused them quickly and then looked at me sharply.

"Madame," he warned, "you could lose any sympathetic ear you might have if this proves untrue."

"We don't have any sympathy here," Beau answered for me.

"It's true," I said softly.

Octavious walked slowly to the witness stand, his head down. When he was sworn in, he repeated the oath very slowly. I saw that the words were heavy on his tongue and on his heart. He sat quickly, falling into his seat like a man who might otherwise crumple to the floor. Monsieur Polk hesitated and then shrugged to himself and stepped forward on our behalf.

"Monsieur Tate, after your son had first proposed marriage to Ruby Dumas, did you visit Ruby Dumas and ask her to refuse?"

Octavious looked toward Gladys and then he looked down.

"Sir?" Monsieur Polk said.

"Yes, I did."

"Why?"

"I didn't think Paul was ready to marry," he replied. "He was just starting his oil business and he had just built this home."

"That seems like a good time to think of marriage," Monsieur Polk said. "Wasn't there another reason for your asking Ruby Dumas to refuse your son's proposal?"

Octavious looked at Gladys again. "I knew my wife was unhappy about it," he said.

"But your wife has just testified that she was happy Paul was doing the right thing and she testified that she fully accepted Ruby Dumas into her family. Was that not the case, monsieur?"

"She accepted, yes."

"But not willingly?" Before Octavious could respond, Monsieur Polk followed quickly. "Did you believe the baby was your son's baby?"

"I . . . thought it was possible, yes."

"Yet you went to Ruby Dumas to ask her not to marry your son?"

Octavious didn't reply.

"Did your son tell you Pearl was his child?"

"He . . . said he wanted to provide for Ruby and Pearl."

"But he never said Pearl was his child? Sir?"

"No, not to me."

"But to your wife, who then told you? Is that the way it was?"

"Yes. Yes."

"Then why didn't you think he was doing the right thing?"

"I didn't say he wasn't."

"Yet you admit you didn't want to see the marriage happen. Really, monsieur, this is very confusing. Wasn't there another reason, a more serious reason?"

Octavious turned his head slowly toward me and our eyes met. I pleaded for the truth with mine, even though I knew how devastating that truth was.

"I don't know what you mean," he said.

"Please," I cried. "Please do the right thing."

The judge slammed his gavel down.

"For Paul's sake," I added. Octavious winced and his lips trembled.

"That's quite enough, madame. I warned you and—"

"Yes," Octavious admitted softly. "There was another reason."

"Octavious!" Gladys Tate screamed. The judge sat back, shocked at the outbursts, one from each side.

"Don't you think it's time to tell that reason, Monsieur Tate?" our attorney said with a senatorial voice.

Octavious nodded. He looked at Gladys again. "I'm sorry," he said. "I can't go on with this. I owe you so much, but what you're doing is not right, my dearest wife. I'm tired of hiding behind a lie and I can't take a mother from a child."

Gladys wailed. Necks strained to see her daughters comforting her.

"Will you please tell the court what that additional reason was," Monsieur Polk demanded.

"A long time ago, I succumbed to temptation and committed an adulterous act."

The audience took a collective deep breath.

"And?"

"As a result, my son was born." Octavious raised his head and gazed at me. "My son and Ruby Dumas . . ."

"Monsieur?"

"They were half brother and half sister," he confessed.

Bedlam broke out. The judge's gavel was barely heard above the din. Gladys Tate fainted and Octavious buried his face in his hands.

"Your Honor," Monsieur Polk said, stepping forward. "I think it would be in the best interest of the court and all concerned if we could adjoin to your quarters to complete this hearing."

The judge considered and then nodded. "I will see opposing counsels in my chambers," he declared, and rose from his seat. Octavious had not moved from the witness chair. I got up quickly and crossed to him. When he raised his head, his cheeks were wet with tears.

"Thank you," I said.

"I'm sorry for all that I have done," he said.

"I know. I think now you will find peace inside yourself."

Beau came up and embraced me. Then he led me away, people stepping aside to create a path for us. I bit off all my fingernails while Beau and I waited outside Judge Barrow's chambers. My heart was pounding and my stomach felt like it was churning butter. The Tates' attorneys emerged first, their faces so stone-cold, they revealed nothing. They didn't even look our way. Finally Monsieur Polk came to us and told us the judge wanted to meet with us alone.

"What has he decided?" I asked frantically.

"I'm to ask you to go in only, madame. Please."

I clutched Beau's arm, my legs threatening to give out at any moment. If we were to leave without my daughter . . .

In his office without his judicial robes, Judge Barrow looked more like a nice old grandpere. He gestured for us to sit across from him on the settee and then he took off his reading glasses and leaned forward.

"This was, needless to say, the most unusual custody hearing in my experience. I think we have sorted out the truth now. I'm not here to assign blame at this time. Some of this was caused by events beyond your control, but there are all sorts of fraud, ethical and moral fraud, too, and you know how much of that is your doing."

"Yes," I said, my voice filled with remorse.

Judge Barrow stared a moment and nodded. "My instincts tell me your motives for your actions were good ones, motives of love, and the fact that you were willing to risk your reputations and your fortunes by telling the truth in court bodes well in your favor.

"But the state is asking me to judge whether or not you should have custody of this child and be in charge of her welfare and her moral education or whether or not it is better for her to be assigned to a state agency until a proper foster home is found."

"Your Honor," I began, ready to list a dozen promises. He put up his hand.

"I have made my decision, and nothing you say will change that," he said firmly. And then he smiled and added, "I will expect an invitation to a wedding."

I gasped with joy, but Judge Barrow became serious again.

"You may and must beçome yourself again, madame."

Tears of happiness flooded my face. Beau and I embraced.

"I have given orders for your child to be returned to you. She will be brought here momentarily. The legal ramifications resulting from your previous marriage, straightening out the identities . . . I leave all that to your high-priced attorneys."

"Thank you, Your Honor," I said through my tears. Beau shook his hand and we left the office.

Monsieur Polk was waiting for us in the corridor. "I must confess," he said, "I had my doubts as to the veracity of your story. I am happy for you. Good luck."

We stepped outside to wait for the car that would bring Pearl back to us. There were still people who had been in the courtroom lingering about, discussing the shocking events. I spotted Mrs. Thibodeau, one of Grandmere Catherine's old friends. She had trouble walking now, but she hobbled her way toward us and took my hand.

"I knew it was you," she said. "I told myself Catherine Landry's granddaughter might have been a twin, but she had lived most of her life with Catherine and she had her spirit in her. I looked at your face in that courtroom and I saw your grandmere looking back at me and I knew it would turn out right."

"Thank you, Mrs. Thibodeau."

"God bless you, child, and don't forget us."

"I won't. We'll be back," I promised. She hugged me and I watched her walk way, my heart heavy with the memory of my grandmere walking alongside her friends to church.

The peekaboo sun slipped out from under the mushrooming clouds and dropped warm rays around us as the car with Pearl in it was driven up. The nurse in the front seat opened the door and helped her out. The moment Pearl saw me, her eyes brightened.

"Mommy!" she cried.

It was the best word in the world. Nothing filled my heart with more joy. I held out my arms for her to run to me and then I flooded her faces with kisses and pressed her close. Beau put his arm around my shoulders. All around us, people watched with smiles on their faces.

As we started from the courthouse, I saw the Tates' limousine drive away. The windows were dark, but as the sunlight grew stronger, the silhouette of Madame Tate became clearly outlined. She looked as if she had turned to stone.

I felt sorry for her, even though she had done a very mean thing. She had lost everything today, much more than her vengeance. Her illusionary life had been shattered around her like so much thin china. She was going home to a darker, more troubled time. I prayed that somehow she and Octavious could find a renewal and a peace now that the lies were stripped away.

"Let's go home," Beau said.

Never did those words mean as much to me as they did now.

"I want to make one stop first, Beau," I said. He didn't have to ask where.

A little while later, I stood in front of Grandmere Catherine's tombstone.

A true *traiteur* has a very holy spirit, I thought. She lingers longer to look after the loved ones she has left behind. Grandmere Catherine's spirit was still here. I could feel it, feel her hovering nearby. The breeze became her whisper, its caress, her kiss.

I smiled and gazed up at the light blue sky streaked with thin wisps of clouds now. Mrs. Thibodeau was right, I thought. Grandmere had been with me this day. I kissed my fingers and touched her stone and then I returned to the car and to Beau and to my darling Pearl.

As we drove away, I gazed out the window and saw a marsh hawk strutting on a cypress branch. It watched us and then it lifted into the wind and soared beside and around us for a while until it turned and headed deeper into the bayou.

"Good-bye, Paul," I whispered. But I'll be back, I thought.

I'll be back.

Epilogue

My dreams of having a glorious wedding were still not to become a reality. The publicity and all the commotion surrounding the custody hearing continued to hover about us when we returned to New Orleans. Beau thought it was better for us to have a small ceremony away from the din, and since his parents were not taking it all very well anyway, I couldn't disagree.

We debated for days about whether or not we should sell the house in the Garden District and build a new house just outside of New Orleans. Finally we both came to the same conclusion: We were happy with our servants and we wouldn't find a more beautiful setting. Rather than move, I embarked on the task of redecorating, tearing the rooms apart, floor to ceiling, and replacing the drapes, wall hangings, flooring, and even some of the fixtures. It was as though I were caught in a maddening frenzy to purify the house and purge it of any and all traces of my stepmother, Daphne.

Of course, I kept all the things that I knew had been precious to Daddy and I didn't change a thing in the room that had once been Uncle Jean's. It remained a shrine to his memory, something I knew Daddy had wanted. I put all of the things that even smelled of Daphne into the attic, burying away clothing, jewelry, pictures, mementoes, in large trunks. Then I gathered Gisselle's things together and gave much of it away to thrift shops and charities.

With the rooms repainted, new drapes on the windows, the changes in the artwork, the house took on my and Beau's identities. Of course, there were still memories lingering like cobwebs, but I believed, as did Beau, that time was the best vacuum cleaner and these troublesome memories would someday become vague and insignificant.

After I had done what I wanted with the house, I directed my energies back into my artistic work. One of the first pictures I drew and then painted was a picture of a young woman sitting in a gazebo with a newborn baby in her arms. The setting placed her in a home and on grounds like ours in the Garden District. When Beau looked at the picture, he told me he thought I had done a self-portrait, and then, a few weeks later, I woke with the symptoms of pregnancy and realized that the inspiration for the picture had come from a deeper realization inside myself.

Beau swore it meant I had some of Grandmere Catherine's *traiteur* powers.

"Why can't it be so? Your people believe it's inherited power, right?" he said.

"I never felt anything like that, Beau, and I never even dreamt of healing people. I don't have that sort of mystical insight."

He nodded and thought a moment and then said a startling thing. "Sometimes, when I'm with Pearl and she's jabbering away in her baby language, I see her fix intently on something, and suddenly her face seems years [illegible] than four. There's an awareness in her eyes. Do you [illegible]hat when you're with her?"

"Yes," I said, "but I was afraid to even mention anything like it for fear you would laugh at me."

"I'm not laughing. I'm wondering. You know," he said, "she's even beguiling my parents these days. Mother tries not to show it, but she can't help but dote on her, and my father . . . when he's with her, he's like a little boy again."

"She has her way with them."

"With anyone," Beau said. "I think she's charmed. There. I've said it. Just don't tell any of my friends," he added quickly. I laughed. "Next thing you know," he said, "you'll have me believing in some of those voodoo rituals you and Nina Jackson used to practice."

"Don't discount anything," I warned.

He laughed again, but two weeks into my ninth month, he managed to surprise me with a wonderful present. He had located Nina and he brought her to our house to see me.

"I have a surprise visitor for you," Beau said, coming into the sitting room first.

"Who?"

Then he reached around the door and brought Nina forward. She didn't look very much older, although her hair was completely gray.

"Nina!" I struggled to my feet. I was so big, I felt like a hippopotamus rising out of a swamp. We embraced.

"You be big, all right," Nina said. "And close. I can see it in your eyes."

"Oh, Nina, where have you been?"

"Been travelin' a bit up and down the river. Nina be retired now. I live with my sister."

She sat and talked with me for an hour. I showed her Pearl and she ranted and raved about how beautiful she was becoming. She told me she thought she was a special child, too. And then she told me she was going to light a blue candle for my new baby so the baby would have success and protection.

"It don't be long," she predicted. She reached into her

pocket and produced a camphor lump for me to wear around my neck. "It keep germs away from you and your baby," she promised. I told her I would wear it even in the hospital.

"Please, don't be a stranger. Come see us again, Nina."

"Be sure I will," she said.

"Nina," I asked, taking her hand into mine, "do you think the anger I threw into the wind when I went to see Mama Dede with you about Gisselle has blown away?"

"It be blown from your heart, child. That's what matters most."

We hugged and Beau took her home.

"That was a wonderful present, Beau," I told him when he returned. "Thank you."

"I see she left something," he said, eyeing the camphor lump around my neck. "Figured she would. To tell you the truth," he admitted, "I was hoping she would. Can't take any chances."

We laughed about it.

Four days later my labor began. It was intense, even more so than it had been with Pearl. Beau was at my side constantly and was even there with me in the delivery room. He held my hand and encouraged my breathing. I think he felt every stick of pain I felt, for I saw him wince each time. Finally my water broke and the baby started to enter this world.

"It's a boy!" the doctor cried, and then screamed, "Wait!"

Beau's eyes widened.

"It's another boy! Twins!" the doctor added. "I thought it might be. One was hiding the other, covering his heartbeat with his own.

"Congratulations!" he said, and the nurses held two blond, blue-eyed baby boys in their arms.

"We're not giving either of them away," Beau joked. "Don't worry."

Twins, I thought. They're going to love each other from day one, I pledged, day one.

Pearl was overwhelmed with the news that she would have not one baby brother, but two. Our first great task was going to be finding names for them. We had already discussed the possibility of a girl and then a boy, thinking the boy would be called Pierre, after Daddy. I knew what I wanted to do, but I wasn't sure how Beau would feel. He surprised me in the hospital room afterward by suggesting it himself.

"We should call our second son Jean," he said.

"Oh, Beau, I thought so, but . . ."

"But what?" He smiled. "I told you. I'm a believer now. It was meant to be."

Maybe, I thought. Maybe.

Beau had a photographer waiting at the house the day we brought the twins home. We had pictures taken of the five of us. We were quite the little family now. We hired a nurse to help with the twins in the beginning, but Beau thought we might keep her on longer.

"I don't want you neglecting your art," he insisted.

"Nothing's more important than my children, Beau. My art will take a backseat," I told him. I wanted to be close to my boys and make sure they were taught to love and cherish each other. Beau understood.

A week after I had returned from the hospital with our twins, I sat out in the gardens, relaxing and reading. Pearl was upstairs in the new nursery, intrigued and fascinated with her two infant brothers.

"Pardon, madame," Aubrey said, coming out to me, "but this just arrived special delivery for you."

"Thank you, Aubrey." I took the envelope. When I saw it came from Jeanne, I sat back, my fingers trembling as I tore it open. There was a photograph within and a note.

Dear Ruby,

Mother insisted every iota of anything that reminds us of you be thrown out. I couldn't find it in my heart to throw this away. Somehow, I think, Paul would have wanted you to have it.

Jeanne

I looked at the picture. I couldn't remember who had taken it, one of Paul's school friends, I thought. It was a picture of the two of us taken at the *fais do do* hall when Paul had taken me to the dance. That had been my first real date, and it was before I had learned the truth about ourselves. Both of us looked so young and innocent and hopeful. We had nothing ahead of us but happiness and love.

I didn't realize I was crying until a tear fell on the photograph.

"Mommy!" I heard Pearl cry from the patio. I turned to see her running toward me, Beau coming along behind her. "They looked at me! Pierre and Jean! They both looked at me and they smiled!"

I quickly wiped any remaining tears from my cheeks and stuffed the picture and the note between the pages of my book.

"They did," Beau vouched. "I saw it myself."

"I'm glad, darling. Your brothers will love you forever and ever."

"Come on, Mommy. Let's go see them. Come on," she urged, pulling on my hand.

"I will, honey. In a moment."

Beau stared at me. "Are you all right?" he asked.

"Yes." I smiled. "I am."

"I'll take her back. Let's go, princess. Give Mommy a little more rest, okay? And then she'll come."

"Will you, Mommy?"

"I will, honey. I promise."

Beau mouthed *I love you* and carried Pearl back to the house.

I sat back. In the distance a cloud shaped like a pirogue drifted across the blue sky and I thought I heard Grandmere Catherine whispering in the breeze again, filling me with hope.